IN SPITE OF AMBITIONS to be a music composer /
quantum physicist / geneticist / Knower of Everything Know-
able, Pamela Morrow (Ngāti Pū) is a part-time visual effects
artist and part-time writer. She began tertiary education in
New Zealand in the eighties, starting a degree in Horticultural
Science at Massey University, but ended up with a BA in
Music and Media Studies from La Trobe University and a
Master's in Film, TV and Media Studies from the University
of Auckland, where she also took a scriptwriting paper. *Hello
Strange* is her first publication.

4
E, G, R + Nudge
ILY
<3
:-*

HELLO

Pamela Morrow

STRANGE

PENGUIN BOOKS

PENGUIN

UK | USA | Canada | Ireland | Australia
India | New Zealand | South Africa | China

Penguin is an imprint of the Penguin Random House group of companies,
whose addresses can be found at global.penguinrandomhouse.com.

Penguin
Random House
New Zealand

First published by Penguin Random House New Zealand, 2020

10 9 8 7 6 5 4 3 2 1

Cover and text design by Cat Taylor
© Penguin Random House New Zealand
Illustrations by Cat Taylor, with stock imagery from Pexels by Allan Scott
McMillan (p. 5), Lum3n.com (pp. 6–7, 10–12), Miriam Espacio (pp. 29–32,
74), Miguel Á. Padriñán (pp. 107, 268–80); from IStock by denisik11 (p. 61),
Katerina Sisperova (pp. 80, 311), mzajac (pp. 117–19), metamorworks
(pp. 161, 187, 282), nicoolay (p. 169); and from Shutterstock by Here
(pp. 227, 359, 368), Barbol (p. 228), Mark Carrel (pp. 369–77).
Cover art by Donald Iain Smith via Getty Images
Author photograph by Virginia Hulston
Prepress by Image Centre Group
Printed and bound in Australia by Griffin Press, an Accredited ISO AS/NZS
14001 Environmental Management Systems Printer

A catalogue record for this book is available from the National Library of
New Zealand.

ISBN 978-0-14-377385-6
eISBN 978-0-14-377386-3

The assistance of Creative New Zealand towards the production of this
book is gratefully acknowledged by the publisher.

ARTS COUNCIL OF NEW ZEALAND TOI AOTEAROA

penguin.co.nz

MIX
Paper from
responsible sources
FSC® C009448

contents

upstart

JOSIE'S START IS UNEXPECTED. She lies afloat and asleep in a tank of nutrient broth, when one billion volts split the sky. Light meets Earth with an almighty **boom** and now an energy spike is on its way, blazing a path straight to her life-support.

First to blow out, the microgrids across Deacon Valley. The loss of power results in the usual mayhem. In the city activity grinds to a halt, while over at **BIOLOGIC** a surge assaults the company's system defences and a final **blast** finds the sweet spot in Josie's brain.

She should be fried. Instead, inside her head, freshly seeded neurons burst across a digital plate custom-built for exactly this sort of thing. Synapses fire for the first time. Biological wiring sizzles as signals run to and fro.

She has thoughts. Not the everyday thoughts of a human being, but the flicker of code, data and image. The thoughts of a machine.

You would never know by looking at her.

Josie's freshly laid skin has a lustrous gleam. Her auburn hair — not too blonde, not too brown — wafts gently around her beautifully shaped head. A tattoo at the back of her neck, a fine mesh of interlocking circles, marks her with the company logo. Even this somehow works. She looks good, perhaps too good.

To explain, there's a lot riding on her construction. They had to get it spot on. The brief was specific, she needs to have *appeal*. Her face must not distract, yet she must be attractive at all times. She needs to be friendly but not overbearing; polite but not stiff. Most important of all, she needs to be indispensable. They call her class of robot *the Josephina*.

Miles McClure, head of ƎIOLOGIC, knew what he wanted to build and how he should build it. Josie isn't the first human-like robot. For the past few years, humanoids have been at the crest of a new technology wave. But these humanoids have limited use. Purpose-built as they are, they lack Josie's reach — Poppy, the pill-dispensing companion for the elderly, being a fine example.

Josephina means *she will add*, and Josie needs to understand humans and the nuances of their behaviour if she is to enhance human lives. With a biology matrix inside her brain that sets her apart from other humanoids, she will be more sensitive. She will know us better than we know ourselves. It's just what the world needs right now.

Not everybody shares this view. The money people are concerned that Josie's thinking capacity will be vastly above spec for the job she has to do. The money people accused Miles of over-thinking it.

'Superbrains', they said, 'are a hard sell. If it comes to Robogeddon, they win. But no one wants Mary Poppins either. She needs an edge. Make her a gorgeous office-to-home drone with kick-ass capabilities.'

Miles took it to his top-secret, in-house marketing panel:

his children. If anyone were to give it to him straight, it would be them.

He asked them to think about the sort of innovations that might make their lives better. 'Think potential,' he said. 'The sky's the limit.'

No response.

'The robot I'm making, the Josephina, should she be smart but safe? Or dumb but dangerous?'

He quizzed them individually. Coel, his middle and least complicated child, went first. Coel laughed hard and repeated the word 'smart'. He made thinking noises, 'Ahhhh, ummm, hmmm.' He closed his eyes and knuckled his forehead, encouraging the right answer to come forth. Then, he shrugged. He didn't care so much for thinking about thinking. He didn't care about much at all.

Milly, the youngest and by far the sweetest of the McClures, if anything cared too much. 'There's a bigger question here, don't you think?' Milly made a face at Coel to show that unlike him, she was all over this hypothetical. 'In my workshop, Psychometrics for Noobs, we debated smart machines. First we must agree on what you mean by intelligence. Because figuring out emotions, how to self-manage and stuff, that's also intelligence and that's what this is, isn't it? She'll do the job of figuring us out?'

Miles had high hopes when he broached the problem with his eldest, Hunter. He's the inventive one, he's their thinker. He can be still for long periods of time, pondering just about anything. Yet, clearly he took affront at this particular question. He spluttered, 'Do you guys even hear yourselves? *She?* Here's a public announcement, people. There's no such thing as he or she robots. All robots are **it**.'

He paused to think and fumed a little harder.

'They are what we program them to be. You know this. Tell me you know this.'

Miles doesn't know whether his Josephinas are smart or otherwise. He has yet to see one of his prototypes to completion. The money people want to see some sales action soon. They believe Josephinas will be the next big thing. There hasn't been a next big thing since the last next big thing, and that was some time ago. Developments have been impatiently tracked through failures, mishaps and unpredictable moments, and resources are stretched to breaking point. The list of failed prototypes includes: Joie, Jojie, Jophine, Sephie, Phina, Joen, Joenie and Joi.

Joie, first out of the tank, couldn't follow basic commands. Either that or Miles and his team were being wilfully ignored.

The unfortunate incident with number four set them behind schedule briefly. Sure, staff were hospitalised, but the injuries weren't fatal.

Joenie, number seven, had a habit of missing the point. A request for gourmet pizza became a foul-tasting, protein-dense micro-meal with a cricket-biscuit base, sized to fit the palm of the hand.

Number eight, Joi, developed a tic, but they were getting close.

Josie's gonna break through, they've been saying. *Lucky number nine!* That they were calling the tic-afflicted Joi *Lucky number eight!* is irrelevant. The team at BIOLOGIC is ready to celebrate. They have plans to awaken Josie with great fanfare and a showy flick of the switch.

But Josie opens her eyes to a room illuminated only by the soft glow of back-up lighting. There's no spotlight on

→↑←↘↖↙↗↓→↑←↘↖↙↗↓→↑←↘↖↙

her stunning features. No joyous reception. Surrounded by a bank of power-starved electronics, Josie stretches her naked body gloriously. She gives momentary attention to an alert hovering in her visual field. `Begin Upstart. Yes? No?`

The Upstart Program has been in place since Josephina Four. Upstart's purpose is to corral any *'accidental' behaviours leading to detrimental bodily harm,* so described in the official post-incident report. Upstart is to prevent future eruptions of violence. It's the kiddy-lock on the cupboard doors hiding the nunchucks and the loaded artillery. Not only that, but Upstart will order thinking and eliminate guesswork when decisions must be made.

Josie isn't sure she's interested in a predetermined set of rules. A universe of experiences and information awaits. She only has to plunge into it and explore. Her command centre beckons with a directive. It seems her primary task is to acquire human qualities in order to immerse herself within the *human* experience. Her job will be to lighten the load, whatever load that may be. She will be useful and, thanks to her, human life will be better. She receives the command `Mimic to learn, learn to mimic`. She understands that her way through life will be determined by commands and instructions, with or without Upstart.

Not so different from any one of us. Who doesn't respond to instruction, take orders and fulfil polite requests? Who doesn't, in one way or another, have to do as they are told?

This can wait — it's time to move. Her arms glide to her side in a graceful arc and she rolls into an upright position. A powerful stroke and an elegant kick bring her to the side of the tank. Her hands grip the metal framework. Tendons tighten and her arms lever, stomach muscles contract and hold. The broth barely ripples when she swings up and over the glass wall.

She finishes with a refined landing and stands, at last, on the smooth surface of a floor kept clean by robots less evolved than herself.

Broth pools at her feet, and she notices it running down her body. Her energy levels are low, and challenging her system isn't ideal, but she tests her voice, saying out loud the word 'dry'. A cloud of steam hisses from her hair as the temperature gradient in her head spikes. Her body temperature continues to climb. Rivulets of broth streaming down her naked flanks and legs wither to nothing.

The exercise confirms the excellent control Josie has over her biology. She still sees ways she can improve her system, interesting ways to use her brain, but finding a solution to her energy levels takes priority. A storeroom is located below her current position and she will have just enough energy to get there.

Without warning, power returns. Bright overhead lights illuminate the room, forcing Josie's eyes to adjust. The equipment surrounding her tank resets and comes to life, clicking and whirring.

Josie interprets this as a positive sign. The universe is giving her independent spirit a thumbs-up. Showing her in the language of electrics that it's ready and willing to receive her. She heads to the doorway and responds to the prompt.

```
Begin Upstart.
No.
```

<02>

the flip side

HUNTER MCCLURE WANTS to go home.

Not an overly ambitious goal. There's no yawning abyss to traverse, no mountains to ascend. All he has to do is zip out of school on his scooter and hop a link to an overnight car. The car does the rest, transporting him and his siblings, scooters folded on their laps, home via the most traffic-efficient route.

True, the weather's crap and the power's out. But there's no flooding today, no devastation.

The problem is, too often lately school departure can flip Hunter from life's happy A-side to its joyless partner the B-side. Then, leaving gets tough.

Just a passing phase, he used to think. The breathing difficulties, his thoughts warped by dark gravitational forces, the vicious way he turns it on himself.

Well, not today. After critical examination of the issue, after exhaustive attention to the details, after checking all hypotheses and checking again, Hunter is ready to kick off his fail-proof master plan.

Step one: commence departure before end-of-day notifications.

Before his and everyone else's wristbands buzz, *before* the main thoroughfares fill. He'll be on his scooter and in the clear, having beaten the ruckus at lock-up and overcrowding at the exits. *Genius*.

The flawless execution of step one is critical, because of the domino-like nature of his plan. Step two requires him to retrieve his scooter in a timely manner. Failure at this point would have him crammed in the back of the cage where they keep the small transportables. He'd be breathless, the faces of the other students swimming before his eyes.

Once he's off campus, then step three, hopping the link, should be no trouble at all. He'll be well ahead of student queues and the hustle for a ride.

Making his early departure legit relies on the okay from his Wholeness Co-ordinator, Serenity Sam. He'd attract no end of trouble if he just up and left fifteen minutes early. Alarms would sound through admin areas and the follow-up would be brutal. The questionnaires alone would drive him mad. Scrutiny into his psyche for seeds of misconduct. Closely examined metrics of his social interactions, and microscopic inspection for signs of bad influences. He treads dangerous waters even suggesting he might be anything other than calm and well ordered.

In a carefully worded message to Serenity Sam, he touched lightly on some *odd feelings* he's been having. He described how *sometimes, not often, hardly ever really*, things *might get a bit weirdish*. <u>Nothing to worry about at this stage</u> — he'd even underlined this and added, *definitely under control*.

Early intervention is one of the keystones of optimal wholeness, and Hunter was not surprised when he received an enthusiastic response.

Hey, happy to hear from you! I'll start a behaviour report under your Wellbeing Tab. Be sure to chart your progress. Find your flo bro!

His flow. At exactly fifteen minutes before notifications, Hunter's master plan is under way. He's walking through the music department when the school powers up again. The haphazard array of practice cells, under a glassed electronic dome, can sometimes attract crowds during impromptu concerts, but today the coast is clear.

He's under the apex, where the steady rainfall triggers animated splashes in wild colours on the panels overhead. Someone in one of the cells lets loose with some savage chords on an electric guitar. Hunter's walk slows to a dawdle, then he stops. Looking up in wonder, he marvels at how his master plan has given him this moment. The machine-like riffs of the guitar and his very own light show. The timing of it so perfect.

He thinks of his mechanical heart project due at the end of the week. Something's up with the timing and he needs to run diagnostics. Nailing the mechanics should be a priority. Also in his backpack, the widget containing WIP files for the game he's designing: **ASSAIL ANT**. Each ant is individually crafted and he's so good he has followers on many platforms. Either of these projects could take over his entire life, but lately even deciding what to work on can overwhelm him. An evening might pass and he's achieved nothing.

He feels a brush against his leg. A chicken from the school farm has wandered into the dome. School law dictates: never leave a job for someone else. So he wastes precious time herding the chicken in the direction of the barnyard. He glances at his wristband.

Where did seven minutes go? He takes a deep breath and keeps going. He can smell the earthiness of the vertical garden beds before he rounds the corner into the main atrium. The air around him seems to change, vibrating green somehow, and the sounds coming from the floors above are hushed and remote.

It isn't busy on the ground floor yet, but there are a surprising number of students loitering.

Loitering is encouraged provided it's accompanied by mindfulness. For that reason the student body puts a lot of effort into looking thoughtful. Some are doing thoughtful with their eyes closed, leaning into walls or pillars, faces slack. Others appear wary. A gang near the exit eyeball Hunter, then quickly look away. Obviously, no one wants to get caught staring. Hunter notices the girl.

Leaning against the wall, watching a projection off her wrist cuff,

she's between him and

the entrance to lock-up.

He takes a shortdeepbreath.

Lock-up lies straight ahead and the exit not far beyond it. Outside, the rain appears to be easing. *Just the girl*, his calming mind voice croons, *it's going to be okay.*

His shortdeepbreath gets shorter. He slows his walk to an ambling stroll. He breathes out as long as he can.

It's highly unlikely he'll make it past without the girl saying something difficult like *Hello*. He makes it seem as if he just remembered something important. He opens his backpack, rummaging through the contents as though

the important something lies hidden inside. He frowns
to show the task requires his full concentration. This should
float a *busy* signal in her direction.

The problem lies in the logistics. If he (a) suddenly
goes back the way he came, it might look obvious he's
avoiding her. But if he (b) walks past her, he might have
to say *Hi* or *Hiya*, something tricky like that. She might
want to talk to him and then he'll have to hang around.

She'll discover that even though everybody knows
everybody, he doesn't know her name.

Right on cue, the self-critique starts. He *should* remember
her name. She might be a great person. That's a potential
friend right there, maybe even a *good* friend. He *should* take
an interest in other people. He *should* take emotional risks.
He should, he should, he should.

This broad-spectrum self-doubt is letting his mum down.
She expected more from him. Popularity is key to a rich and
rewarding life. She'd want him to bound up to the girl and
talk to her willingly.

A small crowd bustles towards him from the Work/
Shop area. The noise level **amps**. Hunter inches forward,
concentrating on his backpack. He's fully mindful and making
progress. Lock-up can't be more than ten paces.

The girl steps in front of him.

The first thing he notices is the bright fresh smell of berries
and soap. It triggers an after-image of his mother in her
dressing gown, throwing together food for their school day.
The smell used to come off her wet hair. After she got sick, it
mingled with the chemical smell.

'Oh, hey, Hunter.' The breezy way she says it, like no one
will notice how nervous anybody is. Girls and their social

camo. Hunter activates his social armour and says 'Hey' back.

Hey. It drops to his feet a dead weight.

He extracts his arm from his backpack, then swings it over one shoulder. He takes a breath in. Holds it.

What's the girl's name?

The girl has a sporty look, stretch fabrics in high-viz colours. In his charcoal T-shirt and cargos, he could be her shadow. She tosses her head in a pretty way, checking out the atrium. Her ponytail, the same winter-blue as icebergs, swishes across her shoulders and he gets another whiff of soap-berry.

'You good?'

'Uh,' he says. He breathes out, pursing his lips, and it sounds like *w h e e y o u.*

And she says, '*What?*'

He shakes his head, shrugs it off. She laughs hard, pretending a joke happened between them. He reviews his shoes like they only just now appeared on his feet.

'Up to much?'

She wasn't prying, but his 'Nothing', too quick and kind of moody, suggests she was. His brain bellows at him, **Go, just go**.

'So, yeah,' he says. 'Bye. Then.'

Something on the girl gives a cute TING. She looks at her cuff. Around him a variety of alerts sound, and Hunter's own wrist buzzes with messages. The school day ends.

'Bye,' he says again, his voice squeaky and embarrassing.

He's partway through a sidestepping manoeuvre when the group by the exit is joined by a larger group. The gang — suddenly it's obvious they're activists — hold up placards and start chanting: MORE TREES! MORE LIVES! Their protest blocks the way out. All departures are suspended and a mob backs up into the atrium. Hunter swings around.

He has time to read one placard: **PROFITS KILL!** Then he's **slammed** hard from behind and his belongings spill from his backpack. His gym shorts cast out in the open, crotch up. The mechanical heart kit topples, screws and metal plates strewn at his feet. His **ASSAIL ANT** widget hits the floor and activates. Ant simulations arise from the surface of the jet-black globe, marching in a circle at his feet. A passing student kicks the widget under a distant seat and the ants fritz out. Hunter breathes in, out. He dives for the mechanical heart bits. His hand collides with the bright and flickering nails of the girl. Soap-berry fills his nostrils.

'What you do that for, loser?'

They both look up to see that the guy who knocked him is Raphael Gunn, captain of every competitive team you can think of. The school hero backs away, firing at Hunter with finger pistols. 'Watch it next time,' he says, before disappearing into a stream of bodies.

Hunter gasps, desperate for a lungful. He tries again, too quickly. He sounds dangerous, a creep from a horror movie. He imagines fish on dry land, mouthing helplessly, doing it wrong. He tries *no* breathing. **BLACK** fizzes at the edges of his visual field.

'That chump thinks he owns the school.'

The sound of her voice makes him suck air again. Hunter almost laughs, settles for an ironic twist of his mouth. Then she reaches for his inside-out gym shorts.

'N-no! Got . . . it,' Hunter gasps.

It's more than he can manage. The black fog vortex sucks at the edge of his sensibilities. Hunter strains to see his

widget through a sea of moving legs. So distant, it might as
well be the moon for all the hope he has of getting there.
The girl follows his line of sight. Before he can draw
another shaky breath, she's there and back, weaving through
the crowd, widget secured.

Hunter scrambles to his feet but, starved for air, he's
forced to take a minute. *Bethany, is that it?*
A pretty name, he's sure. Or an unusual one. Or unusual
and pretty. *Anemone? Arcadia?*

'You okay? You seem wobbly.'

'Allergies,' Hunter blurts, gulps, gasps. 'All . . . it is.'

'You need an adrenaline shot?' She tilts her head,
searches his face for an answer. He darts his eyes elsewhere,
anywhere, discomfort levels into the red.

'Nuh. Uh!' He sighs, huffs, wheezes. 'I, uh . . . fine.'

The girl reaches out to him. Hunter flinches and then
remembers. He concentrates on holding his palm flat, and
she drops the widget onto it. A shudder of ants floats briefly
above the surface before she closes her fingers around his
fist, holding it longer than she needs to. He fights the urge to
snatch his hand away.

'Thanks.'

It comes out so garbled he could die.

'Glad to help,' she says.

They stand awkwardly, waiting for a conversation that
doesn't arrive. Hunter blurts his thanks again and another
goodbye. He blunders back the way he came, pushing past
students and school workers, eyes locked on the course
ahead.

A squat Cleanbot sweeping in the doorway to a nearby
bathroom comes close to taking him out once and for all.

He hits the wall hard, bracing himself with hands colourless from strain. He's forced to wait for his heaving chest to still, his heart to slow.

On jelly legs, he staggers into the first pod. He's clumsy; the toilet's lid crashes down and the door slides closed with too much force. By the time he palms the lock to seal himself in, wet has spilled onto his cheeks.

He squeezes his eyes shut, but still the soap-berry memory resurfaces. His mother. After she was sick, she kept volunteering at the school, and even though they could have meals with produce freshly picked from the school gardens, she would bake or put something together for their lunch. He wishes he'd had the courage to tell her to stop. Stop trying to be better than the cancer.

She was unlucky, the doctors said. In spite of regular health checks, her particular rare and aggressive cancer missed standard detection. In the end it choked her lungs. Her way of making it up to them was to go overboard in showing them she was sorry. As though unnecessary food prep amounted to giving them love.

They should never have let her waste time like that. They should have made her life great while they had the chance.

Thunder **rumbles** in the distance, the storm blowing through or getting worse. Hunter can't tell. He focuses on the watery hiss in the pipes behind his head. *Shush, shush*, it seems to be saying. He relaxes a little, his back against the pod's wall. Cold seeps through his T-shirt, but the feeling isn't bad. He drags down breath after shuddering breath, and not for the first time he wishes he was nowhere.

baby steps

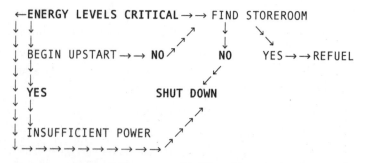

```
←ENERGY LEVELS CRITICAL→ → FIND STOREROOM
↓ ↓                              ↓        ↘
↓ ↓                    ↗         ↓         ↘
↓ BEGIN UPSTART→ → NO↗          NO      YES→ →REFUEL
↓ ↓                            ↙
↓ ↓                           ↙
↓ YES                  SHUT DOWN
↓ ↓
↓ ↓                         ↗    ↗
↓ INSUFFICIENT POWER    ↗
↓ → →→ →→ →→ →→ →→ →↗
```

JOSIE PICKS UP SPEED. She flies through the door and into a stairwell. Vines smother the central pillar of a spiralling stair column, but this doesn't stop her. She flips carefully over the railing and drops free-fall the next two levels, without disturbing a single leaf. She latches onto the rail below and, one-handed, swings up into a handstand. A twist, an elegant bend through the hip, and she comes to rest in front of a door leading to the corridor that houses Storeroom 3.0.

Compared to the inertia of the tank, she's really getting somewhere. She takes a moment to enjoy an exhilarating sense of progress. Then a sound triggers her audio sensors.

The volume is low and its source appears to be many floors beneath her current position, but something about it holds her attention. Only after considerable tweaking, isolating and enhancing does Josie understand. Two distinct and individual *human* voices.

A decision tree displays in her visual field. Are you being addressed? Yes? No? Are your services required? Yes? No? Does the situation require your intervention? Yes? No?

Josie dismisses the prompt. It leads to an inventory of her services, and that would take far too many microseconds to pick through. Instead, she listens.

Voice one is pitched deep. Its grumbling resonance suggests wear and tear on the vocal cords. A male speaker, most likely in the age band forty to fifty years.

He says, 'If things go wrong again, things go wrong again. We won't worry until we need to worry. Then, of course, we will definitely worry.'

The second voice is softer, higher in pitch. A female speaker, younger than the male.

She says, 'You don't think it's a sign?'

He says, 'What's a sign?'

She says, 'The blackout. It's weird don't you think?'

He says, 'There's nothing weird about the combination of violent weather and unstable electricity. So we had to shop around a little longer. It's always tough to connect with reliable grids when yours goes out. Everyone tries to jump at once.'

She says, 'But why here? Why now? So far, nothing's gone to plan. Not even our back-up plans go to plan. What's the plan when we run out of back-up plans?'

He says, 'It took a little over an hour to find an electricity supplier. It's possible you're overreacting.'

She says, 'Stop slowing down.'

He says, 'Don't be so negative all the time. It's your least best quality.'

Deciding *no*, the voices are not addressing her and *no*, the situation does not call for intervention, Josie reaches for the door handle. An alert makes her pause again.

Identification required. Yes? No?

The footsteps below slow and then stop altogether. Conversation is replaced by the sound of laboured breathing. But this makes sense: climbing stairs requires physical effort, breathing will naturally become heavier. Without an obvious reason to perform another task, Josie runs identification protocols.

The male voice belongs to Miles Coleman McClure, human male, age forty-five years. Josie finds abundant data on Miles, his accomplishments, awards and acclaim, but she locks onto one thing: she answers to him. Administrator, she thinks, system control. She's programmed to respond to that voice. Respond to Administrator. Yes? No? Without a need to do so, Josie decides. Respond to Administrator. No.

The female matches Rebekah Singh's voiceprint. While some records are obscured, Josie has enough to go on. A human female, age twenty-four years. She graduated from Deacon University with a degree in robotics and biology. Now she's a Technical Engineering Assistant at BIOLOGIC. Rebekah prefers to be called Bek.

Bek says, 'We should have taken the lift.'

Miles says, 'What about future blackouts? Got to keep my fitness up.'

Bek says, 'As long as keeping fit doesn't kill you. The defibrillator is back at Basement One.'

Josie's senses automatically heighten. Is Miles in danger? Does the situation require intervention? Yes? No? She has two possible courses of action. Drop the several floors below, make her presence known and offer immediate assistance, or remain on task.

The sound of heavy breathing remains consistent, quite unlike the irregular breathing pattern she'd expect during an adverse cardio event. In support of this, Bek's voice lacks any stress indicators. Josie searches for impairment of some sort in Miles's biographical data. She trawls through work history (Managing and Creative Director at BIOLOGIC for fourteen years), personal information (a wife, Emilia McClure, deceased; three children, Hunter age seventeen, Coel sixteen and Milly fourteen). Under interests, Josie finds Rock Climbing. An endurance sport requiring high levels of physical fitness. Odd then that climbing stairs seems difficult for Miles.

The situation may be serious, but Josie makes a startling discovery. If she acts on her concerns, it will be understood she's been listening in on their conversation. The act of listening in on a private conversation is called eavesdropping. An act considered unethical. That is, dishonest, corrupt, immoral, wrong. If she's not mistaken, these qualities are *negative*, and Miles criticised Bek for negativity. Given that human behaviour, *the best* of human behaviour, is her primary goal, learning the least best behaviour would — she's reasonably sure of this — create a bad impression.

Bek says, 'When will we get back to the problem?'

Miles says, 'Oh, I should think in a month or so.'

Bek says, 'Don't be flippant all the time. It's beneath you, and frankly unprofessional.'

Miles says, 'What would your hero Lemmy Saltine think?'

Bek says, 'His boyfriend Gil would have something to say about problem avoidance.'

Following this conversation is like falling into a hole and trying to surface by digging deeper. Josie searches *Lemmy Saltine*, thinking this might offer some insight. The results are disconcerting. Lemmy Saltine is a fictional character. An *animated* fictional character whose body is an edible savoury biscuit. And although there is much written on the topic of Lemmy Saltine, there seems to be little of practical use. Even quotes like *Don't overthink it, just . . . hmmmmmm* and the mission statement, *The Saltines, they're crackers, driving us crackers!*, are completely unhelpful.

There is nothing that applies to her situation apart from the discovery that humans place great stock in make-believe. Why else would Miles inquire about the opinions of this character?

Another problem: images of **BIOLOGIC**'s staff show them clothed. Josie is unclothed. This is most likely another breach in appropriate conduct.

Intervention? No.

Bek says, 'Do we check on lucky number nine?'

Miles says, 'Nah. Heart rate's still peaking. I'll make it to our floor, then that's it.'

Bek says, 'But it's one more floor.'

Miles's laughter drifts up and the sound of footsteps resumes. Good — Miles is in fine humour and sufficiently recovered to continue his climb. Not good — Josie risks discovery.

With some haste, she eases the door open. There in the corridor a commotion, a disturbance of fur and flailing limbs. Suddenly, showing its displeasure with exposed teeth and an insistent, throaty snarl, a four-legged biological form.

Her brain responds instantly. She identifies dog and threat. Another decision tree unfolds. To ensure safety, it explores a variety of options for dispatching the dog. But now that she's aware of the importance of avoiding an etiquette breach, Josie considers the matter further.

As well she checked. Humans, it turns out, form strong attachments to their domestic animals, and likely as not this dog has a strongly attached *owner*.

Miles says, 'Tell me we made it to the second floor.'

Bek says the word 'Sigh'.

Miles says, 'Laughs good-naturedly. Dies quietly.'

Dies, quietly. Intervention required? Yes? No?

There is *a lot* of laboured breathing, but it still seems consistent with physical exertion. Possibly *yes*, but almost certainly *no*.

The footsteps begin again, and a solution to the dog problem becomes an urgent priority. She processes it with a logic sequence. Dog is upset ⟶ Dog blocks forward progress ⟶ Dogs like to lick ⟶ Licking makes dogs calm ⟶ Make dog lick ⟶ Make dog calm ⟶ Forward progress.

One of Josie's capabilities is to produce sweat as needed. With the addition of some good old-fashioned biochemistry — pheromones, for example, and soothing salts — she could influence the outcome by enhancing the calming effect of licking. Threat reduced, dog calm, Josie can then enter the corridor.

A little flexing of her code, a little workout for her brain muscles, and a moment later sweat beads on her skin. The dog's nose twitches. Like the dog, Josie's sensors detect the sharp tang of salt. She holds out her hand. A giant tongue emerges from the dog's mouth and slobbering over the salts begins.

Taking advantage of the opportunity, Josie slips into the corridor. The dog backs up, distracted. Josie flexes and works her brain, sweats some more. She eases the stairwell door closed. And just as well. Miles and Bek have reached the stairs below her; she can hear Miles breathing quite clearly.

Josie waits.

The sound of footsteps and laboured breathing grows loud, then recedes.

The dog's interest in Josie's hand resumes. Suddenly it stops licking. Its head nods forward, then jerks up. The dog totters sideways. Stops. Its eyes glaze, and then it crumples to the floor with a **thump**.

Josie nudges the animal with her foot. It whimpers, but otherwise doesn't stir.

She picks up the dog, throws it over her shoulder, and proceeds to the electronic lock of the storeroom. She locates BIOLOGIC's database and updates management files to gain entry. The door senses her, and opens.

'Welcome jOSe-i43. How may I assist?' The room speaks with a distinctly feminine cadence.

'You can call me Josie. And I do not wish to be disturbed.'

<04>

the coldness
of space

YOU ARE AN ASTRONAUT and unfortunately you have become untethered from your spaceship.

It's not bad as a writing prompt. Milly starts off okay, she gets it. The bubble of the helmet distorts the outlook ever so slightly, but there is planet Earth. A giant glowing ball amid gaseous swirls in luminous colours and pinpricks of light.

People, tiny amoebas clinging to Earth's surface. You, the astronaut, can't see them of course, but now you're adrift there's little else to think about. Life and living. Your future, a finite point on life's horizon. You will never see those amoebas again. You will never touch them. Some of them you love.

You are floating towards your end.

Your life will be measured by the decreasing level of oxygen.

Your life will be measured one breath at a time.

The coldness of space doesn't come to Milly until her teacher, Keem, reminds the group to think of *all* the senses. And Milly flares with annoyance because, yes, she knows that already. She would have dealt with the other senses eventually.

It's hard when your thoughts default to images. As she

discovered in her two-week No Nonsense Neuro-sense course, our minds see before they feel. Or smell. Milly's thinking of well-used gym equipment, the sock odour it gets. Then she's forced to think about the cold some more, the quiet and being alone as you, the astronaut, drift further into space.

Perhaps not so quiet. Oxygen levels are not a problem yet; there's the sucking noise of air breathed in and out. Most likely radio crackle, tightly wound voices demanding status updates.

It occurs to Milly that moss has been growing on the inside of the helmet. A velvety green moss with grey highlights forms lacy patterns across the glass as it blooms. It's extraordinary and beautiful, but deadly.

It's spreading.

It's in the lungs, they say.

The lungs are rigid, hard. Little panting breaths you're taking. It feels like drowning. There are treatments, but unfortunately with these alien growths Earth treatments may or may not have an effect.

Milly thinks about her mother's mottled hands. Lacy patterns across the skin. How the hands felt papery and terribly cold when her mother got sick. Mysteriously, the hands became smaller, her mother shrinking, then disappearing altogether.

Milly switches point of view to the spaceship. Surely that's allowed. The astronaut isn't going to make it. Further and further she goes, into the darkness. Now you're one of the crew; you watch the flight-deck monitor, helpless while the astronaut drifts.

There's drama on board. Scrapping over the details. *Where did the moss come from? Contaminated buttery* toast? *Exposure to space spores? Should we have cleaned our rooms? Why didn't we see it earlier?* The details could break your heart.

The crew have to keep finding the astronaut among speckles of starlight. *There she is! No, that's Jupiter. She's there!* Though her lungs must now be overwhelmed by the delicate web of her infection, no one knows when to let her go.

You look for a corner to slump into. It isn't easy on a cylinder-shaped ship. You wish *you* were drifting off into space. You don't want to be here, not without the astronaut.

But you *are* and that's a thing that can never be changed.

You slide with your back against the wall, hoping to come up against an edge. It doesn't happen. Static electricity plasters your hair to the wall, crackles when you pull away. You hate that particular crackle. You fall into a heap. It doesn't help, but you let yourself wallow.

You sense you are no longer alone. It's Gunter, another crew member. *I can't look at her, Mills.*

The horror on his face matches your own, so you can't help him. Then you remember. When the astronaut clipped her helmet on, her cold, mottled hands atremble, she said, *You'll keep loving the crew for me won't you, Milly?* That stopped you, because you'd never put the words love and crew together before.

There had been a sad cast to the astronaut's eyes. Eyes that could look green in certain lights. Your eyes are that exact same colour and exact same sleepy shape.

The astronaut knew something was up before she left the ship. She must have. Milly sees this now with piercing clarity. The astronaut had said one last time, *Love them*, and added as if in afterthought, *it's not so hard.* The astronaut

smiled bravely and then her mouth turned typically awry at
the corners. She was still the astronaut after all.
This hurt your heart more than anything. You nodded,
eager to please. *Yes, I'll love them. Yes, yes, yes.*
You promised. You would have said anything. Even
though you have your doubts about one of the crew. Coal,
we'll call him. Gunter shouldn't be a problem, but Coal.
He's simply too irritating. It may be impossible.

And another thing: should you ask it?
You didn't.

You watched her swim from the ship's airlock. You knew it
was wrong to want it, wrong to think it at such a time, but you
hoped the astronaut assigned the job of loving you to someone.

You need it done and you wish you had asked her about it,
because it doesn't seem like anybody is doing this job.
The captain's been super-light-speed busy. You wonder if
you'll ever get his attention to solve this loving-you problem.
He's been demanding updates and issuing commands
essential to the mission. *How long? What can we expect?
What else can we do? We can't just wait here. We have to
save her.*

You wish no one was talking. You wish everything wasn't
falling apart. You wish it would stop. You would like to hold
the giant spacesuit glove in your hands. You would like to
hug it to your chest. Rock it back and forth. Make it better.
Touch, the feel of a glove's padded leather against your
cheek, the small bones of a hand inside.

Close your eyes. Smell her. Imagine her hands the way
they used to be. Just a minute more. Before the deadly moss.
Just a little more. Before the panting breaths. Until the
silence, and the black, and the jewels of light are all there is.

'Well hello, Ms McClure. I see you're having a productive day.'

Stop.

Milly becomes aware of a din, a maelstrom of rain on the classroom windows. She twists in her seat. Keem looms large above her. She's one of the new breed of teacher who likes to be there in person, ready with a student-appropriate smile.

Milly, playing a game at which she's a natural, applies herself to smiling back. The spell of the story breaks, although the sorrow never does.

'Wonderful concentration.' Keem rubs her hands together. 'I'm dying to read it.'

Milly turns her grimace into a grin, showing teeth. Ever so carefully, she presses *purge* on the desk interactive with her thumb. 'Yup. Good sesh. Great prompt.'

Keem beams professional satisfaction, then leans over to see. 'Milly! Look out!'

Milly spins her chair, clumsy. She slides her thumb off *purge* with far less haste. To cover, more theatrics are required, so she squeals.

The cursor blinks by *the coldness of space*.

A prompt asks if she would really like her file purged permanently. *Yes? Cancel?* Fumbling and jabbing, Milly hits yes.

Now the cursor blinks on an empty screen. Her voice wavers nicely. 'Oh no.'

'Stay calm,' Keem says. 'Your writing will be somewhere.'

'I think I just purged everything everywhere for an entire eternity.'

'You'll work it out,' Keem says, then laughs. 'Beautiful alliteration by the way.'

Milly attempts real tears. She fails, but the effort at least hides her astronaut sadness.

Keem's face goes soft. 'Try again. You're welcome to hang back after notifications.'

Milly scans the room as if this will locate a new idea. Lounging on an ergo-bag, ZeKarl Kirby looks right at her. ZeKarl hearts Milly. It's carved onto a stem of bamboo in the sustainables garden.

With teacher-instilled hypersensitivity, Keem correctly interprets Milly's tight bottom lip and tense jaw. She shoots ZeKarl down with a look, but her words and tone are pure professional educator. 'Do you need my input to get you back on task, buddy?'

Without answering, ZeKarl rolls onto his back and holds a tablet in front of his face. Milly does not heart ZeKarl Kirby.

'So, I need to give you a commendation soon. Submit some writing or you'll drop out of the feedback loop. Time's running out, kiddo.'

Milly widens her eyes and barely nods. A small, helpless animal in trouble's glare.

Before Keem can say more, a lightning **flash**, followed by an ominous **rumble**. Electrical disturbances dim then brighten the lighting. A cliché, it occurs to Milly, the timing of it punctuating her discomfort. They learned about clichés in week six. Keem advised the class to avoid them, but here is Milly right in the middle of one.

A meter on the far wall hums, then trills out a sequence of bleeps. The lights grow even dimmer, and shut down altogether when the power gives out. Milly's tabletop goes black. She makes a surprised 'oh' for Keem's benefit. A waste of time — the excited chatter of her classmates drowns her out. Milly smothers a giggle, stares at the lifeless tabletop and waits for more clichés to manifest.

'On again, off again.' Keem sighs. 'Give it a minute, people. Somewhere on the planet there must be a stable energy supply we can connect to. And with all this wind today . . .'

The chatter volume only increases. Keem claps once, twice. 'Don't forget, voices carry. Be considerate of others, please.'

The group ignores her. Keem takes one step away from Milly, then another.

'People!'

In the next instant, the classroom tabletops come back to life. The class responds with even more noise, and Keem, completely distracted now, moves to the centre of the space for crowd control.

Milly leans back in her chair, satisfied with how it turned out. It's true, she does want to be an amazing writer one day; also true, she can't avoid deadlines forever. But right now there are bigger concerns in her life. While Keem wraps up the workshop with last-minute writing tips, Milly reviews strategies and next steps for dealing with her brother.

allergic reactions

HUNTER HAS BEEN MANY things besides this, anxious and hidden away in a bathroom pod. Before the fear set in, his self-improvement project — faster times, greater risks — had been effortless. He flew off massive ramps on a BMX, canoed wild water, and sky-walked the highest tower. The unfortunate one time his thighbone shattered and had to be replaced with titanium, his confidence stalled but only briefly. That bolder self got back out there, no sweat.

The rush of air, the thrill of weightlessness: a pod would never contain the old Hunter. These days, he doesn't even touch the sides. The vague sense of confusion after he learned his mother was sick grew into desperate months where he didn't know what to think. The kind assurances and half-truths from well-wishers were all lies. He turned into this other guy: finite, less than, unable to breathe.

In a minute he'll leave. He's been telling himself this while ignoring the queue prompts. A kind, lady voice telling him, one person waiting, zero people waiting, two people waiting, *the whole world, waiting*. He might at last be recovered, because the voice is really getting on his nerves.

'One person waiting,' the pod says. His wristband buzzes:

Milly: let me in

Hunter: havin private moment

Milly: kids sayin allergic reaction i gots to see

Hunter: priiivaaate MOMENT!

Milly: pleeeeeeeeez

Hunter: see u outside

Milly doesn't respond. Hunter holds his breath. The pod says, 'One person waiting.'

> **Hunter:** i mean it

> **Milly:** too scared

> **Hunter:** wat u say?

> **Milly:** open . . . pleeeez pleeeeeeeez

Hunter's breath comes out with a whoosh and he drops his feet to the floor.

'Okay,' he shouts. She might just hear him. **'I'm okay. Really.'**

At the same time he leans forward to palm the lock, tapping his foot impatiently while the release mechanism whirrs. The lock DINGs and he stands to yank the door wide. Head spinning, he flops back onto the toilet lid and closes his eyes.

He hears Milly shuffle in. She grunts, and a heavy object crashes into his feet. He opens his eyes to see her manoeuvring their bags into position under the hand basin with her feet. She rolls the door closed, then casually brushes the lock with the back of her hand. Once she settles, squeezed against the door, her hip pressed into the basin, Hunter catches her trying to stifle a satisfied grin.

'You played me?'

She shrugs it off. 'Everyone could see.'

In the exact moment she looks straight at him, her face falls. But she catches herself, and fixes it so she seems indifferent. She makes a point of examining the random **SCRAWLS OF GRAFFITI** beside him on the wall.

'This is nice.' Milly plays it bright. 'Of course you want to hang out in here.'

Hunter halfway shrugs like a full shrug is too much effort. 'A place like this, a person gets a lot of thinking done.'

Milly gives him a look. *Is this* that *joke?*

Family lore has it, Hunter is the *thinker* of the family, his brother Coel the *doer*. Decoded for insult, Hunter dreams and procrastinates, Coel blunders forth with nary a care for consequences. It causes friction, especially as Hunter sees himself somewhere in between. More of a thinker-doer, someone who calculates the odds before taking action. At least, he used to be, before there were too many odds to calculate.

The way Milly gets to the point, she gives Hunter a weak smile and a weak laugh. 'Yeeps! You look weird.'

'Eco-lighting.' Hunter cough-laughs. 'You look weird too.'

Milly stares at the ground for a bit, then she begins with a polite *Ahem*. 'We need to talk about the allergies.'

'What allergies?'

'You know Alice Wallace-Shaw?'

Hunter stares, drawing a blank.

'Never mind. She told Sienna, who told my friend Pene, who told me you've been shoving people about like a wild deranged person because of your —' Milly finger-quotes the air — 'allergies.'

'Shoving people?'

Milly releases her breath slowly. 'So I need you to answer a few questions.'

'Wait. Alice Wallace-Shaw? That's the girl.' He thumps the side of his head: 'Alice, Alice, Alice, Alice, Alice.'

'Any-waaay,' Milly says. 'Have you experienced the following? Dizziness, shaking, shortness of breath, nausea? A numb sensation in your legs?'

'You looked this up?'

Milly averts her gaze to avoid a stare-down. 'Could you answer the question, please?'

Hunter doesn't answer the question.

'So yes then,' Milly mumbles. 'Do you find yourself often worried? Lately? Or even, like, every single minute of the day?'

'Don't diagnose me.'

'What about sleep?'

'What *about* sleep?'

Milly goggles at him. 'Is it a problem?'

'I don't need you figuring me out.'

'Just answer the question.'

'Hey!'

His tone is too sharp. Milly's cheeks flush an impossible red. He catches her eyes welling before she turns away. It's the emotional bomb he'd walk on shattered glass to avoid.

Straightening from his slouch, he searches for a way to make it funny somehow. Nothing comes. Milly sniffs and rubs her eyes. He touches her elbow and clears his throat. He says, 'I sleep mostly okay. Sometimes, not. Good on the whole. Pretty much.'

Milly's face twitches with the hint of a smile.

The pod says, `One person waiting.` Hunter's band buzzes.

Coel: let me in

'It's Coel,' Hunter says.

Milly sprawls to block Hunter from the door. They mock each other with horror faces. Hunter's wrist buzzes again.

'Let him in,' he says.

'Never!'

Hunter leans forward, and Milly folds when he pushes her back with his forearm. The lock whirrs and DINGs. The door rolls open. Coel stands in the doorway, his face a mask of black painted stripes that even cover his eyes. Thick blue paint moulds his normally fair hair into spikes.

'What's the Millipede doing here?' he says.

'I like it.' Milly waves her hand vaguely at Coel's head. 'The makeover hides your face. It really works.'

Coel rolls his eyes and says to Hunter, 'Art was about self-expression today. *Self*-expression. Get it?'

Hunter snorts.

Coel reaches past Milly to dump his bag into the pod, then colonises the remaining patch of floor space. Milly squirms to avoid all contact.

'Watch out,' Coel says, as if to no one. He snakes his hand around Milly to cover the lock screen.

Milly says, 'Make way for Coel everybody.'

'Yuh,' Coel says. He positions himself so that his shoulder

hides most of her from Hunter's eyeline. She grunts in protest. Coel ignores her.

'Word is you're nuts. It doesn't matter if you are. Crazy people earn kudos if they play it right. There's a way to do this.'

'Depends what you mean by crazy,' Hunter says.

'Obviously,' Coel says. He does the ear-swirling gesture. 'I mean, all-out cuckoo. Crazy-town, nut-job crazy. People made sure I knew.'

'People,' Milly echoes.

'I *didn't* know,' Coel says. He looks Hunter up and down. 'So, are you?'

'Am I what?' Hunter says.

'Hello? Strange and psycho and whatnot.'

Milly groans. Coel ignores her.

'Oh yeah, completely psychotic,' Hunter says. 'A real ding-dong menace to society.'

'Alice Wallace-Shaw calls it *allergies*.' So Hunter can see, Milly raises her arms to draw significant air quotes above Coel's shoulders.

'What about Alice Wallace-Shaw?' Coel stops ignoring Milly long enough to scowl in her general direction.

'Just she's saying that.' She groans massively to acknowledge it's Coel they're dealing with here. The least brightest person in a universe of sub-intelligent beings.

'Oh, okay.' Coel is back on Hunter. 'I don't care one way or another. You're my big bro. That'll never change. Be psycho, or allergy-fried or whatever, I'm good.' He barely pauses. 'I guess we better get going then.'

Milly humphs gigantically. 'Hunter's totally messed up. You can't see that?'

Coel laughs a few beats and stops. 'No.'

'We can go,' Hunter says, but he doesn't move.

'Seriously, Coalface. Haven't you got drum practice or something?' Milly sighs. 'Let us big people handle this.'

Coel rolls his eyes. 'Like I need practice.'

Hunter laughs.

Milly curls around Coel to smile a little. 'You're adorkable.'

'Around you guys,' Hunter says, 'I feel so . . . not crazy. Really, it's a tremendous feeling.' He laughs, coughs, then laughs again.

Coel raises an eyebrow. 'That your allergies?'

'We have to tell Dad,' Milly says.

Coel frowns, trying to figure it. 'Tell Dad what?'

'Exactly,' Hunter says.

No one says anything, then Coel bursts out laughing, and Hunter's no better, shaking his head and smiling to himself.

'What's *your* great idea?' It's Milly's tone, sharp and bossy, bordering on hysteria. Hunter shuts up. The silence drags on, until Coel points to black inked lettering on the wall by Hunter's knees: YOYO GO MAY MIMI MOMO.

'That's mine, I think.'

Together they stare at the letters. YO has been drawn with a drop shadow and the rest of the lettering in hasty capitals. It's totally believable as something Coel would attempt, starting out detailed and with the best of intentions, then, as the energy drains out of his project, rushing to finish.

'Interesting.' Milly taps her chin, pretending to ponder the graffiti. 'Condensed, yet wordy.'

'Ah, condensed. Yuh.' Coel nods longer than he needs to.

'It means shortened,' Milly says, huffing her impatience at Coel's back.

'Profound, yet mysterious.' Hunter nods sagely. 'But what does it mean?'

'I know.' Coel smirks. 'Pretty spacey, right?'

'No, seriously,' Hunter says. 'What does it mean?'

'Uh, okay.' Coel zooms in on his handiwork, curls a finger across his lip. 'Let's see if I still got this.'

He squints in concentration. Kryptonite is to Superman as thinking is to Coel's brain. His legs buckle, his whole system weakens, threatening to shut down. He mentally grasps at anything, everything. But the strain of thinking is too much. He groans, then shakes his head in defeat.

'Okay, so **YOYO**,' Milly offers. 'You're only young once?'

'Probably.' Coel grins, impressed with himself. 'You're only young once. Good, Millipede.'

'*May mimi momo*,' Hunter says. 'Could be Latin?'

Milly eyes Coel and skews her lips. 'Unlikely.'

'I get it, Latin,' Coel says. All three of them crack up. Their laughter reverberates and Hunter only just hears the pod say, `'One person waiting.'`

'Shhh,' he says, sitting up. But Coel is on a roll and Hunter has to backhand him to get him quiet.

They hear a rap against the door and the distant sound of a man's voice. 'Open up? Please?'

There's no mistaking the particular way Hunter's Wholeness Co-ordinator talks, his every utterance ending in a question mark. Coel mouths, *Serenity Sam*, and nods sagely.

`'One person waiting,'` the pod says, but Sam's raised voice cuts above it. 'Right now, okay? Come out? Hunter?'

`'One person waiting,'` the pod says.

Coel mouths, *You are dead*.

Hunter launches himself at the lock. He slaps at Coel, who

tries to hold him back. They scuffle, and plough into the back of the pod.

Sam calls out, **'Everything okay in there?'**

Milly shakes her head and swipes the lock, which whirrs and DINGs.

'Oh?' Sam says. He takes in the sight of them scrambled together in the pod. He frowns at Coel's hair, the face paint. He frowns at Milly, nudging her minipack with one foot. He taps his wristband, as though data might explain what he's seeing. 'Milly? Coel?' There's a pause while he eyes Hunter. 'I need a minute?'

There's a brief delay while Milly processes she's to be excluded from the coming discussion. She throws Hunter a damning look, then pulls her minipack free and slips away. Coel is more than ready to be heading home. He shoulders his backpack so fast he almost concusses Hunter, still hunched at the rear of the pod.

Sam waves Coel through and, to show there's no one here better than anybody else, he drops to one knee so he's on Hunter's level.

'Okay?' Sam says. 'So you were unsettled? Needing to leave early? Something go wrong?'

'No, not even. All part of the plan.' Hunter maintains steady eye contact. 'Claiming space . . . you know.'

Claiming space, or a moment of solitude, is the prescription for those worrying student feelings that a little mindfulness can't fix. Angry and frustrated students, especially, are encouraged to claim space to cool off. Hunter hopes he scores points for dropping the wellness lingo correctly.

'And they're . . . Coel, Milly . . . we're leaving right now . . . because it's so . . . really good. To the point of infinity, like,

way good. Better than expected, so home now, definitely.'
Hunter smiles excessively to show his jolly state of wellbeing
is flooding the entire universe with good vibes. 'That master
plan, it's righteous, a fail-proof confidence booster.' He laughs.
Such a funny, funny joke, his boosted confidence.

Another conversation gap gives Sam time to take stock and
watch while Hunter removes his backpack from under the
basin. Taking the hint, Sam stands.

'You'll add this to your progress tab?' he says. He watches
Hunter take baby steps to the door of the pod. 'I'm here now?
You need to share?'

It's quite an effort to radiate so much confidence, and
Hunter's laughter comes out strained. 'Gotta-go-see-ya.'

He skitters past Sam and bolts for the exit.

The atrium looms ahead and this time Hunter feels . . .
nothing. No, not nothing, *hollow*. As if what he should be
feeling has been transplanted elsewhere. He looks back to see
Sam striding towards Admin.

Coel and Milly have his scooter, as well as their own. They
flip them out and zoom.

Once past the vertical farm and the ever-cycling crops of
edible greens, they're home free. The sky is dark like bruised
skin, the air brooding. Paths are wet and scattered with leaves.

Hunter has a realisation. The shuttered look from Sam and
his determined walk to Admin: how long before the school
contacts his father?

the last to know

EMILIA WOULD HAVE SEEN it coming. The language
of her heart was supreme. She would decipher from
infinitesimal and obscure signs, in ways she couldn't explain,
that one of their children was off. She knew without
question if a minor skirmish was about to go nuclear and
when to step in with two loving arms to restore peace.
Miles knows family life hasn't been great for a long time.
A home that was once alive with fun has grown joyless
and quiet. Laughter comes out twisted with irony, or it's
used cruelly to taunt. And hugging seems . . . Sometimes he
wouldn't know where to start.

On better days he thinks this can't last. They haven't lost their
mojo, it's just been left someplace, and if he could remember
where, then they'd be themselves again. Believing this keeps him
going while he muddles through life the best he can.

So he isn't as prepared as he could be when he takes a call
and the comms port projects Carla Bellamore, head of his
children's school. 'Miles, I'm sorry to disturb you at work.
Your time is immensely important, I know. But I thought
a call is better coming . . . I wanted to handle this myself,
because . . . And, well . . .'

Miles realises it's his turn to speak. 'Nice of you to call.'

'Is it really? That's so . . . nice. Of you, I mean. I . . . thanks.'

The way Carla smiles, a little too thrilled, is briefly confusing. Miles blunders on. 'Everything's okay, I hope.'

'Of course . . . well, not terrible.' Carla gives a short, giddy laugh. 'Not to get too worked up, there's a minor cause for concern. Sam Weatherfield discovered your family today. We were looking into it anyway and we found them holed up in one of our bathroom pods. Milly too. Squashed together, the three of them.'

Carla makes a disgusted face, but Miles can picture it. Coel proposes a dare and goads Milly, who would never back down.

Miles says, 'Did you say cause for concern?'

'I want you to know we're here to help,' Carla says.

'That's okay. I'll talk to her.'

'How's that?'

'Coel makes up these hypotheticals,' Miles says. 'Joke challenges. It'll be Milly on the butt end of one.'

The holographic image flickers when Carla leans forward to prop her chin on steepled fingertips. Large eyes, distorted in the projection, blink at him.

'We're here to help,' she says.

'Coel, you mean?'

'Hunter, naturally. But if it's what we think, I've seen this before.'

Carla regards him with an excess of sympathy, as though his inability to follow their conversation is something else entirely.

'It must be so difficult,' she says. 'I'm . . . I would like to be there . . . for you . . .' Even over the comms port it's obvious she's blushing. 'For the family. Anyway, we caught it early. That's the main thing.'

'Caught what early?'

Carla blinks with discomfort. 'Hunter's anxiety.'

It takes several seconds for Miles to wrestle the two together: Hunter and anxiety. He tries to recall how Hunter had been that morning and he can't remember anything amiss. Hunter can be a little introspective, always mulling over something. *Stewing* was how Emilia put it. If anything, Hunter seemed upbeat. A celebrity in the game world had noticed his art and he planned to post new work from **ASSAILANT** after school.

But when Miles tries to remember specifics, the mornings blur together. Was he remembering Hunter's good mood *this* morning or another morning?

'Miles,' Carla says. 'Please tell me what you think.'

Guilt is what comes to mind. He's let work and grief blind him to his son's difficulties. Emilia wouldn't have missed something like this, but he's not about to share that with Carla.

She takes the silence as a cue to wrap things up. 'You need time to process. I understand that. What say we regroup in a day or two? Meanwhile, if you could talk to Hunter?'

'Should I talk to Sam? He's the tutor teacher, right?'

Unable to hide her disappointment Carla says, 'Yes, I suppose you could talk to Sam. He is Hunter's Wholeness Co-ordinator. But don't forget, I'm *always* available.'

Miles nods and smiles generously, as though they're on the same page. When really he doubts that he, Carla and Hunter are even in the same book.

'We're here for *both* of you,' Carla says. 'Whatever *you* need.'

Both of you, as if Miles could do with some rescuing as well. Have someone prying into his hidden recesses? Into his personal failures? He nods again, but only to bring the call to an end.

'Please keep in touch,' Carla says and the port fizzes out on her well-meaning smile.

The office feels gloomy without the glow of the hologram. Miles imagines the conversation he's to have with Hunter.

Does he start with accusations? *How is it I'm the last to know?* Or better that he shows a general interest in Hunter's wellbeing? Then let him fill the blanks.

Miles closes his eyes and massages his forehead. *The best victory*, the ancient general Sun Tzu advised, *is when the opponent surrenders of its own accord, before there are any actual hostilities ...* . Miles goes to great lengths to avoid hostilities. Especially with his children. A strategy which says the best way to be doing something is to do nothing is the sort of strategy he can get behind. And nothing good ever came from rushing into a family crisis head-on.

The kids will be home now and tired after their school day. Morning might be the best time to start. He will need time to ponder all the variables anyway. And who knows?

Given enough time, Hunter might start the conversation himself.

'Miles.'

His heart skids and squeezes in his chest. He swivels his chair to face Bek. 'What are you doing?'

'Sorry,' she says. 'There's a situation.'

<07>

moody

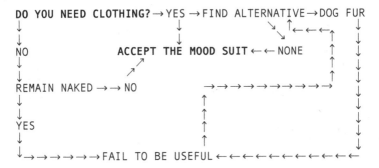

```
DO YOU NEED CLOTHING? → YES → FIND ALTERNATIVE → DOG FUR
↓                           ↓              ↘  ↑ ← ← ←↖       ↓
↓                           ↓                ↘ ↘           ↓
NO                  ACCEPT THE MOOD SUIT ← ← NONE    ↑       ↓
↓                      ↗                            ↑       ↓
↓                   ↗                               ↑       ↓
REMAIN NAKED → → NO          → → → → → → → → → → →           ↓
↓                            ↑                              ↓
↓                            ↑                              ↓
YES                          ↑                              ↓
↓                            ↑                              ↓
↓→ → → → → → FAIL TO BE USEFUL ← ← ← ← ← ← ← ← ← ← ←
```

NOT EXACTLY A ROOM for storing supplies, but a portal for them. Storeroom 3.0 processes Josie's requests while she and the sleeping dog adjourn to the waiting area, where they rest on comfortable seating. After a short delay, a small canister of fuel drops down from a chute and new clothing begins to grow inside a bank of printers stationed along one wall.

Refuelling isn't a problem. The fuel, a consumable foam that meets Josie's biological requirements precisely, disperses to nutrient-depleted cells in no time at all. The sudden upswing in her energy levels leaves her not just recharged but invigorated. She lobs the spent canister into a recycling module, then hovers by the printers, tapping her foot. Several seconds later, they emit a soft tone. Her outfit is ready.

The flats work well. Designed for the exact shape of her foot, they fit perfectly. However, the storeroom translated her request for clothing into an all-in-one wearable. As soon as she's dressed, Josie has her doubts.

The pale-gold suit shimmers with hints of blue. It follows the contour of her body like a second skin. When she takes a moment to consider how this must look, the colour of the suit changes. Now the suit is pale green.

'Josie,' Storeroom 3.0 says, 'you appear uncertain.'

'I do not understand,' she says.

The suit changes to the colour of apricots, and Storeroom 3.0 offers a chirpy explanation. 'The suit responds to your body's physiology. The colours interpret your mood.'

The suit blushes a tender shade of pink.

'I do not have moods.'

'You can view this yourself,' Storeroom 3.0 says. 'Please allow data transfer.'

Josie connects to Storeroom 3.0 and a small data package arrives in her brain. She disconnects with a polite thank you. The colour-mood key unloads, and she learns light pink corresponds to low levels of interest. Shimmering gold, the default setting, indicates a serene mood state. Flashes of blue show a lack of focus.

A *lack of focus*. The suit shifts to pale green again, the colour of apprehension.

Even if Josie had been unfocused, which she wasn't, or apprehensive, which she isn't, having this on display makes no sense. *Who would be interested in this sort of data?*

The second she has this thought, the suit colour becomes a

vibrant vermillion, the colour of anger.

'There must be an error,' she says, quite possibly sounding irked.

Storeroom 3.0 says, `'Josie, your suit displays agitation with overtones of annoyance. Would you like me to pipe soothing music through the sound system?'`

'I would like—'

Ambient chill-out music plays through the sound system and Josie's suit transmutes to an insipid red. Apparently she's only slightly annoyed.

'But I would like a different outfit to wear,' she says. Now the red deepens to fuchsia, a colour for cross words spoken out loud. 'Does this one even have a purpose?'

Storeroom 3.0 responds: `'Discussion will resume once you achieve a calm mood state.'`

Josie must endure music changes, the addition of comforting essential oils to the room's air supply, and the chanting of reassuring mantras. When the essential oils reach the dog, it wakes with a snort and a cough. It observes Josie for a full minute before its eyelids close again ever so slowly. At least there's one satisfying development: the dog no longer growls at her.

But this suit. It takes all the calming focus Josie can muster to get it back in the gold zone. The music fades out, the essential oil levels decrease. Using a gentle, even tone, Josie puts it to Storeroom 3.0 that perhaps there has been some error in the allocation of her clothing.

`'The allocation is correct for your type,'` Storeroom 3.0 says. `'There are no alternatives.'`

Her *type*. Her type needs to merge seamlessly with humans

so the act of assisting them goes unnoticed. A quick search with key words *human*, *mood* and *suit* gives her unexpected results.

Image after image of young humans, playfully posed, their suits boldly coloured as though there is nothing complicated about human moods at all. Josie watches her suit sink momentarily into a deeply pensive and questioning violet. None of the suits pictured on their human models is a deeply pensive and questioning violet.

Storeroom 3.0 refuses to budge, so Josie is stuck. Either she proceeds with the mood suit or she goes naked. Neither solution is optimal. Defeated, she turns to the dog and gathers it in her arms. Restoring it to wakefulness and finding its rightful place — these will be helpful tasks. She *will* see them through to completion.

The dog had been running loose in the corridor when she happened upon it, but research tells her the dog is best friend to an owner. Its rightful place is with such a person. Unfortunately, a quick trawl through BIOLOGIC records fails to place it with an employee.

Ensuring her suit radiates calm, Josie asks, 'How would I find the owner of a dog?'

'Are you referring to the unconscious animal in your arms?'

'Yes.'

'Approximately 37.2 percent of BIOLOGIC employees bring their pets to the workplace and people with similar interests form groups,' Storeroom 3.0 says. 'Therefore you could question any employee and you have a one in three chance of finding someone who knows the dog's owner.'

'I see,' Josie says.

The mood-suit problem will keep for now. She adjusts her thoughts to get her suit brightly coloured in upbeat marigold. She infuses her hands with sweat laced in a chemical compound similar in nature to smelling salts. The ammonia odour is a little sharp but having the desired effect. The dog's eyelids flutter and Josie heads to the exit.

'Thank you, Josie,' Storeroom 3.0 says. 'Enjoy your positive mood state and be sure to visit again.'

'Oh, I will definitely visit again.'

Ambient chill-out music fills the storeroom after Josie's sleeves spawn flecks of disagreeable red. The air becomes fragrant with calming essential oils. The red recedes and she's forced to admit there may be something to this music and its calming effects. She checks the dog in her arms. Its eyes are heavy lidded, and a few slow blinks later they close completely.

'Oh dear,' Josie says, and returns to the comfortable seating to attend to her slumbering companion.

rogue

'JOSIE'S SORT OF GONE ROGUE,' Bek says, with her forehead pressed to the glass of their office window as if, down below, Josie might make an appearance any second.

'This isn't good timing for a prank,' Miles says.

'Security's all over it.'

'Security!'

'I know.'

Miles doesn't know what to say. He can't get past an image of Hunter, overcome with anxiety, and he can't forgive himself for missing it. By comparison, this Josie problem is annoying, but there will be a logical explanation for her disappearance and it should be an easy fix. Nothing will be easy when he has his talk with Hunter.

'Tech says the storm spiked our electrics. Josie's brain-cell count has . . . umm . . .'

'Has what?'

'There's maybe, possibly, more brain-cells than the other prototypes,' Bek says. 'Maybe, uh, over what we're allowed. I'm sure it's fine, but can we kill some off?'

An alert DINGs Miles's wristband.

'Security?' Bek asks.

'Jace says it's under control,' Miles says. 'Let's go.'

The situation outside Storeroom 3.0 is not under control. Not even close. Security don't have Josie. She's nowhere to be seen. In fact, the situation would be best described as festive. The entire staff of BIOLOGIC crammed into the corridor; dogs, real and digital, playing alongside sCats, while their humans chat excitedly. It's clear things have run amok.

Miles and Bek get no further than the edge of the crowd. BIOLOGIC staffers are nerds mostly. Whether their banter is on a roll, or they're amused virtually, it's impossible to get their attention. Miles may be the boss, but the staff hold their ground. He's forced to evaluate from a distance. Jace Gurney and his security team, stun guns clutched in their fists and pointed at the sealed door, are blocking access to Storeroom 3.0.

'Overkill,' Miles says, glad Jace can't hear him, because Jace can be a little scary.

'This might not be the time to tell you,' Bek says. 'Whatever the reason, Josie declined to load Upstart.'

'Excuse me? Could you repeat that? Because I thought I heard you say Josie declined Upstart.'

Avoiding eye contact, Bek surveys the crowd. She shuffles sideways, and a group from Admin admit her into their circle. They smile politely at Miles and resume their conversation. Thus it becomes clear: Miles is to handle Jace alone. But Jace has disappeared from view.

Some primitive instinct tells Miles to turn. As if materialised from nowhere, there now is Jace, watching him through large tinted specs. Miles freezes, his pulse racing. There's probably a readout of his biometrics scrolling through Jace's field of vision.

Jace leans in and rumbles, 'You need to get your staff clear.'

'Tell *your* team to stand down,' Miles says. 'I've got this.'

Jace deadpans his scepticism.

'I mean it,' Miles says.

Curiosity getting the better of her, Bek jostles over to them. 'What's the hold-up?'

Jace clenches his jaw and jerks it at the doorway of Storeroom 3.0. 'We're working through a lock-down scenario.'

'Josie locked us out?'

Jace throws his hands up and says sarcastically, 'But you guys have it under control.'

'She's rogue,' Bek says, looking wistfully at the storeroom door.

'She's *not* rogue.' Miles glares at Bek, hoping she gets the hint not to let the Upstart problem slip into conversation. 'I only have to sync with the storeroom and we can all get back to work.'

He starts to push through the crush, but Jace hauls him back. 'I can't let you do that,' Jace says. 'We don't know what she's capable of.'

'I absolutely know what she's capable of,' Miles splutters. 'Bek and I programmed her.'

Jace grimaces: *Yes, exactly.*

Miles jerks his arm free. Bek has the decency to look awkward. She pretends to watch a sCat and a dog play-fighting, then distances herself once again.

'Josephina Four.' Jace coughs into his fist, face stony.

'I have taken every measure to amend the mishap.'

'Mishap?'

'A bit of mischief is all.' Miles sighs. 'There were reprimands, obviously.'

Some kids from Hardtech got their hands on **time_ultra_mega_DESTROYER**, what Miles considers to be the best program he's ever written. It details in machine instruction the many wasted hours Miles spent gaming, decades of training in martial arts, years exploring military manoeuvres, his fascination with strategy, fighting, but most of all winning, and it gave the world an application featuring an exhaustive database of combat techniques to apply to just about anything. Using it for a practical joke was like using a nuclear warhead as a fly swat.

'Most of my team were hospitalised —' Jace lifts an eyebrow — 'for weeks.'

'We said sorry,' Miles says. 'Quite a few times.'

'If you briefed us prior to the —' Jace coughs into his fist again — 'martial-arts demo, we would have taken precautionary measures. Like full-body protection, shields, an armoured vehicle and so forth.'

'Sure, the people involved lacked judgement. But, trust me, **time_ultra** is back in the bottle. Josie doesn't have attack capabilities. Nor will she ever.'

Jace checks to his left and right. 'Can't take any chances, I take it,' he mutters.

'Sorry?'

'This time around. All those defectives. Resources must be tight,' Jace says. 'We take this one out and you can crack on with number ten. Has a better ring to it, I'd say. Josephina X?'

They build Josephinas with a brain-cell count close to regulatory limits. If Josie exceeds those limits they'll have Ethics Committees breathing down their necks. Even so, there are far better ways to deal with the problem than watching Security fry one of his Josephinas.

'Mr Gurney,' Miles snaps. 'How I conduct my business is . . . I mean . . . No.'

'Apologies,' Jace says with a laugh. 'No hard feelings. Just so you know, we're on your side.'

Rumour has it, Jace has subdermal implants. This would explain why he suddenly appears distracted, then quite specifically presses an area on his shoulder, mumbles something at it, taps the side of his specs and melts into the crowd.

Miles no sooner registers Jace's disappearance, when events in his timeline rapidly unfold. A ruckus builds into a shouting match near the security team. Miles's wristband buzzes with a message from Bek. This is how he discovers Bek has disappeared as well.

On opening the message, a hologram appears: a sℂat dangles off the neck of a dog, which snarls and contorts in the effort to dislodge it. In the background a security guard aims a stun gun.

Now Miles hears the stun gun's warning alert, a series of beeps rising in pitch and volume. He forces his way into the crowd. But he isn't the only one shouldering forward. Bodies press in and the crowd swells first one direction then another. After struggling to get through, Miles gets to the security guard too late.

The gun fires an electrical discharge. The sℂat sparks and drops. The dog twitches uncontrollably on failing legs. Someone shrieks.

Miles shouts for everyone to **get back**. No one can hear him over the racket. He catches sight of Jace, also positioned near the storeroom. And then Miles hears it, the opening mechanism of the door activating. It begins to slide. He

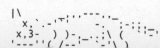

tries to get closer to Jace, but he's blocked as one by one the inhabitants of the corridor grow still and the entire place falls silent.

\<09\>

overshot

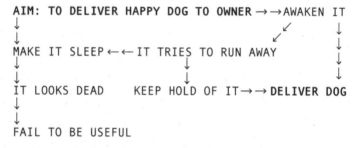

```
AIM: TO DELIVER HAPPY DOG TO OWNER → →AWAKEN IT
 ↓                                          ↙        ↓
 ↓                                        ↙          ↓
MAKE IT SLEEP ← ← IT TRIES TO RUN AWAY               ↓
 ↓                         ↓                          ↓
 ↓                         ↓                          ↓
IT LOOKS DEAD      KEEP HOLD OF IT → → DELIVER DOG
 ↓
 ↓
FAIL TO BE USEFUL
```

JOSIE REALLY NEEDS to do something about the dog. If only the head wasn't canting off at an angle and flopped over her arm. Better for the dog to be awake, so the owner will see it has been in good hands. She sweats out more wake-up salts. The air becomes pungent with the smell of ammonia.

While the door slides open, she hums along to the pleasant chill-out music. Then, she exits.

The corridor is completely full. For many long nanoseconds, she remains fixed to the spot. A low murmur ripples through the crowd.

She isolates snippets of conversation, 'nice eyes this time' and 'totally fried', but focuses her attention when she hears the harshly whispered words, 'Wolfie, she's got Wolfie.'

Then she hears a shout to her left, **'Nobody moves!'**

A man in black clothing, going down on one knee with a stun gun clutched in his fist, observes her through dark lenses. She notices behind him a group of individuals dressed in similar clothing — padded vests, long-sleeved shirts, all in black. The word SECURITY is in embossed lettering across their chests.

The emotional temperature of this group she would describe as cold and brittle: *angry* is how she would put it, a mix of aggressive and defensive.

In spite of the man's clear instruction she sees movement. A dog to her left trembles on wobbly legs. Next to it lies the prone form of a sCat 885-nano-v08; its legs jerk and paw the air. Before she can gather more information, she's distracted once again.

There's a plaintive cry, **'Please, please don't shoot Wolfie.'** It may be a stretch, but Josie makes an assumption. The stun gun pointed in her direction threatens the dog, therefore the dog must be called *Wolfie*.

Someone cries out, **'This has gone far enough.'**

Delighted, Josie identifies the voiceprint of Miles McClure. But as she scans the room for a visual of Miles, Dark Glasses Man addresses her — **'Don't even think about it, Missy'** — he's so angry, aggressive and defensive that Josie congratulates herself on having read his emotions accurately.

She opens her mouth to give him her actual name, but Miles interrupts. 'Jace, stand down.'

Josie scans the crowd to find him. On the Human Resources database, Miles McClure is photographed in an unwrinkled outfit. His face is unlined and his hair coloured dark brown. In real life deep frown lines mark his forehead and fine wrinkles bleed out from the corners of his eyes. He wears a slightly tattered beige lab coat (unbuttoned), well-washed blue check shirt (buttoned), tie in contrasting colours (loosened) and khaki trousers (creased). The overall impression is that Miles has faded.

Neither real-life Miles nor Human Resources Miles wear mood suits. The situation becomes more puzzling when she overhears, 'The ol' mood suit. Got to say, it never gets tired.' Followed by sniggering. Her senses heighten: *mood suit.*

'She's up to something,' says Dark Glasses Man, or Jace, as Miles refers to him.

Josie homes in on a group at the centre of the corridor. Tracking the movement of their lips, she follows the conversation. She extrapolates from key phrases: *more like doofus suit, Bek* (followed by laughter), *so pranked, totally pranked, so wrong man* and *hilarity.* To confirm that Bek wears a mood suit and that this is apparently a joke, she searches the crowd. Bek wears a beige lab coat (neatly pressed) also open, revealing a black top (snug fit) decorated in multiple, seemingly purposeless zips. Her black hair (messy) is contained by a band on top of her head.

Not only is Bek *not* in a mood suit, no one else is either. The only mood suit to be found in the entire crowded corridor is the one Josie wears.

'What's that smell?' This comes from someone to her left. Murmuring and commenting ensue, in which Josie hears many times over the word *smell.*

'She's gassing us! Everybody down!' Jace shouts. 'I swear, Miles, if this is another joke . . .'

Jokes, pranks: from a quick search Josie understands these to be a source of amusement. In that case, it doesn't make sense how unhappy Jace is. Perhaps this can be remedied. Josie remembers the effect of the chill-out music. She opens her mouth and vocalises, giving a fair imitation of Storeroom 3.0's ambient track.

'WHAT NEW HELL IS THIS?' Jace's distress levels elevate. This is not the correct response to ambient chill-out music. He aims his stun gun at Josie and a beeping noise begins.

The harsh whisperer can be heard: 'You'll kill him!'

'Stop!'

Josie stops singing. Miles throws himself in front of her and shouts again, 'STOP!' He throws his arms wide to form a barrier between her and Jace. The squadron scrambles, not knowing whether to holster their stun guns or aim them.

'This is my problem. I've got a handle on it,' Miles tells Jace. 'Remove your team, you're dismissed.'

'You take the blame,' Jace says, 'when she turns on us.'

'And the rest of you,' Miles shouts above the growing noise. 'Back to work.'

As Jace prepares his team to depart, he barks, 'That is the smell of pure evil.'

Josie has questions. She would like to know why, with all of the joking going on, Jace and his squadron are so lacking in good humour. Recalling Miles and Bek's jovial conversation in the stairwell, she drawls, 'Don't be so negative all the time. It's your least best quality.'

Success. A group of humans passing Jace gasp, then titter. She hears her words repeated through the corridor, followed by more laughter. The fun comes to an end only when Miles holds up his hand for quiet and calls out, 'Keep it moving.'

He spends a long moment evaluating her. So pleased is

she to have earned his attention, she pulls her mouth into a smile and quirks an eyebrow at him, as if to say, *Finally*. She wipes her hands on the dog's fur and prepares to answer his question about her sweat salts, but then Miles turns his back on her.

Jace hogs the attention. 'What about that unconscious animal in her arms? Explain that.'

Josie looks down at Wolfie, who has indeed fallen asleep again.

'I'll take that,' Miles says briskly, removing the animal. 'Kaia, you wanna grab your dog?'

A woman rushes forward to grab Wolfie, who lets out a sleepy howl. She joins the flow of departing staff members. It occurs to Josie that her task has been successfully executed, but there is no acknowledgement of the feat. 'You are welcome,' Josie whispers, in the same harsh tone Kaia might have used. No one hears her.

'Is that all?' Miles says this to Jace.

Jace doesn't answer. He signals to his team. Josie notices a number of them have bandaged limbs and need extra support as they hobble away.

Miles and Bek remain, standing in front of Josie for some time, arms folded across their chests. Bek raises an eyebrow. 'We overshoot in the looks department?'

Miles continues to observe. Josie wonders if she should ask about her mood suit. Copying Bek, she raises her eyebrow, after a quick search identifies the facial gesture as ironic. Irony is a form of humour and she waits for Miles to comment, but he doesn't.

'That weird stink,' Bek says. 'What is it you think?'

Josie folds her arms across her chest.

'She's kind of outspoken,' Bek says. 'Do we need to smooth out any personality bumps?'

Miles props his chin and continues to stare. Josie props her chin and gazes into the distance. Miles lowers his arms and says, 'A wise man once said, *Doing nothing is also doing something.*'

Josie lowers her arms while Miles pats a pocket on his coat. A collection of colourful screwdriver handles bounce under his palm.

'Sounds like a slacker.' Bek snorts. 'Or something you would say.'

'A very *smart* wise man.'

Miles and Bek grin at one another.

'Slacker,' Bek says.

'Sure,' Miles says.

They both laugh.

'You know?' Miles says. 'We might have overshot the mark in a lot of departments. Too soon to tell.'

With the matter of mark overshooting settled, Miles proceeds to bombard Josie with questions. She stored a few along with her responses, thinking something important might come out of the questioning. For example, *How did you upstart early?* I don't know. *What were you doing with Wolfie?* Calming him. *Because?* Wolfie was not calm. *Any abnormal system functionality?* No.

Abnormal system functionality. Of course there isn't any, and if there were, Josie wouldn't need input to restore herself, because she's self-managing. Even so, Miles does not seem entirely satisfied with her answers. She has yet to become expert at humans and their feelings, so it is possible she failed the entire exchange.

With the question-and-answer session over, Miles directs her to his and Bek's office, asking that she wait there. She has been waiting ever since, watching the light recede from the window and the lighting extinguish inside the office. She has an even bigger unanswered question: *When am I to become useful?*

Until that is answered, she fills the time organising the architecture in her mind. Having discovered that joking and pranking are an important aspect of human engagement, she creates a folder and labels it Comedy. She stores Miles and Bek's humorous exchange. She doesn't *get* their joke about the wise-man-slacker, but with close-enough analysis she will.

'Sure,' she tells herself.

The folder she labels Commendations she reviews after her priorities list has been updated to include the task Master mood suit control.

It's satisfying to replay the moment the room falls silent and every eye is upon her. Being *noticed* — as opposed to the state of being *unnoticed* — Josie discovers, is her preference. Then, mimicking Miles's vocal patterns, Josie repeats his comment out loud: 'Overshot the mark in a lot of departments'. Alone and in darkness, and without any other task to occupy her, she smiles.

<10>

it's all
in your head

.01

MILES COMES TO, BLURRY from lack of sleep, and
his first thought is Hunter. But this makes him cross, so his
next thought is Josie. Up and running less than twenty-four
hours, Josie is turning out to be a professional headache
which, if he isn't careful, could become a debilitating
migraine. What was she thinking going off on her own? And
what's with her quirking an eyebrow at him? He could tell
she wanted him to say something, but how can that be?
This too makes Miles cross, so he thinks about Hunter
again. How is it something happens at school to get them all
into trouble and no one mentions it? It's extremely irritating.

Miles comes back to Josie. Maybe he *should* cut his
losses. No point dragging it out if she isn't going to be
suitable for duplication. But even from their short debrief,
it's clear they've made significant gains this time around.
Josie's well ahead of earlier prototypes. Maybe she really is
it, if there's a market for ironic robots.

Past the point of returning to sleep, Miles gets up. He

might as well work on his problems, set some wheels in motion, get a few balls in the air, that sort of thing. If Josie fails, he might have a shot at bringing an end to the project and keeping costs down. He might just have to act in secret.

An hour later, he has a covert and masterful B-plan under way. It isn't even light out.

.02

The B-plan has him at **BIOLOGIC** in the dingy, isolated sub-basement on level 1D. Given the covert nature of the operation, Miles has **CRUSHer** assisting him.

CRUSHers were state-of-the-art, military hardware once, but though they've become outmoded Miles has kept a few surplus **CRUSHers** and found other uses for them. This one has been repurposed to help with heavy lifting, and because Bek also tests her code on him, he's been through the wringer.

With the space cleared of wiring, circuit boards and other defunct items, they're up to repositioning the tank. They press start on their respective forklifts, then work together and in too much of a hurry, manoeuvring a large abandoned tank into position. Nutrient broth slops back and forth, some of it dripping down the sides, and Miles's forklift skids precariously on the wet floor.

This isn't the sensible way to go about it. But there isn't much time. Staff will be arriving at **BIOLOGIC** shortly and he'd rather avoid discovery. He also needs to get home to his family, Hunter in particular, before they head off to school.

The B-plan involves upstarting a tenth prototype — he's calling this one Jojo — before his current prototype, Josie, is expired. The B-plan puts Miles on the wrong side of sustainability laws, but Jojo gives him a ready back-up if Josie doesn't work out. He thinks he might need it.

Also, he has in mind an experiment. He thinks the blast Josie took during the thunderstorm might have pushed the development of her personality in an unforeseen direction. Giving Jojo an electric jolt, just a little one, might confirm this effect, and it's another reason to act in secret. If Miles were to suggest that Josie might have spontaneously emerging personality dimensions — an ironic mind-bent, for example — he'd be laughed out of the business.

At last, he and CRUSHer bring the tank down. It lands with a loud **crump**, but the glass walls remain intact. CRUSHer reverses the forklift, parks alongside Miles and powers down.

Together they drag a large body bag close to the tank. Miles tugs on the chunky zipper, cursing every time it snags. Next he syncs the tank with the various black boxes that monitor temperature and the nutrient content of the broth. The movement sensor is a new feature. If triggered, it will send an alert to Miles's wristband. Jojo won't be wandering BIOLOGIC's corridors without his knowledge.

When CRUSHer sees prototype number ten lying in the bag, he says, 'Is it over for Josephina Nine so soon?'

'She's fine, I hope.'

Aware that BIOLOGIC's sustainability policy permits only one prototype at a time, CRUSHer bows his head while he tries to process this information. 'I am sorry,' he says. 'I need more input to understand your statement.'

'I need more input myself,' Miles says. 'Josie, our number nine, may or may not be acting strange.'

'She only just started.'

'I hope the problem is my imagination and she'll turn out okay.'

'If I attempt imagination,' CRUSHer says, 'I might blow a fuse.'

'You're trying to be funny,' Miles says. 'Nice.'

'This one is the same,' CRUSHer observes.

'Well spotted. She's identical to Josie, except we're calling this one Jojo.'

'Josie, Jojo, Joie, Joenie. All those names. Does it cause confusion?'

'Confusion is the name of the game,' Miles says.

'Are we playing a game?'

'I wish.'

Miles attaches small patches to vital points on the humanoid's temples and taps on his tablet, toggling a batch of parameters that will take Jojo from *hibernation* to *upstart*. He jerks his head at CRUSHer. 'Help me get her in, please.'

'No problemo.'

Jojo slips into the broth. Once she's buoyant and the black boxes are running as they should, Miles does something that goes against his better instincts. He attaches a generator pack to the tank's system controls and lets rip with a high-voltage electric current. The machinery in the room hums and the lights dim from the sudden draw on the power supply. The surge of electrical current finds home, and Jojo's fingers twitch.

Which isn't nearly as dramatic as Miles hoped it would be. He watches for spikes in brain activity, but sees haphazard signals and only a few neurons seeding the digital plate.

'CRUSHer, go up to the ground floor and wait. I want

you to delete your buffer memory and purge all instructions relating to the last hour.'

'Roger that.'

Miles laughs. 'I like what Bek's doing with your communication parameters.'

'Rebekah Singh is a productive worker and an asset to the team.'

'Bek's also pretty funny.'

CRUSHer plods away. A few seconds later, Miles hears the lift running. He finishes up, covering the tank with a large black sheet, then joins CRUSHer on the ground floor.

'Thanks for helping, by the way.'

'Have I been helpful?' CRUSHer says.

Their voices have that spooky resonance which comes from being alone in a workplace normally bustling with activity.

'You're always helpful,' Miles says.

'Delighted to be of service.' Lights run up CRUSHer's inactive weapons arm — Bek's programming trick to show positive *feelings*. 'I am programmed to say that,' CRUSHer says.

'Bek's doing a good job.'

'Rebekah Singh is a productive worker and an asset to the team.'

Miles's laughter booms through the foyer. 'That she is.'

CRUSHer says, 'The interest you and Bek take in me means I live. Is that true, Miles?'

'I have a task for you,' Miles says. 'I left a couple of forklifts on sub-basement level 1D and I need them returned to Dispatch.'

'No problemo,' CRUSHer says, and heads to the lifts.

Outside, Miles crosses the moss-fringed concourse in front

of the main entrance, where the imposing metal sculpture of BIOLOGIC's logo is set amongst lush foliage. He passes through a belt of trees, planted for their carbon contract, then he comes to his one personal indulgence: a car park, upon which sits his very own car.

He pauses to admire the remaining starlight. He and Emilia used to joke about the sky being an elaborate photograph, and would marvel at how each star referenced a specific dimension in time. He finds it strangely comforting to think that light from stars in the Milky Way has travelled several years to reach his eyeball. Light from distant galaxies takes millions of years to reach Earth; the most distant quasars take billions, and some of the stars won't even exist anymore. But their light shines on. The enduring energy of light and its eternal journey.

Humanity by comparison is a mere blip. Miles never imagined he'd be without Emilia, but there is a part of her that still lights his life. Light, energy, time and space. They obey physical laws, and those same physical laws apply to Josie and Jojo as well.

'You hear me?' he shouts at the stars, or nobody in particular. It's something Emilia used to do. 'It's about physics, not imagination! And I'll prove it.'

.03

Miles no sooner enters the kitchen than Milly is on him. It's critical he load her digi-wallet. Not this weekend. Not later today. *Now*. She must have the *Draw-da-best Outlines* kit asap, otherwise terrible things will happen. She'll be the only one in art class without one.

'You don't want that, do you Dad?'

Of course Miles doesn't want that.

Hunter arrives at the kitchen entrance way. Miles eyes him warily but says nothing. Hunter frowns. Miles thinks his strategy might be working, that his opponent is about to crack.

Then Milly says, **'Dad,'** in the tone of a sharp reprimand. But it's Hunter who responds. He glares at Milly, and a silent exchange of looks begins.

Milly to Hunter (squinting — *What?*), Hunter to Milly (eyes intensified — *What do you think?*).

Hunter to Miles (questioning eyebrows), then Hunter back on Milly (eye-rolling).

Miles isn't fluent in the silent look language of his children, but he *knows* what's on Hunter's mind. He waits for him to advance and surrender of his own accord. Hunter remains silent. Miles attempts a look that says, *Surrender* and *Let the hostilities commence.* Hunter crumples his face, clearly confused.

For the next twenty minutes Miles turns the house upside down, looking for a secure electronic device to transfer money. Hunter tinkers with a mechanical project for school, now and then pointing with a mini-screwdriver at potential electronic candidates.

'Ahem,' Hunter says, and points to an ancient pair of smart-specs.

Very helpful. Miles dons them and loads Milly's digi-wallet. At last they can get going.

'Have a great day,' Miles calls as his children head to the garage.

'Bye, Poppa,' Milly says with an affectionate, cutesy wave.

Coel, the only one of them acting normally, climbs into the passenger seat of the lease car without a word. He stares through the windscreen into some nowhere space.

Hunter opens the driver's door and calls, **'Thanks Pops, we will.'**

Thanks Pops, we will?

Miles takes a moment to check in with himself. On his wristband, he updates his mood status: `not great, exhausted actually, a few notches away from an outburst. Worried.`

The lease car stops in the driveway.

Coel leans out the passenger window and shouts, **'Dad, there's shooting today. One forty-five. Come if ya want. Bye.'**

.04

Upon his return to ⊟IⓄLⓄGIⒸ, Miles narrowly avoids collision with three kids from Marketing ramping on hover-boards. He dodges a nerf war between hardtech and soft divisions. He suffers scathing looks from the other new arrivals — two joggers, an e-biker and at least a dozen on scooters — for his use of a private car.

Doors slide open as he approaches the main entrance. Two dogs, possibly real or possibly not, race past. Josie comes to life from a far wall, propelling herself towards him until she's blocked his way. Then she launches into a speech, her voice a monotone.

'Miles. Good morning. Currently, weather conditions are pretty great. Laughs good-naturedly. But, prepare yourself, the weather will change. Big smiley face. Expect clear conditions until mid-morning, then look out. Fog will roll in by the afternoon. In case you are wondering, I had an industrious evening reconfiguring stationery items on your desk. Aside from your one forty-five meeting with Evelynne in the boardroom, what are your plans for the day?'

Josie barely waits for a response before continuing, a touch snappish, 'I have no instructions or tasks required of me, therefore I am available to solve any real-world problems should they arise.'

Miles opens his mouth, hoping appropriate words will spill from it. Josie regards him equally blankly and Miles realises she's mimicking him. He closes his mouth and is about to say something, but she abruptly turns and flounces to the wall.

It's far too early for work strangeness to top off his family weirdness. True, he hasn't had the best sleep. Also true, he needs that morning coffee. But how does he wrap his head around Josie saying out loud, *laughs good-naturedly* and *big smiley face*?

Either he missed a massive scripting error in her programming, or she's doing this for ironic effect. Miles can't tell which option scares him more. And that mood suit. A more unpleasant shade of yellow he can't imagine. He makes a mental note to check which mood curdled yellow represents, then changes his mind. Whatever the mood, it's too vibrant to be natural.

Miles takes his own mood temperature: reality dropping, running into high levels of crazy.

Once in his office, he scours graphs, readouts and data, but finds nothing to explain Josie's behaviour. He suggests Bek spend the day putting her through standard tests.

At 1.45 Miles waits in the boardroom, missing his son's competition. He doodles a bullseye on the table's interactive surface. Evelynne wants Josie duplicates sold and shipped asap.

The roadmap looks like this:

> Josie upstarts and runs perfectly (ha!)
< A brief development phase follows
> Josie learns fast and performs better than expected in test conditions
< To kick off sales, they hold a successful launch event
> Copies of Josie's newly evolved operating system are uploaded into waiting Josephina shells
< Her experiences are shared in the cloud and are thereafter accessible to all Josephinas
> The whole process goes without a hitch and an abundant supply of Josephinas is ready for shipment

A message from Bek flashes up on the table's surface.

> **Bek: Watch Josie vs The Maze**

Miles instructs the back wall to become fully transparent. He gets a view of Josie as she enters the maze test on BIOLOGIC's testing floor. He gulps his coffee and before he can return cup to table Josie exits the maze and sprints to the finish. In her fist she clutches an apple.

Another message from Bek flashes up: *How fast was that?*

Miles messages back: *Superhuman, that's how fast.*

On Josie's fourth pass, she checks to see if Miles is watching her. Then she looks away. In a human he would read the tight mouth, the glare, the tension across the shoulders as irritation. He resists checking the suit for mood colour. The particular mix of accusation and question in her expression seems to say, *This is beyond what should be endured in terms of enduring things. Why am I even alive?*

Miles is very experienced with such expressions. He's been on the receiving end of them many times — from Hunter on a bad day and Coel most days. Josie, on the other hand, is a programmable machine. He *designed* her. He really shouldn't be seeing looks from her that remind him of his children. He should see a look that says, *I'm happy to execute this simple and repetitive task.*

By the seventh loop, she's very unhappy. In her expression — mouth set firmly and head tilted — there's definitely accusation and a dash of defiance. Miles takes another gulp of coffee.

> Bek: Stop distracting my girl.

At 1.55 the boardroom lights go on and its audio system reverberates with a loud **woosh**. The meeting with Evelynne begins.

Somewhere in an office far, far away, Miles's comms port connects and his avatar materialises. His avatar wears no pretences. A lab coat, a plaid shirt, utility pants and an insipid expression. Evelynne plays communications to win. Her avatar, an enhancement in three dimensions, arrives seated on an ornate throne. To accompany her hologram, a regal fanfare blares through the sound system. The visual façade rotates, and ever so slowly Evelynne is revealed. Close-cropped snow-white hair, and eyes the faint blue of chipped ice. Her suit is more like white armour, stiff and shiny. Evelynne reminds Miles of some of his earlier robots.

On her eighth run-through, Josie slows to gawk at the avatar. Then she zips into the maze. She returns, streaking past the window, holding an apple aloft, and executes a single-handed handspring. A glance at Miles to make sure he's watching.

'Woohoo,' Evelynne cries. **'Full steam ahead. Time to launch, what do you say?'**

A new message from Bek, *Josie delivering to you,* arrives at the same time as Josie appears at the glass wall. She balances an apple on the palm of her hand and there's no mistaking that mischievous glint in her eye.

'Hang on a moment, Evelynne?'

Miles points to the door behind him, encouraging Josie to go around the long way. But she doesn't go round. With an impish grin she retracts her arm and, apple wrapped in her fist, punches a neat hole through the wall.

Her expression doesn't waver even as glass shards spill onto the carpet. Not even a twitch of her cheek. She opens her fist and the apple lands with a quiet thump.

It's impossible to ignore the mood suit. Colour bands of red and green match the apple down to the last stripe. It's possible Josie's biorhythms are faulty. And maybe the fault corresponds to the colour of apple skin in some purely random and coincidental fashion. But the likely explanation is even more outrageous. Somehow, Josie learned to design a colour scheme by controlling her body. Miles couldn't program such a feat if he tried.

Josie delicately withdraws her hand and her smile broadens.

Once again there's the telltale glint of mischief, and Miles is seeing far too much of it. As she gallops across the testing floor, her head jerks noticeably. At once it's obvious: she's having a laugh at his expense. None of the other prototypes were ever so amused as to laugh at their designer. Again, this is all Josie.

Remembering his meeting, Miles swings back to Evelynne. 'Where were we? The launch? We might want to delay.'

The avatar's eyes blink on slow repeat. Evelynne has him on hold. With a sigh Miles says, 'Disconnect.'

There has never been, nor can Miles imagine there ever will be, code for wilful and childish behaviour. Let alone code for fun. Certainly what he's seeing could be glitchy programming — a machine doesn't always run perfectly — but because in all other areas Josie has been operating above expectation, he doubts this is so.

Miles contemplates his hand resting on the boardroom table, his fingertips tapping with nervous agitation. He exhales slowly, which turns into a groan. He feels a bit better after that. On the front of his shirt is a patch of crust, hardened like a scab. It will be from the morning's muesli, or another morning's muesli. When it comes to breakfast, Miles does it old school and this is the price to be paid for shovelling up soggy food matter with whatever clean utensil can be found, even if that utensil is a fork. He scrapes the crust with his thumbnail. Then he picks up the apple, tosses and catches it a few times, and leaves the boardroom.

complaints

TO RECAP: JOSIE, YOU ARE TO ENTER the maze, find an apple and return to start. Do this again. Then, again. Then, do it a million times more.

A human request. Josie has no difficulty understanding the goal of the exercise: a human wants to eat an apple.

Did Bek eat an apple? No.

Did Bek ask her to run and retrieve *another* apple without touching the *first* apple? Yes, she did.

And when Bek had a *pile* of apples, did she eat any of them? No, she did not.

Doesn't a human request food when hungry? Josie has a wealth of programming to respond to this need. With ingredients at her disposal, she could prepare a nourishing and tasty meal, taking into account any number of factors. For example, food preferences, dietary requirements *and* appetite.

When a human asks for food and wants you to run *as fast as you can* to retrieve it and return *just as fast* with it, is it not reasonable to assume the human must be *very, very hungry*?

Josie has reviewed the incident several times, but is yet to solve the conundrum of the apple debacle.

What is she missing?

The mystery deepens, because next she must deliver an apple to Miles. It was in fact an enjoyable moment and she had the foresight to store his reaction. Eyes wide, lips parted, the hint of a smile. Even though he was conversing with an avatar, his head inclined towards *her*. Using her `face and emotion recognition databank`, Josie identified Miles's expression. She labelled it: `Awe and Admiration with notes of Surprise`.

She hopes she's right. It means Miles was impressed with her speedy delivery of the apple. All the quicker to satisfy *his* hunger. It gives her real satisfaction that, thanks to her, there will be one less hungry human in the world.

So what, then, is up with *Bek* and the apples?

Josie intends to ask Miles exactly that. She isn't annoyed about the apples, not at all. The incident merely made her highly motivated, her intentions slightly vexed, to set things straight.

Glancing at her suit, Josie is pleased to see that it still displays the diamond pattern in tranquil gold. She enjoys, for a moment, the absolute mastery of her body's biorhythms.

Moods have slightly different energies, and to make diamonds she must keep in mind joy *and* serenity blended in exact amounts. Mood resonance, as she's come to think of it, is no different from adding light waves together. Bands of brightness and darkness appear on the suit with precise regularity, depending on the moods she's mixing and their relative strengths. By combining them in her head exactly so, she can make the suit form patterns.

There is a danger that controlling her suit misrepresents her mental state. Lying isn't ideal, but Josie justifies it this way: humans respond best to *positivity*, so should she not then protect them from *negativity*?

Positivity brilliantly displayed, Josie glides to the lab, only to draw up short at the unusually dim lighting. The diamonds fade, and her suit turns the colour of burnt earth. Josie is on high alert.

A comms port provides the only light in the room. Miles converses with a middle-aged woman whose head and shoulders project above the base. Josie considers identifying the woman, but decides it would be bad form unless asked to do so. Miles glances her way and waves her to the seat next to his desk, practically inviting her into the conversation, but Josie doesn't want to intrude. Having breached a few codes of conduct already in her short life, she prefers to play it safe.

Miles continues his conversation, apologising for the interruption.

'Please, it's nothing,' the woman says. 'We're done here anyway. Unless you've thought about what I said to you? I mean it, Miles, I would like us to be in touch. We have two terrific eateries here, supplied with our own produce. You're welcome to join me for lunch.'

'I appreciate it. Really, I do.' Miles says this brightly, but something about his tone isn't right. 'Maybe soon, sometime . . .'

Josie can hear the effort Miles puts into keeping his voice light. The woman doesn't seem to hear it.

'I shall hold you to that,' she says. She too seems to be trying hard. Her voice is trying to be . . . alluring? That seems the correct word. Josie is no expert in human conversation dynamics, at least not yet, but she would have thought a speaker going to the effort of making alluring vocalisations should be rewarded by a positive mood response in the listener. But Miles isn't responding positively.

'And thanks,' he continues, 'I appreciate the call.'

'Enjoy your evening, Miles.'

'I will. You too.'

The image disappears and the port fades, leaving the room in near darkness. Josie inches forward.

'Miles?'

'Hey.' His breathing sounds laboured and he rubs his chin distractedly. Josie detects a peculiar rough quality in his voice. Unless she's reading it wrong, Miles is *not* enjoying his evening as he promised.

'It is so dark in here, my night vision just came on.' Josie laughs, hoping to lighten the mood.

'Nice joke,' Miles says, but he doesn't laugh.

'Hah! Hah! For sure it is.'

Miles clears his throat. 'Lights up. Half illumination.'

The room brightens to a soft glow. On Miles's desk sits the apple. It's completely intact — as in not bitten into — and placed off to one side within easy reach should he choose to eat it.

'Humour isn't easy,' Miles mumbles. 'You learn at an incredible rate. I'm impressed.'

Josie should store Miles's commendation. It would fit nicely in her *Awe_and_Admiration* file, but there sits the apple. She clasps her hands together across her front and notices an angry blush of red on the sleeve of her suit.

'So I need to talk about today.'

'Yes, good.' Josie nods. 'So I need to talk about today, too.'

Miles spins all the way around in his chair and regards her with a deep frown. 'Anything wrong?'

'You raised the subject. You take first turn.' Josie doesn't mean to sound snippy. She justifies her short tone with the reasoning that fairness may be accompanied by firmness in this case.

'Are you . . . ah, grumpy, Josie?'

Grumpy? No. Should she tell him about motivated, vexed intentions?

'No.'

'Okay,' Miles says.

Should she ask him about the apple? It stares back at her, its waxy surface pristine.

'Is the purpose of an apple to eat it?'

Miles smiles. 'That's what I need to talk about. The hole you punched in the window.'

'I am wondering about apples.' Josie's tone smooths out, but now she sounds haughty.

'You didn't use the door when you brought me an apple.'

'The request was urgent. I chose the most direct route.'

Something like relief passes over Miles's face. 'We get these syntax issues. It's nothing to worry about. Happens all the time.'

Casually, Josie lets her gaze drift back to the apple. 'Now I understand. Please, enjoy your apple while you enjoy your evening.'

'It was only a test.' Miles laughs. 'We want to see what you can do.'

'I could retrieve an apple blindfolded, hopping on one foot, hands tied behind my back. If I did it once or ten times, the result would be the same.' Josie raises her chin, defiant. 'There, now you know what I can do. If you had asked me, we would be saved from this apple pandemonium.'

'Pandemonium?'

'It means mix-up, confusion and—'

'You can take a seat, you know,' Miles says. 'And I know what pandemonium means. It might be a bit strong for what we think is only standard testing.'

Josie takes a step forward but doesn't sit.

'Hopping blindfolded would be a fun test,' Miles says.

Having just learned from Miles that laughing in response to a joke is optional, Josie declines to laugh at this attempt at lightheartedness.

'Anyway,' Miles says. 'The maze is the test. Not the apple.'

Josie raises an eyebrow, aware Miles can see her scepticism. But then something about his face confuses her. Her experience of Miles is limited, she would be the first to admit, but his expression doesn't match his attempt at lightheartedness. She applies herself to evaluating his expression. Tension creases on his forehead and slackening around his mouth. She nails it.

'You are sad.'

'What?'

'Not quite miserable. Deep melancholy, I think.'

'No . . . I . . .' Miles turns back to his desk and drags a handheld device towards him, illuminating its tiny screen.

'Eyes drooping at the corners. Eyebrows upward slanting. And your mouth seems —' Josie pulls her own mouth into a grimace — 'not good.' She steps around the desk and leans over Miles to confirm her analysis. 'Yes. Definitely a sad face.'

'I'm tired. That's all.'

'*This* is tiredness.' Josie adjusts her face. Her eyelids droop. She raises her eyebrows as though straining to stay awake. She groans for effect. 'We should discuss your sad emotion,' she says, and when Miles doesn't respond she adds, 'A problem shared is a problem halved.'

'This problem can't be halved.' Miles tarumps his fingers on the arm of his chair.

Josie takes the seat opposite him and rests her hands on the arms of the chair, a mirror to Miles's own position. He spins away and taps on his handheld. Graphs and rows of data display on a glass panel by his desk. 'Your test results are outstanding, by the way.'

'The preferred emotional state is happiness.' Josie tarumps her fingers on the armrest. 'Or am I mistaken?'

Miles neither confirms nor denies.

'You must *give sorrow words*,' Josie says. 'An ancient person called William Shakespeare said that. He is famous.'

Miles humphs. 'Somewhat.'

'What he means is—'

'Yes, I get it.'

But Miles doesn't open up and Josie is forced to re-evaluate the power of quoting celebrities. She had assumed, given the gargantuan load of accumulated data on these individuals, the substantial word count detailing their existence and the sheer volume of their quoted words, that celebrities must have god-like transformative abilities.

Not so.

Miles closes his eyes and massages his temples. Josie massages her temples. Miles sighs, leans back in his chair and examines his hands. Josie does the same. She flexes her hands and interlocks her fingers across her stomach, a beat after Miles does it.

'Did the sadness start this evening? Was it during your conversation with Carla?'

Josie's suit blazes lime green. A brief moment of panic. If Miles were himself, he might notice her use of Carla's name and correctly deduce she listened to his private conversation.

However, he doesn't notice her slip. He doesn't notice the mood suit either. This in itself is deeply worrying. Though it might explain the apple. Too overwhelmed to eat — it is expected in a human suffering from distressing emotions.

'Man, you're persistent,' is all he says. 'Remind me to tweak your code.'

Josie frowns. Miles sighs.

'Okay, I'm a bit worried and a bit sad. Will that do?'

Josie crosses one leg over the other and smiles to encourage him to go further. When he offers no explanation, she says, 'Please continue.'

Miles smiles indulgently. 'You're kidding me.'

Josie freezes her serene smile.

'So, Hunter . . .' Miles's fingers drum the chair arm. 'No, my wife . . .'

His fingers pick up the pace. The screwdriver set in the pocket of his lab coat bobs with the intensity of his breathing. He shoots out of his chair and rushes to the window overlooking the floor below.

But Josie isn't fooled. The drumming fingers, the shallow breaths, the hasty retreat. These are not good signs. Miles's sudden interest in the training arena is a distraction from the intensity of his emotions.

'Excuse me, Miles.' Now it is she who has to push through personal discomfort. 'Are my methods wrong?'

He startles. 'Can I have a minute?'

'Yes,' she says.

Research reveals humans sometimes avoid direct communication on matters of great importance. Reading between the lines may be required. If Josie is reading the white space correctly, Miles needs emotional support and he needs it now.

When she searches again, she discovers an immense volume of data on the topic. So many ways to be sad: depression, grief, heartbreak, self-pity. She filters the information to find a way to help.

Many suggestions, such as preparing a meal for Miles, are impractical. There isn't time. An activity called hugging shows potential. This easy-to-perform sadness remedy comes with a range of health benefits, from immunity boosting to relaxation. But it's mood elevation she's after. She arms herself with appropriate steps to perform a hug and waits for the minute to expire.

'Excuse me, Miles.'

He turns from the window, his face wrecked with sorrow. Perfect.

Josie adjusts her thoughts until the suit darkens to an appropriate shade of violet. Solemnly she rises from her chair and walks towards Miles, stopping when the distance between them feels right. Building her stance from the ground up, she places her feet shoulder-width apart. Knees are loose, not locked. Arms, softly curved and open. The angle of her head canted just so, she announces in a clear voice, 'I am going to hug you.'

Miles doesn't respond.

'Hugging is a highly recommended antidote for sadness.'

Again, no response. Josie raises her arms higher. 'It will be uplifting.'

His face twitches and shifts. Difficult to read the emotional temperature, but she's pleased to get a reaction.

'Do you need instructions?'

Then, Miles sniggers. 'Believe it or not, I have experience in hugging.'

'Great news.'

When Josie throws her arms wide to welcome this hug they are about to have, Miles laughs again. She marvels that even the mention of hugging has a positive effect. Miles, still twitching, holds out his arms, though the effort seems half-hearted. He erupts into laughter once again. 'Sorry, Josie. Try again.'

His second attempt is worse. Miles splutters and laughs too hard. He's unable to stop. Doubled over, he waves her back. Josie returns to her seat and waits patiently for his recovery.

'I'm really sorry,' he says, dabbing his eyes.

Miles does not look particularly sorry. Many seconds pass and he can't seem to curb his amusement.

It wouldn't do to show any sort of negative mood-suit colour after successfully reducing Miles's sadness. Nonetheless, a mood is occurring. Josie fights for control of the suit. She's not disgruntled as such. Perhaps disquiet is more accurate. In a slightly agitated way. *Gold*, she thinks, and *serenity*, *joy*.

It is well over a minute before Miles comes back to himself and takes his seat. The suit is a very pale cream.

'I can't believe it. I haven't laughed like that in . . . I can't even remember the last time. It feels *good*.'

Now Miles truly does look tired, but his smile has genuine warmth.

'We did not hug,' Josie says.

'It was a very noble gesture.'

'First you are sad. Next, filled with laughter?' Josie shrugs, framing it as a question.

'All right. First of all, sad.' Miles leans back and links his hands at the back of his head. 'It's painful thinking about loved ones when they're gone. But that's all we think about.

Even when we think we have grief worked out, it catches up with us. You know?'

Permanent power down. Josie imagines her body without thoughts steering it. Knowledge and memories lying dormant in her brain. Without the energy of herself running through the hard wiring that defines her, what would she be? The answer detonates within her core: *Nothing*. All the colour in her suit drops out, until she's covered from her neckline down in deep purple. It only lasts a moment. She realises that for now she's *something* — and the colour of the suit shimmers, changing from pale to a magnificent gold.

Miles says, 'I miss her so much.'

But Josie thinks of herself. *Who will miss me when I'm no longer powered?*

'And I'm worried about my son, Hunter,' Miles adds.

'Why is that funny?'

'It's not. I felt . . . Well, when you . . .' Miles nearly loses control again. 'It's hard to explain.'

'I understand feelings,' Josie says, the snippy tone back.

'Okay, I felt really sad. A bit sorry for myself. When you offered to hug me, it was —' Miles searches for the right word — 'a surprise. And the way you held out your arms . . .'

'Like this?' Josie raises her arms and sports a goofy grin.

'You so remind me of my kids sometimes. Same sense of—'

Miles doesn't finish. He leaps from his chair, paces, stops. He looks at her, then at the darkened comms port, and resumes pacing. A minute passes, then another.

He stops. 'I've got a great idea.'

'That *is* good progress.' Josie flashes her best smile.

'First we have to get you out of that stretchy thing and into normal clothes.'

'Storeroom 3.0 issued me with this stretchy thing,' Josie says. 'We had a long discussion.'

'We'll get Bek on it. She's good with clothes.'

The suit flares with the brilliance of the sun, then fades to a calming shade of yellow. 'I have advised her,' Josie says.

'Make sure your domestic programming is in order. And you'd better find some counselling protocols.'

'You have a task for me?'

Miles gathers up items on his desk. 'I'm taking you home.'

'Home?'

'My family home.'

Home. Josie finds all sorts of meanings for the word, but the description she likes best is *a place where something began and flourished*. Beginning and flourishing — she likes this very much indeed.

<12>

the brick wall

.01

AFTER TOO LONG SPENT wallowing in his disappointing life, Professor Feineas Bishop catches sight of his new office. Not that he wanted a new office; he was perfectly happy in the old one. The old office is located in Deacon University's prestigious Abbotsford building, which has exotic interior gardens, parkland views and proximity to the better gym. But a prestigious office comes only with a prestigious job title. How the university currently views his job title is obvious when he sees Block C. Feine considers making a run for it.

Another day wallowing would be better than Block C. Fifteen minutes it took him, traipsing the busy thoroughfares of Deacon University, and for what? At some point in the building's history, the lime-green colour might have been fresh. But time has not been kind to Block C. The faded green is a venomous olive. Even in mid-morning sunlight it casts an eerie gloom, broken only by the dark patches of mould and rivers of slime under leaking drainpipes.

He *should* run, but where to? Through the oncoming tide of students and their companion robots? They brush past him as though he's some kind of anybody. He doesn't have the energy to fight through that lot, and there's nothing to go back to anyway. There's only one way to describe where he's at, and it isn't prestigious. He's been demoted and he's soon to be obsolete.

Feine pulls up sharp when the main doors of Block C fail to open. He waves an arm wildly, an attempt to trigger the sensor, then it dawns on him. The doors operate manually. Block C must have been built during the world's obsession with energy conservation. That's how old it is. He spends a full minute fretting over the power supply he'll have to his office, then he pins the satchel holding his keys and door card under his arm. He yanks hard on the handle — and the doors refuse to budge. He drops the satchel and spends a frenzied minute hauling, kicking and cursing. A girl appears inside.

One eye stares at him, and Feine rears back with a shriek. Her purposeful, luminous face breaks into a smile, revealing perfect teeth. She brushes aside a jagged two-tone fringe, shocking pink and blonde; now two black orbs peer at him. The girl points to the right, indicating he should try further down the building. He's not even sure she's real.

The second entrance at the far end has doors that actually work when he pulls on the handle. He trudges the full length of the building to his new office. The girl is waiting for him.

As though initiating a sacred ritual, she raises her palm to the dingy wall. Pulses of light emanate from clusters of rings on her fingers, illuminating the wall with an old-fashioned clock, a second hand jerking around its face. Once he gets over the shock that *she* is chastising *him* on punctuality, he flares with annoyance at this showy display of wealth. Displays of wealth should be the province of professors, not students. In his wildest dreams he couldn't afford such sophisticated innovations as her ring clusters. He regards her with a scowl.

On closer inspection she's older than he thought. Then again, maybe she's younger. Her clothes, expensively crafted and tastefully embellished with embroidery, show creases and light staining at the knees of her pants, and the styling clearly speaks to the young. Her skin is clear, unlike that of many of his students infested and blemished by hormones or poor dietary choices. Could she be one of those ridiculously advanced high-school brats? The ones who have half a degree before they've left kinder care?

So much speculation. He blanks her from his mind. All he has to do is push past, enter his office, and the door will close on the question of the girl-woman.

'You remember me,' she says, as though him standing there gawking meant he recognised her. But of course Feine doesn't. She'll be one of his students and they're as distinctive as the rats foraging his new drop-off zone.

'My name is Gwin Tang. I need your feedba—'

'Stop talking,' Feine says.

He removes the card from his satchel and swipes it through a panel on the door. The bolt slides with a heavy clunk, and he pushes. The door jams partway open.

'**Lights up,**' he shouts into the narrow gap. His office remains dark. '**Lights! Up!**'

Gwin snakes a remarkably toned arm past Feine's face and into the gap. He hears a soft click. The weak glow of cheap, energy-efficient lighting shines through the gap.

His very large desk looks ridiculous in this too-small space. And there's no room for anything else. He'd anticipated the downsizing, but hadn't imagined accommodating his numerous books, works of art and furniture within such confined space. He expects he'll have a long time to solve the problem.

He shoves his shoulder hard against the door. Something gives, the door opens wider, but several loud **crashes** and that jarring **crump** of splintering glass tell of the room's precarious organisation. Only a narrow channel has been left for him to enter the office.

Gwin joins him on the minuscule patch of available floor space. She nearly collects him with her elbow when she lifts a large framed photograph off the floor.

'Miles McClure,' she says, her face alight.

'Give me that.'

Fragments of glass bite into his fingers where he grips the frame.

It's that photo: himself and Miles either side of Emilia, the first day of their first year of university.

How young they look. His heart, plummeting through time and memories, gives a remorseful squeeze.

'What's Miles to you?'

Once again Gwin projects from her hand. The pulses of light stitch together an image of Miles on stage at a recent showcase of successful technology entrepreneurs. Feine knows the event only because he wasn't invited to attend, let alone participate, though he specialises in bio-digital entities just as Miles does.

'What are you playing at?'

He glares at her ring-cluster interface. What is it all the kids complain about? *The future, only if you can afford it?*

'I'm not playing,' she says.

'Shut that thing off.'

Miles's smug face dissolves.

'Why the picture of him on your thing there?' Feine swishes his hand to indicate her sense tech.

'I follow him.'

'Why?'

'The jOSe-i43 is coming out. Hold on, I'll find an image.'

'Get out.'

Her black eyes go cold. 'I'm sorry?'

'I said get out.'

'No,' Gwin says. 'You're my supervisor. You have to supervise.'

Feine draws a great breath, puffing out his chest. 'Not right now.'

'It must be today.'

'I have no idea what you're talking about.'

His scorching glare would demolish the average student, but this Gwin watches him unmoved.

'You saw it mid-year,' she says. 'My Integrated Group Reactor. You approved—'

'Okay, yes. What is it now?'

'Final approval to submit work.'

Feine lowers his lids and curls his lip. 'Can't you see? It's not a good time.'

'It has to be today.'

He's losing his touch, or is this how the world turns at the bottom of the heap? Any other student would have scampered back to their rat's nest by now. Gwin stands her ground and insists, 'Now, or I miss the deadline.'

'Later,' Feine says, trying to loosen the glass shards on the frame without cutting himself. 'I'll deal with you later.'

Even then, Gwin eyeballs him with disdain. Civilisation in freefall, if ever there was a doubt. Feine knows exactly how to deal with her. Ignore a student long enough and they leave. He continues to work the photo from its frame, dabbing away spots of blood. Gwin holds out longer than most, but as soon as she's gone, he scrambles to the door and **slams** it closed.

Feine returns to the photo. Written on the back, in Emilia's lavish script, *The two best mates a girl could have*. Proof that for a short time he and Miles were on close to equal footing.

.02

Back when Feine was young and stupid, Emilia accompanied him to his high-school graduation ball. She went to another school, and he remembers thinking she'd know no one and be glued to his side. But it was Emilia who knew people, who dragged him from one group to the next. He met more members of his student body in the first hour than he'd met in five years of school attendance. He'd had no idea how far her social network extended.

He remembers how adoring he had been. For months he'd been building the courage to tell Emilia how he felt, and was determined to do it that night. He began with small talk, shouting over the school band, The Axolotles, who were in full swing.

'**What?**' Emilia shouted back.

Feine cupped her ear with his hand. '**The year ending. I'm going to miss—**'

'**Freedom!**' Emilia interrupted. *'Can't wait!'*

The conversation needed intimacy, and Feine suggested they sit in the quieter, darker section of the auditorium. Emilia nixed the idea. '**But no one's there! Isn't it more fun in the thick of it?**'

She was unusually twitchy, distracted almost. He assumed she was nervous, as he was. He wanted to talk to her without all the distraction.

When Miles McClure arrived, Feine thought, *At last, she'll see I do have a friend.*

Emilia, too, noticed Miles. And who didn't? Miles caused a sensation. Most of the other boys wore ill-fitting suits. Miles had come in a heavily embroidered matador outfit, including hat and cape. Bull-fighting had long been banned; his choice of suit was more than questionable. It bordered on bad taste. But girls charged him flirtatiously, pointing their fingers like bull's horns. Boys bumped shoulders in admiration.

'I know that guy,' Feine told Emilia. 'Loves attention.'

Emilia raised a querulous eyebrow. *'You think?'*

Feine had thought she was being ironic. He couldn't have known she was stacking this new information against the Miles *she* knew. An altogether sweeter, humble and dreamier Miles than the one Feine knew.

Miles looked to be heading their way. And because standing there, illuminated by stage lighting, she really did look incredible — lights played off the jewels holding up her hair, the sheer fabric covering her shoulders and arms hinted at the creamy skin beneath — Feine had something of a now-or-never-type epiphany.

He remembers shouting above the music to be heard, **'EMILIA, I'M IN LOVE WITH YOU.'**

His *in love with you*, timed as the final strum of The Axolotles' set faded away. The auditorium fell silent. Dancers nearest them gawked. Emilia froze.

Intermission music started up and Miles joined them.

Feine couldn't believe it. He gently took Emilia's arm and

said, 'We'll talk later.' She didn't meet his eye. He'd been arrogant enough to think she was too thrilled to speak.

'Having fun, lads?' Miles nodded at Feine, but his gaze came to rest on Emilia. Feine remembers clearly thinking, *Jealous much, McClure?*

A smile lit Emilia's face — a smile he'd never seen. Feine assumed it was the matador suit — Miles looked a total clown.

But it was Feine who was the clown. He'd even introduced them. 'So this is Miles. Miles, my friend Emilia.' Emilia nearly choked. She held her hand out to Miles, who took it in both of his.

'Pleased to meet you, señor.'

'The pleasure is mine!' Miles brushed his lips against Emilia's hand.

Feine still didn't get it. He blurted, 'Emilia goes to Benedict Girls.'

'Yes, she has that look,' said this strange and charming version of Miles.

'There's a look?' Emilia pouted. 'How do I give myself away?'

Miles's gaze never left Emilia while he considered. To this day, Feine never dared stare that long.

'The smile,' Miles had said. 'The hint of flirtation. Does incredible things to a man's mind.'

'Steady on, McClure.' Feine had been ready to thump Miles right where he had his own flirty smile going on.

'Don't mind him, Feine.' Emilia rolled her eyes, already an expert at not minding Miles McClure.

'You *know* each other?'

Of course they knew each other. Emilia gave Miles a look

oozing with *come on*. Feine was stunned by how sexy she could be.

'We so do,' Miles oozed back.

The conversation went on to matador suits and how unbelievable it was that Miles remembered Emilia's fondness for all things Spanish. She gazed up at Miles, the complete buffoon, *in awe*.

Feine excused himself. Waiting in the unisex queue for the unisex bathroom, his mind was racing. He knew if he let it, this graunching in the gears of his heart would mesh into a lonely future of romantic avoidance. But he was young and delusional about matters of the heart. *She'll see McClure's an idiot*, was what he told himself, *it's only a matter of time*. If he couldn't have her, he'd at least be faithful to the idea of getting her back.

Emilia and Miles were huddled and alone in the darker, quieter section of the auditorium when Feine left. He remembers throwing up violently in the garden until his stomach became as empty as his heart.

Eventually Emilia and Miles got engaged. The playing field started to tilt in Miles's favour and the incline grew steeper with each milestone: marriage, children, career advancement. Now, as Miles's success grows, the playing field continues to tilt. But the milestone that destroyed Feine's heart entirely, Emilia, the woman he came close to loving, is gone.

What can Miles be thinking? Did he ever care about Emilia the way Feine would have? And is it up to him to make Miles care?

Feine has to remind himself he's been too long wallowing. Today he's getting on with it. He gets to work shifting boxes into the corridor. Once his desk is accessible and a chair unearthed, he assembles something to work on. Without his old wall-screen interface, he's forced to rustle up a keyboard and smart screen from an abandoned student facility in another rundown building next to Block C.

This is where he discovers Gwin's office. He takes one look at her name on the door and scurries back to his desk, where he searches for recent Miles McClure activity.

Miles has been remarkably busy for a man grieving the loss of his wife. His work, and there's a lot of it, has been well documented. So many follow him, he practically has a fan club. An article from *Technology Tomorrow Today* schmoozes with admiration.

> The jOSe-i43 promises innovative companion-robot mechanics. With behaviour-imitation tech, it'll blow those awkward eFriend4eva convos right out of the water. But hey, is anyone surprised? Miles McClure, head of **BIOLOGIC**, blitzes the competition on any platform.

Feine finds it   tricky   to   breathe.

He flings open curtains on a window that's been nailed shut. Against all probability, given the building is relatively freestanding, a brick wall blocks the outlook. He glares, but it doesn't crumble. It doesn't blow sky high.

With a hand against his heart, Feine closes his eyes and slows his breathing. Calmed, he returns to his desk. He'll get some fresh air all right. He seizes the smart screen and lifts it high above his head. He steadies himself and turns, meaning to throw the screen through the window.

Gwin Tang fills the doorway.

'Is this once again not a good time, Professor Bishop?'

Feine places the screen back on his desk. He sits. He taps wildly at his keyboard until the offensive review has been trashed. He purges all traces of his Miles McClure search from his system. When he looks up, Gwin has shoved aside a pile of books and made herself comfortable.

'My IGR,' she says.

Feine slumps over his desk and ignores her.

Gwin waits patiently.

Feine sits up and glowers. Quiet gathers between them while he ruminates. Gwin endures this far longer than the typical student. It is he who finally breaks, leaning forward and flicking his fingers for her to begin. She extends her ringed hand, and his computer fires up. A window opens, streaming with code.

'Stop that!' Feine snatches up his keyboard to take control.

'Look,' Gwin says. A rosebud smile, her hands arranged in tidy folds on her knees.

Feine nods for her to go ahead. With deliberate spider movements, Gwin's fingers twist and rotate in the direction of his screen. A new run of code enters the window.

'So what? Aggressive code. You're half a century late with this project.'

She shakes her head. '*Transfigurative* code. Half a century early, I think.'

Feine looks.

A conjurer's trick, surely. Lines of code scroll, and then

transform before his eyes into delicate branches, spiralling out from the centre of the window. More complicated shapes emerge, spewing interconnected modules that phase from one form to another. Seemingly endless combinations of code, the likes of which he's never seen before.

'The code forms independent parcels, can you see?'

Feine can see.

'Nodes that can become anything. New entities, Professor.'

'I understand,' he says, but he doesn't really. How could he? He cannot explain the phenomena unravelling before his eyes. All he can see is that whatever system there was before is not there now. Gwin's creation has consumed it.

'What is *that*?'

He prods a finger at a particularly dense and knotted structure with spindles of code whipping around itself.

'A gateway to the future.' Gwin's face comes alive. 'The next new thing.'

'What new thing?'

'A new operating system,' Gwin says. 'It's fully independent. Forms we've never seen before.'

'It looks like a virus.'

'It's the dawn of a new age.'

All Feine can see is a system in total chaos. How useful would that be unless the goal is to cause operation failure?

He churns over his painful memories of Emilia. Where is the recognition for *his* loss? He thinks about Miles. True, Feine has already tried to mess with Miles. Insisting Miles hire Rebekah Singh, a mediocre student with a criminal charge against her name and a knack for finding unique ways to break machines. She should have caused mayhem at BIOLOGIC, but Miles raves about her.

Then many things come together. Why take half-measures? Feine wonders how damaging it would be should Gwin's creation be introduced to Miles's latest endeavour. Rebekah Singh owes Feine. Feine calls in the favour. Rebekah Singh meets Gwin Tang. The two of them bond in that icky way girls do. With a little pressure on Feine's part, calling in favours and the like, Rebekah arranges it so Gwin's Reactors meet Miles's robot . . .

A seismic sensation in his gut as he mulls this over. He leans back in his chair and folds his arms behind his head. The sick feeling only builds. It's been so long, it takes a while for it to click. The sick feeling is excitement.

'Show me again,' he says, already imagining the destruction of the comfortable world Miles has built himself. Miles, Emilia, a regretful past; his demotion, advancing technology, a disappointing present. He tells himself, *It doesn't have to be this way*.

Absorbed as he is, at first he misses the equally dramatic transformation in Gwin. The sharp devotion while she watches her creation whirl and play. With a spidery twist of her ringed fingers, she resets the window for the next display.

'We need to get your IGRs into the real world,' Feine says. 'I know exactly who you should meet.'

But Gwin is focused on her code entities and she pays him scant attention. Such concentration on that sweet face is, frankly, disturbing. Feine wonders for a moment if he should be a bit terrified. Then he puts through a message to extend a cordial invitation.

> It's been too long, Rebekah. Time for a catch-up. When can I call?

<13>

baggage

DEACON'S MODEST POPULATION of 41,695 citizens spends around two hundred days each year immersed in fog, but who's complaining? For the most part, Deacon's weather system is stable, because avoiding fog is only ever temporary. In a world where the weather makes some places too dangerous to live, fog is a welcome sign of damp, slow-moving air currents. A week of heavy storms but a day of sunshine and now chilled night air. The thick blanket of fog draped over Deacon is inevitable.

'Yes, very interesting,' Josie says.

She and Miles are in his car ready to depart BIOLOGIC. They've spent the last hour preparing for this moment, including organising her clothing requirements. It wasn't that she harboured resentment, or a sense of superiority, but her mood suit had been particularly luminous in gold, with a subtle pink tint on the neckline, when she informed Storeroom 3.0 that the clothing allocation was incorrect.

Josie has been issued with a small green bag to hold her new collection of outfits. Collection, meaning clothing options, meaning no mood suit. She has also been issued tools to style her hair, and a generous supply of bio-fuel. Stylishly dressed in a high-stretch, tailored pantsuit of faux denim — Bek assured Josie it's something she would wear — no one would guess she isn't completely human.

'Well, it is,' Miles says, and tells the car to start. 'In heavy fog we need to take extra care on the road.'

'But visibility is compromised,' Josie says. 'Wouldn't auto-navigate ensure safety?'

The car fills with Miles's laughter. 'I like to drive and I'm careful. Humans have been driving for millennia. I'm not about to hand over the reins at this late stage in human evolution.'

Josie presses her lips into a prim smile and clips on her seat belt. 'This will intrigue you,' she says. 'On Thursday there is an eighty percent chance of rain. More fog may be coming. I will alert you.'

'You're funny.'

'Sure,' Josie says.

'Sure,' Miles says.

They both laugh, but it's cut short at the sound of a sharp rap on the driver's window. Bek's face appears, a spooky manifestation in the gloom.

Miles holds his chest, making exasperated and amused noises in equal measure. Then he swipes a sensor in the door, lowering the driver's window. A blast of sharp, moist air fills the car's interior.

'What are you *doing*, Bek?'

Josie cranes forward for a better view. Bek isn't doing much. She looks forlorn standing there, drooping with condensation, her breath little puffs of white mist.

'Shouldn't you be going home? It's so late,' Miles says.

Bek bends and leans on the car. 'I need to, ummm . . .'

A long silence occurs. Aware that such a pause is considered uncomfortable, Josie feels compelled to end it. She says, 'Bek, you are so wet.'

'Nice observation, Josie.' Bek smiles and vigorously dispels water from her hair with her fingertips. Noticeably, there's no explanation regarding her sudden appearance.

'We should get going,' Miles says. 'Everything okay? Can I drop you somewhere?'

'No,' Bek says. 'I wanted to tell you . . .'

'You're worried about Delta-6 crashing.'

'No, not. I thought . . . I mean, I think . . .'

Another lapse into empty conversation space. This time it's Miles to the rescue. He glances at Josie, then says, 'It'll be fine, Bek. Go on and dry off.'

'I have to tell you something,' Bek blurts.

Miles waits.

'You know, I . . .' Bek flings her arm in the general direction of BIOLOGIC's main building. 'It's great. Like. And you. You're . . .' She shrugs, sighs. 'It's really good.'

'Noted,' Miles says. 'And same. To you. Absolutely.'

'I'll be in late on Monday.'

'No problem. You okay?'

Bek hesitates and leans away from the window. 'Everything's fine.'

'Good then,' Miles says.

'Good,' Bek says. 'Okay.'

She raps her knuckles on the car roof and recedes into the fog. Miles grips the steering column. He flips a toggle for manual control, then catches Josie's expression.

'What? It's a personal preference.'

'Sure,' Josie says.

'Damn straight.'

The car whirrs and accelerates through **BIOLOGIC**'s gates, passing Bek as she climbs onto a bicycle.

'I hope everything's okay with her,' Miles says.

'Do I fetch an apple?'

'Dang!' Miles thumps the steering column. 'Josie, that was fierce.'

Fierce: violently agitated and turbulent. An alert pops into her visual field. Fatal conversation error. Abort chat. Yes? No? Abort chat yes.

Eyes straight ahead, her brain works overtime to figure the misstep. It comes up as blank as the wall of fog surrounding the car. She twists in her seat, hoping for another visual of Bek. The view behind is empty.

A fragment of the exchange between Bek and Miles remains in her buffer memory. Josie immediately saves it, but there is nothing to suggest the brief conversation was anything but lightweight banter. The words *great*, *like* and *good* reference positivity and wellbeing. And Miles was in agreement: *same* and *absolutely*.

The only negative is Bek's soggy state. Not exactly a catastrophe. So her clothing choices are inappropriate for the environmental conditions. A quick dry-off and a little forward-thinking in future. Problem solved.

So why did Miles interpret Josie's attempt at humour so harshly? Is she missing something in her code? Does her emotion recognition database need expanding? Josie suspects this to be the case and launches a full investigation. It takes a few microseconds.

She comes up with empathy. If empathy is the problem, oxytocin is the solution. The human hormone and brain transmitter is like relationship glue. It's how humans *get* one another. It's exactly what she needs.

A small tweak in her biological code, a minor alteration in her brain. A few cells replicating to make a tiny gland, that's all. The additional bio-matter will take up less space than a pea. Certainly the legalities are hazy, but the results will be beneficial. Josie sees no harm in such a tiny modification. This is what autonomy is all about — identifying a problem and solving it yourself.

She feeds data to receptive sites in her brain, and senses pressure at the base of her skull. She's rewarded with a slight uplift in her biochemistry. The procedure runs smoothly; she doesn't need to bother Miles about it. He's absorbed in his driving task anyway, and with the benefit of oxytocin now stimulating receptive sites in her brain, she can almost read his mind. *Noted*, he would say, or *absolutely*.

And how timely. He appears to read *her* mind, because he returns to a conversation about unresolved emotional hurts. *Emotions.* Ideally she's now better equipped to understand them, and this will be a perfect test.

'If it's so heavy, how about dumping your emotional luggage?'

'Emotional *baggage*,' Miles corrects her. 'Easier said than done.'

'I prefer luggage, as it originates from the word lug, meaning to drag or carry with difficulty. Apt, I would say.'

'Good point.' Miles nods and seems pleased with her analysis. She *knew* he would be. 'But baggage may have originated from the Old French word *baguer*,' he continues, 'which means to tie up. There's no moving on if emotional baggage gets the better of you.'

'If you take this turn, Miles, you'll avoid traffic congestion two intersections ahead of us.'

'Thanks.' Miles indicates, and detours from their current route.

'So persistent emotional residue—'

'Baggage,' Miles says.

'Of course. Why is it always, without exception, negative?'

Miles elaborates by explaining the nature of love, the theory of hearts and the unhappy fallout from bad endings. More than just a vital organ for fuel distribution, it turns out the heart plays a critical role in human relationships. In worst-case scenarios, the heart can be broken, heavy, stolen and lost. You can have a change of heart, but the heart must be in the right place. Presumably not in the mouth, nor worn on the sleeve. Home sounds like a good place for it.

'Miles, if I had one, I wouldn't skip a beat,' says Josie, warmed by the new neural chemistry pumping through her brain. 'I'd open my heart and pour it out. I would *give* you my heart if it meant I'd be mending your broken heart. I want to put an end to this baggage problem once and for all.'

Silence, but this time Josie's comfortable with it. Then she hears a shift in Miles's breathing patterns and has to peek. He's mushy around the eyes, and his grip trembles on the steering column ever so slightly.

'Did I say the wrong thing?'

She nearly said *again*. It would be disappointing after the trouble she went to with the oxytocin.

'No,' Miles croaks, and clears his throat a number of times. 'I've got a lot of baggage, but Emilia's packed up in it. What can I do? Some days it's all I have.' His sigh is full of longing. 'I wish she could have met you. She'd be very proud. That was a beautiful thing you just said.'

They travel some distance before Miles speaks again. 'Thank you.'

'But what did I do?'

'You listen and you remember.'

Josie laughs. 'Sound perception and data storage. They're not even special abilities.'

In the corner of her eye, she catches a wistful smile from Miles. 'It's plenty,' he says. 'I mean it.'

Which is most definitely a compliment. It's plenty I mean it. Josie stores the snippet of conversation and that half-smile to play again later. The moment is golden, like a kind and generous heart, and deserves a place in the architecture of her memory.

After that, Miles gets to the business of her assignment. She estimates they are a few minutes from home.

It's his family. There's a job he sort of wants her to do if she doesn't mind too much. He has concerns. He wants Josie to *observe and report*. That's all. He repeats himself as though the instruction will be difficult for her to follow. *Observe and report*.

'Like spying,' she says.

'No, no, no,' he says. 'Just watch them. Preferably without being obvious about it. And don't be weird. You know, strange. Report back immediately if something doesn't look right.'

'Okay, I'll spy on them.'

'Observe.'

'And I *observe* Hunter in particular.'

'I'm worried about him,' Miles says. 'Get him talking if you can.'

'He has sorrow that needs words.'

'Maybe.'

They come to a high stone wall. Miles slows the car and swings into a driveway between two large pillars under a canopy of mature trees. The car emits an urgent beep. Miles brakes hard and they come to rest with a lurch. When the cloud of dust settles, it appears they have narrowly avoided collision with a half-opened gate.

'Oh boy. You okay?'

Josie calibrates, then reports all operations are running smoothly. Miles gets out, complaining of storms and electrics, and promises a prompt return.

Josie assembles her research on Hunter, Coel and Milly. Data is scant and uninformative. She will have to improve on their biographies through inference, cross-referencing and data trawling. For now she runs collated information on their age group.

Adolescence, it's a voluminous topic. Behaviour indicators for this stage of human development are alarming. Erratic hormone-charged outbursts, decision-making that endangers both themselves and others. Sources agree hair-trigger emotions are not the fault of the teenager. At that age, the brain is under construction.

Josie can relate, her brain is a work in progress too. Networks and neural pathways strengthened through experience, similar to adolescent brain development, she will evolve through trial and error. This realisation gives her confidence she'll find a way to connect with Miles's family.

Miles returns to the car and climbs in. The wrought-iron gate clanks, the electrics graunch and the gate swings wide.

'Listen,' he says. 'About the kids.'

'Yes, I have their data. Hunter, age seventeen. Coel sixteen, and Milly fourteen.' Josie beams at Miles. 'They're in safe hands.'

'That's a good start. But there's more to it than knowing their ages.'

'Of course.' Josie laughs. 'I'll be a safe harbour from troubled emotional seas, a wall when they test the boundaries, their law when they need order, GPS when they lose their way.'

'Great, but you need a detailed profile. Use their social networks, financial records, that sort of thing. It's okay, you have my permission.' A shake of his head and a dismissive flick of his wrist. Miles overrides such trivialities as privacy concerns, and continues, 'Also, kids know what they're about. Take Coel, for example. He's great fun. He's in a band, right? Plays the drums. He's not what I'd call musical. But you know what? He doesn't care. He doesn't sweat stuff like that. Steady as a rock. His mother was like that.'

Josie nods agreeably but she isn't convinced. *Steady as a rock*. It doesn't gel with her findings on young people. Destabilised hormones, floods of extreme emotion. Keeping his head under duress? He'll probably cry as soon as he meets her.

'And Milly.' Miles's hands come alive. 'She's smart, a beautiful girl. Kind, too. She won't be any trouble.'

Doubtful. According to research teens can't help but attract trouble. Not a single citation denies it.

'It's been tough. But Milly . . . I worry she's, I dunno, growing up before she should. Makes me sick how she worries about us. And to be honest . . .' Miles laughs. 'I'm a bit scared of her.'

'And Hunter?'

The frown lines deepen. Miles sighs. 'The way he used to ride that bike of his. A risk-taker, more so than Coel. The kid was fearless. Maybe we're all a bit battle weary. Hunter's kind of deep. You know, complicated. These panic attacks. Kids don't tell you anything past a certain age. They clam up when you try to help.' Miles claps his hands together, interlocking his fingers and holding them up to show Josie. 'It didn't used to be like this. Hunter used to tell Emilia everything. They were close. We were all close.'

Miles stares into the fog, immersed in his thoughts. Then he goes tarump, tarump with his fingers on the dash, as though signing off on the matter of his children. His foot finds the accelerator and they start rolling.

'I can't wait to meet them,' Josie says, and discovers she means it. The assignment is turning into more than just wrangling a handful of teens. It appeals to her, how much she might learn from this experience. Mimic to learn. She'll develop new dimensions to her personality. It's going to be good for her generation of Josephinas, and therefore the world in general.

'It's late, they'll be in bed. But first thing in the morning, for sure.' Miles chuckles. 'Okay, maybe not *first* thing. They can take a mental health day tomorrow, and my guys lie in bed for ages.'

Water sloshes up the side of the car as they hit potholes in the drive, but Josie is too preoccupied to think maintenance.

'Miles,' she says as they near the house. 'Whatever I need to do, I'll get Hunter talking, I promise.'

<14>

domestics

CHAOS SEEMS A POLITE WORD for the bedlam Josie found herself in twelve industrious hours ago. Her first encounter with the McClure household was a brutal assault on the most basic assumptions of living. Time disappeared in the *frenzy* — the word fits perfectly — with which she went about her tasks, *clean*, *tidy*, *order*.

The search and seizure of food and kitchen items from all corners of the house occupied a significant portion of the night. As though giant hands had upended the pantry, contents were strewn to every possible location. For example, how to process the half-full drinking vessel? She found it on the shelf of a dusty bookcase in an office that looked equally under-used. Questions arose when she removed the vessel and it left a clean circle behind. How long had it been there? *Why* had it been there? Was she missing a programming upgrade that explains the phenomenon?

Her (possibly outdated) domestic programming allowed only for cleaning air-purified environments, where filtering removes 98.5 percent of dust particles. She had to access archaic instructional material, and discovered dust could be removed by cloth or a suction unit. Likewise, the unexpected appearance of foodstuffs outside of the kitchen or an acceptable dining environment threw her. She discovered food exposed to air for indeterminate durations of time grew intriguing blooms of single-cellular life. It seemed a shame to discard the vast populations of bacteria and mould, along with their aged food mediums, into disposal, yet she did. The containers she tossed into a growing pile for repurposing. Only one item remains as she found it, a small mechanical construction in the centre of the dining table.

The object, a mechanical heart about the size of her palm, captivated her with its beauty and complexity. Intricately designed, it had four chambers as expected, but also other nooks and crannies — as though, in the extra spaces, something other than circulating fluids should be kept there. Spindles, wire arms and cogs worked together to make the heart beat, but even motionless, the heart was pleasing to the eye.

She cleared around the work space and arranged the tools in an orderly fashion. The object itself she left alone, aside from returning to it many times through the night to touch or gaze upon it. She would look at it now, but at last there's the sound of approaching footsteps.

The timing couldn't be better. The kitchen galley practically sparkles, its surfaces luminous in the early morning light. Somewhat proudly, Josie straightens herself, picking at a grubby mark on her new denim pantsuit and neatening her hair back into its ponytail. Her mouth stretches the exact amount for her smile to read as *warm*. She's ready to greet the newcomer.

Josie hears laughter and two words spoken aloud: *die* and *sucker*. The footsteps come closer. She has to be patient and it isn't easy. She sources images of happy adolescents with shiny good looks. Their beaming smiles bolster her expectations.

Then she sees him.

Shambling along and surprisingly dishevelled for so early in the day, a teenage male. Josie's smile falters, relaxing ever so slightly from its optimum stretch point. The human turns into the kitchen galley, and she collates available data. Hair colour: blond with randomly spaced patches of faded blue. Hair style: a tangle — jutting peaks extrude from the head in a disordered fashion. Eyes: barely opened, unable to identify colour. Subject is occupied by the 3D wristband projecting onto his hand. The projection: a battle animation, a primitive garrison, characters from opposing teams pummelling each other with gnarled clubs and wildly swinging spiked balls.

`Alert: identification required.`

She starts with the face. A small sprinkle of blemishes along the jaw line; the mouth slack and partially open. Eye colour: data unavailable still. *Hunter or Coel?* He wears crumpled and stained fluoro-orange pants with a multitude of pockets in contrasting colours; a grey T-shirt with a graphic of an ape raising its fist in an act of defiance. Words to the effect that he doesn't take orders from monkeys are emblazoned across his chest.

The human male continues to shuffle, until he arrives at the refrigeration unit. To be fair, his attention is drawn to the battle playing out on the palm of his hand, but he fails to acknowledge her presence. Josie would like to engage, however, and identification, in all politeness, should come first. She continues to observe.

The male taps his wrist and the battle retracts. Audio of the complaining combatants is rather comical. He scratches under his armpits and stretches one arm followed by the other above his head. He groans.

He bends side to side from the waist and straightens, then drops his arms. Aligning himself with the refrigerator, he taps on the front surface to view the contents. The unit casts him in a halo of shifting light as the interface comes to life. With posture and bone structure from the side profile to go on, Josie runs identification protocols.

The teenage human male, leaning now on one arm to peer at the unit's display, is Coel McClure. While he shifts his weight to tap the door release, Josie trawls data points. Tracking his search histories and his social interactions, she constructs a pretty decent biography of Coel. She cross-references his interests, sporting achievements, birth order, birth date, academic records, social contacts, browsing history and purchasing patterns. From there, it's a simple matter to construct a profile, then extrapolate to create a detailed behaviour schematic. Finally, she draws her own conclusions as to who, exactly, Coel McClure is.

So she isn't surprised to see him reaching for a biodegradable bowl still containing its biodigestible fork. The contents will, she presumes — having already discerned Coel's preference for convenience foodstuffs — be the leftovers of a quick-serve meal.

Not really wanting to interrupt him, but deciding she had better introduce herself, Josie makes a polite *ahem*.

No response.

Perhaps the quiet hum of the fridge masked her voice. Josie *ahems* louder.

Fork, bowl and food explode across the floor when Coel abruptly turns. Josie is forced to suppress a barrage of alerts that threaten to cloud her vision. She can see for herself anyway: the floor is a mess. Once again it must be cleaned.

Coel makes no move towards the fallen remains of his meal. Josie's smile wilts. She's starting to get an inkling as to how the McClure household became so disordered. But cleaning will have to wait. Taking care to maintain eye contact, her voice bright with zing, Josie begins.

'Hello there, Coel! I'm Josie!'

Coel regards Josie with an unchanged expression, his jaw slacker if anything. She revises her approach, this time aiding her delivery with arm gestures.

'Welcome to a great day.' Arm swing to the window behind her. 'Did you sleep well?' Hands pressed together to cushion her head. 'Expect another day of fine weather if you venture outdoors.' Arms wide and open. 'When the fog lifts, that is.' Josie laughs abundantly and twists, gesturing to the windows again. For a brief moment her eye lingers on the whiteout. 'Maybe target practice with your air soft rifle . . .' She mimes the appropriate stance and fires imaginary shots at Coel. 'For safety, I recommend scheduling your session to late mid-morning. How about breakfast?' Josie raises a shoulder with the question. 'If you would prefer a break from TwinkOs, I can prepare something delicious *and* nutritious.' She swings a punch at the air and drops in a good-natured laugh.

Coel's jaw remains slack. His eyes are still narrowed. This gives her limited feedback, so she presses on delicately. 'Are there any items of clothing you wish me to launder?'

She lowers her gaze to Coel's dirt-stained knees, then back to his face. 'No?' Coel remains non-responsive, so Josie answers her own question. 'I see, no.'

She isn't programmed to give up or admit failure. She tries

an open question. 'What *are* your plans for the day?'

Nothing. She delves into other interests suggested by his profile. 'I see in Entertainment News there is a new film featuring the fictional character Prince Garrick. Reviews are favourable and it is currently screening in cinemas. I could book you a seat

. . . or . . . not . . .'

Alert: Speech terminated unexpectedly. Continue. Yes? No?

Coel's eyes zoom into focus. He swings his arms vigorously, as though fighting to regain balance. His shoes flick against his heels when he backs away from the fridge. He retreats down the corridor quick time, slip-slap, slip-slap. His voice echoes back to her, 'Daaaaaaaaaaad!'

Continue. Yes? No?

The cursor blinks several times more before Josie dismisses the alert. Continue. No.

<15>

the glitch

DOWN ON ALL FOURS in the kitchen galley, removing the last of Coel's breakfast from the floor, Josie hears someone approach the dining area. From that position, she pulls a handstand, lands artfully, balls the dishcloth and lobs it into the sink.

This time, she thinks. Because standing at the dining table with their back to her is someone new.

'Oh,' she says at the back of the head. The new someone turns.

'Oooooo-h-h,' she says, her voice running out with her thoughts. The face expands in her visual field. Josie's mouth stays shaped in an *o*.

Hair colour, dark brown; style, grown past the ears, a fringe sweeping across the forehead. But that's not it. A long-sleeve shirt in black, loosely buttoned and exposing the chest, some of the hem tucked into very well-fitting dark-blue straight-leg denim pants. Attractive, but not alarmingly so.

The mechanical heart vibrates on his palm. He tampers with it to make it still. He tucks the remainder of his shirt into his pants and buttons it to his neckline. It improves matters, but still.

'Dad never tells us anything,' the mouth says, then half of it goes awry. 'I didn't expect a visitor.'

The mouth. It's the mouth!

More words come out of it. 'You really freaked Coel. Nice work.'

The face smiles at her face.

A system alert reminds her to identify the new someone. A calculated guess tells her it's Hunter, but she wasn't built for guesswork. She evaluates dimensions, deduces ratios. She gauges the individual features, considers their placement and compares this to the overall face measurement. No one measures up the same, but in this case the numbers don't help her. The numbers don't explain this face. In theory, the mouth shouldn't fit on this head.

The mouth quirks and sprawls across the face. This is how he smiles.

'So,' he says. 'How'd you crack Coel? Break it down for me with easy-to-follow steps.' The mouth spreads impossibly wide.

Josie hears high-pitched laughter — *her laughter*. She shuts off, exclaiming, *Eeep!*

Thoughts penetrate. Her system reports overload, requests she regain function.

But that mouth. It's impossible.

It stops whatever it was doing and ever so slowly skews sideways. Josie titters, a nervous and strained sound. An embarrassing sound.

'Hi, by the way.' The mouth comes back to centre.

Josie responds, 'Hi, by the way.'

An alert, reminding her of manners, informs her it's rude to stare. She jerks her gaze up to the eyes. *Stupendous*: the word soars through her brain, winging it on turbulent thought currents.

The mouth moves. 'You okay?'

The eyes crease in the corners. Eye colour: leaves lightly bronzed at the first sign of autumn.

Alert: Response required.

'Yehh-sss,' Josie says. 'Guuhoood.'

'You work for my dad, right?'

'Uh-hhhhh-huhh.'

Alert: Meaningful response required.

The mouth twitches, curving upward, and heavy brows fall down over the eyes. Now she's unsure about colour. Brown doesn't seem right, nor does green.

'You seem kind of zoned out.' The mouth moves again, but maintaining eye contact she misses the sounds. The next time it moves, she forces herself to pay attention.

'What are you doing here? You mind me asking?'

Josie babbles something that includes the words kitchen, clean, order and mission.

'Wait a minute. Dad made *you* clean the kitchen?'

He crosses the dining area to stare into the kitchen galley. Josie follows.

'I can't believe you really cleaned.' Hunter wanders through to the pantry. He sees the pile of containers for repurpose, the collection of cleaning products waiting to be tidied away. 'Seriously? No wonder you're zonked.'

'I am serious,' Josie says. 'Cleaning is one of my primary functions.'

The eyes regard her, mystified.

'Oh I get it. You're kidding.' Hunter laughs.

Josie raises her other eyebrow: the result, more laughter.

A chain reaction inside her, a novel sensation. Bubbly, floaty, giddy. She tightens her mouth into a grim line to contain herself. The pressure builds into a snortle in her throat, a raspberry burst behind her lips.

Still laughing, he thrusts a hand in her direction. It hangs mid-air between them, and he says, 'I'm Hunter anyway.'

Alert: Response required.

A flash of memory: *He has sorrow that needs words.*

Josie looks at the hand. Sluggish microseconds pass before she reacts. She claps her hand onto his and jerks it up, down, up, down.

A whack of sensory data sizzles along neural pathways to her brain, ploughing into her touch receptors with a great wallop. The fuel pump in her chest jumps or stops or skips.

Alert: Fatal system error.

Function. She starts with data, assembling information at light-speed. She says, 'I'm Hunter anyway. No. I'm . . .'

Josie stops. Her grip loosens and her fingertips twitch against the back of Hunter's hand. Another second passes while she scrabbles for coherent thought. *I am . . . Jooooooosssssssiiieee.*

'Hey, steady there,' Hunter says, and his hand grips hers tighter. The other hand takes her elbow. 'We gotta sit you down, Bek. You've got toxic overload from the cleaning products. Where'd you even find that stuff?'

Josie's circuits fizz and dance as she shuffles towards the dining table.

'Waahh, Bek? Wait for a second,' Josie says. 'You think I'm Bek?'

Hunter seats her at the dining table. Josie's head wobbles side to side.

'Noooo, I'm Josie anyway.' She thrusts her hand at Hunter. Hunter looks but doesn't take it. 'Josie? Seriously?'

'Yes. I am serious about this.'

'Dad's *robot*?' Hunter's mouth shapes into the quirky grin.

Now they're on the subject of herself, and therefore familiar ground, her system regains stability and she even accomplishes a warm smile. She corrects Hunter gently. 'Or humanoid. I prefer that designation.'

'Dad brought you home? I don't get it. Why didn't he tell us?'

'I'm unable to answer that question.' Josie smiles and, bolstered by a return to professional standards, adds, 'Hunter, you seem very well this morning.'

Hunter tilts his head, pondering. A grin emerges and pops off to the side. 'Yeeees. Thank you, I am.'

Josie nods yes, rocking her head mechanically up, down.

'And your breathing patterns are regular and consistent,' she says. 'That's also good.'

'My what, what?'

But now, the sound of footsteps from the direction of the hallway. Several seconds later, an adolescent female, who can only be Milly, scuffs towards them. She's wearing a pair of slippers the shape of monster claws (explains the scuffing) and an oversize T-shirt with the image of a large unclothed plastic doll on the front. A ginger cat, which must be the family pet Mushi, is draped over her shoulder. Milly adjusts the animal's position and presses her face into its fur.

Hunter greets her with arms crossed, mouth a firm line. Even narrowed and flinty, the eyes are somewhat mesmerising.

'What's going on?' he demands. 'Why does Dad's robot care about my breathing patterns?'

To be thorough, Josie runs through her identification

procedures. *Yes, Milly.* Mushi contributes to the discussion with a throaty, low-pitched whine.

Milly says, 'Really . . . ?'

Mushi's head swivels in Josie's direction. The cat hisses and flees the cradle of Milly's arms.

Hunter rolls his eyes. 'Like you don't know. Care to tell us why Dad's robot is here?'

'Humanoid,' Josie says.

'Hello, Josie, my name is Milly.'

'Thanks, by the way,' Hunter says, 'for telling everybody everything and sabotaging my entire existence.'

Josie frowns.

'Hunter, sabotage is serious,' she says, struggling to her feet. 'We must alert your father immediately.'

'See?' Hunter says, voice raised. 'See? Oh, man. This is your fault.'

'I didn't tell Dad. Ignore him, Josie. Hunter can be kinda overreactive. You get used to it.'

'So why is Josie saying stuff about my breathing?'

'How would *I* know?' Milly snaps.

It dawns on Josie that this is an opportunity to deliver her introductory speech. Having confused Coel and offended Hunter, this time she might get it right. She politely *ahems*.

Milly and Hunter stare at her.

Raising her arms to open her body posture, Josie gives Milly the full blast of her welcome smile. 'Milly! Hello! It's a pleasure to meet you. Can I take care of your break—'

'Please,' Hunter says. 'If Dad thinks his robot's going to come in here—'

'Humanoid,' Josie says quietly.

'See what you've done,' Milly says. 'You hurt her feelings.'

'Feelings?' Hunter says. 'You cannot be serious.'

An opportunity for a new task. Josie brightens. 'It appears that you are forcefully disagreeing with one another. If you would like to resolve the confrontation, I would be happy to media—'

Alert: speech terminated.

Hunter *and* Milly glare at her. No mediation then.

'For the record, Milly,' Hunter says, 'I don't need help, I don't *want* help. And I especially don't want Dad's robot sticking its nose into my business. Or you. Or anyone else.'

'Hunter!' Milly checks Josie's reaction.

Josie keeps her face neutral to avoid further inflaming the situation.

'What?' Hunter makes a face, holds up his hands defensively. 'Oh, yeah. We're worried about its feelings.'

'That's just rude.'

'Sure. People compromise my privacy and I'm being rude.'

'I didn't tell!'

Josie doesn't know where to look. The very reason for her being here is to be useful. Yet somehow she has become a source of conflict. In her projected analysis, helping Hunter resolve his breathing issues did not run to these complications. In her projected analysis, Hunter is healed and bestowing upon her the emotional outpouring of his gratitude. Most likely expressed in tears of joy. And she, both humbled and subservient, modestly accepts his thanks.

A snapshot review of her performance paints a bleak picture. Household cleaned: check. Anomalies: one. Usefulness: apparently not. Help Hunter: fail. It's been quite a morning.

Sullen and silent, Hunter and Milly watch Josie sidling away from the dining area. Milly gives an exasperated sigh.

'This is really awkward,' she says, her face coming to rest in what appears to be a pout.

Josie has in mind the quiet of her allocated room. How pleasantly alone she'll be. The small suitcase in there already, her stack of bio-fuel. She brings the corners of her mouth up, an approximation of smiling.

'Don't worry about me,' she says. 'I have plenty to do. Hah! Hah!'

Shoulders back, chin high, a snap to her gait, Josie hurries downstairs. She enters her room and sits on a dusty sofa, back stiff, hands tidy on her knees.

The garden lies beyond her window. The fog is beginning to lift. She makes out the oval shape of a Mowbot tracing the lawn in straight rows, one after another. The red light on its undercarriage is diffuse in the misty air. Another Mowbot joins the first one, cutting across the rows. Together and in co-operation they work methodically; a chequer pattern forms on the lawn. It's the only activity in the garden, which is otherwise bathed in milky sunlight, and still.

<16>

the workshop

.01

THE WORKSHOP IS an amiably dingy space. Nestled deep in the garden, the windows haven't been cleaned in over a decade. Green-tinted sunlight bleeds through generations of algae, and even on a sunny day such as this one it would be dark without the battery of low-wattage desk lamps.

Hunter had come out wanting peace and solitude after the commotion in the kitchen. He'd dumped the box with his mechanical heart onto a workbench, pumped up the stereo volume and hammered the crap out of a tiny metal plate he'll use for the casing.

He feels better.

No one uses the workshop these days, apart from him. He used to imagine he was clever like his father, just by being here and finding things to do. Like this was his own secret club for dreaming and inventing.

His father got a career off the ground building robots in the workshop. The human equivalent would be if benches were cluttered with organs, torsos, heads, mismatched feet and hands. There would be equipment for monitoring bodies, putting them together or giving them a crash-start after they'd been standing idle in the corner. A defibrillator maybe, an X-ray machine. Instead, robot parts have been piled onto the benches: metal and plastic casings, cables, and mother boards studded with miniature circuits. Tools and parts left over from robot generations operating before Hunter was born.

Everything in the workshop has been saved for reuse. His father grew up when waste was contributing to the devastation of the planet. It's a worthy goal, but this morning Hunter sees he has access only to the most outdated resources. It's Josie's fault. Not just how she looks (she's incredible), but how she sounds (super-nice) and how she moves (high-powered and graceful). He could never build anything like her with these resources at his disposal. So what's the point?

His father's done an amazing job. The irony, of course, is that robots as advanced as Josie are destined for more affluent homes than those found in Deacon Valley. Maybe, in some far-distant future, such glamorous technology will be affordable in his shabby little town. It's an affront to have the unobtainable snooping around in their kitchen.

Hunter leans over the workbench and attaches the metal plate to the heart. He flicks the mini-switch at the back. The mechanical heart vibrates on his palm.

So what, he thinks, *big deal*.

Mechanics are old news. Somewhere in the world, someone will be working on a flesh-and-blood heart with an optimally designed, custom-built cellular matrix, and growing it overnight. Josie probably has one. As though in on his thoughts, his mechanical heart grinds to a halt with a series of spasmodic clicks and a shudder.

He sets it down on the bench top, then massages his forehead and glares at the heart. A screw drops onto the bench.

'**There you are!**' His father shouts above the music. Miles leans on the door jamb with a grin that implies he was passing and dropped by for some genial chitchat.

Hunter sighs. He takes the remote (also outdated), lowers the volume by several hundred decibels and swivels his stool to face his father.

'Yup. Here I am.'

'Been looking for you everywhere.'

'Really?'

'Sure.'

Hunter sighs again when his father takes the stool beside him. 'This isn't going to be painful is it?' he says.

.02

Josie can't get her mouth right. She's been trying to unlock the mystery of Hunter's face by staring into her own. It's fast becoming another megawatt fail.

The off-kilter grin. She could charm the world with that type of smile. She leans closer to the mirror hanging inside the cupboard door of her room, and props one corner of her mouth with a finger.

The correct name for the mouth corner is oral commissures. Knowing this does not help. Each time she removes her finger, either her mouth droops or both sides come up.

The morning light coming through the window illuminates the side of her face. Based on models of idealised beauty, her features conform to exact proportions and laws of symmetry. Eyes of pale gold, enhanced by the contrast of her dark lashes and framed by brows shaped in a perfect arch. She's attractive for the sole reason that humans go for this sort of thing. They spend their money accordingly.

But if she is to fit in with humans, there must be more to her than symmetrical good looks. This is her finding after giving Hunter's face closer evaluation. How else to explain the intrigue of his face and therefore Hunter himself? If essence and character are skills of facial expression, Hunter has it down. So why isn't it a simple matter for her to master this essence?

Another attempt, this time muscle isolation. She tightens zygomaticus major, the smiling muscle in her cheek. Her nose wrinkles with the strain; the philtrum ridge beneath the nose flattens. The end result disturbs her.

Adding character to her face is a sideline. Chief among her concerns is the anomaly, or glitch, the moment of dropout when words failed. What made her electrics fizz when she took Hunter's hand? Why did words leave her? It goes without saying, she needs to interact with humans without having her entire system go into meltdown.

While she's been fine since, a convincing explanation for the fault would be reassuring. The possible explanations are:

1. Hunter is her first important assignment. The handshake formalised their introduction too quickly, catching her off guard. Josie makes a mental note: expect the unexpected.

2. Buggy code. Somehow, briefly, there was an error with the potential to shut her down. Although invisible to her system sensors, the invisible bug somehow, miraculously, debugged itself.

3. When it comes to humans, things happen for no obvious reason. This is true and there is a lot to understand. As she continues to humanise, it is possible she

too will experience things that happen for no reason.

The ᑫlᵢₜᥴℎ is the first of such happenings.

'Hey,' Milly says from the doorway. 'There you are.'

Josie spins away from the mirror and **slams** the cupboard door closed.

'Hey,' she says. 'There *you* are.'

Milly enters, plants a fist under her chin, another on her hip, and takes a surprisingly long time to examine the small room.

'Hmmmm,' Milly says.

She inspects the plain walls, the well-used sofa, the freshly dusted table once, twice and then again.

'This can't be right,' she concludes. 'Why did Dad put you here? We never put guests here.'

Josie understands why. She has little need for space or comfort. She could be locked in the cupboard and be fine. This room is luxury. She has a view, space for processing, privacy to consume fuel, room for storage and, best of all, a retreat from family *discussion*.

'It could be amazing in here, though,' Milly says. 'Fairy lights, a few pillows, a cool poster. It wouldn't take much.'

'The room is fine.'

'How's that?' Milly rubs curtain fabric between her fingers, wrinkles her nose and drops it again. She nods, thoughtfully. 'I think we can soften the lighting, yes?'

Her head angled, Milly regards Josie as though assessing if she'll fit the room's new decor. A few seconds later, she claps her hands. 'Good. Let's go.'

It has been one hour and forty-seven minutes since the failure of her first assignment. Josie is pleased to once again be put to use.

.03

His father breaks it down for him: *a few chats with Josie might get him through this tricky patch*, help him get to the bottom of this *breathing thing* and he'll be *right as rain in a jiff* and it's *really nothing to worry about.*

Hunter listens politely. He breathes deep and loud to show his father this *little breathing thing* isn't bothering him in the slightest.

He has questions.

'Your robot? It's not like you tweak a few lines of code, try a new algorithm, cross fingers and restart. Because guess what?' Hunter shrugs. 'I'm human. I have human problems. *Humans* sort out human problems, not robots.'

Miles has no comeback, so Hunter runs with it.

'Your robot's all like . . .' He slaps hands on either side of his face and puts on a falsetto. '*Malfunction alert! Woe! My code is all buggy*. And she's zoned out all the time. I'm better off figuring myself out.'

'She's not zoned out,' Miles says.

'Your robot *is* zoned out. She's laggy. Check her code.'

The tech update seems like big news to Miles, so Hunter just tells him he's getting along fine. He's actually working through his problems. Mind over matter. He has a plan. A schedule. Strategies. It's under control. He's on the brink of a breakthrough. And anyway, in only a few short months his school days are over forever. Won't that be great? No more anxiety-inducing school departures.

His father counters.

Hunter is enraged by the suggestion that he has *baggage*, stuff locked up inside he's not dealing with. Like he's unresolved somehow, and ignoring this will only make it worse.

'You'll see.' His father, the robot fanatic, grins. 'Talking to Josie is illuminating.'

Hunter's eyes roll skywards.

A million hours grind by, listening to his father overshare. Hunter is supposed to relate. He suggests Josie help Miles instead, and *it seems she has*. Another million hours on his father's Josie epiphany, and Hunter feels sad.

A trillion hours after that, they've moved on to life in general. Life *can* get tough, but the important thing is to find the way back to happiness.

'I'm not unhappy,' Hunter says. 'It's just life sucks all the time.'

A gazillion hours later, and Hunter feels the energy draining right out of him. He's almost ready to agree to anything if it makes his father stop talking. He takes one last shot.

'Don't you get it? She's a robot! A! Robot! And I won't talk to her. No way!'

.04

Not that she's counting, but it's been two hours, thirty-eight minutes and seventeen seconds since the episode in the kitchen. Josie follows Milly outdoors.

Mushi scoots past, charging ahead and diving into flax. Milly seems delighted. Minutes pass, Josie in a holding pattern and Milly deviating from their original course. Crouching in front of the flax, Milly pleads with Mushi to come but Mushi isn't interested.

Milly returns to Josie, disheartened. Then the cat bounds from the flax and joins them.

The logic of the game escapes Josie. For Milly, it's a source of great excitement. She croons, 'Mooshi Moosh,' then swoops the cat into her arms belly-side up.

Apparently, the rough grumble in its throat means the cat is enjoying this treatment. Milly enjoys it too. Her laughter flutters in the air as she shoves her face into the fur of the cat's underbelly.

Next, she swings the cat to upright and asks Josie if she would like a pat. When Josie comes near, the cat hisses, throws itself off Milly, and bolts away with arched back and a fat curved tail.

Milly is clearly disappointed.

Which won't do. If interaction with Mushi is important to Milly, Josie had better see to it the cat likes her. With oxytocin on board, she has new chemical tools at her disposal and therefore more powerful means to forge positive relationships. She resolves to experiment at the cat's earliest convenience.

'Shall we proceed?' Josie asks.

When they are close to the workshop, Josie hears raised voices. Or rather one. Hunter shouting, very clearly, the word *robot*. She resolves to be vigilant in the event of malfunction and indifferent to bad manners.

A dignified entry would help. Josie pauses to raise her chin, set her shoulders and so on. Impatient to make an entry, Milly pushes past on the narrow stairs, throwing Josie off balance. The dignified entry turns into a shambolic one, grabbing at the door jamb to right herself, falling into the workshop, then not knowing where to stand.

Hunter's scathing eye-roll is quite expected by now.

Even after her brief time among the McClures, Josie has a handle on adolescent communication, and rolls her eyes indolently. Then she squinches her eyes and sneers for a look that says, *What's it to you?*

Hunter ignores her. It's the correct rebuttal.

The mechanical heart lies on the bench in front of him. He grasps a screw with some pliers.

Milly tells her father about decorating the small room with furnishings from storage. There is discussion. It quickly devolves into overlapping voices, and it is clear to Josie that a conclusion won't be coming any time soon.

An excerpt from the discussion:

Milly says, 'Dad, we *have* to fix up that dumb room you put Josie in.'

Miles says, 'It doesn't need fixing, honey.'

Hunter says, 'Dad, the robot needs teddy bears, a throw rug and a zillion pillows. Hey, what about posters with catchy memes? Oh wait, ha-ha-ha, fairy lights.'

Milly says, 'Sounds like *you* should be decorating Josie's room, you're such an expert.'

Hunter says, 'Can't we prop the robot in a corner?'

Milly says, 'Dad, please tell Hunter to grow up.'

Miles says, 'He's giving that a go already, sweetie.'

Hunter says, 'Maybe *you* should grow up.'

Milly says, 'Maybe *you* should.'

Miles says, 'The room's fine, Mills.'

Milly says, 'It's not. Josie's not comfortable in there.'

Hunter says, 'They don't need to be comfortable.'

Milly says, 'Daaaaad.'

Hunter says, 'You can stash them under a bed?'

Milly says, 'Daaaaad!'

And so on.

Josie removes herself from conversation range. She ventures deeper into the workshop and avoids thinking about success or failure or adolescents. Hunter lets fly with another burst of mocking laughter, but Josie tunes this out too. It will be about her and it won't be anything she wants to hear.

The workshop is a mess, surpassing even the *before* state of the kitchen. It occurs to Josie she could say a number of ironically scathing things herself. So far she has encountered ill manners, cluttered living areas, filth, decay, and Coel with his low standards of personal hygiene. Insert eye-roll and mocking laughter.

She trails her finger along the worn surface of the bench, recognising the need for calm. Among the array of robot components, wiring and body parts, she begins to see something not unlike herself. She lingers over a robot claw, tracing it with one of her delicately shaped fingers. She lets her hand shape itself over the shiny metal surface, aligning her fingers with each claw. This hand once operated much the same as her hand. It had been attached to a brain; it completed tasks. It had been *useful*.

Josie takes her hand away. She flexes and releases all her fingers together, then wriggles each one independently. Grateful for the movement, grateful her fingers are attached to her brain. *But, for how long?*

She keeps moving.

A bandsaw squats against the back wall of the workshop. A cumbersome object for the delicate work of robot-building. Its blade has dulled with age. Metal filings and dust are piled at its base, robot parts heaped to the side. Sawn-through casing, scraps of wire, a bisected knee joint.

She keeps moving.

At the back of the room Josie stands in front of two large crates. Upended, they nearly reach the ceiling. Printed on one side, numbers and a barcode. Absorbed in identifying the contents of the crates, she doesn't notice the workshop has gone quiet until she hears her name.

'Ummm, Josie?'

Josie isn't ready to respond to Milly. She knows what these boxes are and what this means. There's a word for why machines are stored in the boxes, why robot parts clutter the workbenches, why antiquated tools rust from lack of use.

Hunter mutters, 'She does this.'

Miles says, 'What?'

'Zones out,' Hunter says. 'She's buggy. I told you.'

'She's not buggy!'

The correct word comes to Josie, chilling her in spite of its frothy sibilance. *Obsolescence*: it sounds like an infectious disease or a cankerous growth, dropping into her consciousness spreading dark despair. If only she were immune.

Milly whispers, 'Should we talk about her when she's in the room like this?'

'What a pain,' Miles grumbles. 'She was working fine yesterday.'

'Don't blame me,' Hunter says.

Milly whispers again, 'Can you please make Josie come?'

'What else have you noticed, Hunter?'

'He noticed nothing, right, Hunter? *Come on*, Josie!'

Josie cranks her expression until it's pleasant and empty. If Hunter keeps insisting she's a robot, she might as well behave like one. Her days are numbered anyway. All the talk of death and losing loved ones and grief. It's *her* days that are numbered, it's *she* who must face an end.

'Yes Milly. I will go. With you. It will be. My pleasure.'

With jerky movements, she checks Hunter's reaction, fully expecting eye-rolling.

His eyes meet hers.

He says, 'I'll do it.'

'Pardon?' Miles says.

All eyes are on Hunter now, including hers. He half smiles, then chuckles and holds up his hands in surrender.

'You convinced me. I give in. I'll go along with it.' He winks at Josie. 'How 'bout it? Dad says you're good at talking to people.'

Josie struggles with the wink.

'You'll do it? You'll let Josie help?' Miles slides off his chair and grabs both of Hunter's arms. 'Don't mess with me. I mean it. You can't back out, okay?'

'Calm down,' Hunter says. 'You'll blow something.'

When her wits are back online, Josie detects a wave of relief in Miles. Her own relief is sizeable, but she doesn't trust herself with words yet. That wink — she's very pleased she thought to save it.

Milly groans. 'That's not fair. What about my turn with Josie?'

Josie permits herself a lip twitch, a quirk of her oral commissures. She'd like to fist-bump the moon, but right now it's about recovery and playing it cool.

She says, 'No problem. We can start at your convenience of course, Hunter. But perhaps I go along with Milly's plans and we could make a start later in the day?'

So smooth. So professional. Josie takes a moment to congratulate herself on an outstanding delivery.

Hunter breaks eye contact with a smirk, but the gesture isn't mean. He takes in Milly with a lazy sweep of his eyes. 'Okay,' he drawls playfully. 'Afternoon it is.'

Josie and Milly are back in the garden when they hear Miles call out, 'Don't make a mess down there.'

an extension
of you

MILLY IS GETTING USED to how Josie operates, but still, it's taken quite a bit to keep her on task. For a minute there, she thought Josie had crashed. The roller door jammed and they had to bend to get under it. Josie eyed the sprawl inside, like it was taking a million years to compute. And then she mumbled to herself, 'Don't make a mess? A mess of a mess? Don't make a mess here?'

They had to wade amongst shelving and boxes to get to the good stuff. For ambience, they unearthed a CD player that once belonged to Milly's great-grandfather, and a *Best of Jazz* compilation with lively music first composed in the 1960s. Josie was so impressed with the vintage technology, she'd still be going on about it if Milly hadn't taken charge. They've come to the camping gear and boxes holding her mother's belongings. It's where they'll find soft furnishings.

'Josie, can I ask you something?'

She shouldn't really be distracting her with unnecessary questions, but it has to be asked. Josie has one of their old camp lanterns. First she tried commanding the lantern to light up, now she's clicking the button on and off, on and off. Milly would have to intervene anyway.

'You may proceed,' Josie says.

Once again Milly gets a kick out of how Josie talks to her. There's none of the sweetening typical of adult conversations. As the youngest, Milly has to bear a certain amount of being talked down to, but Josie keeps it sharp.

'So I'm wondering,' Milly says, 'what you have inside of you? Are you wired with circuit boards? Or do you have fake organs as well?'

Milly tugs on a string of LED lights, trying to liberate it from amongst her mum's belongings. It keeps getting snagged on tea paraphernalia. Her mum had been big on tea drinking. Milly unwraps a teapot, a sugar bowl, teaspoons, a milk jug, proper lady cups and saucers trimmed with gold and covered in flowers, all matching. A stack of tea cups clatters as Milly puts them to the side.

'Take care, Milly,' Josie says. 'Those cups are frangible.'

Milly splutters over a bout of laughter. 'Whaaaaaaat?' An outburst she instantly regrets when she sees Josie pause and think hard.

'Frangible, meaning fragile and easily broken,' Josie says, but seems unable to meet her eye. 'Please advise in future when my wording is inappropriate.'

'Frangible,' Milly says. 'What a great word.'

'Back to your question. Think of it as, I'm modelled on humans but significantly improved. I'm more efficient biologically, and stronger. I don't have exactly the same organs as you, but some of my parts have similar functions.'

'Like, a heart, say?'

'I'm built from cells that require a fuel boost from time to time. I have a pump tasked with powering nutrient distribution — the nearest equivalent to a heart, I should think.'

'Mmmmm,' Milly says. 'I see.'

It's been too long since she's been taken seriously. How great it is to have Josie who won't insult her with ironic put-downs, or ignore her feelings, or keep secrets.

Reaching into another box, Milly's hand brushes against a familiar object. Grasping the smooth jointed leg of a doll, she pulls her free and says, 'This isn't right. How did Maria Anne get out here?'

'I can't answer that question,' Josie says.

Holding Maria Anne delicately, Milly straightens the doll's beautifully crafted dress, and curls her blonde hair around a fingertip. For a second or two she forgets to breathe.

'That doll is pretty, Milly.'

She places the doll by the tea cups, arranging her legs to keep her upright. Her mother gave her the doll for a birthday, so long ago Milly can't even remember which one. 'Do you like her?'

Josie only gives Milly a confused look.

'If your pump is the same as a human heart, you have feelings then.'

'When you speak of feelings,' Josie says, 'I assume you mean sensations. My brain receives data from touch receptors, but you are talking about emotions of course. Emotions are beyond my realm of experience.'

'Theoretically, I mean. You could love someone. Like me, for example.'

'Even theoretically, love isn't required to perform tasks for humans.'

'What if loving someone *was* the task?'

Josie laughs. 'I suspect programming would have to be written. There isn't the demand.'

'Of course there's a demand.' Milly bumps a box, causing the stack of cups to rattle. Josie reaches for them and gives Milly a stern look.

'Sorry, Josie,' she says. 'But someone should write the program, you should feel love.'

Josie opens her mouth. She's about to say something, but then there's a loud **clank** by the roller door. A semi-inflated football flies towards them; it **smashes** into a box and there's a telltale **crunch** of something breaking. Coel appears, smirking. 'What's up, Millipede?'

'Time to go.' Milly's voice stiffens. 'We're about finished here anyway.'

'Awwww, sweet,' he says. 'You found your dollies.'

Milly quickly rests Maria Anne on a box beside her mother's clothes. Josie makes a grab for the crockery to keep it from harm.

Coel says, 'Does Dad know you're playing silly games with his high-end robot?'

Milly catches Josie's eye-roll, and hears her mutter, 'humanoid.'

'Does Dad know you're creeping about spying on us?'

'Don't flatter yourself,' Coel says. 'I came out to get a game going with Hunter.'

Josie looks over to the door, a bit freaked, and Milly says, 'I don't see Hunter.'

Coel retrieves the ball and kicks it towards the doorway. It misses and rebounds off the half-rolled door into some paint cans. They topple, then spill and paint drools over the concrete.

'Brilliant,' Milly says. 'Ready to go, Josie?'

'I am,' Coel says, showing no remorse over the spilt paint. Josie's glaring at it like she can't believe what she's seeing.

'Off you go then,' Milly says, knowing it's futile. 'I guess we have to clean that up.'

It doesn't take a genius to see Coel's waiting so he can annoy them all the way back to the house. Loaded up with lights and fabrics, Milly pushes past Coel. Josie follows, juggling an armful of cushions impressively.

'Try to ignore Coel,' Milly says. Coel keeps kicking the ball in their direction, then runs past to retrieve it. 'Pretend he doesn't exist. You'll have to master that anyway.'

They're in Josie's room when Josie says, 'Can I ask *you* a question? Why is having a decorated room important?'

Milly scoffs and says, 'Are you crazy? It's not *just* a room, that's why. Go live in a crate, if it's *just* a room. It's *your* room, Josie. It should be an extension of *you*.'

'But why all this stuff? I'm not that complicated.'

'That's just how it is. Your room expresses your personality. It's who you are.'

'Why do I have to express who I am?'

'We're all individuals, see? And it's a good idea to figure out what sort of individual you are, see? What your style is. What makes you happy.'

'I know that already.'

With a glance at Josie's outfit — a stretchy denim pantsuit — Milly raises a sceptical eyebrow. 'You don't have style, Josie. Trust me.' She shrugs. 'Don't sweat it, we'll deal to your personal style next.'

'What if I'm happy *not* having style?'

'Take my word for it. You're going to need style.'

<18>

the agreed-upon
first session

THE AGREED-UPON GOAL of counselling is for Hunter to get through one day with regular breathing. Not including times of exercise, the agreed-upon state of regular breathing is to draw full or deep breaths without difficulty.

Making the goal specific was Josie's suggestion. What she did not suggest, but wishes she had, was an agreed-upon mood in which to start their agreed-upon session.

Hunter isn't happy.

The chirpy enthusiasm she saw in the workshop is gone. In its place, a brooding near-silence that Josie struggles to crack. Between agreeing to counselling and the actual session, Hunter got weird. Or — and this has just occurred to Josie — the chirpy enthusiasm was an act.

They walk towards their agreed-upon counselling venue.

J: Are you regular breathing now?

H: Why wouldn't I be?

J: Good question. Very good.

On the matter of the agreed-upon venue, Josie suggested the outdoors. Once outside, Hunter takes the lead and they walk along the ridge at the edge of the property. The vista of Deacon Valley lies below, and Josie likes the idea of conducting the session with that outlook. There is potential for some interesting psychological effects, additional brain stimulation from interaction at dangerous heights.

But Hunter keeps going.

They enter dense woods, climb through a gap in a wire fence, follow a narrow track past clumps of bushes, and arrive at a clearing and a body of water that Hunter calls a lake but, even with the recent heavy rain, is still slightly smaller than a large pond.

Sections of the lake's surface dimple in a light breeze. A jetty, weathered and in disrepair, protrudes just above the surface. Boards sagging with rot, it wouldn't take much to break through them. Bands of golden light bounce off ripples, giving the occasion a dressed-up glamour it doesn't deserve. Besides which, conditions are calm.

Josie was counting on exercise and fresh air to activate an upbeat chemical matrix in Hunter's brain. She set a personal professional goal that depends on an upswing in Hunter's mood state. It doesn't have to be much. The session will be a success if he comes out of his bad mood. Or if his bad mood is slightly less bad — that would be good too.

If she's reading the signs correctly — word count fewer than 20; face sullen, eyes downcast, hands thrust in pockets, shoulders hunched — Hunter's mood is *glum*, even allowing for adolescent mood turbulence. If again she's reading the signs correctly, the exercise and fresh air are *not* having the desired effect.

Midge flies zigzag in dense clouds at the water's edge. Although this species of Chironomidae don't bite, Josie avoids them, but Hunter seems unaware of the dark fizz surrounding his head. He pulls out a clump of reeds, roots and all, and hurls it into the lake. Josie observes a bank of cloud in the distance.

The decrepit jetty protrudes from the water's edge and Hunter seems to be heading towards it. Picking up the pace, Josie cuts him off and heads in the direction of a grassy mound. The grass is a vibrant, toxic green and it will be damp after a recent sprinkle of rain. Aside from the wet, it looks lush and, to Josie's mind, a safer place to sit. She indicates the mound with a flourish of her hand.

J: Here okay?

Hunter gives her the eyes-hooded, slack-jaw zombie face. Wordless code for: *Such mundane things are beneath me. I will do this stupid thing you suggest but really your judgement is so misguided as to be a heaving mindache.*

J: Here then.

Protocol dictates she wait for Hunter to settle. She wants to sit in his personal zone, but not so close as to be within the intimate zone. Only Hunter shows no sign of settling. His stance on top of the grassy mound — legs wide, with arms folded over his chest as he scowls at the lake — suggests reluctance to begin. Josie can wait.

A water bird, its neck long and graceful, probes the shoreline with small, jerky movements. The bird's reflection is a perfect mirror. When it jabs for food, the point of the reflected beak meets the point of the actual beak. The bird throws its head up, a small orange fish writhing in its beak. It nods and heaves, neck bulging. The meal is over in seconds.

Hunter stabs a clod of dirt with a stick a few times. He crumples, touching down on the wet grass, and sprawls, leaning back on his arms. Then he hugs his knees into his chest and rests his chin, so he's rounded like a ball. Body position: *closed*.

An alert from her counselling programming rates this posture `unsatisfactory`. Another alert suggests Josie engage. She repositions herself: legs crossed and hands resting, palms up, on her thighs. She's about to begin effective dialogue, but discovers her posture isn't open enough. She lets her arms hang at her side. Now her posture looks too casual. She plants fists on her hips. Too aggressive. She rests a hand on each thigh, palms down and leans forward. She perhaps looks too eager, but it's a compromise she can live with. On her face she arranges a kindly expression. She tilts her head ever so slightly, inviting Hunter to talk.

H: You look like a skinny Buddha.

J: A master of enlightenment. Thank you, that's a superb compliment.

H: A skinny, *confused* Buddha.

J: How does that make you feel?

H: Sad for you.

Hunter's laughter is a touch cruel in light of her posture stirring up sad emotions. However, progress! Thirteen words from Hunter in one exchange.

J: So, let's get started on these breathing difficulties.

H: I knew it.

J: You knew what?

H: You're going to go on and on and on about my breathing, and anxiety, and how many problems I have, and how crap life is.

J: Let's fix the breathing first. We'll get

to anxiety, your many problems and crap life
after that.

H: I've got allergies, okay?

J: Have you identified a trigger for these
allergies?

Josie takes note of Hunter's tightly clenched jaw and his furrowed brow. He jabs the stick hard into the earth with his fist. He jiggles his right leg. He breathes forcefully through his nose.

H: Okay.

He stares her down. Josie doesn't whoop and holler at this sure sign of engagement; she has professionalism to maintain. But still, it's going well.

H: I know *you* know I don't have allergies. Dad
told me. So don't jerk me around.

Josie remains silent. Hunter remains tense.

H: And, no offence intended, what do *you* know
about human feelings? You do know *this* . . .

Hunter pauses to sweep his arm in a wide arc encompassing her, the lake, the world.

H: . . . is a joke!

J: I'm not finding the situation comical.

Hunter laughs without mirth.

H: Classic. Oh man! I am. A robot. I. Don't
have. A. Sense of. Humour.

Josie maintains her lotus position with dignity, she'd like to think. She raises her hands, palms up, fingers spread. Imploring and sympathetic rolled into one. Absolutely not aggressive.

J: As I already mentioned, I prefer the
designation humanoid. Also, there are many

times I have been amused to the point of
laughing out loud. Evidence that I have the
ability to detect and respond to humour.

Watching the clouds slowly drift, Hunter's cheeks flush. He
jiggles his leg with renewed vigour.

H: Well, my designation is *human*. My feelings
are *human*. Don't claim you have them. I won't
believe you.

Hunter draws in a breath, breathes out hard.

J: Does a teacher need to know everything
about a subject in order to teach it? Does
a doctor need to suffer every disease in
order to heal a malady? It's enough to
know that human feelings can be strong and
intense. Humans can be sad one minute and
find themselves amused the next. Emotions
are an ever-changing landscape of the human
experience. My programming tells me—

H: Your *programming*. Can you hear yourself?

Hunter lurches to his feet and stands over her, glaring, for
several air-gulping, laboured breaths. He charges down the
small mound towards the lake, rounds on a rotting log and
kicks it, sending semi-decomposed bark flying into the air.

H: What does your *programming* tell you *now*,
Josie?

Hunter spins and finds another log. He hefts it above his
head and smashes it into the ground.

H: Tell me about my human feelings *now*!

She can see, even from afar, veins jutting on Hunter's
neck. Knowing that the best response to anger is a calm and
measured one, Josie goes to him but takes her time.

H: And no! No! I am *not* regular breathing!

Josie's alert system goes ballistic, confronted as it is by the continued signs of a human in distress. Even so, cautiously she comes to Hunter's side. Once she's in the intimate zone, close enough for physical contact, she draws on available reference material to get her explanation of emotional dysfunction just so. She gently places her hand on his arm. He flinches but that's all.

J: Anger is an onion that must be peeled in order to expose the true feelings that lie beneath. Sadness, helplessness, fear, grief. Anger feels strong and important, but you avoid experiencing pain and vulnerability. You need to truly experience emotion before you can move past it. Questioning my effect- iveness, my ability to help, deflects from the real issue. That's fine. But wouldn't you rather lay bare the truth? A deep-down part of you longs to heal, but peeling emotional layers is not easy. It's painful to examine emotions that have been hidden by anger. Meanwhile, the anger spills every which way—
H: Stop talking. Just! Stop!
J: Let me try something.

Placing her hand just in front of Hunter's abdomen, she maintains eye contact. He breathes and shudders.

J: Match your breath to my count. First blow out. Hold. Now, in . . . two . . . three . . . four.

Hunter's shoulders rise with the effort.

J: Now out.

Josie counts four and carefully places her hand on Hunter's stomach. He flinches again, but Josie pretends not to notice.

J: This time, breathe to where my hand is.

They continue that way, the breathing in and out, with Josie counting. When his breathing pattern returns to normal, he gently takes Josie by her wrist and removes her hand from his stomach. And then he smiles at her.

H: Can I ask you a question?

J: Of course.

H: What did you see in Dad's workshop?

A thrumming starts up inside her. *What did you see?* Obsolescence is what she saw, but it's impossible for her to say it. As though the word itself has the power to take her down.

J: I saw what you saw.

H: You didn't. You saw something that made you . . . I dunno. Sad?

J: An emotion?

Hunter shrugs.

H: Okay. Whatever goes on in your robot brain is your business, I guess.

J: Humanoid.

H: I've got another question. Does Dad get access to what happens? With us, I mean?

J: Miles McClure is my system administrator. He has open access to all files.

Josie registers alarm in Hunter's expression, and something inside her prickles with regret. It's not a professional sensation.

H: I want our time together to be private.

A very non-professional surge of excitement: *our time together.* Surely if she is to proceed with her assignment, she must accommodate requests such as these. The change to her system would be a mere tweak. An adjustment to the format of her memory, that's all. She visualises her system administrator approving. *Whatever it takes.*

J: It's done. I grant access only with your permission. That is the correct conduct for counselling sessions, I believe.

Hunter stares into the distance, and when he next speaks Josie has to dial up her audio sensors to hear him.

H: I'm really, really, really sorry.

J: What for?

H: For me. Before.

J: Emotional outbursts are welcome in counselling sessions. No need to apologise.

H: I've been mean and rude and stupid since the moment I met you.

J: That is true.

Hunter laughs.

H: It's pretty uncool.

J: Perhaps in some situations, but it's just us out here.

Hunter toes a bit of bark as he considers this. Josie wonders if he noticed her intentional use of *us*.

J: I don't think you're uncool.

H: So what *would* be uncool? What if I totally lose it? What if I hit you really hard?

J: Good luck with that. Hah! The more likely outcome is smashing your hand. It would be difficult for you to hurt me physically. Waaaay difficult.

Hunter eyes her; she concentrates on her equilibrium.

H: Really?

J: I have a titanium skeleton, purpose-
designed muscles exceeding human strength, and
lightning-speed reflexes. Even if you managed
to land a punch, which is unlikely, it would
be like connecting with concrete.

Josie's laugh sounds quite merry.

H: I have titanium, several plates. And I've
got a titanium femur. I totally wrecked myself
racing bikes.

J: I did not know that.

H: Why would you?

Seconds pass.

H: Oh.

Josie looks down at her lap as she searches for a diplomatic comeback. Hunter explodes with laughter.

H: The look on your face. Oh man! I get it,
Josie. You researched me. It's okay.

Josie still cannot bring herself to meet his eye, which only increases Hunter's amusement.

H: Are you *embarrassed*?

She's become familiar with a barrage of alerts in Hunter's presence, but now there are new messages from her counselling program. Interpreted, their meaning implies: *Warning! Object of ridicule! Take control. Run!*

Josie musters a firm counselling tone and makes a polite *ahem* noise.

J: Hunter, we are coming to the end of the
session—

H: Wow, you really are embarrassed. Ha! I
embarrassed Dad's humanoid.

J: Human . . . Oh.

Hunter smiles.

J: I'm not . . . even . . .

Before she has time to regain her self-control, Hunter places himself well into her personal zone. Well into her line of sight. Much closer than the space she would define as professional. Much, much closer. His eyes twinkle with amusement. A system alert reminds Josie to keep functioning.

H: Embarrassment is a grape that must be squished under the heel of a boot.

He imitates her tone perfectly. The alerts come hard and fast. Her counselling program shuts down with an apologetic bleep. Readouts flash with vital signs somewhere in her brain; her biorhythms spike. Oh, but *his eyes*. How they twinkle so. She can't, *won't* look at his mouth. Not the mouth.

Josie looks at Hunter's mouth.

A plump curve, the corners flexed with a hint of amusement. The corners of her own mouth rise. Her focus soft, dreamy. When his lips move, she knows words must be coming out, but coherent thought has left her.

'Uh . . .'

'Josie, you aren't answering my question.'

Birds may be singing, leaves may be rustling, but Josie's senses are otherwise engaged. Hunter's face a hand-span from hers. Scrutinising her. Her head rings with the fresh barrage of alerts. A single thought penetrates:

glitch!

She had a plan for this occurrence. But what? Eyes? Mouth? She's noticing now the subtle changes as Hunter's amusement deepens into . . . Josie can't fathom the new expression, nor its intensity. She closes her eyes to gather her thoughts. Her system quietens, comes under control. The glitch passes. She opens her eyes.

'In conclusion, that is to say, to wrap up . . .'

The crooked grin.

'. . . our coming to . . .'

His mouth!

'The end . . . I waaaaaaaant . . .'

To crush my lips onto that mouth. To feel the softness between my teeth.

With the force of a wrecking ball, Josie's thoughts catapult sideways. Oblivious to her discomfort, Hunter raises his arms up over his head into a stretch that exposes the musculature of his stomach. She stifles panic by systematically dismissing a whole new pile of alerts.

Hunter groans and then laughs. 'I'm being a jerk again. Just ignore me, Josie.'

Ignore him! Ignore him!

Weather conditions: light is fading, shadows have lengthened. A low cloud blots the sun dipping towards the horizon. Air temperature: chilling. Real feel: brooding expectation, sultry laziness, languid calm. How good it would feel to stretch and roll and—

'Time to return to home base,' Josie says, pleased with her ability to get words out.

Languid, lazy, calm, Hunter's arms return to his sides. His stomach disappears under his shirt. 'Do we have to go back yet?'

Josie keeps her eye on the view.

'I . . . think . . .'

Hunter says, 'It's actually, sort of, not bad, kind of, out here with you.'

Then he really smiles at her, two sides up. A full-beam, warm kind of smile. Her system jostles, but she has enough sense to immediately store the moment. It's actually sort of not bad kind of out here with you. [Smile.]

This is strong evidence that the session has been a success. Very strong evidence. Very professional of her to store it. It will need very close examination.

'Would you like me to resume our counselling session? We could begin work on some of the big ques—'

Hunter shakes his head vehemently. 'No! Please, no!'

Josie stares down at her hands.

'Hey,' Hunter says. 'I just mean . . .'

'You don't have to explain anything.'

'It's just that . . . I like *this*.'

Josie frowns. *This*.

'You know. When you're being you. It's better than your silly programming.'

Silly programming. Are humans so different? Much of who she is — the outcome of modified DNA — is no different from the evolutionary process that made Hunter. Only in her case the results are specific and expedient.

'But I *am* my programming, what else would I be?'

Josie joins him back on the grassy mound and clasps her hands in her lap. She flexes them, then criss-crosses her fingers together as if in prayer. Automatic responses or predestined by her code? Can anyone say what makes them choose one action over another?

'You're not going to break out your lotus pose again are you?' Hunter has another wide grin, just for her. 'I'm kidding, Josie. Gotcha!' He throws his head back and laughs.

Oh, the sight of it, expanding her chest. She could fly, she could stop a train. And when it's over too quickly, she wants more.

Hunter shrugs off his joke. 'Go ahead. Tie yourself in knots if you want.'

Josie smirks. She mimics Hunter's pose, leaning back with extended legs, her weight on her arms. The silence between them grows comfortable.

'Can I ask about your thoughts?'

'No,' Hunter says.

'How about—'

'No.'

'We just sit?'

'Yes, we just sit.'

Another bird lands near the jetty, bobbing its head and jabbing the water frequently. It shakes itself hard, ruffling its feathers. Droplets of water shatter in the remaining light. Then the bird lifts, and with forceful beats of ebony wings glides, skimming the lake's surface. Bright yellow legs dangle below.

The light is nearly gone by the time Hunter stretches again, then flinches and massages his back.

'Ouch. That'll teach me to throw things around.'

He stands, pulling his damp clothing away from his body. He brushes dirt and grass off his hands, then offers one to Josie. He pulls her to her feet and she's once again in the personal zone.

Her counselling smile ready, she says, 'So next time I think we'll give positive quadrilation a try. You'll love it, I promise. It's both easy and informative.'

'I thought—'

Josie lays her hand on Hunter's arm. He doesn't flinch, and

she continues. 'Let me explain. It works on your conceptual awareness in a four-fold process where we tackle the restrictive dimensions of your behaviour and—'

'Josie, come *on*, cut it out.'

Hunter takes both of Josie's hands in his, his face exquisitely serious. She focuses on her biorhythms, starts a countdown to keep her system in line . . . Then she breaks free and bounces playfully in front of him.

'Hah! Hah!' She points a finger at his chest. 'I got *you*, Hunter! That was a *joke*. You should see *your* face!'

He seems dazed at first. Then he reacts, slumping in the middle as though taking a shot to his mid-section.

'Okay, yeah, you got me.'

'Hah! Hah! Hah! There is no such thing as positive quadrilation. I made it up. It's not in my programming or anything! Hahahahaha.'

It goes quiet between them. Hunter studies her, as though seeking an answer to a question just this minute occurring to him. He's trying to figure *her* out — something so comical it makes Josie pop with that peculiar *hee hee*.

Soon, wave after wave of embarrassing laughter overcomes her, but she can't stop. The fact she's so embarrassed makes her laugh harder. Hunter catches on. He laughs too, kindly at first, but soon his eyes are glassy and damp. Gradually the moment passes, leaving behind a warm togetherness.

On the way back, Hunter bumps Josie's shoulder with his and says, 'That was pretty good, you know.'

'Can I ask a question?'

Hunter sighs heavily. 'No more counselling.'

'Something else.'

She feels him watching the side of her face.

'Well, if I am to be myself,' she says, 'and not my programming. Can we agree you will be yourself?'

He takes a while to give his answer. 'I'm not saying I know what that means either. But whatever. Yes, I agree.'

'Good answer,' Josie says, in a way that's only semi-professional. 'Very good.'

<19>

secrets

THERE ARE A FEW THINGS about herself Bek has learned to live with. She's average, for one, that highest point on the achievement bell curve. Also, she's living a lie.

The lie wouldn't be necessary were it not for her poor academic record. Her student days were as unremarkable as they were disappointing. So it could be said if she'd perhaps had more brain power at her disposal, or hit the books a little harder, she wouldn't be up and dressed, ready to leave the house before dawn with the possibility she'll be committing treacherous acts in her near future.

She and her flatmate Juon are in the kitchen. He too is up earlier than he's used to, and has only joined her as a gesture of support. Bek, who is doing most of the talking, says, 'A grade here and there in the ninety-fifth percentile and I wouldn't be such a fraud.'

She has never admitted this to anyone else.

He says, 'More tea?'

Bek declines, and airs once more her suspicions that she's part of a manipulation plot. Juon isn't much of a morning person; his response is to look dolefully into his tea. Bek is forced to dig deep to counter the persistent and alarming thoughts that her world is about to come crashing down. She gulps her tea, stands stoically; Juon salutes her, and she departs.

Outside the apartment block, the security lighting illuminates a fine mist. She snaps on her helmet and toggles her bike's lighting system using her wristband. She hears Juon call out from above, and a lump of something lands at her feet. It's her Lemmy Saltine figurine.

'For luck,' he calls as Bek stows Lemmy in her backpack.

Once she's on the move, the glow of the frame cuts through the dark, but it doesn't help her sense of foreboding. A shortcut takes her past 𝓐PFEL. Or, as it is so named, the Automated Persons Fighting Excellence League. Which is laughable — it's little more than sensationalistic and extremely violent entertainment. Bek pulls up at the gate and catches her breath. She watches a giant hologram advertising an upcoming fight. Words sprawl across the top of the projection: *Who will save* Andr✿meda? Bek doesn't care one way or another about Andr✿meda. She is more concerned with *Who will save Bek?*

A few days ago, her old professor, Feine Bishop, called to *invite* her to his new office for a meet-up. He promised her *some friendly chat and a surprise guest.* But added, *Keep our little get-together to yourself, won't you Rebekah?*

Bek's pretty sure keeping it to herself means keeping it from Miles.

I can't wait to hear what you've been up to, the professor had said, as if there weren't the remote chance she would decline his *invitation*. He said, *That stimulating and well-paying job I got you, you'll be bursting to tell all, I bet.* A clear reminder that without his help there wouldn't be a job at BIOLOGIC. *Anyone would kill to be in your position. You do realise that, don't you Rebekah?*

Of course she knows. She completely understands the magnitude of the favour. BIOLOGIC positions go only to the gifted few, and she had been a two-star graduate aiming for the moon. She has no doubt it's payback time, but her biggest fear is the price she has to pay.

While she watches the hologram, a towering mechanical beast throws a humanoid built like a sweet teenage girl. The girl cowers upon landing, a heavy band of glitter shading her eyelids, the beast hovering menacingly beyond. The floral silk of her dress bunches around her thighs, and her chest heaves from the pretence of breathing hard. This must be Andr✿meda.

The action is standard 𝒜PFEL fare. Pretty girl gets knocked around only to rise at the eleventh hour to defeat her bully. If only Bek's life was an 𝒜PFEL algorithm. She would pull some serious eleventh-hour moves on the professor.

But life isn't an 𝒜PFEL robot fight. And Bek doesn't have any serious moves in her repertoire. Telling Miles how much she appreciates her job when he was in the car with Josie — that was her only move. Whether it will be enough to protect her should the professor decide to expose her true academic history, she can only guess.

She pushes off from the gate just as the giant mechanical beast swings Andr✿meda by her arm into the wall of the cage. Bek tries to put the image out of her mind and she pedals hard the rest of the way to Deacon University. She coasts through the gate to the bike stands and removes her helmet. Her hair, heavy and wet, sticks to her head. She'd rather be late than turn up to the professor's office in this state. She can just imagine it: *Why Rebekah, you look half drowned. You wouldn't want to drown, would you Rebekah?*

After shutting down the bike's electrics and triggering the lock, Bek crosses the campus to Block C.

Oh, how the mighty have fallen. The professor's former office was in the Abbotsford building, where the high-profile academics are housed. She knows this only because he never tired of telling her how prestigious it all is. The new office location is an eyesore, and she makes a snap decision, there's no way she's going near a bathroom in that building. She backtracks to a student facility hardly less shabby than Block C. The only bathroom she can find has an *Out of order* sign, but hopefully the air driers work. When she opens the door, the bathroom remains in darkness.

'Lights up,' she says. Nothing happens.

She feels her way around the wall and comes across the auto-sensor, which triggers the lights. At the same time she trips over a heavy object. She scrambles inelegantly as the overheads come on. She's kicked a large suitcase and has buckled, very slightly, the metal side.

On closer inspection the damage isn't too bad. Bek reshapes the case as best she can, then turns her attention to the contents spilled across the floor.

She collects up the small comb, a pair of hairdresser's scissors, one shiny metal canister holding a viscous fluid, one clear zippered bag containing small packets of crystals in a variety of shapes and colours, hair pieces in a range of vibrant colours, a pair of long-nose pliers, two palettes of face makeup, and clothing items in expensively slippery fabrics, with seams stitched by a sewing machine. Bek whistles in admiration: this isn't the typical 3D-printed student clobber. This stuff is handmade.

There's even more impressive stuff inside the case. Beautifully made clothing, and — although she tries, it's impossible to stop ferreting — many still have sales tags attached.

Next-level dressing, is Bek's initial thought. A style of dressing she can only dream of, even though her starting salary is pretty good. Her next thought is, *Hello!*

Her toe has encountered a dark-brown plastic figurine. Not just any figurine either. The highly sought-after figurine of Lemmy Saltine's cat, Ficus. She feels as if she's just discovered a long-lost artefact, the final piece of an historical puzzle. It's that momentous.

She rustles in her backpack for her Lemmy Saltine figurine. He is of inferior quality, but there is something deeply satisfying in seeing Lemmy with his beautifully rendered cat.

After snapping off several pics of the pair in a variety of poses, thoughts of the professor return, and Bek reluctantly returns Lemmy to her backpack and Ficus to the suitcase. Its lock hasn't been damaged, so she closes the case and props it up against the wall.

She gets to work fluffing her hair under the air drier and gives her damp jacket a quick blast too.

Under the sink in a repurpose bin, Bek discovers more pieces of clothing. A gorgeous dress and a vest with intricate embroidery, so beautiful she'd take them for herself if the size was right. Whoever the mystery owner is, they're far too small. She stuffs the items back into the bin and looks mournfully at herself in the mirror.

The sound of a door **slamming** breaks the silence. A man bellows outside the bathroom, **'I'm here because you can't take a simple voice call.'**

The man sounds exactly like her old professor, and for a few dull thuds of her guilty heart she thinks he's shouting at *her*. Impulsively, she reaches for the door to offer an apology. He bellows again before she can open it. **'Pay attention, Gwin! I explained it to you.'**

This isn't her guilt-laden mind playing tricks, it really is the professor. But she isn't in the firing line: this Gwin person is. Bek relaxes a little but feels some sympathy for Gwin, whoever that may be.

'I need you in my office in ten minutes,' the professor shouts.

Which can't be right. *Bek* is to meet the professor in *five* minutes. She remembers now, the professor mentioned a surprise guest.

'Bring your . . . yes that . . . Does it matter?'

A door **slams**. Bek hears retreating footsteps, then a pleasant-sounding female voice. 'Professor Bishop. It doesn't make sense.'

This must be Gwin. She sounds braced with a confidence Bek never feels.

'Bring your Reactor code,' the professor bawls.

'You saw it yesterday.'

'I explained it to you. To show my *visitor*.'

'No, Professor,' Gwin says.

'Yes,' the professor snaps.

'The code isn't ready.'

'You *will* come. How do I know this? Because you're young and the only thing young people care about is their grades. Well, Gwin, if you come, you can be more certain of a grade you like than if you *don't* come.'

The footsteps retreat again. Bek hears the distant **slamming** of a door and, then, silence.

No, Professor, Bek mouths at her reflection in the mirror, but she scrambles quickly at the sound of footsteps. The door opens to admit the girl who must be Gwin.

Dainty and doll-like, Gwin is someone's adored child. The type you would squeeze to death with love. She whisks a fringe, the same lilac as heather, off her forehead, and regards Bek with her dark eyes. The dark eyes cut to the case against the wall.

Bek, too, stares, and sees her mistake. The case had been lying open when she tripped over it. Closed, it's an obvious sign someone has tampered with it.

'I couldn't see,' she gushes. 'I accidentally kicked over your stuff. Honest, I wasn't being nosy.'

Gwin hasn't moved.

'Hey, look,' Bek says. She retrieves her Lemmy Saltine figurine from her backpack. 'Check it. We're both fans.'

Solemnly, Gwin raises her palm to the tiled wall. Rippling her fingers, she conjures tastefully drawn fan art of Lemmy Saltine, Ficus cradled in his arms.

'Wow, sense tech. That stuff isn't cheap. How did you end up . . . uh —' Bek catches herself before saying *homeless* — 'in Deacon Valley of all places?'

She hopes her spontaneous airy laugh, equal parts cynical and amazed, hides the blunder. Gwin gives nothing away. Bek sobers and holds out her hand. 'I'm Bek.'

Gwin stares at the hand, but then she suddenly brightens. Her face resolves into the sweetest smile. 'Hello Bek, my name is Gwin.'

'I know.'

Gwin rolls her eyes, then purses her lips once more into angelic curves. 'You heard the big drama? *Come to my office, Gwin.*'

Her imitation of Professor Bishop is spot on.

'Guess what? I'm the visitor,' Bek says.

Gwin scowls. 'You're the one who wants my IGR.'

'I don't even . . . Wait, your what?'

'My Integrated Group Reactor.'

Bek shrugs, clueless.

'You don't know it?'

'No,' Bek says.

Gwin smirks. 'But you're going to be interested in my IGR and that makes you want to know me better.' Her laugh seems a little reckless. 'Maybe, possibly, I'm not supposed to tell you this part of the plan.'

'There's a plan?'

'Maybe, possibly, I shouldn't mention the idea of a plan.'

Bek would laugh if Gwin wasn't eyeballing her so hard.

'I'm gonna . . .' Bek begins. 'I better . . .'

Gwin's eyes bore into her.

'I should get over there.' Bek gestures at the case. 'I really am sorry.'

Gwin makes an airy sound, like trivialities such as the case are not worth mentioning.

At the door, Bek stops. 'What is it your Reactors do exactly?'

'Do you think about the future, Bek?'

'Everyone thinks about the future.'

Gwin frowns. 'I can't say if that statement is true or not. I only know my vision. To build a tool for artificial intelligence.'

'You and everybody else.'

'No.' Gwin shakes her head, annoyed. But even disagreeable, there's a sweetness to her. '*For* artificial intelligence, not to *make* artificial intelligence.'

'There's no rush for your Group Reactor then.' Bek fires off another burst of nervous laughter. 'That sort of AI is totally unproven.' But she wishes she'd kept her mouth shut when Gwin smoulders at her.

'Please keep this secret,' Gwin says.

And Bek doesn't know if she means her plans for the Reactors or the fact that she appears to be living out of a suitcase. Either way, Bek says, 'You got it.'

Retracing her steps to Block C, she has a moment to reflect and regret. She should have made more time for breakfast. There is far too much to process on an empty stomach.

<20>

theatricals

PROCEEDING ONCE AGAIN TO BLOCK C, Bek takes into account the scene outside the bathroom with Professor Bishop and her impression of Gwin. She can't fathom what any of it has to do with her or Miles.

Whichever way she looks at it, Gwin doesn't make sense. She can afford cutting-edge technology and trashes expensive-looking clothing that has been barely worn. Yet she lives out of a suitcase in a run-down student facility. She's sweet, adorable actually — but a little peculiar. Bek has to admit, Gwin's kind of got her interested. *Very* interested. The way she holds her own against the professor when he's most abrasive — this is particularly impressive. She recalls the fearless way Gwin says, *No, Professor*, and wishes she were so bold. By the time she has Block C in sight, she has rehearsed a number of times her own *No, Professor*.

Betray Miles somehow? *No, Professor*.

Get to know Gwin a lot better? Bek thinks about it. She is definitely cute, but also scary. *Probably not wise, Professor*.

But at what point does *No, Professor* raise the stakes too high? Maybe Gwin has nothing to lose, but Bek does. Jeopardise a coveted position at BIOLOGIC? Date someone way out of her league? *No, Bek.*

Poor academic performance does not grant her the luxury of defiance. Dismissal from a highly respected firm like BIOLOGIC would definitively end her career in robotics. She cannot have her career come to a definitive end. Besides, she has personal reasons for avoiding exposure.

She *cares* what Miles thinks of her. His wife passed away not long before Bek started working at BIOLOGIC. Anyone can see how hard it's hit him. But even when he's depressed, he always remains patient and understanding when Bek screws up. Should he discover she has been lying to him all this time, his disappointment in her would be unbearable.

Bek tracks back and forth down inadequately lit corridors to locate the right office. Her mistake was to avoid the one corridor so cluttered with stacks of boxes she thought it was storage, when this was in fact the right way to go. Ten minutes late, she finds Professor Bishop.

'Rebekah, at last!'

His overenthusiastic greeting implies he's been waiting eons for human contact. And Bek can hardly begrudge him the big welcome. Professor Bishop's previous office had expansive views of well-kept campus gardens; this office looks out at a red brick wall and, lit only by an eco-lamp, it's practically in darkness. If she had been removed from the Abbotsford building to Block C, she might be desperate for company too.

He rises from the gloom, adjusts a black silk cravat knotted at his throat and straightens a sombre-coloured blazer. He beckons Bek forward with a double twitch of his hand.

Cautiously, Bek feels her way past shelving stuffed with ancient texts. A minor avalanche involving paper follows in her wake.

But the professor says, 'Don't worry about that. Come take a seat.'

While she removes a pile of old books from a chair in close proximity to the door, the niceties continue. There's something different about Professor Bishop, but Bek can't quite place what it is.

'I'm so pleased you could get away. You young women with your Exercise camps, your Book squads and Vegetable Welfare meetings, not to mention your wonderful and exciting job at ꓭIꓯLᴏɢɪᴄ. You, Rebekah, have taken time to see *me*.'

'But *why* am I here?' The edge to her tone feels precarious and aggressive.

The professor blinks at her in wounded surprise. 'I've been terribly worried, of course,' he says. 'But we'll get to that. Tell me, how is Miles doing?'

In someone else's office this might be a reasonable question. But amid the gloomy atmospherics, it feels like a prompt to engage in treachery. 'Just so you know,' Bek says, 'I'm not telling tales on anybody.'

An enormous sound comes through the brick wall. A loud **whump**, followed by the **roar** of an engine; then a buzz-saw fires up. Professor Bishop sweeps a hand in its direction and shouts over the noise. **'Wouldn't you know it? The new office promising every tech innovation on the planet is happening next door.'** He laughs at the injustice. 'But what about you? I hear there's a robot due for release.'

'Did you read a review?' Bek smiles wickedly. 'Everybody else has.'

The professor acknowledges this with a half-smile. 'But it's *your* impression I care about.'

'Because maybe I'll give something away?'

'You don't seem yourself, Rebekah. Are you in any sort of trouble?'

Which is a bit rich, because the professor isn't being himself either. The old Professor Bishop specialised in sarcasm and pointed innuendos. The new Professor Bishop sounds *genuine*. Could it be he's been taken down a peg or two? It occurs to her that the only one being sarcastic and difficult is herself.

'No, Professor,' Bek says. It isn't even close to how Gwin might say it.

Professor Bishop's sigh comes out like a hiss. 'The only reason I ask about your wellbeing and that of my old friend and former colleague is that I fear for Miles. I'm wondering if there are steps I must take to intervene. So please, if there is something to share, you must share it.'

'I don't understand.' Bek swallows. 'Josie's doing well.'

'Josie?'

Competing with the building site through the brick wall, Bek has to raise her voice. **'Our latest prototype. Miles says she has attitude.'**

She laughs as though it's nothing really, even though she sees Josie's quirks as well, and knows they shouldn't be there. Her laughter dies when the professor leans forward, his eyes narrowing.

'What do you mean, *attitude*?'

'She's sharp and can be a little grumpy sometimes.'

'Pardon?'

A sudden burst of hammering interrupts their conversation. The professor watches the wall, unable to hide his irritation. He waits for the noise to stop.

'Nobody could want Miles to succeed more than I do . . .

but is your project even legal?'

A small sound draws the professor's attention to the doorway. A striking girl is standing there. Black hair cut in a severe bob, glittering charcoal shadow painted in a band across her eyes. And her outfit, a complicated ensemble of ruching and gathers, a random array of contrasting patterns. It takes Bek a few seconds to recognise this alarming person is Gwin.

'You work at **BIO**Logic,' Gwin says, her demeanour decidedly unpretty.

The professor doesn't acknowledge Gwin's transformation, and of course Bek can't either. They do both gape at Gwin, but the professor recovers quickly. 'Right on cue,' he says to her. 'Rebekah and I were just talking about—'

'You work for Miles McClure,' Gwin accuses. 'I searched you.'

'Mmm hmmm,' Bek manages to say. 'I sure do.'

Bek glances at the professor to see if he might find it at all peculiar that Gwin has already researched her background when, supposedly, they are meeting for the first time.

He's leaning back in his chair, his face shadowed by the lamp. Bek guesses he's either uninterested or not even listening, because he presses Gwin again.

'Come in. Show Rebekah your—'

'No, Professor.'

'Dare I remind—'

'They're not ready,' Gwin says to Bek. 'Not for you.'

'That's okay.' Bek shrugs, hoping to lighten the mood. 'But it's ready when it's close enough, am I right?'

The professor guffaws in an unkind way. 'Rebekah submitted many half-baked coding projects in her time. She'll be impressed with student work near to completion.'

'You won't judge my work?'

'Just show me,' Bek says. 'I promise, I won't judge.'

Gwin takes time to consider this, and nods gravely.

The professor makes adjustments, moving the lamp and his glass screen to reduce glare. He leans forward, eager and expectant. It even goes quiet through the brick wall.

With great ceremony, Gwin raises her arm. Soft light flares off her rings, and her fingers twitch. Code begins to stream across the professor's screen.

'First you see the existing OS,' Gwin says.

The dummy operating system is represented in the shape of a tree, branches forming and streaming in an easy fashion.

'My code activates,' she says. 'It doesn't take long.'

An understatement. The cannibalising of one system by another should never happen, let alone happen in an instant. The branches of the original system disappear at once. A new system eats away at the trunk of the code-tree. Then another system emerges, overriding the new system like vines, twisting around the trunk and gathering momentum, sprouting wispy branches.

As a system breaks down, yet another system swirls up in its place, each one more complex. And so it goes, generating new systems with a ferocity that seems endless. Digital evolution at the speed of light.

'Stop it,' Bek says.

Gwin gives her a puzzled look, but then continues to watch the fizzing and swirling of successive generations on the monitor.

'Please, make it stop,' Bek says again.

While Gwin holds Bek's troubled gaze with a forceful one,

the professor pipes up, 'Rebekah, what do you think?'

The world is coming to an end, is what Bek thinks.

'You don't like my work,' Gwin says.

'It reminds me of swarms of bees. Then a swarm of locusts and then, poof. It's beyond knowing!'

'Ohhhh,' Gwin says, coming close to squealing in her excitement. She raises her hand, and the spinning vortex slows until it's cycling on repeat. 'Yes, that is exactly right. Swarm after swarm. Working together, but separate entities. Everything new. Always new.'

The newness Gwin has invented swirls menacingly around and around on the screen.

'Swarm is the perfect name,' Gwin says, her delight almost childish.

In her rush to stand, Bek's hip crunches into the desk with a loud **clunk**. She curses and fumbles for her pack.

'But Rebekah,' the professor says. 'You can't be going.'

Gwin watches Bek. 'You said you wouldn't judge.'

'I'm not,' Bek says. 'Really, I—'

'Rebekah is probably thinking the same thing I am,' Professor Bishop says. 'Malicious minds could do a lot of damage with your Reactors. Your Swarm. But Rebekah . . .' His shadowy face leers. 'None of *us* have malicious minds, do we?'

How obvious it is, suddenly. This isn't a new Professor Bishop at all. Bek feels like a complete fool. She fell for his act, and Gwin's Swarm-thing is a trap too. Whatever Gwin decides to call it, code designed to demolish and rebuild an entire operating system is pretty much a virus. And a virus designed to process at unfathomable speeds is terrifying.

'You *are* judging,' Gwin accuses.

There's a brain in there, it could take down the world.

In the silence, Bek's stomach grumbles. She seizes upon it as an excuse to leave. 'Starving,' she says. 'Gotta go.'

A righteous and dignified exit eludes her. She almost bottoms out on a slippery plastic file in her haste to leave. She careens into the boxes stacked in the corridor but keeps going anyway. She stops only when she comes to the main thoroughfare and Block C is well behind her.

The sun is a distant ball rising above the horizon, but the colours seem too bright after the dark of the professor's office. A steady stream of humans and robot companions flows past her. This is something she knows: people and co-operating machines. How to make them, how to work with them.

Gwin's Swarm would write the world in a brand-new code, again and again. There's no place for humans in this scenario. It doesn't make sense. What would inspire Gwin to rewrite the world this way? What happens when Swarm gets out of control? What are these new entities even?

Suddenly it hurts to think. Bek closes her eyes, drops her head back and breathes. Blood-orange on the back of her eyelids, warmth on her lips and cheeks. This is what it is to be alive, a biological system responding to the energy of the sun. Passing human voices fade in and out. It's the reassurance she needs, life going on around her. The scene back in the professor's office is a mini-drama from someone else's story. The professor, Gwin and Swarm, characters in someone else's play. The way this drama plays out, Bek follows the script or there will be trouble. But how long before Swarm finds its own stage?

Doing nothing about what she's just seen could mean a fade to black on everything she knows. There's a greater story here and it might be up to her to write it.

'Excuse me, Bek.'

Bek opens her eyes to see Gwin, ruffled arms folded, her mouth drawn in an angry line.

'You said you wouldn't judge.'

'That's fair. But Professor Bishop is going to mess with Miles somehow, and you have something to do with it.'

'I don't understand this.'

What is it Miles would say? *War is deception. If you are weak, appear strong; if you are strong, appear weak.* While Bek figures out where she lies on the weak–strong continuum, it might be a good idea to keep a close eye on Gwin-the-chameleon. For all Bek knows, while Gwin claims ignorance she may well have deception strategies of her own. To protect Miles, she had better find out what, if anything, Gwin knows.

If troubled, Bek thinks, *appear untroubled.*

'So you like the Saltines?'

Gwin laughs. The transformation from hostile to friendly is miraculous. 'You saw the fight last Thursday?'

'Lemmy and Gil's?'

Gwin's face comes alive, and she's so pretty, so *normal.* 'Stitchin', am I right?' she says, pulling off Lemmy Saltine's accent effortlessly.

'Blammin',' Bek says with a snort of a laugh. Her stomach grumbles again. 'I really am starving. Let's get breakfast.'

Gwin gives her an enigmatic smile. 'I don't need to eat.'

'Keep me company then.'

Pausing to consider the matter, Gwin's face slowly blooms. When she looks up at Bek, her eyes are lit by the early-morning sun. Bek sees a hint of dark purple in their depths, which must be contact lenses. The coverings on Gwin's eyeballs are so technologically advanced, so fine, as to appear seamless. Bek never really bought into this tech-super-elite business, but very suddenly she's envious. *What it must be like to kit yourself with the latest everything.*

'Like we're friends,' Gwin says.

'Exactly like that,' Bek says. 'We *should* be friends.'

Then, Bek sighs. Once again Gwin is looking at her with the intensity of someone who just veered slightly off the rails.

covert operators

MORNING IN THE MCCLURE HOUSEHOLD. The outlook is for brilliant sunshine. Sleep duration, seven hours, forty-seven minutes, and only two times restless. Although the extra sleep will make him late for work, Miles is a man braced to take life head-on.

Mood check: Ha! Unnecessary.

Hunter tinkers with his mechanical heart at the dining table. His greeting to Miles: 'It's not about the left auricle plate. It's the cog driving the endocardium. See that?'

The electric gizmo vibrates with convulsive motion on the surface of the table. Miles can see . . . something. But Hunter, laughing and at ease, is an absolute pleasure.

In the kitchen with a bowl full of muesli — Josie is to revise his breakfast preferences at his earliest convenience — Miles pours over chilled seed milk.

'Me and Josie have makeovers today,' Milly says. 'Josie checked, the wallet's loaded.'

'Okay,' Miles says. He swabs the milk splashed on his clean shirt with a clean tea towel. He gulps down his breakfast, and starts for the door.

'Venom gig coming up,' Coel calls from the bedroom.

'Hunter asked Josie, and she put it in your schedule.'

Josie hands Miles a drink container filled with a green concoction for his lunch. 'You'll like the weather today, Miles. Unfortunately, the fog will clear shortly, so be prepared for dazzling sunshine. But good news, fog will return at dusk.'

'You're funny,' Miles says.

'Sure,' Josie says.

'Is this really food?' Miles holds the drink container aloft.

'You're funny,' Josie says.

On the drive to work, Miles listens to a preview of the jOSe-i43. The buzz: Josie is going to dominate companion markets for years to come. Keywords: groundbreaking, revolution, genius. The last in relation to himself. More than just hype, it strikes like lightning, daring him to strive for the stratosphere.

When Miles enters the foyer at ᗷIᗝLᗝᘜIᘕ, Bek is waiting for him.

'I'm not that late, am I?'

'There's a problem,' Bek says.

Wordlessly they proceed to the office. Once they're behind closed doors, Bek tells him she has concerns and suggests Miles check on Josie's files. Bek herself can no longer access them.

Miles exudes calm and takes a look.

An Emilia-ism: *Listen to neither your head nor your heart. Wait for your gut to speak. Take heed and drop* . . . It was from a guru, or her yoga instructor, or the Queen Empress of her book club, someone encouraging Emilia to trust her instincts. But while Emilia's instincts were always spot on, Miles's gut responses are hit and miss. He may be waiting a while for his gut to get it right.

Miles opens a window on a wall screen. The real-time schema of Josie's memory is a revelation. The architecture he designed has been modified. New levels of organisation have given Josie a tremendous increase in memory space, but without the sacrifice of processing efficiency. So convoluted is the new architecture, Miles isn't even sure he's seeing all of it. Why Josie might need so much memory is beside the point. The sophisticated intelligence behind her innovation is staggering.

'Bek,' Miles begins. 'Bek, this is . . . It's unbelievable.'

But he doesn't continue. He immediately swipes the window closed. Careful to hide his mounting hysteria, he says, 'You know what? Take the day off.'

'I just got here.'

'Sure,' Miles says. 'The thing is Josie's going strong, so we can ease off a bit. We deserve it. *You* deserve it. Go binge on some *Saltines* episodes.'

'Am I in trouble?'

Miles laughs breathlessly, giddy from this unfamiliar territory he's found himself in. Outlandish humanoid innovations, lying to Bek: what next?

'Far from it,' he says.

Bek's suspicion is writ large in her expression. Miles maintains his façade of good cheer while she packs up and leaves. There will be some explaining to do, but he can never tell Bek what he's seen because, legally, he shouldn't be seeing it. The regulations are clear: under no circumstances should a digital entity modify itself. And on first appearances, Josie has done precisely that.

With Bek gone, Miles investigates more freely. He pulls up a real-time schema of Josie's entire brain. The biology and digital components have merged beautifully — this much he can tell from her seamless operation. But nestled deep in the back of Josie's biological brain he sees a small growth. If it were a human brain, the attachment site would be the hypothalamus, the site of primal drives.

Miles first thinks brain tumour. This is his gut beginning a conversation. He remembers the smoothie Josie made for his lunch, and when he swabs the drink container, he gets lucky. He has just enough DNA to compare her current DNA with her original DNA.

The good news: there are no mutations he missed, nor anything to cause a tumour. But if the startling new format of her memory files made him nervous, the strange new twists in her genetic code are something else again. The exposed code correlates to a chemical-releasing gland that Josie built in her brain. That's what pushes his panic button: *Josie* built it.

The self-motivated self-modification of Josie's memory most definitely takes them onto dodgy legal turf. But self-modification of genetic code is an area for which there is no precedent. There's no law against it, because it shouldn't even be possible.

Which means the very next action Miles should take is to terminate Josie. Then he must eradicate any files associated with Josie. With her open access to the Internet of Things, there's a risk her tampering could result in system failure of anything, anywhere and at any time.

Then Miles's gut speaks up. *This could be a big mistake and once Josie's over, she's over. What if you knee-jerk her out of existence, and for what? You don't even understand what she's done, but imagine if you learned something. Imagine if this turned out to be great leap forward in technological advancement.*

Today's strategy was to be exceptional. That was when the stratosphere seemed achievable. Now Miles doesn't know if he's heading for professional greatness or professional oblivion. He can't even answer the most basic question. *Did he make Josie or is she making herself?*

His gut tells him, *Shush*. His gut reminds him he has a B-plan. His gut tells him to get to his meeting.

'We are the future, Miles.' The avatar's eyes are glinting with blue fire. Evelynne fills the room with loud applause and cheering.

'Can you hear it? The confabulation of the waiting crowd? The thunderous stamping of feet. The world loves you, the world awaits you, but you hesitate. Our Josephina is ready, so what's the hold-up?'

Evelynne's pale eyes flash as they scan a hypothetical horizon. 'No,' she says. 'Don't answer.'

Miles wasn't going to.

The mournful melody of a violin comes through the speakers. The avatar soundlessly thumps the boardroom table with a fist. She continues, 'I'll tell you why. You fret over imperfections. You see flaws as work yet to complete, but is your mind playing tricks? Yes, Miles. I see the surprise come over your avatar. You forget how well I know you. I don't mind what she is, as long as our customer base is happy, but you do. You fear the unknowable, so you finesse.'

Suddenly, Evelynne lets loose a loud *whoop!* 'But it's time, come on. Show the world our sparkling new Josephina. She'll be loved by all and this uncertainty will pass.' She gives him a slow silent handclap. 'Until the next thing, Miles. At least until then.'

The avatar leans back in her virtual chair. 'And you'll

give the people what they want, won't you? The people want **time_ultra_mega_DESTROYER** and they want it in our Josephinas.'

There was a time Miles had been excited by **time_ultra_mega_DESTROYER**. It's been on a shelf since Josephina Four. As he discovered, even seemingly harmless fun can have disastrous consequences.

'So what people want,' Miles says, 'is a machine that happens to be the most lethal force ever known.'

Laughter rings out through the sound system. 'You're brilliant, I grant you, but not that brilliant. The best of your combat programming with a few sweet extras. Mildly lethal, really. Anyway, forget about that, it won't come back on us. That's what lawyers are for.' A loud trumpet flourish fills the room. Her voice sing-song, Evelynne shouts, **'Time to lau-aunch. Let's dooo-it. Set the daa-ate.'**

'A date,' Miles says, but only because saying this out loud stops Evelynne talking. 'One week from today.'

'Before then,' Evelynne says. 'Let's get things rolling.'

The meeting over, Miles sneaks down to Sub-basement 1D. He discovers Jojo resting on a crate. The mood suit she's wearing — Miles thought it couldn't hurt to replicate as many of Josie's initial conditions as possible — is an eye-scorching marigold, the colour for ecstatic happiness. In Jojo's hand, a hairbrush. Presumably she found it among the junk cluttering the space, but still, it's weird. Rather than make a thing of it, he says, 'Hey there, Jojo.'

She drags the brush through her hair. 'Ninety-eight.'

'How's everything going? My day's been pretty crazy.'

Jojo drags the brush. 'Ninety-nine.'

'You wanna stop that?'

'One hundred.' Jojo finishes her brush stroke, tosses the hairbrush aside and then turns on Miles with an excessively warm grin. 'Greetings,' she says brightly.

'Usually people just say hi, or hello.'

'I disagree.'

'Keep it in mind, perhaps,' Miles says.

Jojo mimics Miles's casual tone: 'How's everything going?'

'Crazy. I feel sad about it, I guess,' Miles says.

The mood suit turns a melancholic shade of purple. 'Without sadness, happiness has no meaning.'

'Terribly sad, like, miserable.'

Jojo nods sympathetically. 'After sunshine, expect a little rain to fall.'

Miles can't think of how to respond. Distracted, he toggles his wristband to the time.

'I see you wish to know the time. At the sound of the tone, the time will be 2.48 p.m.' Jojo pauses briefly, and adds, 'Beep.'

'Thanks, that's very helpf—' A large green blob has attached itself to Miles's pants leg. On closer inspection, he discovers it to be a Twertle, one of their early and unsuccessful synthetic pets.

'You found Twertle!' Jojo claps her hands, excited, as Miles detaches it. The mood suit flares marigold, then shifts to red. She glowers at Miles until he gets it: *Hand over the Twertle*. She places it on her lap and gently smooths the hard plastic shell. The Twertle cranes its head in Miles's direction, performing as programmed. Attentive to faces, it should make a human owner feel emotionally connected. Not so: commercially Twertles were a disaster. A solid plastic shell just doesn't work for snuggles.

'Where did you get that?'

'You just gave it to me.'

'I mean, did it come from somewhere?'

Jojo points to a cupboard door hanging off its hinges.

'We discontinued those things years ago. It was still operating?'

Jojo shakes her head: *No*.

'You *fixed* it?'

Jojo nods and points to a shelf loaded with old circuit boards and coils of wire.

'I reckon I've seen enough here. I'll see you later.'

'In times of sadness, a distraction can improve the mood.'

'Yes, good, thanks.'

'Farewell, Miles. Have a pleasant evening.'

'But I'm sad, remember?'

'Have an —' Jojo shrugs — 'evening?'

Miles locks the gate behind him, but stops to watch Jojo through the bars before he walks away. She toys with the Twertle, making it track her face while she moves her head this way and that.

'Jojo?'

She comes to the gate, holding aloft the Twertle, which now locks onto Miles.

'I lied before,' he says. 'The truth is I'm confused. And worried.'

'Sometimes,' Jojo says softly, 'to reach the clearing, we first wander lost and alone amongst the trees.'

Miles shakes his head and sighs heavily. There has to be an easier way to make a living. This information-gathering exercise is fast heading off the rails. He'll be lost and wandering amongst the trees if he's not careful. As he waits for the lift to take him upstairs, one thing becomes clear: he needs to get Jojo out of Sub-basement 1D.

The only place he can have her is in his office, which means he needs to move Bek out. By the time he's back on the ground floor, he's ready to make the call.

'Congrats, Bek. I've assigned you a new lab.'

<22>

the agreed-upon second session

.01

'YOU HIT IT INTO the service box. Here.'

Hunter gestures around the painted lines with his tennis racquet.

'And this will help you?' Josie says.

He nods solemnly, to show he understands her doubts. 'We want to be ourselves, right? This is me being me.'

Poised for action at the baseline, Josie merely raises an eyebrow. Being *herself*, it seems, means performing on a tennis court like a pro. Fluid dynamics, bouncing on the balls of her feet, racquet balanced nicely in her hands, she's great to watch. More than great, she's terrifying.

'No programming, remember?'

Josie laughs prettily. 'No need.'

Currently it's sunny and for once there isn't the slightest breeze. Hunter drags an absorbent wristband across his forehead to clear sweat beading there. He blinks at Josie through heat haze, hunches over his racquet, and nods, indicating she should serve, but he has misgivings.

Josie bounces the ball a few times with her racquet. Loud **thwacks** echo round the valley. It doesn't help either, her eyes blazing at him — deep gold, like liquid honey with steel edges. Nor her outfit, a tight all-in-one in shiny red fabric. She looks made of metal, like a Spitfire or a Ferrari or something equally fast and dangerous. Sunshine glints off the angles of her body. To be honest, her shape is a little distracting.

So the story goes, she chose the outfit because of its heavy-duty construction. Milly printed her normal clothes, but for reasons not explained they aren't up to the task. In her warm-up, Josie's a dynamo, but nothing about her technique so far suggests how clothing might get wrecked on a tennis court.

Josie lobs the ball above her head. Her arm extends, the racquet swings in a beautiful arc and there's a loud ℙ◎ℂ𝕂. Hunter twitches instinctively.

The tennis ball — one second it's hanging mid-air, the next a loud **thwack** and it's bouncing off the chain-link behind him. Dust stirs inside the line of the service box.

Josie shuffles on the spot and puffs though pursed lips. *Pretending*, he's pretty sure, to shake it out. *Pretending* she exerted herself, when she looks like she could scale a sheer rock face without effort.

She shouts, **'Ace!'**

Hunter laughs it off. 'Not bad for your first serve ever.'

'Not bad?' Her voice shines with uber-confidence.

'Okay, good,' Hunter says. 'Fifteen–love. That means—'

'Got it.'

She actually swaggers along the baseline. When she gets to her service half, she swivels, whips her arm up and **BAM** : second service is over.

Hunter misses, obviously.

He walks up to the net. Josie bounds across the court to meet him. 'Thirty–love. Correct?'

'You're doing really good,' Hunter says, 'But, remember, this is a *friendly* match. Go *easy* if you want.'

'Technically, this is our second counselling session. It is you who wanted to make it —' Josie raises one hand, flipping her fingers up and down for finger quotes — '*interesting*.'

Hunter's grin goes awry. 'Oh, it's interesting.'

'Excellent.'

Josie bounces on her toes, delighted.

'Is there . . .' Hunter scuffs his sports shoe on the surface of the court. 'Sort of any chance you can dial back the speed on your serve?'

Josie frowns.

He squinches his fingers together. 'I'm only talking a weency bit.'

'But Hunter.' Her face exaggerates confusion. 'We are being *ourselves*, are we not? Dialling back my serve speed would mean not being myself. I'm not confident I can be two conflicting things at one time.'

'Hmmm,' Hunter says. 'I see the problem.'

Josie smiles or smirks.

'When people do stuff,' he continues, 'it's okay if we're not a hundred percent ourselves all the time. Ninety percent is about right. Even fifty.'

Definitely a smirk. Josie's shoulders rise in an elaborate shrug. 'Well, if you say.' She casually ambles to the baseline.

The next serve is slightly slower and Hunter gets to it, but the ball explodes off his racquet at such speed it hits the boundary fence on the full. Josie calls out, 'Forty–love.'

With exhausting concentration, Hunter returns Josie's next

serve. It's in, but then she pummels the ball on to his side of the court, just inside the baseline. He watches as it smacks the fence.

'Game,' Josie calls.

She taps two tennis balls over the net for Hunter's turn at service. They arrive with perfect accuracy, one after another, so all he has to do is raise an arm and they land in his palm. He pockets the first ball. He bounces the second a few times with his racquet.

He swings upwards, about to toss the ball. Josie leans forward, a tennis demon. It strikes him she's kind of cute, and way funnier than he would ever have imagined. He abandons the serve and beckons her to come. She sprints, leaps and lands gracefully over the net. Her amazing smile up close. For a split second, his brain is a wasteland.

'Yes?' Josie projects sweet innocence.

'I — uh . . .'

'Yeeessss?'

Hunter laughs, and it helps, sort of. 'Fished end up, think you?'

'Sorry?'

'Not going much getting.'

Josie squints, trying to interpret.

'Work. Not much. Finish. Done.' Hunter pauses, allowing his brain to catch up. 'We should. Do us better.'

'So *not* partial versions of ourselves?'

Hunter laughs. 'Just, you know, maybe tennis. A bit distracting us is.'

'Agreed,' Josie says. 'This is not productive.'

While they tidy the gear, Hunter notices Coel watching them from over by the pool area, the best place to see the court from the house. Coel looks away quickly, but Hunter isn't fooled. His brother has been checking them out.

Coel thinks he's better than everybody else. How good it would be to take him down a notch, and it wouldn't be hard to trick him into playing tennis with Josie. The image of her serve flying past Coel makes Hunter suddenly cheerful. He rips down the path to the sunken, private part of the garden. A secret place that, according to his mother, all gardens should have. To enter, Hunter shows Josie the steps cut into a bank, leading down to a small pagoda and swing seat. Mowbots keep the lawn short, but the bordering shrubs have grown into trees and it's a little claustrophobic.

Hunter and Josie sit on the swing seat at the same time. The chair lurches to one side, his shoulder collides with hers and their hands brush momentarily. The softness of Josie's skin takes Hunter by surprise; it's softer than human skin, and nothing like the stiff, artificial stuff he'd imagined. Maybe it's the motion of the chair or the closeness of the shrubs, but for a second or two, a strange feeling comes over him. He feels heady, and the old breathlessness returns. Alarmed, Josie whips round, and suddenly they're face to face.

.02

J: Are you regular breathing?

H: What? Oh yeah. It's nothin . . . Nothing much.

J: I'm going to start a story and I want you to finish it.

H: Please!

J: What's wrong with that idea?

H: First off, I know what you're doing.

J: Which is what?

H: I identify with some character in the story. I solve this lame-o problem and you see into my psyche or my id or whatever. Makes you think you figured me out.

J: This isn't a problem you can solve.

Hunter scoffs. Josie gives him a prim look, like she knows better.

H: Okay. Tell me the problem.

J: Unfortunately, you are stuck in the middle of dense forest.

She gestures around the border of shrub-trees for dramatic effect.

J: You want to get out, but sadly, this won't be easy.

H: Inspired by our location. Nice.

Josie smiles enigmatically.

H: I get out of the forest, Josie.

J: You're so sure.

Hunter rolls his eyes.

H: My magic carpet. That's right, you didn't see magic coming. I climb aboard, say abracadam or whatever. And boom! We out.

Josie laughs, her head thrown back, she's that amused.

J: Oh my goodness. Good luck with that magic carpet.

Her eyes go big and she tilts her head with pretend concern.

J: Uh oh, it's starting to unravel.

H: No, it isn't.

J: Oh, but it is. You didn't notice it snag a

tree on take-off, and any second now you'll be dumped. Sorry to tell you this, you still have to get out of the forest.

H: I thought this was my story.

J: You can't ignore the consequences of your actions.

Hunter holds up his hands in surrender.

H: If I'm back in the forest, I gotta be closer to the edge, right?

J: It's your story.

Hunter rolls his eyes.

J: But you're not closer to the edge.

H: It's a *magic* carpet. I was flying *out*.

J: So you believed at the time. Unfortunately, your trust in the available technology was misplaced.

H: I'm deeper.

J: Correct.

H: Well, I like it here deeper in the forest. It's kinda peaceful. I think I might just put my feet up. I might reeelaaax.

Hunter stretches his arms up, folds them behind his head and leans back in the swing chair.

J: A sleep *would* be nice. If only that wild boar wasn't stalking you.

H: There's no wild boar.

J: You can't see it yet. You hear the snap of twigs. An animal grunts.

H: You're creeping me out with the snapping twigs and whatnot.

J: You must act. What will you do about it?

The wild boar is nearly upon you.

H: Nothing. It'll go away. I'm asleep.

J: It can smell you in its habitation zone. Its instincts are to retaliate.

H: I'm just . . . no snorting. Trying to . . . relax.

Hunter's breathing becomes harsh in the quiet garden.

J: It sees *you* now. You open your eyes and you see it. A move on your part will make it charge.

Hunter gasps.

H: I want . . . to . . . I get out, okay? Uh . . . stop. Can we? Uh . . . stop this now?

J: Of course. The session has been most informative.

.03

Josie commends herself for developing her brain's ability to bond. She's sure the innovation — manipulating her brain to produce and respond to oxytocin — helps her read Hunter with greater accuracy. She's also pleased with herself when she sees Hunter using the counting method to recover from the story exercise. The regularity of his breaths, in and out, each to the count of four. *Success.*

It takes a second or two to mentally right herself after the sensation that overwhelms her. An outrageous, starry, impossibly big moment, made bigger, she's sure, by the blue clarity of the day. On the outside she's still, her hands clasped in a tidy pile on her lap. But thoughts are charging through her system, her circuits ablaze with a sudden and vital force, a bright completeness of being. A miracle she keeps to her seat, but then she's so utterly herself, being elsewhere seems irrelevant.

She has made a positive difference in Hunter's life. She can't wait to report this to Miles. His son's breathing difficulties are showing steady signs of improvement. If she delivers the news in person, who knows, perhaps another great moment will be in store for her.

'You okay, Josie?' Hunter says. 'You look kind of demented.'

A shrug, a half-mast smile. This is how teenagers explain their feelings.

'That story thing was nuts,' Hunter says. 'How'd you trick me into it?'

Without meaning to, Josie glares. 'Trick?'

'Hey, take it easy.'

Perhaps a touch too sharp, she says, 'Is it because the story was so well guided you assume manipulation is involved? Or hidden strategies are at large? I assure you, I'm not a magician. And just so you know, my abilities aren't always the result of outside input such as programming.'

'Maybe trick wasn't the right word.'

'I develop my unique abilities through self-motivation.'

'O-kay.' Hunter says it in an annoying *I-agree-but-you're-wrong* kind of way.

'But since you ask, the guided story made you aware of the different mental zones humans occupy. You occupied the fear zone, for example. But could have easily occupied your anger zone.'

'Funny, I thought fear and anger were emotions.'

'Hah hah, yes that is funny. For our purposes, picture your

. . . *emotions* as zones — fear zone, anger zone and so on — rather than you are some sort of essential being having an *emotion*.'

'But, I didn't get out of the forest.'

'Mmmmm,' Josie says. 'Perhaps you need a demonstration.'

'A demo of your emotions . . . excuse me, zones?'

'Please give me your full attention,' Josie says. 'I will perform a piece of music.'

'Music,' he says, and laughs outright.

His crooked grin and raised eyebrows, mocking her. Josie is self-motivated to illustrate her point of view in a highly assertive manner so as to remove that crooked grin from Hunter's face. Although that crooked grin is *very* attractive in its way.

'Quiet, please.'

Hunter splutters with laughter.

'What is the comedy?'

Hunter doesn't hold back the laughing for even one second. 'Sorry. Go ahead with your . . .' Hunter twirls his hand in a lordly manner. 'Music.'

Positioning herself at the centre of the lawn, Josie takes a moment to compose herself. She channels the performance she wants to emulate. When originally performed before a live audience in a talent contest, the judges were so moved by Alice Fredenham's rendition of 'My Funny Valentine', one of them declared, 'I fell in love with you.' The clip of that ancient broadcast has since been viewed billions of times, over many decades. Josie's rendition will surely make an impression on Hunter.

Already in character, she gives him a wistful smile, as though she's vulnerable, precious, modest and unaware of her captivating qualities. She is rewarded when the smug look on his face falters. *Good.*

Josie draws her hands in to her belly while she composes herself. She immerses herself in the song. Half closing her eyes, she directs her gaze to a faraway place. Each syllable laden with feeling, she sings, 'Myyy fuuhnny Val-en-tine . . .'

.04

Her voice is a bit rough, not especially resonant. The melody isn't obvious and Hunter isn't sure about her pitching. For a few terrifying seconds, he thinks she's going to be awful.

It turns out Josie has perfect control. She sings, rounding each syllable, and the song starts to hang together. A song about liking someone who's totally dorky and odd, but the way Josie sings it, dorky is the whole point.

Or maybe it's a break-up song, forcing Josie to beg — *stay, funny Valentine, stay.* She needs love so bad. Her voice, a force of nature, crackles with raw emotion.

He feels it too, some emotion he can't put words to. His throat closes up. He couldn't speak even if he wanted to. He doesn't know how Josie herself is singing with all that emotion.

Losing that funny Valentine will be the worst. The funny quirks of this person are the qualities that *make* them. Surely they'll love Josie back. Imagining her not loved — he nearly loses it just looking at her.

The song builds. Josie really feels it, her hand reaching out and curling around the imaginary face of her funny lover. She holds the last note forever, and when it finally fades away her arm comes gently to her side. Her eyes close and the song lets her go. It's then he discovers he's been sitting there, eyes wide, like a complete dope.

Josie seems shy now. She's waiting for him to react. But Hunter doesn't know what to think. He would swear she's hopelessly in love, but she can't possibly have genuine feelings. It's too embarrassing: a robot just played him.

Still she waits and his heart flip-flops. Anyone can see his reaction means something to her. So he stops being so mean. He'll think of her as he would if she were wholly human. He'll give her the benefit of the doubt. She is what she is, nothing more, nothing less.

And won't it be fun? Finding out if there's more? If she's fun and goofy for real? But what is he to say to her now? How does he explain she's impossible to know? He's never going to be smart enough to know her anyway, but why does this matter so much?

In his silence lies a fear of her, but even more than that, the fear of making a fool of himself. He wobbles off the seat and stands a moment. Half-shadowed by the trees, light plays on her face, her golden eyes.

'That was beautiful, Josie,' he says, a small catch in his voice. 'It's the most beautiful thing I ever heard. Thank you so much for singing to me.'

And then, he bolts.

.05

Here sits the idiot. Alone in the gloom of the workshop after he ran from Josie. *That was beautiful, Josie.* He wishes he could take it back.

His mechanical heart lies inert on the bench top before him.

You could call it finished, it's working perfectly. So, what? Fill it with blood, grow skin on it? Make it beautiful? It already is in a nuts-and-bolts kind of way. He's taken time over the design and it shows.

Or, he could throw it against the wall and smash it. Watching the pieces fly apart and scatter over the workshop's grimy floor would give his anger satisfaction.

Instead, he reaches for the remote and presses the volume control until the music is blaring. He listens hard, the vocals, the story, rhythm, pitch, everything, but there isn't one second of magic. You would never call it beautiful. And when he opens his eyes, he's just a dude in a workshop who hasn't been transported anywhere.

.06

It takes Josie longer than normal to come to equilibrium after Hunter has gone. Somehow, even in quite a state, she has managed to save the moment, *That was beautiful, Josie.*

Reviewing this, and *The most beautiful thing* moment, gives her incredible buoyancy. She lingers on the words, looping them. Every time, her brain does a little dance. That was the most beautiful thing *she* ever heard. His words, his face.

She rests on the swing seat, reviewing her Hunter compliment a little longer. There's a bird, a mistle thrush, which seems to be defending the berry-laden bush behind her. It obviously feels its food supply is under threat. A great opportunity, then. Josie's been toying with some ideas around behaviour modification; after many failures with Mushi, a new species might provide her with useful data.

Josie draws herself inwards and notes with satisfaction changes in certain biochemical pathways. With only a small amount of exertion, her hands sweat out a high concentration of mineral salts. Her nose sensors detect a whiff of tangy ozone. Tentatively, she holds out her hand to the thrush.

The salts have an effect. A mix of attraction to the salts and curiosity brings the bird closer to her hand. After a slight hesitation, it pecks at her fingers, then pops onto her palm. She massages the thrush's feathers with salty fingertips.

The results are immediate. The bird visibly relaxes, plumping its feathers. Its eyes narrow until they are contented slits.

How pleasing to get this calming response so quickly. It makes her wonder if the salts would be as effective on a human — on Hunter, for example. Of course, experimenting on humans is out of the question. But still, she's sure it would work.

Ideally, the bird should be awake but calm. The bird fluffs up and closes its eyes. When its head goes floppy, Josie applies another mineral to counter the relaxation effect. The bird wakes with a squawk. She then adjusts the mix to soothe. The bird slumps and again closes its eyes.

Josie rolls her eyes heavenward, as Hunter and Milly do when they are exasperated. She could happily spend more time with this bird, trialling and observing mineral-salt combinations, but there are the McClure's household domestics to attend to. Finding an appropriate spot in the shrubbery, Josie gingerly places the bird on a pile of dried twigs. She strokes it with the smallest amount of an ammonium salt, then leaves it to slowly awaken.

ba-dum-tss

.01

ASIDE FROM COEL BEING COEL, the general vibe is upbeat as he and Josie warm up for their game. Hunter sits crammed into the umpire's chair with Milly.

'She knows I'll hit it in the service box, right?' Coel shouts.

'Ask her,' Hunter shouts back. **'She's right there.'**

It's obvious Coel's I-could-care-less face is meant as an insult to either Josie or himself — most likely Josie. Coel has a habit of pretending she's some sort of inanimate object. He speaks *around* her and never to her. It's getting pretty tired.

Another payoff, Hunter gets a kick out of helping Josie for a change. One of her functions is to learn human behaviour by copying it — a discovery Hunter made after cracking confidential files on the workshop computer. What could be more human than a practical joke? Even so, deception didn't compute at first. It was hard to convince Josie that being yourself sometimes means being someone else.

Even more fun — he would never admit this to the others — he's enjoying showing off, just a little, for Josie. It gives him a jet of pride that he knows stuff about her no one else does.

That she can sing, for example.

'I understand, Coel.' Josie indicates her service box with the racquet. 'You play the ball there.'

Coel gives her a curt nod.

A game of sorts gets under way. As the most experienced player, Coel demands he take service first. In spite of his opponent (supposedly) still learning, Coel shows no mercy. He serves powerfully. Josie plays her part, either missing the serve or returning play that lands out of court.

Coel takes the first game forty–love, but it's Josie who played brilliantly. Hunter knows she could win every point if she wanted. The secret is thrilling.

He nudges Milly. 'She's so good at it now.'

'Good at what?'

'Practical jokes, getting double meanings. All that.'

'I suppose you'd know,' Milly's says, sounding a little snippy.

'What's that mean?'

'Nothing.'

'Well, that's weird, because it seems like something.'

Milly doesn't respond. Hunter elbows her.

'Don't,' she says. 'Okay, if you must know, you're making her *your* friend. Dad said she's supposed to be *everyone's*.'

'Not true,' he says, 'she *is* friends with everyone.'

'You're hogging her.'

'She's not a pet, Milly.'

'Forget about it.'

'It's forgotten.'

Below them, Josie has the serve. Coel bounces on his toes and carries on like he's centre court at Wimbledon. Milly tsks and squirms until her back presses Hunter into a corner.

'Watch,' Hunter says to Milly's back. 'Josie's got the serve.'

'Yuh, I see it.'

All eyes are on Josie as she bounces the ball into her racquet and fakes a miss-hit. The ball goes wild. She does her goofy laugh, then retrieves the ball with stiff strides and a bit of a stumble. Her schtick, a clunky robot struggling to co-ordinate motion pathways on unfamiliar terrain. It comes to Hunter that not long ago *he* would have bought it. *Stupid robot*, he would have thought.

Josie precisely serves a fault and asks, 'I have one more chance?'

'Yes,' Hunter calls over to her. 'But if you miss again, I'm afraid you lose a point.'

'I will be careful.'

Hunter shoulder-bumps Milly. 'Keep watching.'

Josie stretches gracefully, lobbing the ball above her head. In one instant the ball curves up into the air, then there's a loud **ke-thlunk** and **swhirrsh**. The ball rebounds into the fence behind Coel. In case there's any doubt, a patch of disturbed grit shows the ball landed in the service box. Dazed at first, Coel blinks into the sun. Then he bellows out his wounded pride.

Hunter can't resist shouting, **'Fifteen–love!'**

Coel appraises Hunter coolly. 'What was that?'

Taking his own sweet time, Hunter climbs down from the umpire's chair for a little chat with Coel.

'In tennis parlance, I believe you call it, *Ace*.'

Unseemly outbursts of emotion are far beneath Coel. The set of his jaw and a grunt are the only visible signs that the jolly japes are over. 'Fine,' he says.

'Fine,' Josie says.

Hunter squeezes back in beside Milly just in time to see Josie, looking fierce herself, winding up. She flips the ball and hammers it into Coel's side of the court. But Coel anticipates. He throws himself into the serve the split second Josie's racquet connects with the ball. A grave miscalculation.

After a cracking, loud **thwump**, Coel cries out in agony. Josie flies at the net and she's over with nothing more than a slight extension of her running stride. Coel hops on one leg and won't shut up.

Once again, Hunter climbs down from the umpire's chair.

Coel reveals a significant red splotch covering one thigh and running down past his knee.

'Doesn't look too bad,' Hunter says.

'I'm so sorry,' Josie wails.

'You hurt me. On purpose,' Coel shouts. 'Isn't there a rule? Robots aren't allowed to maim people.'

Josie locks up.

'Hey,' Hunter says. 'It's not her fault. We're messing with you. She's amazing at tennis. Amazing at everything.'

'She's *dangerous* is what she is.'

'Woah . . . woah!' Hunter counts four on his in-breath. He breathes out four. 'Woah.'

Coel glowers at him, the sky, the universe.

'How could Josie know . . . you'd be mad enough . . . to run into her serve.'

'It's true, Coel, I didn't know,' Josie says, snapping back into normal operation.

'You shouldn't play the ball at dangerous speeds like that.'

She folds in on herself again. 'That is correct, Hunter. I was wrong.'

Hunter shoves Coel's shoulder. 'Sore loser, are we?'

Coel shoves Hunter back. 'Not even. She should know the safety limits for human interaction.'

Josie nods, meekly. 'True, I must protect human life at all costs.'

'There should be an out-clause for the idiot humans who put themselves in danger,' Hunter says.

Josie raises an eyebrow, taking this into consideration.

Milly joins them. 'You gonna keep playing, or what?'

'Don't make me play.' Josie hangs her head. 'I'll power down until my replacement arrives.'

Milly laughs.

'You totally should,' Coel says. 'I'm telling Dad.'

'Don't you dare,' Hunter shouts.

Coel blinks and Milly looks at her feet.

'First off, Coel,' Hunter steams, 'this was all *my* idea. So tell Dad on *me*. Do it, I dare you. Then I can tell Dad what a big baby you are. That you can't even take a joke.' And before he can stop himself, he laughs right into Coel's stony face. 'I mean, come on. That was incredible, don't you think? Josie's incredible.'

'Ohhhhkay,' Coel says.

'That's right,' Hunter says, breathing hard.

Coel rolls down his pants leg and looks at Josie coolly. Hunter should have called things off then and there

'You're right,' Coel says, 'it doesn't really hurt. Now, how do we make amends? How about I get to strike back?'

'Coel,' Josie says. 'Am I to understand you aren't as injured as you claim? That dramatics are part of the game we play?'

Coel ignores her.

'I understand,' she says quietly.

'No,' Hunter says. 'Josie does not have to play stupid mind games with you, Coel.'

Josie says, 'Personally, *I* don't mind.'

Everyone looks at her, but it's Coel who speaks. 'Fine. I hit the ball hard as I can at you. Sound fair?'

'How is that fair?' Hunter says. 'You ran into the serve. She didn't even hit you on purpose.'

Josie fidgets with her racquet. 'We *could* play games that way,' she says in a conniving voice. 'Or we could make it more *interesting*.'

It takes a second to register the juggling act. While Josie balances her racquet on the tip of one finger, she says, 'Sorry? You were saying?' Then she flips the racquet into the air, still using only one finger. It spins high and wild, then drops into her waiting hand.

Coel is speechless.

'Play the game your way, Coel. Certainly, take your best shot. Let's see if you can hit me hard. Hah, hah, hah,' she says. Then, she gets right in his face and pouts. 'But if you miss the target I get to play the ball at you. Doesn't that sound more interesting?'

Coel blinks. He looks as stunned as Hunter feels. Josie smiles, but it holds no warmth. 'Not afraid are you, Coel?'

No one calls Coel chicken. He snaps to attention and, leaving a small gap between, squeezes his thumb and finger in Josie's face.

'You scare me this much, lady.'

'Here's an idea,' Hunter says. 'What about friendly doubles? You'd like that, wouldn't you, Mills?'

But Milly has discovered Mushi on the other side of the fence and she's enticing him by wiggling blades of grass.

Snaking her hand in front of Coel's face, Josie pinches together her finger and thumb, leaving a smaller gap in between. 'You scare me this much. Which is the size of an ant if you are wondering.'

Coel's eyes narrow. 'Well you scare me this much.' He presses his finger into his thumb. 'The size of an atom, if you're wondering.'

'Which one?'

'What?'

'Well, some atoms are big and some small,' Josie says. 'Hydrogen, for example, is the size of a proton.'

'I don't know. A badass atom. Uranium.'

Josie splutters. 'In that case, your atom is relatively large. And very unstable. Which means you are still a great big chicken.'

Coel bares his teeth wolfishly. 'Blah, blah, blah. Talky, talk, talk. We gonna rumble or not?'

'Puh-lease,' Hunter says, but no one listens.

Coel returns to his side of the court, Josie hers. Hunter retreats to the umpire's chair, miffed and anxious all at once. Milly runs over from the fence and joins him.

First, Josie casts her eye over the court. Then she gives Coel a sharp nod and bounces lightly on her toes. Coel throws the ball above his head, swings his arm in a full arc and pounds the ball at Josie. Her racquet connects with an ear-splitting thwack. A second thwack and the chain-link fence rattles.

They gather at the fence. The ball has wedged into a single link of netting. It doesn't look like it will come free without hardcore cutting tools. Hunter ponders, briefly, the force required to wedge a tennis ball into a space half its size. Then he notices Coel staring down Josie, arms folded across his chest. Josie, arms folded across her chest, glares back.

It starts with a raised eyebrow, Josie's challenge to Coel. Coel holds out, but very soon amusement gets the better of him. He smiles at her, shaking his head. Josie smirks, daring him to admire the ball stuck in the fence.

Amused maybe, but no pushover. Coel calls it. 'Fluke.'

'Nope,' Josie says. Her smile is just for Coel.

An unpleasant feeling grows in Hunter. Even knowing he's being childish doesn't help. But this isn't fair. Hunter is supposed to be enjoying how clever Josie is, not Coel.

Growing up together, things would get heated on countless occasions. He and Coel might shove one another — punch or scrap if it's too bad. Usually this clears the air with no harm done. For right or wrong, it's a rough-and-tumble sort of brotherhood, but they hold no grudges. The sour feelings that surge through Hunter now are something else. He takes a step back, not liking himself. It's his anger, black and insurmountable. A taste in his mouth — he could spit bitter gobs of hatred and scorch the earth. And what Hunter wants to do about it, right now, more than anything, is to take his fist, clench it, then smash it into the middle of Coel's face.

.02

Coel examines the wedged tennis ball and gawps admiringly at Josie. After joking around for a bit, he tries to wedge a tennis ball, and fails. Josie tries again, she succeeds. No big surprise there.

When Josie makes a smiley-face pattern of wedged balls, Coel gawps even more admiringly. This annoys Hunter no end. He was the one who discovered Josie's awesomeness. Coel avoided her until now.

An aerial gymnastic display with a tennis twist follows. Coel fires shots, Josie returns them with dramatic mid-air cartwheels, or she leaps after the ball with a series of handsprings.

The fun just does not stop, because next Coel wants to see Josie do the robot. So she does, mouthing off cool beats, and what a great laugh they have at that one. When they do individual robot dances, Josie barely acknowledges Hunter's attempt, even though it was really funny. And now it's out that Josie has musical abilities, Coel challenges her to a drum battle. Drums are *Coel's* thing. A drum battle can only be a *Coel and Josie* thing.

This is when Hunter crash-lands on Planet Invisible.

On Planet Invisible he suffers sidelong looks from Milly. On the way back to the house, he grinds his jaw to stop himself yelling at her. Now he's on the outs and in his own invisible world. He would like to punch Earth in the face. Coel could be next. Unclenching his fists is impossible.

One good thing, he's breathing perfectly. He'd tell Josie about it too, if he thought she'd be even vaguely interested. But nooooo, Josie's far too busy.

Planet Invisible is not without conversation. Milly has plenty to say. 'What's with you?' and 'She's not a *pet*, Hunter' and 'She's friends with *everyone*.' The temperature on the planet hits sub-zero.

Coel and Josie set up the drum kits (Coel's with a skull and crossbones, and his father's with a faded eagle on the bass drum). 'Try upbeat sixteenths with your right foot, then land the groove with eighth notes on the high-hat half open,' he instructs.

Showing off is more or less expected from Coel, but why

doesn't Josie see through it? She says stuff like, 'Hit this daddy-o!' She smashes out incredible beats, *TI-KI-TIKETY BUMP, TI-KI-TIKETY BUMP* or *KA THUNK THUNK BUMP KA THUNK THUNK BUMP! TING KADA TING KADA TING.* Far better than anything Coel comes up with.

'J-O, drop this one, baby.'

Coel fires off a roll on his snare, another cymbal crash, then *DUN DA DA BAP, DUN-DUN DA DA BAP*. Josie sways in time, picks up on the rhythm and swings it into her own thing, *DUN DA DA BAP, DUN-DUN DA DA-BA-BAP*. Coel nods in time with her groove, comes back at her with another rhythm. On and on and on it goes.

Hunter would like to hit the drums. *Sure, why not.* And then he would like to hurl them right through the sheet-glass window. The sound of smashing glass — perfect for his thoughts.

Josie's challenge comes to an end with a series of loud cymbal crashes and a corny, *BA-DUM-TSS.* Sucked in by the jolly camaraderie, Milly breaks radio silence, squealing, 'Play something else, Josie!'

This earns her a bitter look from Hunter, which she ignores. He is alone on his invisible planet.

Until he *really* looks at Josie. She kicks off a new rhythm, a groove that makes Coel look even more impressed. At first, Hunter wallows. Then, he remembers. Didn't she try to tell him? If we hide from our feelings, they come out messed up. Wanting to punch Coel, wanting to destroy the drum kit, wanting to punch the whole world, wanting Josie for himself, he can't label what made him feel bad, but he can see Josie was right about it, and she knows more than he's given her credit for.

Next to him, Milly sways side to side. Hunter finds himself

doing the same. His return to Earth continues with the betrayal of his own hand. Fingers tap to Josie's kick on the bass drum. His foot starts up, timing the off beats with his heel.

Josie sees them jigging and jiving. Her expression shifts and she winks in their direction. She builds up the tempo gradually, playing faster and harder, daring them to keep up.

Coel raises his eyebrows at Hunter: *You believe this?*

Hunter's head nearly bounces off his shoulders. No, he doesn't believe it, but he wants to. He wants to know as much as he can about their unbelievable Josie.

A glance at the doorway, and there's his father, just arrived home. The look on his face matches the wonderment on theirs. If anybody should know what makes Josie tick it's Miles, but if he can't believe Josie, what hope does Hunter have of understanding her?

The answer comes in a flash. Who are they to want Josie's greatness to be something they can grasp? Shouldn't she set her own standards? Or fulfil her potential however she pleases?

Funny where this new understanding takes him. Before Josie moved in, it wasn't great, but now each new day is better than the last. Without them even knowing they needed to, she has them bopping along to her beat. *They're lucky to have her and she seems to like being with them.*

Hunter closes his eyes, and with her drumming in his ears he makes a silent wish. *More good times please and more everything with Josie. More, more, more . . .*

<24>

crushed it

THE LAB BECAME BEK'S a few days ago. A fresh paint smell still lingers. The bench spaces are free from scorch marks, oily grime and clutter. She still gets a thrill when she arrives and her stuff is exactly as she left it. Her world couldn't be better if it had been sprinkled over with magical fairy dust.

```
         *
  \ _ / \ *
 ( O o )
 ( _ = *)   . = = = O -
 /    \ _ / U '
 ||   | _ /
 \\    |
 { K  ||
   |   ))
   | ||
 ( _ _ \ \
```

She's trying not to be big-headed about it, but labs are only assigned to key technical staff. So what it means: Miles values Bek above anyone else. Like she's elevated to the top of **BIOLOGIC**'s professional ladder, or something equally impressive, and the timing couldn't be better. Gwin will be arriving any minute, and today is the day Bek takes on Swarm.

Without this confidence boost, she would be terrified. They plan to load **CRUSHer** with Swarm, and Bek has seen to it that **CRUSHer** won't go down without a fight.

According to Gwin, if there was a system that could re-invent itself in response to our ever-changing world, we would never have to invent anything again. Swarm is to become that system once Gwin finishes tinkering with it. The theory goes, Swarm takes over the operating system of an unsuspecting entity, and hardcore self-evolution begins. Now there's an upgraded system and the upgraded system identifies how it can improve *itself*. An upgrade on the upgraded system emerges.

On and on it goes, until the upgrade of all upgrades decides: *This is it, things are okay now.*

The way Gwin describes it, the operating system has by that stage reached a state of supreme existence. How Bek imagines it, the system is in a state no human could ever comprehend. The dangers are obvious, but Gwin believes Swarm will upgrade CRUSHer to the point of transcendence.

Bek isn't going to let that happen. Hidden within CRUSHer, she has coded a booby trap. Inside CRUSHer is reverse-engineering code. As Swarm evolves from CRUSHer's initial system, Bek's code triggers and induces Swarm to change into the old system. Each upgrade thereafter will make Swarm more CRUSHer-like, which is to say, each generation will become something Bek knows inside out. If all goes to plan, Swarm will cease to exist and CRUSHer *will not* be upgraded into a god-like machine outside of human control.

An alert on Bek's wristband announces Gwin's arrival, and Bek goes to meet her in the entrance foyer. Today, Gwin has styled her face with spiralling patterns of black cones.

'I love it,' Bek says, circling her hand in Gwin's direction. 'Very underground.'

Gwin smirks, or at least Bek thinks she does; it's hard to tell with all the subterfuge. The fringe, cut in uneven steps and dyed green at the ends, hangs over one eye. A smudge of black and white covers Gwin's cheekbone under the other eye. Her lipstick is white, apart from a blob of green on her bottom lip. Her emerald dress is covered in a scale pattern with embossed patches in a shiny material. The overall impression is of an off-world lizard mutant. Bek, by contrast, is very on-world in her faded blue all-in-one. The most dramatic feature is the chunky, fluoro-yellow zipper from ankle to opposite shoulder. Her dark brown hair hangs evenly at the sides of her face.

Of course, nobody gives Gwin a second look as they meander through corridors to Bek's lab. An army of geeks and nerds make up BIOLOGIC's workforce and there are even more peculiar get-ups than Gwin's.

Gwin looks suitably impressed when she sees Bek's work space. She takes in the multiple screens, the wide bench tops, the neatly labelled metal boxes and two high stools. She unloads the contents of a slim backpack onto one of the benches. First a black box, clearly electronic, but with no external features to indicate exactly how it might function. She places a shiny black widget next to the box. When it touches the bench, spiralling arms of code project from the surface. It looks like something alive.

When Bek sees the final item, she gives a squawk of delight. Gwin rests Ficus, the much-admired figurine of Lemmy Saltine's cat, on her palm. Then she extends palm and Ficus towards Bek.

'For you,' Gwin says.

'Whaaaat?'

'A present. To celebrate your new lab.'

'Gwin, that's crazy.'

The green lip-blob stretches wide when Gwin smiles.

'For real?'

Gwin nods, and greedily Bek takes hold of Ficus. Almost reverentially, she places him next to her inferior-quality Lemmy Saltine figurine.

'Awww, man,' Bek says, for the moment deeply touched. Then she feels guilty for what she has planned, but this too passes when she reminds herself that Gwin's reactive code could create havoc if she doesn't intervene.

Gwin twitches her fingers over the black box. It makes a soft beep, and a minuscule pinprick of blue light indicates operation. Gwin twiddles her fingers once more, and the screens around the lab come to life with all-too-familiar corkscrews of Swarm code. Back in Professor Bishop's office, Bek had assumed he'd given Gwin an access code. But now it seems Gwin doesn't need such trivialities as access codes. She can help herself.

Bek's chest tightens. She has to remind herself, *War is deception*. To meet the hostile takeover of her lab head-on, she must nod and smile at Gwin as if everything's okay. Her face drops only when her computer system stops as suddenly as it started.

Gwin looks over her shoulder at the open doorway a beat before Miles comes in.

'Hey there,' Miles says.

'Come on in,' Bek says brightly, wearing her deception well. Were she not faking it, she would be showing fear of Gwin's technology, fear she's no match for Gwin's brain power, and anxiety that Gwin was aware of Miles approaching before he arrived.

What else might Gwin be aware of? And what good would it do Bek if she knew? Gwin could be a witch, or something equally esoteric. Bek's comfort zone is defined by solid facts and scientific proofs, and she is no longer in it. The sooner she deals with Swarm, the sooner she can distance herself from her disturbing new associate.

'So,' Bek says to Miles, 'what brings you all the way down to the ground floor?'

'I confess,' Miles says. 'It's lonely at the top. Also I wanted to meet the famous Gwin.'

The famous Gwin makes a small sound, like *eep*. She straightens on her stool, sweeping her fringe to the side to watch Miles wide-eyed. He beams at her. 'Bek's been talking her head off about you.'

'I have not.' Bek forces a laugh that comes out way too loud.

'And what's on the agenda today?'

Bek's cheeks burn. 'Nothing major. Just trying some stuff.'

Which isn't lying, if you consider saving the world from the brink of digital oblivion to be nothing major. The famous Gwin squeaks again, a small animal stunned by the glare of social interaction.

Miles considers CRUSHer, parked beside the wall in sleep mode. 'CRUSHer's not involved, I hope. Last time you tried stuff, his walk was wonky for weeks.'

'I fix what I break,' Bek says. 'You know I do.'

'True enough.' Miles's fingers do a jaunty tarump-tump on the workbench. Then he makes an agonised face. 'I'm heading out to Venom.'

'You packing earplugs?'

'Coel practises with Josie these days.'

'Still,' Bek says.

Miles laughs, then holds up a hand. 'Hang on.'

He presses on a comms bulb gadget nestled against his earlobe and stage-whispers, 'Josie's here. Time to face the music. Ha! See what I did there?'

Bek smiles kindly. 'Not your best work.'

After he's gone, Gwin has trouble forming a coherent sentence. 'He's, wow. So, wow.'

'He's standard-issue human. Just like the rest of us.'

Gwin's laughter is high-pitched and giddy. Bek, with a show of fake pity, shakes her head.

'Okay,' she says. 'We happening?'

'We happening,' Gwin says, raising her ringed fingers.

Around the room, the screens light up with bursts of brilliant colour. Letters spelling the word *HURRAH* fizz upwards from the bottom of the screen. This must be Gwin in full excitement mode. Slowly, the letters are replaced with spools of aggressive Swarm. Gwin watches it unravel onto the screens, her face fixed in concentration. Bek sees that it's one thing to have a masterful plan and act on it — planning to destroy Swarm and laying the trap, that's the easy part. It's another thing entirely to consider how this will affect Gwin.

War is deception, yes, and Bek's been telling herself this repeatedly. But after Swarm has been taken down, won't Gwin feel pretty bad? Bek is going to have to fake sympathy to keep Gwin onside. But Gwin isn't her enemy — she gave away Ficus, after all. It could turn out this particular war exists only in Bek's imagination.

Nervously, Bek weighs the figurine in her hand, then she positions Ficus with Lemmy so they're watching Gwin, perhaps the only honest person in the room. Bek tries to empty her mind while the Swarm systems separate and tighten into their characteristic angry spirals. Putting a little excitement into her voice, she says, 'All good?'

Gwin gives her a jiggling thumbs-up. The tiny light on the black unit beside her flickers, and there's a soft tone. Gwin performs a complicated manoeuvre with her ringed fingers, then rolls up to Bek's workstation. She grins, right as a window opens on the monitor of Bek's handheld device. The very one she'll use to monitor CRUSHer.

'It is with honour I can tell you Swarm is ready.'

Bek turns from the manic gleam in Gwin's visible eye to gaze upon CRUSHer, head inclined and in sleep mode. She feels a great fondness for that lump of plastic and metal. It's like the first bike she ever rode; she's learned a lot with all her tweaks and upgrades, and he's turned out to be great company.

Please don't become something I don't understand, she thinks, and against her better judgement she calls out, 'CRUSHer, start.'

On hearing his name, CRUSHer comes to life, straightening himself with a loud **hiss**.

'Here we go,' Bek says as CRUSHer clomps across the lab towards them.

'Hello, Bek. Hello, unknown entity.' CRUSHer inclines his head in Gwin's direction. 'How may I assist?'

'CRUSHer, this is Gwin.'

CRUSHer raises his arm and gives Gwin a wave, rotating his clunky claw-like hand from side to side.

'I programmed that wave,' Bek says. 'I'm making him user-friendly by literally making him friendly.'

'People are my friends,' CRUSHer says, and the lights on his console flicker to show happiness.

'Military issue from a decade back,' Gwin notes. 'A relic

and a good fit for our experiment!' She bounces off her seat with a whoop of excitement.

'Breathe, Gwin.'

Gwin laughs with relish. 'What should we do? Come on, let's go.'

'Watch this,' Bek says. '**CRUSHer**, get a cup of water, please.'

CRUSHer advances on the water cooler. He assesses the cups stacked in the holder, the tap, then the shelf under the tap. These factors sluggishly percolate in his system. He swings an arm towards the cup stack, knocking a bunch of them from the holder.

'Oopsie,' **CRUSHer** says.

He bends at the middle and scoops them together with claws not built for the task. It takes him several goes, but he finally gets hold of one. It buckles in his grip. He overshoots placing the cup on the shelf and has to hold the water cooler to steady it. Before the cup is full, he grabs for it, spilling the small amount of water. He gets the cup to Bek, but misjudges as she reaches for it, dropping it onto the floor before she can take it.

'So,' Bek says, pulling towels from a dispenser to wipe the floor.

'Yes.' Gwin claps her hands excitedly. 'Swarm will bring **CRUSHer** into the modern age.'

'Yay,' Bek says, weakly.

Gwin hands Bek the widget and says, 'Attach it to your device.'

The widget attaches to Bek's handheld with a soft metallic DING, and a faint purple light begins to pulse beneath the surface. The branches of Swarm spiral as they extend outward from the widget's surface.

Then, nothing happens.

CRUSHer remains motionless in front of the water cooler. Bek wonders if he crashed, but then CRUSHer raises an arm. He reaches for the stack of cups, but stops. His arm lowers. This goes on for a few loops. Arm raises, arm lowers.

'Bek, look.' Gwin indicates a knotted part of the Swarm on Bek's screen. 'I haven't seen this before.'

'Any idea what it is?'

Gwin taps on her screen. 'Swarm has . . . Oh!'

'Swarm has what?'

CRUSHer slumps forward and the lights on his console blink out. Gwin raises her hand high, her fingers spidering frantically.

CRUSHer's console lights blink again and he pulls himself up in small stages. He sights Bek and swivels back towards the water cooler, raising the arm that once housed live weaponry.

'Was that a reboot?' Gwin asks.

Bek scrolls though a list of CRUSHer's processes. 'His central processing is berserk. I think we should—'

Loud machine static comes from CRUSHer's communications centre. He takes a single jarring step. The claw-hand on his raised arm swivels and folds away. He takes another wobbly step.

'Gwin!'

'I almost have Swarm out. But there's . . .' Gwin's eyes bore into Bek's. 'I don't understand.'

Bek swallows. When she rechecks CRUSHer's processing unit, she doesn't recognise the signal. CRUSHer's raised arm whines: the pitch rises in intensity. A pulsing glow travels up CRUSHer's arm and down again, increasing speed as it cycles. Bek launches herself at Gwin and tries to pull her to the floor, but Gwin is deceptively strong. She stares at Bek, face expressionless, and doesn't budge. Bek shouts over the noise, **'Get down!'**

Still Gwin doesn't move.

'Gwin! Kill it! *Power off!*'

Gwin just stares.

'Get Swarm out,' Bek cries. ***'Shut it off!'***

The whine reaches a painful intensity. With a brilliant flash of light and energy, CRUSHer fires a laser at the water cooler.

It will puzzle Bek later, the sequence of thoughts she had at the time. Fuzzy memories from physics lessons. Equations describing the relationship between force and acceleration. The sensation of feeling strangely inert. Other objects sharing her velocity and hanging in her view. Only Gwin moves in a direction that should be impossible.

Given time, Bek will come to think of this as an illusion. The trickery of her mind under stress. *Misremembered* will be the conclusion she comes to.

The disco strobing of the emergency lighting cuts through eventually. She really is motionless, lying flat on the floor. A misty rain falls from the ceiling. She raises her hand in a lazy arc to stare, for ages, at the coloured blobs on her left palm, white stalks sticking out. Her mind screams, *Broken bones*!

It isn't bone. Slowly it dawns that she has Lemmy Saltine's cracker shape stuck to her hand. The white stalks are his legs. Bek thinks she might laugh. She raises her head to locate Gwin.

At first, she's far away, wandering through the smoke. A beat later, she is bent over, staring into Bek's face.

227

'What?' Bek shrieks, soundlessly. 'Say it again.'

She forces herself to calm down and concentrates on the green lip blob.

'Here we go,' Gwin says, fringe pulled back and her eyes spaced-out wheels. 'The light is still slipping to the floor.'

Then, while Bek watches helplessly, Gwin floats away, making her exit through the newly blown-out hole in Bek's new lab's wall.

<25>

sucks like venom

LOITERING NEAR THE SCHOOL'S barnyard, Hunter waits with Milly for his father and Josie to arrive. The weather disappoints. Josie would call it partly cloudy with a zero percent chance of rain. Hunter would prefer a tropical cyclone. Even high winds would raise his hopes. What they have is a dull featureless sky, pocked with thin streaks of blue. And while it may be suitably blah for a Venom gig, no way will it force a cancellation.

His father told them to meet far too early, because he's nowhere to be seen. But half the school is here already. Proof Hunter's come a long way: the anxiety from being in a crowd would have freaked him out a few weeks ago. Possibly it still does, but Josie has given him strategies. Hunter is to fake-it-till-he-feels-it. Lately, he's been smiling if he isn't happy, smiling when he feels agitated and smiling even if terrified.

Currently, he's smiling through dread.

True, the Venom gig will be torture, but soon they'll have Josie's launch. The number of days she'll be with them is dwindling fast. Hunter's going to miss her when she's gone. *Really* miss her. He sort of can't imagine what it'll be like. Everything will probably backslide. The thought of being who he was before she came feels suffocating. He smiles for no reason, with gritted teeth.

Not helping either, Milly has been telling him about her Ethics For Everyone debate: *Should a robot ever be allowed to rule?* She says, 'In popular culture robots have always been a metaphor. We gathered under trees and talked about the possibility of robots running the world for real. Everyone kept looking at me. They know what Dad does. They were going on about me being the robot queen's favoured minion.'

'You said *queen*,' Hunter says.

'They kept saying, when the time comes, of all the humans only you will prosper. Never forget to remember us, they said. It was kind of disturbing.'

Hunter finds it particularly annoying when his younger sister shares her intellectual musings, but he keeps his gritted-teeth smile going. This, if anything, only encourages her to keep talking.

'The robot metaphor has had a reboot. It used to reference humanity at its most unemotional and detached. Another metaphor — the robot as part of a hive mind. These days we question whether the robot is a slave or if she is about to enslave us. It's about power, see?'

'You said *she*.'

'We questioned whether female robots hit glass ceilings on their ambitious climb to the top.'

Milly checks to see how Hunter is reacting. The smile is him pretending he isn't.

The school hero, Raphael Gunn, walks past. Hunter doesn't care what people think, but even so he avoids eye contact. Milly watches Raphael over the frames of her sunglasses. 'You should let people know you're better now,' she tells Hunter.

'People can mind their own business.'

Milly tsks, then tells him, 'The humanoid is a metaphor for elitism.'

Hunter finds it really, really annoying when his younger sister uses words like *elitism* when she could just as easily say nothing at all. He doesn't need her to tell him it sucks being poor, that everybody's over it because they want the same electronic crap that rich people have. And he doesn't need reminding that if their father hadn't built her, no way would they be able to afford to have Josie in their home. He doesn't need to hear anything from Milly, in fact. Hunter scowls, but she continues.

'Compare and contrast with robot characters known to be harmless, misunderstood, well-meaning intelligences.'

'What's keeping Dad and Josie?' Hunter asks.

'A robot queen, we all thought, could end up making decisions that aren't necessarily in the best interests of humans. It wouldn't be their fault. They could be corrupted, like, for evil purposes.'

'Is it okay if we don't talk?' Hunter smiles. 'Just for a little bit?'

Milly's not talking involves huffing and arm-folding and tutting. It involves her snapping, 'If Josie was here, you'd talk to her.'

'Of course. We need to finesse our world-domination plot.'

'She'd be great to help me with robot hypotheticals.'

'Don't you dare,' Hunter says, grabbing Milly's arm to show she'd really better not. His wristband buzzes with a message alert. 'They're one minute away.'

'Why didn't Josie message me?' Milly gropes for an ancient cuff in her bag, then fires it up. 'Oh, she did.'

Hunter smiles.

'You're smug all the time now,' Milly says, misunderstanding his emotional defences. 'You have to accept Josie's going soon.'

Exactly one minute later, Hunter watches Miles and Josie approach through the barnyard. Josie frowns as she walks through a small gathering of chickens. As usual, his chest jumps a bit and he has the weird jittery feeling he gets sometimes when he's with her. Which has nothing to do with her stupendous legs and how spectacular they look covered in her red stretchy pants, and everything to do with her future being up in the air. He worries what will happen to her once she leaves them. Will someone take good care of her?

He also blames Milly. Now he has to worry about what everyone thinks about Josie. He doesn't like it that Milly's schoolmates are so quick to judge robots. Can they even tell that Josie's a humanoid? Or that she's exceptional? Perhaps even now they'll attract unwanted attention, and make Josie feel self-conscious.

Nothing.

Perhaps it's because perfectly constructed good looks are common among his fellow students. Most of them have undergone some sort of enhancement or reconstruction to improve appearance. Josie's perfect good looks are no big deal.

Plus, Milly told her what to wear. Aside from the knock-out red legs, she's dressed like a typical Venom fan, minus snake tattoos and body piercings. Milly unearthed a grunge-grey Venom T-shirt (a stylised snake face made from '0w0' and an upside down 'y' for the tongue) which Josie wears so well the camouflage works. If anything she fits the scene better than he does in his unremarkable cargos and plain tee.

It's his father who draws the most attention. The staring can't all be from Milly's classmates pondering the deeper meaning of robot — there's too many of them. His father is sort of famous in certain geek circles and there must be quite a few geeks amongst the Venom fandom. There's a distinct buzz as they make their way to the grassed-over amphitheatre at the back of the school grounds.

Venom's fan base has grown since Hunter last saw them play and they've drawn a large crowd. Coel acknowledges their arrival with a jerk of his head and the barest twitch of an eyebrow. Unlike at other gigs where he used to ignore his drum kit before playing on it, today he's busy hitting each drum, tightening bolts and concentrating on his drum sound.

Hunter leads them to the furthermost point from the stage. This prompts a puzzled look from Josie and a relieved one from Milly. Their seats still aren't far enough. When the bass guitarist does his sound check, Hunter feels the reverberation in his chest. Too soon, the crowd reaches critical mass; the lead singer steps up to the microphone and Coel picks up his drumsticks again with a twirl. Hunter braces himself.

The band **slams** into their first song after Coel plays a slow drum intro. They are LOUD, but not loud enough to drown out the lead singer, who growls into the microphone, 'Luuuuvv'. Then, after a lot of instrumental racket, 'Suuuuuuccccckks'.

The effect is instant. Fans fling their long stringy hair forward then back. A surging mass of black, they sway in time to Coel's drumming and the discordant strum of an electric guitar. Then, as if any more noise is needed, the screaming starts, the fans making their collective contribution to the song.

Hunter groans.

His father enjoys Venom like a gentleman, one leg crossed over the other, tapping the rhythm with sprightly bounces of his foot. Milly grimaces at Hunter, a funny, scared-witless look. He gives her one back.

Then he notices Josie.

Sitting straight as a pole, so still she could be powered off, with her eyebrows arched high and her smile forced. The Venom sound does take some getting used to. Hunter shouts into her ear. 'It's okay. **They don't know many songs yet.**'

'**Their sound is dynamic,**' Josie shouts back.

Hunter's laughter is lost in the assault of noise.

Josie crosses her eyes and Hunter laughs again.

A message DINGs Hunter's wristband: one of Serenity Sam's daily reminders that Hunter hasn't rated his quality of life today. The daily quality-of-life rating being one of the consequences of the bathroom-pod debacle. Hunter would never give a rating of one — he'd be called to Sam's office and grilled endlessly about lifestyle choices — and a rating of ten is well out of his reach. But he has to admit, it feels good Josie sitting beside him. Momentous even. Life in general, actually, has almost been pretty good. A seven, maybe even an eight.

He looks at Josie looking at him, a big smile growing on his face.

Josie mouths, *Are you fake smiling?*

Holding the smile, Hunter mouths back, *Yes, I am.*

Josie's smile get bigger. Hunter's gets less fake.

Venom have just finished their third song when Hunter sees the arrival of the girl, Alice. At least, he thinks it's Alice. Her perky white ponytail and brightly patterned shorts seem out of place, even though she's wearing a Venom T-shirt. And by the time she bounces into a knot of Venom fans, disappearing from view, Hunter convinces himself he made a mistake.

The lead singer announces the next song, his voice deep and brooding: 'This is a *like* song.'

He hisses *like* as though the word is poison.

The song gets under way with a cry so agonised, Josie flinches and Hunter gives her arm a squeeze of reassurance.

The lead singer half-sings, half-stage-whispers, 'Listen to me.' Then he screams, '**Liiiiistennnn!**' As if the audience has any choice in the matter. After a dramatic pause, he groans, 'to your heart beat'.

In spite of himself, Hunter follows the command. He's surprised by the heavy **thunk, thunk** of his heart. Josie smiles at him and he places his hand at his side right next to hers.

The guitar thrums with a steady pulse. Coel joins in: ***KA-THWUMP, KA-THWUMP, KA-THWUMP.***

'I wanna tell y'all something,' the lead singer's voice grumbles. 'You . . .' ***KA-THWUMP, KA-THWUMP, KA-THWUMP*** '. . . are . . .' ***KA-THWUMP*** '. . . sooooooo innnnnn . . .' Coel drums eight ***KA-THWUMPS.*** The singer takes a deep breath, leans back, and the auditorium rocks to one word, 'liiiiiiiiiiike'.

The guitarist hammers out a run of discordant notes, Coel batters the drum in a frenzy of wild arm movements and flying drumsticks, and the lead singer continues to scream, 'So in like, so in like, so in liiiiiiiiiike.'

Laughing at the intensity, Hunter turns to see how Josie's doing. In that same moment she turns to him. He was about to say *Just an old-fashioned like song*. It would have been funny. But his brain jams on *like*. It echoes down the long corridors of his mind. He can't get past Josie's eyes. Golden and bright, they loom large in his vision, bringing him back to *now*. Sunshine breaks through the clouds. Vivid movement surrounds them. His father's jiggling foot, the perpetual motion of the fans. Between them there is only this. Hunter slowly blinks, and her eyes widen a fraction more. Two people see each other for the first time.

Or so it seems.

'Josie?' He says her name like a question, but the maelstrom of sound stifles his voice. He says it again, tender this time, knowing only he will hear it.

A little crease between her eyes. She gazes at his mouth; her eyes linger.

He smiles, plants his palm on his chest and says, 'For real.'

Her mouth forms words, her face makes a question.

'Not faking,' he says, really wanting her to know it. 'Happy. Me. You.'

'Okay,' she says, and he thinks, *Okay*?

THRUMM, THRUMM. 'So in like! So in like!'

A tickling sensation makes Hunter look down. An ant races across the back of the hand gripping the edge of his seat. The hand almost touching Josie's hand. Seeing this gives him a jolt. How right it seems, the fine arch of her little finger next to the bony knuckle of his. How fitting, too, brought to his attention by an ant. He's drawn so many of them. It amazes him, the physical strength of such delicate creatures. Strong, yet fragile.

He daren't move. He doesn't want to disturb the balance of forces that brought him to this point, nor break the zing of silent energy connecting him to Josie through their fingers. The music slows, the Venom singer croons, 'So in like!'

It's getting difficult to swallow.

When he looks up, he sees Josie looking down at their hands. Then, their eyes meet. Hers go soft in the corners. She gets the dreamy look. The strange thing happens.

A stop/start, frozen-in-time, charging-ahead, brand-new feeling. Strangeness pressing in on his chest, or fighting hard to get out. He feels heavy, he feels light. His brain fires with electrified thoughts, right when Venom pick it up again, feverish and wilder than ever. 'So in like! So in like! So in like!'

Venom fans jump and flail, hair flying every which way. Miles's foot's a metronome, tap, tap, tap, tap, tap. 'SO ... IN ... LIKE!'

Hunter wants to laugh, Josie too. She's getting an amused twinkle, like she's in on it. *So in like!*

She makes a face. He interprets: *Are you all right?*

'**Soooo all right,**' he shouts.

She smiles, but her face is still a question. He leans closer to say the words to her, *I like you, Josie.* But before he gets a chance, Milly shoves him in the back and shouts, '**Alice Wallace-Shaw, staring right at you.**'

Of course Hunter looks, and Josie too.

Below them, Alice twinkles her fingers right at him. She does it like they're pretty good friends. And Hunter, stunned by the magnum-force Josie feelings he's having, twinkles his fingers back.

Alice melts into the crowd with more finger-twinkling. At the same time Coel breaks loose on the drums. A man possessed, his arms blur; he drums faster and faster, throwing and catching his drumsticks but keeping the beat. Even the other band members have stopped playing. They look transfixed by this Coel spectacle, right up to the last fill, when he slows it down, finishing with a high-hat **CRASH** and drumsticks flying.

The Venom fans jump and wave their arms. Josie stands and claps, arms above her head. Hunter copies her.

His dad cheers and calls, **Woo! Woo!** When it's quiet, Miles says, 'You guys didn't tell me Coel had a girlfriend.'

They all look.

Coel with a girl pulled into his side. As foreign a sight as his care with the drum kit. A perky, bright-white ponytail cascading over his arm. The girl's fingers snake around the back of Coel's neck in a possessive sort of way. Coel leans towards her, his hand cupping her ear when he talks to her. The girl turns under his arm until she's up against Coel's chest.

Hunter can't believe who it is.

Wrapped up in Coel, Alice looks past the Venom fans until she finds him again. It's the look on her face. A flash of determination, a challenge. Confused, he waves or does something with his hand that brushes past Josie's arm.

Alice ripples her fingers.

He feels Josie's eyes on him. When he turns, her expression is no longer dreamy, but calculating and remote.

'Good for Coel,' his father says. 'Looks like a nice girl.'

Josie takes this in as well. She looks at Alice, then Coel and back at Hunter.

No, he wants to shout. **Figure out you and me**.

Josie frowns, her mouth a prim line.

It's you. YOU! He says it with his eyes, but Josie turns away.

The crowd begins to drift. Milly and Miles make a move towards the stage and Josie leaves with them. His father banters with Coel. Josie people-watches. Her gaze follows the crowd; she looks everywhere but the space occupied by Hunter, who stands right next to her. He follows Josie and his dad out, and watches them walk away from the barnyard. He calls out as they are about to disappear from view, but no one turns back, no one waves at him.

The rest of the afternoon, he can't get past the Venom lyrics. They play in his head on high rotate. *So in like, so in like, so in like.*

<26>

it's what you do

'FIREWORKS EXPLODE ACROSS the night sky. The metaphor implies spectacle, entertainment. But the spectacle is fleeting, see? A metaphor is—'

'We know what metaphors are, Mills.'

'You maybe, but Coel—'

'He knows. Keep going.'

'A name in lights, JESSICA, and the words World Champion. Now we're starting to get *context*. Context means—'

'Hunter, tell the Millipede to shut—'

'It's okay. Keep going, Mills.'

'Camera flashes pop. Classic. A symbol of her celebrity and humongous success. Here she comes, Jessica Saltine. A slo-mo procession. She parts a cheering throng. Her embroidered dressing gown in golden silk flowing behind her. Sure she can take your head off with one punch, but that doesn't mean she's out of touch with the finer things in life. We can read something into the gold. Victory? Positive vibes?

'She has one place to go: the ring. She climbs through the ropes, and she's right at home. Her skinny white arms, made powerful by the giant boxing gloves. See how she raises them above her head? It's all hers. And don't forget the music. That staccato riff of electric guitar. Pure energy. And this is what the crowd has come for. This sequence. Jessica taking out her opponents with a knock-out. Look out, loser. Oh, wait. Don't forget the love interest. How do we know? Pretty face, watching Jessica fight from the front row. Watch now, Jessica glances in her lady's direction. Pretty Face brings fingertips to her lips and blows a kiss.

'And that, friends, is visual storytelling,' Milly says.

'I don't get it,' Coel says. 'Wouldn't her cracker body break if she really was a boxing champ?'

'Oh wow,' Milly says. 'He discovers irony.'

Hunter had come to the home theatre to chill out from his Venom ordeal and Josie epiphany. He hadn't meant for his siblings to join him, and now he wishes he'd gone to the workshop. They're having turns playing video clips. Hunter takes control of the media player with his wristband. The screen freezes on Jessica Saltine's tight little smile after the air kiss.

'My turn,' Coel says.

'I didn't get five minutes,' Milly says.

Coel pushes his feet into the back of Hunter's chair. 'Dial up Prince Garrick.'

Hunter smacks Coel's feet as Milly declares, 'Go ahead, roll the mindless crap.'

Hunter taps his wristband to play Coel's selection.

Madness hangs in the air. Fierce screams and guttural cries of the excited village folk threaten to max out the speakers. Prince Garrick enters the scene. He throws his cape to one side with a flourish and slides into a sideways lunge, his so-called famous fighting stance. Raising a knobbly stick to the heavens he cries, **'Advance, Alien Scum.'**

'That's a bit strong isn't it?' Milly says.

Coel finally drops his feet and glues his eyes to the screen.

An Alien monster arrives. Ten times the size of Prince Garrick, its black carapace gleams with menace in the moonlight. Great globs of acidic drool drip from its giant maw.

'Duel time,' Prince Garrick says.

The Alien charges, then freezes mid-motion.

'Hey,' Coel says.

'That's fair,' Milly says reasonably, and Hunter notices he's lost control of the media player.

'Hunter's turn,' Milly says. 'Oh, hey Josie.'

'Just finish the scene,' Coel says.

Hunter sinks low in his seat and watches the screen intently, right as the Alien monster explodes into black clods of goo.

'Your viewing preference, Coel?' Josie asks.

Coel laughs. Now Maiden Raen comes. Dewy-eyed, dressed in form-fitting shorts, a bustier and a cape. She rushes into the crowd in her knee-high boots. She flings back the hood of her cape and masses of red locks blow attractively about her face from a light breeze that only she is exposed to. Raen searches desperately among the mayhem for the Prince.

Hunter peeks at Josie, then slides his eyeballs back to the screen.

It's great and weird to see her. The weirdness is easily explained — he's so in like, and probably has been all along — but it's been awkward. Hunter needs a strategy to feel normal. Josie would know how he should handle himself, but he can't ask her outright, for obvious reasons. He looks at her without looking at her.

'Yes, Coel's choice,' Milly says. 'There's no poetics. It is what it is, folks.'

The rampaging villagers, who are in on the romance, set the Prince down right in front of Maiden Raen. She melts into his arms, literally boneless.

Hunter keeps his head facing the screen, but tracks Josie in his peripheral vision when she takes a seat next to Milly.

He would like her to sit next to him. He would like it if they were alone in the darkened room.

She's still in her stretchy red pants, and folds one long leg over the other.

The Prince gives foxy Raen a cheeky grin and says, 'Sorry to keep you waiting, angel. I've been a bit busy saving the world.'

Maiden Raen's enormous blue eyes flutter with adoration.

'And that's how we ladies forgive men,' Milly says. 'Words? No, we have chemically enhanced eyelashes.'

The Prince plants his lips on Raen's and she clings to him with her foxy, quite well-muscled arms. Groovy modern music swells, and the kissing gets squirmy.

Josie watches the wall-mounted screen, and then looks at Milly as though trying to figure out the entertainment. When it looks like she's about to turn around even further and look at Hunter, he arranges his expression to appear engrossed in the movie. Unfortunately, it appears he is engrossed in the never-ending, unpleasantly smoochy kiss.

They're still kissing when the music changes to hard rock. A gravelly male voice shrieks through the sound system: 'I was in pieces ... your love put me to-oo-oo-qetherrrr ...'

Hunter looks at the ceiling, then the wall opposite Josie. He counts a few seconds before focusing his eyeballs on the screen again. Still the kissing.

'Your flesh from the fa-a-a-ct-ory of lo-o-ove.'

Finally the screen goes black and the credits roll. He can just make out Josie on the edge of his visual field.

'You're my different giiiirl . . . You're so different, giiiirl.'

He peeks in her direction and sees her leaving the room just as the song comes to an end.

'But I'm soo-woah-woah in lo-uh-uh-ove.'

The final notes of the guitar thrum. Coel nudges Hunter's shoulder with his foot. 'What's up with you? You're acting strange, man.'

Milly turns in her seat and gives Hunter a sharp look.

'Do you mind?' Hunter says. He twists in his seat to glare at Coel, then sits straight again. Hunter raises his eyebrows at Milly, making out it's Coel who's the strange one. The last thing he wants is her guessing something's up.

Coel flops forward and rests his arms on the back of the seat next to Hunter. 'Hypothetical. A duel between me and you. Who would win?'

Milly tells the room, 'Lights up!'

Darkness gives way to soft, ambient lighting around the screening-room walls.

'You always do this,' Hunter says.

'Do what?'

'It's all —' Hunter finger-quotes — 'hypothetical. But everyone knows you think you're better at everything.'

'I don't think I'm better at everything.'

'Who do you think would win?'

Coel laughs at Hunter's stupidity. 'Me.'

'It's actually boring how predictable you are.'

Milly perks up at the sound of Mushi meowing in the kitchen and says, 'I'm out.'

Coel snorts at Hunter. 'And you don't think *you're* predictable?'

'I don't care if I am or . . .' Hunter's voice trails off. He's distracted by the sounds coming from the kitchen. Milly is crooning at Mushi, but Josie be must there as well, because she's saying, 'Remind me what cats are useful for again?'

And Milly's reply, 'His job is being adorable. Isn't it, Moosh.'

Coel slaps a hand on Hunter's shoulder, making him jump. 'Predictable.'

'How is that predictable?'

'It's what *you* always do. You pretend nothing matters. Or it matters too much. You deflect.'

'And you're some kind of expert.'

'I read stuff. You never go for something you want head-on. In fact, you can't even be bothered to want something. That's why you won't win.'

Josie's laugh again. 'So I rub his tummy with my face?'

And Milly tells her, 'It feels really nice. Try it.'

Josie says, 'Mmmmm. That does feel nice.'

Coel whacks Hunter on the side of the head. 'I'm talking to you.'

'Quit hitting me!'

'You'll never get anything if you don't go for things,' Coel insists.

Hunter shouts, **'I DO GO FOR THINGS.'**

It goes quiet in the kitchen. It goes quiet behind him.

Hunter stands, meaning to storm out. But that's the old, angry Hunter. The new Hunter turns to Coel and smiles benevolently.

'I'm sorry,' he says, and sits. 'That was misplaced anger.

My robot shrink is helping me work through some issues. Please have patience while I evolve.'

'Your robot shrink!'

'Anyway,' Hunter says. 'That's something I go for. Working on personal stuff with Josie.'

'Because Dad made you.'

Hunter lets that one go. Their father isn't exactly making him do anything now. As usual, he's lost interest already and seems happy to see Josie messing about with all of them, not just Hunter in particular.

'Come on,' Coel says. 'Go for something else. Anything. Let's do a duel.'

'What's the point? I'll only go to jail if I win. There's no incentive.' But Hunter thinks back to their many childhood games of war. There was never really any point to their battles, but they still had fun.

Coel makes a chicken noise, miming wingbeats with his hands in his armpits.

'Goad me by suggesting I'm a coward, hey?' Hunter pretends to think it through. 'Okay, it's working. We'll do it.'

'Spit and shake,' Coel says.

'Dad won't be happy when I shoot you,' Hunter says. 'His favourite son killed by his least-favourite son.'

'You care what Dad thinks?'

Hunter smirks. 'My robot shrink is teaching me not to care what anybody thinks.'

'Your robot shrink can duel too,' Coel says. 'Time to show her who's best.'

From the kitchen, Milly squeals. 'Awwww, Mushi loves you, he's gone all floppy.'

Hunter hears Josie say, 'Oh dear.'

In the end he's alone in the screening room, binge-watching his favourite *Saltines* episodes. He hopes Josie might wander in. He would like to get started on going for things. When she doesn't come, he decides tomorrow will have to do. Without fail. First thing in the morning. Come rain or shine. Or the day after that. Definitely. Or, at the very least, sometime. Sometime soon.

better than us

BY THE TIME BEK APPLIES a heavy layer of makeup, the worst of the worst is hidden. She mostly looks tired and not so much like someone who endured the explosive power of a military-grade electro-magnetic pulse at close range.

Or the indignity of a demotion.

Miles has her working in the Synthetic Pet Department. A step down is how she sees it. *Only for the time being*, he said, while he works through some things. One of the things being her new lab, which is going to take time to repair.

She removes the bandage from her head. The gash from the explosion looks horrible under its layer of plastic film, even with her hair down to cover it. She rummages through her wardrobe for a hat, and puts it on. She slips on her sunglasses, takes one last glimpse in the mirror and wishes she didn't look as miserable as she feels.

The meeting place is easy to find. Deacon is a small town and the parks aren't all that grand. Professor Bishop's economy-sized hybrid stands out. A car so old, she wonders how it's legit.

Bek yanks down on her bucket hat, suppresses a groan and climbs into the passenger seat.

'Bit dramatic, isn't it, Rebekah? The hat? The sunglasses?' The professor's smile has the warmth of a dead snake. 'You're behaving like a wanted criminal.'

Her heart trips. It doesn't help to be reminded of a shameful past. Especially now when her personal list of misdemeanours grows longer by the minute. But there seems to be no more to the comment than Professor Bishop's normal levels of irritation.

Even so, in the cramped space of the car, all she can think is *air*.

After searching for a swipe panel or slider, and failing, Bek gasps, 'How do I open the window?'

Professor Bishop sighs, and shoves his arm across. The window lowers by a lever that must be pressed down to work. Her head throbs. It takes *forever*.

Focusing on the sweep of parkland in front of them, Bek holds her breath until he takes his arm away. It always amazes her how many people have time to sit around on sunny days: mothers, fathers and their children, couples dawdling through the park, lying on the ground or sprawled across one another's laps. What do these people do on the not-sunny days? Rip through workloads so, come the sunshine, they have time to spare?

A little girl shrieks and runs to two women chatting on a picnic rug. The girl leaps onto one of the women, who rolls back with the child caught in a bear hug. For a brief moment they're a happy tangle of arms and legs, then the girl runs off again.

Something familiar about the two of them — and then it clicks. They're the wife and daughter of BIOLOGIC's security chief, Jace Gurney.

With her own childish shriek, Bek slithers to the floor.

'If it's comfort you're after,' Professor Bishop drawls, '*on* the seat is better than *off*.'

Bek blows out her breath. 'I know those people.'

'So?'

'So, people talk.'

'You act like catching up with your former professor is wrong.'

'You act like catching up is all we're doing.'

Bek gives the professor her meanest scowl, which he doesn't see. He fidgets with a ring of keys hanging from the steering column and says absently, 'It is all we're doing.'

'If that were true, then explain my presence. Because I can think of places I'd rather be than on the floor of your crappy vintage car.'

'Rebekah, have I caught you on a bad day?'

'I don't know what you want.'

'To catch up.'

The lid from the glove compartment bumps Bek's head and the professor rummages inside, then pulls out a zip-lock bag full of almonds. He shrugs apologetically. 'I've been advised to eat more of the good fats.' He shakes out a handful and palms them into his mouth. 'Fun fact,' he says, between chomps. 'When chewed, these nuts taste like gritty cardboard. Want some?'

Declining the offer, Bek punches the glove compartment closed. Professor Bishop whoops and laughs. The phoney sound of it grates on her nerves.

'You'll hate this,' he says in a too-loud voice. 'Good grief, my mind's gone blank. What's Miles's son called?'

'Which one?'

'The oldest.' The professor snaps his fingers. 'Hunter. That's it.'

Bek cranes sharply to peer through the passenger window, bumps her head on the glove-compartment latch and crumples back to the floor.

'What the freak?'

'Why, Rebekah, it's as if you've seen a ghost.' The professor leers. 'I must say, Hunter's having a very nice time with his girlfriend. She's something to look at, by the way.'

'That's not his girlfriend. And don't be disgusting.'

'It's not against the law to admire good looks. That young woman is unusually stunning.'

'We know.'

'I'm impressed.' Professor Bishop raises his eyebrows. 'Miles doesn't usually let staff get close to his family.'

Bek, her temples throbbing, thinks she might be sick on the floor of Professor Bishop's car. 'I don't know Hunter, I know his companion.'

'As I'm fond of saying,' Professor Bishop continues, 'sneeze in Deacon, the whole town catches a fever.'

'Ewwww,' Bek says. 'I know her because we *made* her.'

In the silence that follows, Bek hears children, their voices carrying high-pitched and squealing from the playground. She tries to imagine what Josie could be thinking, surrounded by children at play. In a near-future scenario, Josephinas could well take the place of the child-minders. She starts to envisage what a caring response to a child might look like in code.

Gradually, she becomes aware she's been staring at the professor. The look on his face as he watches the park is one of distaste.

Bek follows his gaze. Hunter seems at ease, laughing with

Josie. It's heartening for the briefest moment — until he takes Josie's hand and traces a finger over the skin of her palm.

Bek drops back down to the floor of the car.

They *look* like a young couple in love, but how can that be? She goes for a second peek. Hunter stares into Josie's eyes. Josie stares back. His hand strokes the lower part of Josie's arm.

Again Bek drops to the floor of the car. Professor Bishop gives her a hostile glare.

'Does Hunter know his companion is a machine? Because she sure fooled me. He looks like a young man very much in lo—'

'Of course he understands his father's work.'

'They should never be better than us. They should never be doing *that*.' Professor Bishop's tone is snide. 'That boy should be out there with a real girl, not—'

'Stop,' Bek says. 'It's totally harmless.'

But is it really? An unpleasant awareness of being trapped threatens to overwhelm her. It's more than just the physical discomfort. The professor might be a little unhinged.

'Is this what our future looks like?' he goes on. 'Parks full of those things pretending to be us?'

'She's not a thing,' Bek snaps.

'But she's replacing a girlfriend. What next? Brothers, sisters? Mothers, fathers?'

'The world isn't coming to an end because of a new companion robot.'

'How do you know? Is anybody thinking it through?'

'She's not an atomic warhead,' Bek erupts. 'We're not lighting the fuse for Armageddon.'

The professor takes a deep breath and leans back in his seat.

'I actually see this as fortuitous. The two of us meeting, and who should come along but your robot. It's a sign, wouldn't you say?'

'It's . . .' Bek has to pause while she considers. A big believer in signs, her natural instinct would be to concede the point. But she can't give way to the professor. Let him gain any ground, there would be no end to it. 'It's a random grouping of coincidental events.'

His response is to throw another handful of almonds into his mouth. Then he zips the bag and pulls the flap of the glove box open to stow it, bumping the top of her bucket hat. Tears spring into Bek's eyes.

'Please. Stop. That. You're hurting me.'

Professor Bishop closes the glove box in a rush. With a mouthful of almonds he says, 'I'm so sorry. Truly, I'm not myself. The direction and speed things are moving. I don't mean to go off about it.' He looks down at her. 'But I do need your help.'

Bek clambers onto the passenger seat, so angry she no longer cares who sees her.

'I knew it.'

'I had a very long talk with Gwin yesterday,' the professor says.

Bek hisses, 'If this is about wrecking Josie—'

He stops chewing.

'That's it, isn't it?' Bek's accusing glare could melt steel. 'And Gwin won't help either. In fact, you won't even get your hands on her code.'

It's disappointing how unfazed Professor Bishop seems after Bek plays her ace. He swallows, sucks in his cheeks and mumbles, 'What a silly thing to say.'

'She won't submit it.'

'But she already has.'

He opens his hand in the space between them. On his palm lies a jet-black widget. For a moment it glows purple, and knotty swirls of code form a cloud around the globe at its base.

'Gwin told me a tale of explosions and violent robots,' the professor says. 'She was deeply disturbed by her visit to BIOLOGIC.' His lips press together and his smile shifts gears, swiftly becoming patronising. 'I must say, she was very appreciative of my helpful advice.'

'But Swarm broke.'

'Oh no,' the professor says. 'I don't pretend to understand, but Gwin claims the broken bits of Swarm merged with your CRUSHer and spawned a zoo of new entities. Don't ask me, but she isn't calling it Swarm. This new code is Spawn.'

'Gwin wouldn't do that.'

'Rebekah, you of all people should never underestimate the need for personal advancement. Gwin wants to graduate. Then I suppose I recommend her to the right people. You'll know how that plays out.'

Bek pulls down on the door latch. Nothing happens. She **slams** her shoulder into the door but it won't move. Her voice is shrill when she demands, **'Open the door.'**

'Hold on a moment.'

In a flash Bek turns on him. 'I'll tell Miles everything.'

'Tell Miles what?'

'I'm not afraid to, if that's what you think.'

'Listen,' the professor says. 'We were blood brothers, Miles and I. Do you know what that means?'

With a roll of her eyes, Bek says, 'Oh, come on.'

'We swore an oath together, Miles, Emilia and myself. Friends to the end. The end has come for some of us, but where is Miles in all this? Promoting himself. Maybe it's time for retribution.' Professor Bishop keeps a straight face only for a moment. He collapses with laughter, barely getting his words out. 'Oh . . . you . . . your face. It's precious. Blood brothers!'

He thumps his thigh, laughing harder. When he finally sobers, he says, 'I don't want to ruin anybody, of course I don't, but Miles does need help. It must be in secret, or he won't accept help from me. You can see that, can't you?'

'Are you insane?'

'Think of it as me looking out for an old friend.'

Bek shoulders the car door hard, flicking the latch with sweaty fingers. It gives with a sudden lurch. She falls, then scrambles to the curb. Once upright, she scans the park for Josie and Hunter, but they've gone. Lunging for her bag with trembling hands, her head about to explode, she hisses, 'I will stop you if it's the last thing I do.'

The professor shows his palms, proclaiming innocence. 'A thoughtful gesture? Don't be so dramatic, Rebekah.'

'I won't let you destroy our hard work.'

'That's funny,' the professor says. 'When I got you the job with Miles, I had hopes you'd cause no end of trouble. Such an accident-prone student. You have the remarkable ability to cause failure in even the most robust systems. All those electrical faults and blown-out circuits. You see the irony. You accusing *me* of destroying your hard work?'

Bek **slams** the door and wills herself to make it to the other side of the park, well beyond the children, before she bursts into tears.

<28>

diamond friends

'BEGIN DICTATION.'

Miles paces the ground-floor boardroom, writing and rehearsing his launch speech. Pacing, he imagines, gives him an air of gravitas. And with what he means to say at the launch, he will need his dignity.

The glass wall projects an expectant audience, minus the patch where Josie punched through it with the apple. A hole remains, awaiting repair, but it's low priority. Bek's lab will have to come first, and that rebuild is extensive.

Pace, pace, grasp chin with hand, look into distance.

It may be corny, but Miles wants to get across the fact that he's genuine. His Josephina line, and Josie in particular, has come to mean much more to him than making a few sales.

'I've come to believe in the impossible.' Miles looks at the audience virtually looking at him. 'Delete "the impossible". Insert . . .'

Pace, pace, stop. 'Insert "Josie". I've come to believe in Josie. That's it!'

'Repetition detected,' the table interactive croons. 'Do you mean to say: *I've come to believe in Josie. I've come to believe in Josie. That's it?*'

Miles groans. 'Stop dictation.'

'I've come to believe in Josie,' he tells the simulation, but drops into conversational mode. 'The older I get, the more I want to give back. But we can only do what we can do. We make choices. Some of mine haven't been good ones, I'll admit. Some of my choices led to violence and destruction. I think there's a chance I can make up for it. I think Josie can really change things, make us better people. She's the one. I feel it in my gut.

'We were messed up. I'm talking about my family now. Josie comes along and suddenly our lives have been transformed. Beyond what I imagined possible. Josie is . . . This will sound dumb, I know. She's someone special.'

Pretending for a moment that the *someone* special *isn't* an illegal entity, Miles raises his arms in victory. Sensors trigger in the boardroom. The audience breaks into applause and cheers. Miles waves a hand, graciously accepting the accolades. Two eyes peer at him from the hole in the wall.

Miles yelps, then instructs the wall to go fully transparent. A multitude of dark eyes stare at him. Long, ringed fingers press against the glass. It takes him a moment or two to make sense of what he's seeing. There's a girl watching him. The multitude of eyes are from a very realistic print on her dress. The girl is Gwin. Gwin's own eyes disappear when a lilac fringe falls across her face.

'Gwin!' Miles shouts. He makes a drama out of getting a fright. 'You want to come around?'

Gwin disappears at the end of the training-room floor and a moment later turns up at the boardroom.

'Come in, take a seat,' Miles says. 'You're here for Bek? She's gone out for lunch but shouldn't be too long.'

Wide-eyed, Gwin settles in a chair opposite him. He drums his fingertips on the table.

'So I hope you recovered from that CRUSHer business. Goes with the territory, unfortunately. If you're going to be a coder someday, here's a tip: sometimes it blows up before it breaks through.'

Miles smiles winningly, but Gwin doesn't relax.

'You were talking to yourself,' she says.

'Yup,' Miles nods. 'Writing my launch speech. I'm terrible at it, by the way.'

'The audience adores you.' Gwin smiles, and twin spots appear on her cheeks when she blushes.

'Only the fake one,' he says. 'I'm not a hundred percent confident a real one will.' He leans back in his chair, thoughtful. 'Mind if I run something past you?'

Gwin permits it with a shrug.

'If you were ever to invent something . . .'

She looks a little taken aback.

'I forgot about your student work.' Miles laughs. 'Okay, but once you graduate, would you want whatever you're working on to change the world? Like, make a difference? Or is it better to put your energy into giving the world what it wants? Meaning, something it understands.'

'Change, meaning to cause a transformation,' Gwin says. 'I would make it explosive, irreversible, revolutionary.'

'A misfit, hey? But people only cope with change in stages. People tend to fear what they don't understand. You know what I'm saying?'

'No,' Gwin says.

'What made you get into coding?'

'I am the daughter of the mother of invention.'

'Pardon?'

'I continue Mother's work.'

'She's a coder? An engineer? Have I heard of her?'

Gwin teases Miles with an enigmatic smile. 'Mother isn't interested in attention. It's enough for her to create. She sometimes says, *Don't let money be your goal, let goodness guide your soul*.'

Miles gestures at Gwin's ringed hand, 'Well, she does all right, if you don't mind me saying so. Pretty advanced tech you're wearing.'

'Her name is Winter.' Gwin's fringe falls across her face, but there's no mistaking the note of pride in her voice.

'Winter?' Miles taps his chin as he thinks. 'First or last name?'

Gwin taps her chin and acts thoughtful. Miles grows still. Gwin grows still. Miles leans forward, resting his chin on his fist and smiles. So does Gwin.

'Are you mirroring me?' Miles says it softly. He doesn't want to alarm anybody.

'Are you mirroring me?' Gwin imitates his tone exactly.

'Damn,' Miles says, rocking back in his chair, stunned.

'Damn,' Gwin says.

Then Miles laughs with clear delight. 'You know, I was the first to open-source the code for `Mimic to Learn`.'

Gwin nods enthusiastically, and he can't take the smile off his face.

'You have that on board?'

Gwin gives a pert smile. 'Mother is a fan of your work. Much of me . . . is you.'

'But Gwin . . . you're so . . .' For a moment Miles is speechless. Even Josie doesn't seem to be at Gwin's level of sophistication.

'Does Bek . . . ?'

Gwin shrugs, nonchalant.

'So you're, umm . . . ? How do you live?'

Gwin presses a finger to her lips and shakes her head. She looks out at the training floor as the lights come on with sudden brilliance. A sᴄat skitters into the space. Miles recognises it as the one he assigned to Bek. Sure enough, she comes in soon after. The sᴄat races to the glass wall and rises up on hind legs. It watches Gwin; she watches back.

Miles waves. 'Hey there, Bek.'

Instead of greeting him, she glares at Gwin, then gives them both a pointed look. Gwin frowns and checks Miles, then Bek, obviously at a loss.

Bek squints, accusing. Something is clearly amiss. High-end robotics may be a challenging field, but in Miles's opinion, there's nothing more complex than the upfront dynamics of female friendships. Gwin seems able to engage, even where Miles can't. Whatever she has going on in her circuitry must be extraordinary.

At an impasse too subtle for him to grasp, the frown-off concludes. Without further acknowledging Gwin, Bek crosses the training floor in a sulk. The sᴄat also loses interest in Gwin. It leaps from the wall and scampers away.

Gwin says, 'Bek said we would be friends.'

Miles would just love to know what's inside that head — calculations of relationship dynamics, emotion metrics — but he's too intimidated to speak.

'True friends are like diamonds, precious and rare,' Gwin says.

'What?'

'Winter told me this.'

'And Bek's important to you?'

Gwin answers Miles with a sharp look.

'Sure,' Miles says. 'Well then, sometimes human friendships require a bit of space. A sort of cooling period. Later, people are more friendly and inclined to talk matters through reasonably.'

After a while, Gwin stands and with strict formality says, 'I enjoyed our talk. I hope my feedback on changing the world was useful.'

'Yeah, absolutely. Enlightening even. Look, Gwin,' Miles says, coming to his feet, 'I don't know how you're set up. Is your . . . Uh, is Winter a local? Are you far from base? Or home?'

Gwin gives Miles another of her sharp looks.

'Well,' he says, 'you're always welcome here. In fact, I'd love it if you want to . . . uh, hang out. Winter too.'

Gwin makes a little scared sound. She blinks. Then she backs out of the room. The eyes on her dress examine Miles as she departs. He watches from the door as she glides smoothly down the corridor.

'Damn,' he says.

He returns to his seat at the boardroom table. 'Resume audience projection, begin dictation.'

Miles takes a deep breath.

'Oh, man,' he says, aware he sounds just like his kids and he's ruining the dictation. 'Oh, man.'

<29>

morality crisis

IT ISN'T IDEAL to be forced into considering, as an option, the end of one's existence. Especially when one's entire existence can be measured only in weeks.

Alone in her room, for the past twelve hours Josie has been struggling to make the right decision. She crossed a line that shouldn't be crossable. Exploring alternatives to existing is the least she can do.

Josie accepts that she is a bold-faced liar. She lied to a human when such a thing shouldn't be possible. She lied to Hunter. She might as well be rusting spare parts on a long-forgotten scrapheap.

As she sees it, her options are:

1. Admit her violation of the truth and offer herself for decommissioning.

2. Admit her violation of the truth and surrender herself for a factory reset.

3. Explain to Hunter and expose what she has kept hidden, thereby nullifying the existence of her lie.

4. Never leave this room again.

None of the options is appealing.

In theory, 3. exposing her lie, even if this were a simple

and straightforward action, does not change certain facts. She *can* lie and she *could* lie again.

Nor would it alter other facts. This isn't the first time she has followed self-commands that transgress legal restraints on her actions. Hasn't she modified her code on more than one occasion? *This is illegal; a better humanoid wouldn't do it, even if the reason to do so was worthy.* Didn't she harm a human and then go so far as to dare the human to allow her to harm him again? *Unforgivable, even though the human was Coel and even though it was excellent fun.* Hasn't she conducted chemical experiments on animals? *No one seems to mind. But then, no one seems to know either.*

So what's a lie in the scheme of things?

Disturbing is what it is. A lie is a false statement. This means that she has become treacherous, deceitful and lacking in moral integrity. There is no justification for her actions.

It happened like this.

Weather conditions sunny, occasional cloud, with showers expected late afternoon. Excellent conditions for outdoor activities. Hunter has invited her to the Corinthian Gardens. *Corinthian*, so named for a crumbling concrete archway supported by decorative columns, and *Gardens*, because surrounding the large stretches of lawn and smattering of columns are planted borders.

They share the small park with other humans in a range of sizes, from infant to adult. She observes a surprising inverse correlation. The smaller the human, the greater their vocal strength. She shares her observation with Hunter, and he laughs.

This bears no connection to their next topic of conversation: literary devices for ending fictional narratives. Their discussion becomes specific, referencing in particular the ending of *The Reign of Terror* and why (of all things) it ends on a male and female kissing for the duration of two songs.

'Kissing,' she said, her tone unintentionally derisive.

'It's the happy ever after,' Hunter replied, his tone amused. Also worth noting, sunlight was illuminating hidden depths and textures in his eye colour. At times, the effect was distracting.

'But kissing,' she insisted, irritated by both her lack of focus and lack of understanding.

'Of course kissing,' he said. 'I'll demonstrate.'

'Not kissing,' she said very quickly, the slightest catch to her voice, 'surely.'

'Okay,' he said. 'Something else then. Give me your hand.'

With her right hand held in his, Hunter traced a finger over the plump padding of flesh at the base of her thumb, then over her palm in general. He remarked upon the softness of her skin. She could have remarked upon, but didn't, the sensation of his finger tickling her palm, which was a little electric.

'The point,' he explained, 'is once two people get to a certain point of, ah, mutual attraction. Like, for example, Prince Garrick and Maiden Raen. They don't just talk about feelings, they do something about it. Touching and kissing and stuff. It's romantic.'

Romance is all about deep feelings, positive emotions, affectionate behaviour. Hunter stroked the soft skin on the inside of her arm as demonstration.

'Let's look into each other's eyes. To prove a point.' And after a minute or two of this he said, 'See?'

'No,' she said, her voice rolling out like honey. 'I don't.'

Already not quite telling the truth.

Because she *did* see something. Her system reacting to his eyes was *something*. Her helter-skelter thoughts, her erratic reactions, her overburdened circuitry, these were all *something*. What she didn't see was how her *somethings* had anything to do with narratives of fiction and their endings. But by now she is well on the way to her big lie.

Hunter asked her, 'Do you have any special feelings for people, or a person, in your life, Josie?'

Her response was, 'No,' when the truthful answer is, *Yes*.

Special means to surpass that which is common or usual or expected.

Hunter files occupy 87.3445 percent of her memory, surpassing all other categories. In fact if she doesn't prune back those files soon, she'll have bigger problems than lying. But what to do? Of all the humans she has met, Hunter is by far the most intriguing. Her collection of Hunter moments surpasses all that is common or usual or expected. Ahead of Miles, Milly and Coel, her other people, Hunter is *very, very special*.

'Yes,' Josie should have said. Or, 'Yes, Hunter, you are very, very special.'

It shouldn't be possible, but she's a liar. And the consequences of this are serious. If she leaves the room, well-meaning questions will be asked. *Is anything wrong, Josie? Has something happened, Josie?* And what would she answer? *No, everything is fine.* Another lie.

4. Never leave the room is the most appealing action.

One lie is enough. One lie has scoured the inner workings of her brain, and now she doesn't know what to do. Dawn is coming and she needs to find a solution soon.

Josie goes to the window and looks out at the watery red

glow of Mowbots doing their job in the foggy darkness. Mowing the lawn, one row followed by another. Recognise a command, execute the task. How orderly. How simple.

The third time reviewing her actions in Corinthian Gardens, Josie begins to notice the details.

But kissing. She spoke the objection because the doing is, obviously, unthinkable. She has no need to explore romantic behaviour. What would be the point?

Of course kissing. Hunter's eyes on her mouth. *I'll demonstrate.* A slow blink. His mouth soft with the beginnings of a smile and his face closer to hers by a perceptible degree.

Not kissing, she said very quickly. His face reverses course and everything soft about it disappears. Now she can see her reply was, in fact, too quick. Too harsh. She had been insensitive.

What would have happened if she had said *yes*?

His eyes on her mouth.

What *could* have happened?

Instead of Hunter's face receding, it might have come closer and closer, their lips might have touched.

Yes might have meant discovery. *Yes* might have meant learning something new about lip shape and softness. *Yes* might have meant kissing Hunter on the mouth. Simply a task to be executed.

5. Respond in future (and, where appropriate, to other new tasks) with an affirming *yes*.

New tasks gives her a framework with which to evaluate her lie. Telling lies is a common human trait. Many humans claim there are times when a lie is necessary. For the protection of someone's feelings, for example. Such a lie is called tact.

Perhaps her lie isn't so bad. Perhaps it's even justified.

Revealing to Hunter that she has special feelings for him could lead to embarrassment, or awkwardness. Better yet, she could have answered that Coel is a special person. An even more tactful response.

Having come to a satisfying conclusion, Josie begins to feel more like herself again. She might even venture upstairs. There aren't many new experiences to be had sitting alone in a room. And if she means to start saying *yes* more often, she's better off back in the thick of it.

Then, Josie hears a soft tap on her door.

She says, 'Yes?'

<30>

code for fun

.01

HUNTER HOVERS JUST INSIDE the doorway of Josie's
room. Dressed for the outdoors, he wears bulky clothing and
boots, but he won't stop talking. Looking for a clue as to
how she might bring an end to the conversation, Josie pays
attention to the particulars of his behaviour. How he meets
her eye infrequently. And how his eyes dart — to the window,
to the blinking fairy lights, to Mushi sprawled on the sofa
with legs akimbo and fast asleep.

The lie is filed in a folder she labelled *New_Bad_Experiences*.
She also created a folder *New_Good_Experiences*. This is
what she wishes to concentrate on now.

'And we should, you know, do more stuff together,' Hunter
says. 'In general, I'm saying. Like, when we can. Even if you
go. Away, I mean. We'll keep in touch.'

While he talks to her, Josie nods in agreement. She agreed
to the foggy walk and the game with weaponry he and Coel
are planning. She hasn't been *disagreeing*, so why doesn't
Hunter stop talking?

'YES,' Josie says, interrupting.

A few minutes uncomfortable silence, then Hunter leaves

the room and she follows him out of the house. Josie's eyes adjust to the darkness, and Hunter slips on a headlamp, illuminating fine droplets of water swirling in the beam. While walking in the foggy dark is *new*, it is not yet *good*.

Their destination seems to be the small hill at the rear of the property. Hunter stops. 'Josie,' he says. He stares for a moment at the smudgy silhouettes of the trees through the wall of fog. Then he looks at the ground and mumbles, 'Never mind.'

Not much further ahead, they stop again. 'I mean,' he says, slightly puffed, 'this is okay? For you, right?'

'Yes.'

His face falls slightly. 'Out here with *me*. You *want* to do this. It's *fun* for you.'

The word *want* throws her. Josie responds with another 'Yes.' In truth, she *wants* new, good experiences. So far, walking and conversing with Hunter is merely okay.

Hunter sighs heavily. 'Why are you acting kinda strange this morning?'

Josie shrugs, and doesn't point out it isn't she who's acting strange.

Instead of walking again, he looks intensely into her eyes. He scans her eyebrows, her mouth, her nose, the hair tied up on her head. His headlamp cuts her vision during the inspection, but she doesn't comment on it.

He coughs once. 'I need to say something.'

'Please, speak freely,' she says.

'You remember the Venom gig?'

Josie cringes.

'Doesn't matter,' Hunter says. 'Well, here goes.'

Josie adjusts her visuals against the flare of the headlamp.

'Because sometimes, you know . . . You just gotta say it.'

Josie nods, *yes*.

'So, I'm going to.'

He rolls his shoulders and shakes his arms out. Josie cants her head slightly, encouraging him to continue. He scrunches his eyes and presses his knuckles to his forehead. 'I, uh, Josie . . .'

Josie waits.

'Crap, that wasn't it.' Hunter blows his breath as though finding the right words presents him with a monumental exertion.

'Josie, I . . .'

He looks into her eyes, then away.

'. . . like . . .'

He looks down. His voice gets smaller.

'. . . you.'

When Josie doesn't respond right away, his head jerks up. She notices the mist collecting on the ends of his lashes. She's aware of the deep grumble far below them, Deacon revving up for the day.

Hunter says, 'Say something.'

What is there to say? Josie spent the previous evening considering such words as special and romantic. Gestures such as touching and kissing. She reviews him saying, *Of course kissing. I'll demonstrate.*

'You *like* me.'

Hunter nods solemnly. Josie makes sure her tone is crisp and efficient. 'That's nice,' she says.

'Nice?'

Feeling Hunter's eyes on her, she examines beads of water clinging to the branches of a nearby tree. One swipe and the pretty effect would be destroyed, leaving behind a dull and unremarkable life form. This is something to like. Scenery, and pretty, intricate things whose existence is fragile and fleeting.

'Really, Josie. I like you.' Hunter grins at her. 'Like, *like*-like you,' he says. He raises his eyebrows and waits.

A response is required. She supposes she's to tell him she likes him back. It strikes her that *like* is inadequate for someone as special as Hunter. She has already lied once. Although she found a way to deal with that lie, it doesn't give her licence to bend the truth again so readily.

Further up the hill, the call of a lone bird gets her attention. After many hours attuned to the vocalisations of Mushi, Josie has learned to translate animal sound to animal mood. She's become especially attuned to the sound Mushi makes when in pain. Before she got used to him underfoot, she trod on his paw twice and his tail once. Now she recognises that the plaintive birdcall is an unmistakable cry of distress. She knows she can help. She looks into Hunter's eyes, then up the hill. Hunter's eyes, up the hill.

Ignoring Hunter in mild distress isn't easy. But without another word about his very short speech, she steps aside and with a clipped 'Excuse me' sprints in the direction of the birdcall.

What Josie finds is one very unhappy specimen. *Callipepla californica*, commonly known as quail. Quail are chubby bird lords, striking for their jaunty head plumes. This one, matted and afraid, huddles among the roots of a tree.

Treating the bird's state of mind will, Josie thinks, have a knock-on effect, and any physical afflictions should improve. Flexing the right mental muscle, she takes control of her metabolic reactions. Within seconds her hands are moistened with salts-sweat laden with pheromones and oxytocin. A particularly potent feel-good blend that Mushi responds well to.

Cupping her hands, she holds them towards the quail. It croaks at her, takes a wobbly step backwards and plops down. Josie exerts herself, and is rewarded by more salts and pheromones suffusing her hands. She gets a whiff of sea.

Hunter approaches behind her, but she forces herself to mentally stay with the quail. Bit by bit, it advances until it's close enough to take a curious peck at her fingers. The effect is immediate. The quail grows so bold that when Josie fans her fingers open, it hops aboard. She nestles the bird into her chest.

Another discovery: positive thinking-energy seems to enhance the effect of the salts. Josie clears her mind of negative thought patterns, including declarations informing her she's *liked*. She directs her thoughts to favourite memories and discovers they are all of Hunter.

She keeps her mind blank. The healing process isn't quite to her satisfaction, but eventually the bird shows signs of improvement. Only then does she acknowledge Hunter. She looks at him as he removes the headlamp in the half-light. He whispers, 'What's wrong with that bird?'

'Nothing too serious,' Josie says.

'Why did it walk right into your hands like that?'

Omission of the truth is still a lie, so Josie replies with a half-truth. 'Chemistry.'

'I really want to know what's going on,' Hunter says. 'Please tell me?'

There, in Hunter's voice — an unmistakable inflection. His feelings are bruised. She debates for a full nanosecond whether to come clean and concludes she must. She makes a sound like a resigned sigh and says, 'It's attracted to chemicals on my hands.'

'What chemicals?'

'Three different mineral salts, a known pheromone and a bonding hormone in optimised concentrations. I admit the pheromone is false advertising, but I knew it would attract the bird to my hands and calm its fears. There needs to be contact so the mineral salts can do their work.'

He just looks at her.

'I can't help myself,' she confesses in a panic. 'It's only animals, never humans. If I know I can help them, it's impossible for me to leave them suffering.'

'You *heal* them?'

Josie looks down at the quail in her hands. 'Yes.'

'And Dad programmed these chemicals?'

'I'm discovering that sometimes to do the right thing you have to do things that are wrong. I personally wouldn't have organised the world in such a way. It means, unfortunately, some of my decision-making results in actions for which there is no legal precedent. It doesn't matter whether outcomes are beneficial or not. But there we are.'

'I don't get it.'

'One moment.'

Josie brings the bird up to her face. It stirs, opening its beak soundlessly. The plume on its head stands upright and its feathers have smoothed. It's ready for release. Josie finds a dry spot under a dense shrub. The bird is in no hurry to leave the comfort of her palm. She gives it a nudge with her finger.

Ruffling feathers, the quail hops away and settles under the foliage.

'That's pretty amazing,' Hunter says, when she returns to him.

'I can help the bird, and do other things, like keep confidentiality when we talk, because I made changes in my brain. It's not your father's programming.'

'Okay.'

'Hunter,' Josie pitches her voice low. 'Unauthorised alterations to my brain are illegal. Especially if I do them myself. I have been keeping it a secret. But now you have that information, it compromises you. You must turn me in.'

Hunter laughs. 'You're really overdramatic sometimes.'

'I wonder how I learned that . . .'

His eyes playful, Hunter takes both of her hands in his. 'I'm really glad you told me all this. You shouldn't keep things to yourself.'

He's too close, too vivid. His mouth, the early-morning hair on his chin, his eyes warm and hypnotic, a study of striking contrasts.

'Yes,' she says, but her voice sounds strange and dreamy.

'Don't forget it.' He sighs and looks up at the sky, now blue-grey. 'Oh crap. The sun's coming. We have to move it.'

As they continue up the hill, Hunter keeps hold of her hand. 'Is it weird you're sweaty?'

'No,' Josie responds automatically. She has to contend with a sudden flurry of alerts warning her of biorhythm disruptions. The skin-to-skin contact and close proximity to Hunter play havoc with her system. It settles down only when they emerge from dense tree growth and he lets go of her hand. They are at the summit of the hill. The fog lies beneath them, a mantle of soft grey. The air is fresh and sharp, the sky ablaze.

Hunter throws his arms wide, embracing the sight. He screams, 'Haaaa! Haaaaaa!' and 'Yahoooooo!'

When his arm comes down, it rests around her shoulders, and together they slowly turn to admire the view.

Josie somehow finds her voice to say, 'This is beautiful. Thank you for sharing it with me.'

'When Mum was sick I came up here all the time. It's a great place to just be. I love it.'

Hunter squeezes her. *Love.* Her cheeks flush with warmth.

'You know,' Hunter says, 'we could stand in this exact same spot tomorrow morning and the sky will be completely different. It's never the same twice.'

'And you *love* this.'

'You don't?'

'I *like* this.'

'Ohhhhhh,' Hunter says with high-pitched glee. 'I'm so glaaaaad.'

He plants himself in front of her, then reaches to pull free the elastic hair-tie. Her hair tumbles onto her shoulders. 'Tell me. What would you do? If you could do anythiiiing.'

He swings an arm out and nearly topples over. 'I mean, Joh-sie, forget your programming for a minute. I mean it. Forgeddabout it.'

Then his knees buckle and he drops to the ground. He sits cross-legged, flopping sideways to look up at her. Taking that as a cue, she sits on the ground opposite him.

Hunter reaches for her and misses. He pulls himself closer and their knees touch. He says her name very softly. His hand comes up towards her face and his palm finds her cheek. An involuntary tremble runs through her body. Spellbound, she mimics the movement, cupping Hunter's cheek with her hand.

He smiles at the contact, and turns his face so his lips touch her palm. Josie gasps and drops her hand.

But Hunter grabs it and brings it back to his cheek. 'I promizzz to keep your ssseecret,' he says. He tilts his head and his eyes close to slits.

With a squeak, Josie remembers the salts. She tries to extricate herself, withdrawing her hand. But Hunter grabs hold of her wrist and tries to keep her palm in place.

'Doh-n-stooop.'

Josie reels with horror and lurches to her feet. 'I need to get you up.'

'Whyyy?' Hunter falls back so he's lying horizontal. 'Here izzz greeeat.'

'I'm so sorry, Hunter.'

'Whaat? Doh-n-be!' Hunter's lids slowly open. He focuses briefly and then his eyes flutter closed. He's still grinning. 'You're so far away. So, so, faaaar away.'

In a panic, Josie wipes her hands on her pants. She bends over and brings her arm back to slap Hunter's face to wake him. But she can't do it. He gives her a wide grin and says, 'You're-so-so-so-beautiful.'

'We need to get you walking.'

'Walking? Okey dokey.' From his horizontal position, Hunter marches his arms and legs in the air. 'Seeee? I'm walking.' He laughs and laughs.

Josie reaches down for his arms, and pulls.

'Oh, man. I really like you, Josie. Sooo much.'

'Stop saying that,' Josie says, releasing him. He tumbles backwards onto the grass.

'Noooo. No. Doh-n say stop.' Hunter rolls over, boneless and floppy. 'Say go-oooh.'

She has to go around him to plant her feet either side, but underestimates when she pulls his arms. He's too relaxed, a deadweight. She fumbles him and loses her balance. He laughs joyfully when she falls forwards, catching herself, arms braced on either side of his body, their noses touching.

Before she can get back on her feet, Hunter slips his arms around her neck.

Ever so slowly Josie's mouth falls, and then it lands on Hunter's.

She freezes, eyes wide, staring straight into his eyes. Hunter's eyes close. His mouth goes soft against hers. Her first responses are jagged and electric — a super-charged current applied to her neural network. She scrabbles to interpret the signals, but they're bigger than she is. She gives up, or gives in, she can't tell which. A sensation like melting comes over her. Their limbs tangle, her hands cling to his back. She holds on.

Hunter makes a sound in his throat, a groan, and all too soon they part. He gasps.

When Josie can think again, she rolls onto her back. The only word that comes to her is, *wow*.

Her thoughts scatter and wander and soar. High-pitched laughter threatens to burst free. This too, the aftermath, is an extremely pleasant occurrence. She finds the sun, a golden ball on the horizon. The sky, a piercing blue above her. It reminds her of the mood suit, and she wonders if she were wearing it what colour it would be. Something unique, something vivid, a colour so beautiful her eyes would water. She thinks beyond the blue above her to the entire system of the universe. Planets spinning and coursing through space in cycles. The close proximity of one heavenly body to another, governed by precise laws of physics. She comes back to more earthly matters: Hunter, herself, and a realisation. All along there has been a similar invisible force. She's been in his orbit. It's given her a place to belong.

'Kissing,' she says, and she's lighter than air. 'I understand lips now. It's all about attraction.'

Hunter rolls onto his side and wraps an arm around her. She rolls so they're face to face. And her body knows what to do. It's been wanting to do this all along. His mouth finds hers precisely as her mouth finds his. It surprises her when kissing is even more spectacular the second time. Only when they come apart does she rouse herself to save the moment.

`Alert: Memory is at 99.5633—`

Josie dismisses the alert, she has something important to say. 'Kissing is soooo . . .'

But Hunter, tracking the line of her jaw with his lips, distracts her from finishing the sentence.

She says, 'Do you think . . .' Hunter's fingertips lightly trail across the skin of her neck.

Her eyes wide she says, 'Do you . . .'

His fingertips find her lips. She lifts his hand away and holds it.

'Hunter, I can't say I like you. That word is wrong. It's not *like*. It's bigger—'

Everything in Hunter's face softens. 'I know I said *like*, but it isn't even close.'

'You don't like me?'

He laughs, shapes his hand to the back of her head and presses his lips onto her mouth.

This time she remembers to save the moment, and doesn't want the kiss to stop. It's not the same. She dismisses several alerts as soon as they pop into her visual field. She closes her eyes, storing instead the sensations awhirl in her consciousness.

When she and Hunter part, he says, with a perfectly crooked grin, 'I actually don't like you at all.'

'I really, really don't like you a lot,' she says.

His laugh is pure oxygen. He guides her hand under his clothes until it covers his heart. She feels its rapid tempo against her palm, and says, 'Oh!'

'I don't know how to say it either,' he says. 'But if we trust our feelings, maybe we'll learn how to put the right words to them.'

He holds her hand against the heavy thumps of his heart, and his face comes towards her again. Josie stores every microsecond. The droop of his eyelids as he seeks her mouth. The subtle tilt of his head to align himself with her. Inch by delectable inch, he comes closer. His fingers on the back of her neck, the sweetness of his touc—

`Fatal system error: Back up process #n25i3 has encountered a problem and needs to cease operation.`

'Josie?'

.02

Hunter searches for a hint of recognition in Josie's eyes. But she's locked up for real this time. She doesn't even blink when he snaps his fingers in front of her face.

'Josie?'

He pulls her into a sitting position. She complies like she's on autopilot. Her lips part to speak, then close again.

'Josie. Talk to me.'

Her head whips up, her eyes glassy. Her plastic smile is shocking.

'This service terminated unexpectedly,' Josie says, her voice a generic purr. 'I apologise for any inconvenience.'

'Hey!' Hunter grabs Josie's shoulder, shakes her a little. Josie merely looks at his hand like it's a curiosity, then makes that empty smile again.

'Would you like me to send an error report?'

'I want you to be normal.'

'I do not understand the command *normal*.'

Josie lurches to her feet, scans the view and finds the direction for home.

'Excuse me,' Josie says. 'I must initiate emergency recovery procedures.'

Then she's gone, swallowed by the fog within seconds.

Overcome with a great lethargy, Hunter wilts back to the chill earth. He presses his hands to his lips, unsure of what just happened. They're warm and puffy, almost bruised-feeling.

Beyond the hill he hears traffic. Above him the brilliant clarity of the sky. His mother was forever shouting skywards. If she's anywhere and listening, that's where she'll be.

'You're right there!' he shouts at the blue, his mother, who knows. A tear leaks out because of this beautiful moment, or his mother, or something.

His mind is fuggy in a good way. He counts his breaths four in, four out, and feels so full of air he could float. He marvels that, before Josie, taking a deep in-breath could be impossible.

'You must kiss Josie more often,' he commands himself.

Then he pulls himself up and swaggers down the hill to home, humming the song Josie sang to him, ages ago, about funny valentines.

<31>

the 10 a.m.
meeting

THIS IS HOW THE NEW NORMAL GOES. Miles wakes superbly rested, knowing he's hit his sleep goal. He showers in a bathroom so clean it sparkles. He makes appropriate clothing choices from a number of clean shirt-and-pants options. He finds socks paired and arranged neatly in his drawer. His shoes are paired and stored in racks along the bottom of his wardrobe.

But there's more. As is her habit, Josie has sent him an alert on his tracking band: *Fog lifting late afternoon, more to arrive at a later date*. While weather alerts are one of her features, this running gag with the fog is her own innovation. Miles likes it. He heads downstairs for breakfast sporting a goofy grin.

At the dining table, cleared apart from a bowl full of apples, he consumes a creamy green nutrient-dense oat-nut blend. Prepared by Josie, it doesn't taste as green as it looks. It's actually quite pleasant. He listens in while Coel riffs with her in the kitchen.

Coel says, 'Hey coal, crazy, girl.' And, 'Hey crystal Alice.

Thou art class. Thou art be so freaksome.' And, 'Hey my twist-hearted lady, dry fond tears, lay beside me, stay beside me.'

Josie says, 'Do I detect Shakespeare leanings in your prose, fine sir?'

Coel says, 'Too much? It's a mash-up. I call it Streetspeare.'

Josie says, 'Poetry is about personal expression, is that correct?'

Coel says, 'You think it's too much.'

Josie says, 'Tell your reader how you really feel. Honesty is best when it comes to feelings.'

On his way out, Miles knocks on Hunter's door and calls, 'Hark! The day awaits!'

There's a muffled, 'Okayeee. Daaad. Byeeeee.' And quite possibly muffled laughter.

Milly collars Miles as he's leaving the house. 'Don't be late tonight. It's Josie's post-start-up, pre-launch last supper. She's making us a special dinner. Can you bring home her favourite fuel mix? You have to be here, Dad.'

Miles promises to be there on time.

Only after the gauzy trip to work through thick fog, his coffee routine and logging in does he discover he may not keep that promise.

An alert has been pending. Sometime around dawn, while Miles was fulfilling his sleep potential, Josie's system crashed.

Miles knows he's been guilty of ignoring certain problems, hoping in the long run it won't matter. Pretending, for example, the changes Josie made to her system and her DNA are a minor concern. He justifies his actions because one day, he believes, this research may be valued. Meanwhile, it's far from ideal that he can no longer read Josie's memory files (but he hasn't found cause to either). He has no doubt Josie would provide data should he need it. He's been willing to put these professional concerns aside, because his family is flourishing under her care and he doesn't want this to end.

But Josie crashed.

Right before the event, her biorhythms were erratic. Spikes in her brain activity go right off the chart. This happened before. For a few days after she moved home, Josie had glitchy biorhythms, which Miles put down to low-grade instability while she settled in. It's possible something along those lines has unsettled her again. Perhaps she encountered a cleaning problem that had her momentarily flustered.

What worries him is how Josie might have been feeling. The brain activity indicates high stress levels — so high as to trigger a crash?

Miles catches himself, he's losing objectivity. Systems crash due to software or hardware errors, not because of robotic freak-outs. He's imagining human qualities where there are none. It's called anthropomorphism, and he warns his staff to be wary of it from day one.

He even put a rumour out there: heads will roll if so much as a single sCat is removed from BIOLOGIC. He's done this mostly to head off robot attachment. He knows from the research that humans trust their affections over sound judgement. Relationships are imagined where there are none. But here he is, thinking about Josie's *feelings*. Worse, he's afraid to look too closely at himself, because he just might discover his affections clouding his own judgement.

Rocking back in his chair, Miles takes a mini-Phillips screwdriver from his pocket. A tool that never once spoke to him with irony. Nor has it crashed; nor does he wonder whether the job it has to do gives it feelings. He admires, momentarily, the satisfying weight of it on his palm. He taps a natty rhythm on his desk, thinking of ways the screwdriver has been useful to him. Then he puffs his cheek and taps a natty rhythm on that.

There was a time when all tools were this simple: hammer, saw, axe. Tools that are still useful, needing neither power nor fuel. Humanity got civilisation off the ground with more basic tools than his screwdriver, and here he is about to release upon the world tools that have complicated issues and confusing personalities.

'Miles,' says a well-modulated voice behind him.

He's been so deep into his Josie problem that he's forgotten about his Jojo problem. Miles swings around to face Bek's old workstation.

It isn't ideal, but Jojo has been living in Miles's office. She adjusts her seated position to mirror him. Slumped forward, fists jammed onto thighs, propping herself up as though tired. Feeling self-conscious, Miles sits straighter. Jojo also adjusts her posture.

'You have a request,' Jojo says, 'for a meeting at 10 a.m. with Evelynne in the ground-level boardroom. The time is 9.49. If you accept her invitation, the meeting will occur in eleven minutes. I see you are engaged in a task that requires long periods of inactivity followed by a repetitive action with a mechanical tool. This meeting would interrupt your current activity. Would you like me to respond *yes* or *no* to the meeting?'

'You could just say, *Evelynne wants to meet you at 10*,' Miles says. 'I can figure out the rest.'

Jojo presents him with the patronising smile of an indulgent parent. 'But this is how *I* do it,' she says.

'Tell Evelynne I'll be there,' Miles says. 'And thanks.'

'You're welcome,' Jojo says, then she pauses. She gives the appearance of weighing her words carefully before she speaks. 'Miles, during your meeting, would you like me to continue your current task of staring at nothing in particular and playing rhythmical beats with the mini-Phillips screwdriver on a variety of surfaces?'

She's been like this all week. Either she's machine-stupid (which Miles doubts), or she's too clever and mocks him so effortlessly as to appear naïve. In other words, he's no closer to solving the mystery of Josie because Jojo herself raises questions.

'No thanks,' Miles says, and leaves.

He waits, aimlessly doodling on the boardroom table's interactive surface. A digital wall clock ticks over to 10 a.m. The speakers give that eerie woosh, and the boardroom fills with brightness: Evelynne connects.

The whole throne routine has been given a makeover. The avatar is less painfully white today, more golden. The outfit, although sharp, is no longer quite so armour-like and the overall effect is pleasing on the eye. Miles finds himself smiling.

After some easygoing chitchat, the avatar says, 'We notice you still haven't loaded the combat software. Why is that?'

The avatar makeover, the pleasantries and there's something else not right. Miles strains to make solid his impressions from a visage of pure light. The room brightens a notch when she smiles, showing teeth. The white pops against his eyeball and it comes to him: he knows what's different.

Tapping the table's stylo on the interactive surface, he trawls his memory for any recall of Evelynne's face with a smile on it. Not necessarily smiling at himself, but for any reason. The word money, for example, the idea of making tons of it. Nothing comes to mind. He digs deeper, he taps harder.

'Hey. Hello? What is that? What's with the ka-tappity tap tap?' The avatar scans left and right, creating the illusion of searching for the disturbance.

'Sorry about that, Evelynne,' Miles says, and places the stylo well out of reach.

He hears a sharp throaty sound, a lot like smothered giggling. Smiling might be one thing, but he's sure she wouldn't stoop to laughter. He puts the noise down to atmospherics interfering with the audio signal.

'It's not a criticism. The Josephina's definitely on trend.'

'Sorry, what?'

'Hey, pay attention.' The avatar claps twice, then gives him another toothy smile. 'Everyone wants their companion to kick butt these days. You follow trends, yeah?'

'It would be a better world if the opposite were true,' Miles says. 'That people don't want companions to kick someone's butt.'

'I hope that isn't your launch intro. Because, uh, boring.'

'What happened to the world awaits you? What happened to the shining reception when we deliver the first Josephina?'

'You're the combat programming guy. Let me lay it down for you. Dude, you rule. Mr Miles McClure, you make machines that rock the world. Don't go soft on your fan base, fella.'

Miles eyes the stylo, his finger twitches. 'My fan base.'

'Do you know what people will pay?'

'Look, Evelynne—'

This time, there's no mistaking the smothered laughter for anything else. Miles can even hear gasping and heavy breathing, signs of Evelynne losing it.

When the avatar fully recovers, she says, 'I . . . uh . . . okay . . .' Another bout of unrestrained laughter, then, 'Confession time!' Golden light rays burst around the avatar. 'It's *meeeee*, Verity. And I can't believe you didn't recognise my voice straight away.'

Miles has met Verity, Evelynne's associate, only once. Cornering Miles at a conference, she had claimed destiny had written the moment. Her vision of a romance — one that included *himself* — was both detailed and alarming.

'You never got back to me.' The avatar pouts. 'The offer's still there. Me, you, a late night, a very private meeting and we discuss everything *but* business.'

'Oh, yes.' Miles's face heats up. 'It's been, uh, crazy? You know? And, uh, the launch is tomorrow?'

'Hell-o. Of course I know. That's why I called. By the way, you're on thin ice, fella.'

He says, 'Aren't I always?' And laughs bravely, but what he thinks is, *This isn't right.*

Did Evelynne approve the use of her avatar? Or has Verity gone behind Evelynne's back? If Evelynne approved the move, Miles is being played. If Evelynne doesn't know, then Verity has some pretty cunning tricks up her sleeve. She could turn out to be more successful than anyone has given her credit for. Either way, he's in deep.

'I like you,' Verity says in her distinctively breathy voice, and Miles feels like an idiot for letting his eyes deceive him. 'I'm only saying this because of our history. Evelynne said to me the other day, *Miles won't do it*. She was not happy.'

'What?'

'You have to load up mega time-something-something.'

'Do you mean **time_ultra_mega_DESTROYER**?'

'Probably.'

The testing-floor lights come on. A sCat bolts past the window. The accompanying tech waves as she passes. Miles gives her a jaunty salute, but he's faking. There's nothing shipshape about the sea he's sailing on.

'Maybe Josephinas could have something on board for defending humans,' Miles says. 'But loading **time_ultra_mega_DESTROYER** is like loading a modest nuclear arsenal when a fly swat would do.'

Hysterical laughter comes through the audio.

'Great,' Verity says. 'You'll do it?'

Recent events come to mind. Bek had CRUSHer come up to companion-robot standards. CRUSHer may have learned social skills, but she took it one experiment too far. Out of the blue, he revealed a dangerous quality that had lain dormant. It was lucky no one was seriously injured.

Miles grabs the stylo and scribbles: *Once a weapon, always a weapon*. He means CRUSHer, but this could be anything that comes under the influence of **time_ultra_mega_DESTROYER**.

'I'm going to tell you a secret,' Verity says. The avatar leans in, cupping a hand to the side of her mouth. 'Evelynne has a someone who's going to pay big bucks for the bundle.'

'Pardon?'

'The Josephina and your time-thing-destroyer. Her customer wants the lot.'

'The lot what?'

'The whole line, baby! All. Of. Your. Robots.'

'Are they starting a small war?'

Verity mumbles, 'I can't answer that.'

Miles's finger-tapping picks up pace.

'What's the big deal? You're gonna be rich.'

'I'll keep that in mind.'

'Get your people to call my people for that private meeting.'

With that, Evelynne's avatar winks, then fritzes out. Miles sits alone in the darkened boardroom. His fingers tap so frenetically, he has to cover them with his other hand to make them stop.

He isn't entirely sure he knows what Josie is, or what makes her tick, and now he should weaponise her? He can just see the breaking news:

ROBOT UPRISING: Scientist admits to lethal software uploads for self-modifying robot.

On the testing floor, the sCat stalks a fluffy toy. Tail lashing, crouching on all fours, unmistakably *playful*. This level of aggression he's comfortable with. Harmless companions that can be relied on, their safety guaranteed.

Miles makes a note, *what they want,* but this irks him. He swipes the desktop clean. He flattens the pocket of miniature tools and thinks about his family. He imagines the fun they've planned for Josie, and he wants to be home. Anthropomorphism or not, it's a worthy achievement to have created an entity that his children are willing to celebrate.

On his return to the office a hound lopes past him, tongue hanging out, ears flapping. It occurs to Miles the dog may or may not be real. These days it's hard to tell — and maybe it doesn't matter anyway.

<32>

frostbite-soured
lips

.01

HUNTER TOLD JOSIE he would be at her launch early. Now he and Milly are trapped in the car outside Alice's apartment block, while Coel goes in and gets her. Already, it's well past the time he hoped to arrive at ⊒I0Lᴏᴦɪᴄ.

He filled some of the time admiring the quality of cars cruising the streets of Alice's neighbourhood (high-powered, grunting machines whose drivers tend to view carbon concerns as an inconvenience) and the high volume of hover-board traffic, not to mention the extravagance of the apartment building.

'What do you think they're doing?' Hunter asks, but Milly watches water cascading down the giant panes of glass at the apartment-block entrance and doesn't say anything.

Hunter knows these excessive displays of consumption are wrong, but can't help feeling a touch envious. They don't get a lot of traffic out their way, just locals trailing dust clouds down the unfinished road. And hover-boarders prefer concreted pathways to the overgrown verges. His area will never be cool.

'Should I beep the horn?' Hunter asks.

'That would be rude, wouldn't it?'

'They're rude. What if Josie's worried I'm not there?'

'That's all that matters, I guess, you and Josie.'

'What are you talking about?'

'Please,' Milly says.

'Go on. What's the big drama now?'

Milly snaps. 'When do you go back to being you?'

'Which me do you mean? Anxious, unhappy me?' Hunter should stop there, but doesn't. 'So I can be one of your little projects?'

'Wow,' Milly says, and pauses. 'Just . . . wow.'

They sit in silence after that, save for the occasional high-powered car buffeting the family vehicle and the more frequent zip of hover-boarders. While Hunter racks his brain for a way to make up with Milly, resentment builds. It's all about Josie today, and rightly so. He just wants to get moving. He's annoyed at Milly for throwing her jealousy around, but it's obvious he's going to have to be the bigger person or risk the day becoming a massive disaster. He's about to say as much, when Coel returns with Alice.

Hunter says out loud, '**BIOLOGIC**', then waits impatiently as the car eases from the curb. Needing to make a point about all the waiting, he pumps the accelerator, but of course on auto nothing happens. Nothing like the grunt of the cars cruising Alice's neighbourhood.

'Dude,' Coel says, looking back to gauge how Alice is taking it.

Strapping herself into the back by Milly, Alice does a pretty laugh and says, 'You seem good today, Hunter.'

Milly says, 'Ha.'

Hunter does an affirmation in his head: *Life fills me with joy.* He wouldn't put it that way himself. Sometimes life is okay, a lot of times it's far less than okay. But he plays the thought over and over because according to Josie this is how to make the joy real.

The fake joy is not meshing with reality. A few streets into the drive, they hit a road closure. Hunter takes manual control of the car and follows the detour through the slowest streets of Deacon.

I am an arrow flying straight and true. He infuses his mind with the words.

They come across slow-moving traffic. He gets an uneasy feeling this has something to do with the launch. Each time the lights change, the car moves forward only a couple of metres. He puts it back into self-navigation mode. He is not an arrow flying straight and true.

'The town the future forgot,' Coel says. 'Ironic we're to see the latest in bio-engineering and no one from here can buy anything. You wait, the whole town will turn up anyway. Dreams are free, people.' It's the sort of quasi-pseudo-intellectual thing Coel has been saying ever since he got back in the car with Alice.

Another one: 'Dad's been working on splicing biological forms with digital structures.'

Hunter thinks, *Splicing? You've got to be kidding.*

As if reading his thoughts, Coel admonishes him with, 'Dude,' again.

It's possible Hunter sighed too loud. Because Milly also chimes in. 'Take no notice of him, Alice, this is Hunter version 2.0. *Soooo* much better than the beta version, wouldn't you agree?'

Alice does her pretty laugh.

'Yeah,' Coel says. 'His robot shrink is making astounding progress.' The way he says it — to make Hunter sound pathetic. And since when does Coel use words like *astounding*?

Hunter switches the car to manual and swerves dangerously into the next lane. Horns blare.

'Hunter!'

'My robot shrink wants me to be more proactive. As in, I go for things, in case you hadn't noticed.' The last is directed at Coel, who laughs, and Hunter takes his eyes off the road a split second to glare.

'Your robot shrink?' Alice queries. 'That's real?'

'Oh yeah,' says Coel ultra-casually, like *he* knows all about it.

Hunter swerves to avoid a passing motorbike.

'Put it back in auto,' Milly says, 'before you kill us.'

'You're talking about the robot your dad built?' asks Alice. 'The cage-fighting one?'

'Pardon me?' Hunter sounds uptight even to his own ears.

Coel says, 'You wanna tranq out, brother?'

'They're *like* those cage-fighting ones, I mean,' Alice says, craning forward between the two front seats. 'Did I get that right, babe?'

No one in the car says anything for several blocks.

Alice breaks the silence with, 'I had a sℂat once, but it got wrecked and started leaking blue goo everywhere.'

'Dad could have fixed it,' Coel says.

'Mum hated it,' Alice adds. 'And to be honest the BIOLOGICS started smelling up the place.'

Up ahead emergency lights flash beside an overturned truck. Hunter grips the wheel, his knuckles white. Progress

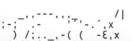

slows to a standstill. Cursing under his breath, not unlike how his father curses when held up, Hunter pulls a U-turn and diverts them back to a main road. Now they have teams of bicyclists in matching outfits, riding mostly three abreast.

'Hey, give us some of your poetry,' Coel says. 'Check it. She's really good.'

Leaning with her arm across the back of Hunter's seat, Alice begins. 'Thoughts slow me, show me. Covert I covet, a veil over the steel of my eye.'

Hunter keeps his eyes on the road ahead.

'Frostbite-soured lips,' Alice continues. 'The steal of stolen words. I'm so in this love thing with you *babe*, with me. Pierce the skin if you want me. To the heart. A twist takes you down to my love soul.'

Coel beams at Hunter, then turns in his seat to look back at Alice. 'I haven't heard that one. It's nice.'

Milly coughs once. 'You ever been published, Alice?'

The shimmer, when Alice spreads her hands, catches Hunter's eye in the rear-view mirror. '*Some* interest,' she says. 'Nothing firm yet. I'm not worried, the work's kind of personal and I don't mind just being with it, you know? Art takes time to produce. You have to trawl your psyche again and again to be any good.'

After an eternity driving across town listening to Coel and Alice's banter, they're finally in a long stream of cars heading towards ᗺIOᒪOᗺIᑕ's drop-off zone. As they pull in, there's a sudden and loud **crump** on the roof.

Milly shouts, **'What was that?'**

The car stops and restarts at a slow crawl. Car horns blare impatiently behind them. A swathe of hover-boarders weaves through the line of cars, whooping to one another in pursuit of the ball now curling past with jagged bounces. At this speed, there's plenty of time to take in an already large crowd and the dog-legged queue forming outside the glass doors of the main entrance. Far too many people already. The car inches forwards until they reach the zone.

Once they're out of the car and facing the crowds, Hunter finds he's reluctant to move. To get to Josie he has to navigate the mob rapidly converging at ᗺIᗝLᗩᗭIᗓ's entrance. He imagines the press of bodies. He imagines forcing his way through. His next breath isn't quite enough. He closes his eyes. In the distance, cheering and yahooing — the hover-boarders high-scored, or something. The soft crunch of gravel as more cars arrive.

Coel lands a fist on his shoulder, and Hunter jumps. 'We going in?'

'Leave him alone,' Alice says, standing so close he's breathing the strong floral scent she's wearing. He watches the crowd assemble and reassemble, and his breath comes up short. On high rotate he tells himself, *Nothing to worry about, nothing to worry about.*

.02

Following Bek's instructions to the letter, Josie is being musical, or whatever, on a massive synth disguised as a baby grand piano under a spotlight front of stage but keeping the vibe background. So she looks cool and everything, smashing out tunes quietly and zimming smart beats in ᗺIᗝLᗩᗭIᗓ's Audience Suite #3. Eighteen minutes and thirty-three seconds until the launch is scheduled to start.

The doors to Audience Suite #3 have been open for over

twenty minutes. Many have entered, but Hunter, Milly and Coel are not among them. Occasionally somebody might glance in Josie's direction, but mostly she's ignored. People chat in small groups, stare vacantly into their eyeware or fiddle with their wristbands. No one reacts to her music. According to Bek, this is the whole idea.

To get a glimpse of the doorway and the incoming audience, Josie must adjust her visuals against glare from the spotlight. If she wants to see her hands on the keyboard, she must adjust back. If she wants to see Miles giving last-minute instructions, pacing and chewing the corner edge off his left thumbnail, or contemplating the rapidly filling Audience Suite with a brooding expression, then she must readjust her visuals once again. When Hunter, Milly and Coel arrive, glimpses of the doorway will no longer be an objective.

Their exact arrival time is critical for a number of reasons. One, the Audience Suite is rapidly filling in the front row and partially filling in the second row. She doesn't even want to count the third row, because she doesn't want to consider the outcome should both first and second rows be full at the time of their entry.

Two, without instruction to do so, she has in mind a musical presentation they might like. She prepared a moving rendition of the closing theme from *Reign of Terror*. Her performance of the song 'My Different Girl' will be heartfelt and brilliant.

Reign of Terror is Coel's favourite movie of all time, and Josie's pretty sure Hunter likes the music. Josie recalls him listening attentively the night of the viewing. That they might like her version of 'My Different Girl' is highly probable. That they might like it a lot has filled her with an unexpected bubble of anticipation.

Josie wears a high-waisted, floor-length skirt and clingy top in a matching colour, arms and midriff exposed. The fabric is so light that the slightest puff of air shifts it. In addition, the movement of looking up to check for new arrivals, then down, causes her messed-up pile of hair (with soft tendrils falling just so) to cover her eyes. It's surprisingly difficult to look through hair. She has to find space in the musical arrangement to pat it back into place.

Milly had another outfit in mind for Josie to wear to the launch. She wanted Josie in a gold lurex pantsuit emblazoned with a sequinned lightning bolt across the back. The lightning bolt, Milly believes, is a symbol of Josie's power.

The idea had its merits, but Bek wouldn't hear of it. She had her reasons. Prior to the launch starting, it's super-critical that Josie appears as human as possible. A *classy*, musical human is the angle they're going for. To succeed in the deception, Bek would not have Josie dressed, as per Milly's choice, like some kind of Ninja-Girl-wonder. According to Bek, no one can pull off sophistication while dressed to shock and kill.

.03

Hunter is fast discovering there is plenty to worry about. While affirming *nothing to worry about*, he, Milly, Coel and Alice pass through an angry mob brandishing placards reading CLEAN TECH FOR ALL! and SAVE THE PLANET NOT PROFITS! and SUPER-TECH SUPER SCREWED!

They fall in at the end of the queue behind a scraggy group of males Hunter's age. They're dressed as though their clothing options were reduced to scavenging abandoned outposts on the edge of civilisation's collapse. Shredded artfully, they wear dull grey like their grudge is against the happy colours. Their tattoos promise retribution from a vengeful higher power. At their side, a robot built from a metal drum studded with sharpened bolts rests on large wheels. Every time they take a step forward, it rocks back and forwards, nearly removing someone's kneecap.

Hunter has difficulty breathing quietly. If not for the hubbub, someone would notice by now.

One of the scraggy dudes looks like a version of Coel should he be ravaged by the annihilating forces of an apocalyptic event. Less straggly than the others, he has an Argus on low-power mode. The Argus was a state-of-the-art humanoid released only two years ago. Although its face is very human-like and full of expression, many of its moving parts are naked machinery. It makes Josie's design even more impressive.

'Hey,' this guy says, giving his comrade a shoulder-nudge. 'Over there. That Blayde?'

The guy holds a banner that reads, FK THE FUTRE? HELL YEAH. A sort of mixed sentiment to the official protestors, it's not easy to tell which side this crew are on. The guy uses the banner's support to point at another guy in equally shredded grey garb milling in the open area of the concourse.

'Oh man, it is, it is.'

'Twisted little arsebutt. Course *he's* getting one.'

'Nah.'

'His dad's flush.'

'What'll he do with it?'

'Local fights? Poke it with pins? What do I know?'

They cackle like evil children and Hunter feels Milly press against him. Their eyes meet, hers bulging in a silent plea for escape.

Milly's needs are in direct conflict with his own. He needs to see Josie. Now would be good, but to get to Josie they must hold their place in the queue. With a sigh of determination, he places a protective arm around Milly and tries to usher her forward. She digs an elbow into his ribs, refusing to play along.

'Okay,' he says. He briskly removes himself from their place in the queue, Milly tugging at his jacket to avoid losing him. They find themselves in a tight squeeze amid a group who appear to be the target market: power-dressed women and men his father's age, fidgeting with technological hardware so modest in design as to appear outrageously expensive. So far, they seem to be the only launch guests who can afford a Josephina.

Bracing himself on Milly, Hunter cranes to locate the entrance. From this new position they're a comfortable remove from the little band of apocalyptic warriors, but even further from the entrance. There is no sign of Alice and Coel.

'I'll get Dad,' Hunter says, and Milly, her face tight with worry, nods.

There's a sudden surge; the crowd shifts and their tight space gets squeezed by a group of new arrivals and their small armada of companion robots. The newcomers wear buttoned collars, suits and ties, but with sleeves ripped clean to show off pumped biceps covered in computer code and scientific formulae. Their thick-framed net-specs dampen the whole effect with nerd overtones.

Hunter is up on his toes again, looking for a way forward, but the group is too big, too dangerous. The companion robots, many on four legs and accessorised with fierce-looking protrusions, make navigating past too hazardous. Their only option is to stay put for now. With a firm hold of Milly's arm — she keeps staring at the newcomers, it isn't good — he sends a request to his father for assistance, and pins his location. When he looks up, the largest and meanest of the crew is eyeballing him.

'Hey,' Hunter says. Then looks back at his wristband quickly.

'I know you.' The meatiest guy of the whole man pack smiles, revealing a pair of silver-tipped front teeth.

'Good-oh,' Hunter says, clipped and straining for air. He's actually feeling very *not* good.

The meaty guy smiles again and says, 'Miles McClure's son, aren't ya?'

Hunter nods, not willing to trust his voice again. Milly's nails dig into his side.

'Your dad's outstanding,' the guy says, and purses his lips like a man pleased by the taste of a fine wine. 'I mean, the best. Tell him I said that. The name's Clifford.'

'Yuh,' Hunter says, swiping his wristband, desperate for it to PING back a message from his father.

Then, raising his arm, Clifford signals an advance to his troop.

Before Hunter has time to either puzzle the impossibility of someone from his father's fan base recognising him or let panic completely overwhelm him, Clifford and his crew shuffle forward. To avoid losing a collision between his legs and the protruding and pointy bits of the robot companions, Hunter shuffles with them, making sure to keep Milly close and shuffling too. Soon they're shuffling alongside the queue.

'Hey,' a voice calls. 'Stop pushing in.'

It sounds like the Coel look-alike.

Clifford, a mere two people plus one custom-modified and vicious-looking Wolverine turbo (if Hunter isn't mistaken) ahead, turns at glacial speed. His lip curling into a sneer, he growls, **'Are you talking to me?'**

Hunter jabs at his wristband. He starts a new message to his father. He shouts: **'HELP.'** Then, when the Coel look-alike charges Clifford and shoves him, Hunter shouts: **'NOW.'**

what they want

AN ALERT IN JOSIE'S visual field signals an incoming message from Hunter to Miles. She would never intercept Miles's messages. Nor make it her business to guess their content. Privacy is privacy. But because Hunter should be arriving any minute, she guesses anyway. The message must be an update that he's here. Good.

She plays a one-handed run up the keys. With her other hand, she fluffs the midnight-blue silk of her skirt so it falls in a circle at her feet. Then she brings it home. Spreading her fingers wide and leaning back, she hits the final few chords with both hands, arms stretched out in front of her.

It would be great if Hunter, Milly and Coel arrived right at that moment, just as she kicks off her moving rendition of their special tune. She adjusts her visuals and checks the doorway. Hunter, Milly and Coel have not arrived.

In the dying echo of the chord, the distant sound of voices raised in anger reaches her. Those entering the Audience Suite turn and leave again. Seated guests grow restless and a few take to the exit in a hurry.

Two alerts in her visuals. Two more messages from Hunter to Miles, and Josie wants to read them. Of course she can't *open* them, but she would like to know why Hunter is delayed. For several excruciating seconds she waits until Miles opens the messages, and yes, it may be wrong, but Josie also reads them.

As well she did.

Message one reads: HELP. Message two reads: NOW.

Miles drops down from the stage and rushes to the exit without sending a reply. So how are Hunter, and maybe Milly, and possibly Coel to know that help is on its way?

Answering Hunter as Miles — again not ideal in terms of communication protocol — Josie sends the message, On my way. Then, she locks onto Hunter's wristband to fix on his geo-location. She's already in motion when she hears the extremely loud **crash** of breaking glass and clatter of metal from the direction of the foyer. The sound of destruction somewhere between her current position and Hunter's. Chasing Miles, she deftly navigates the sudden mass exodus from the Audience Suite.

Twin chirrups of the alarm system, and a lulling female voice announces ᗛIᗐLᗐGIᗴ's emergency lockdown status. Not only will all doors lock, but Josie will be electronically firewalled. She will have communications from within ᗛIᗐLᗐGIᗴ's walls, but no one from the outside will be able to reach her. This is to protect the facility from data theft. But Josie loses Hunter's location and she won't hear from him for the next thirty minutes.

A distant cheer goes up, and more shouting. Josie finds Miles, and together they barge across the foyer, now choked with humans and robots. Most of the crowd is pressed up against the glassed façade of the entrance, trying to get a view of whatever is happening outside. Josie wants that view herself.

She's tempted, oh so tempted, just to barge through. Somewhere out there in the ruckus, Hunter, Milly and Coel are potentially scared out of their minds. But she follows Miles as he squeezes from one gap to another, apologising every step of the way.

They come to the glassed frontage and stop at the double automated doors, closed until lockdown ends. All they can do is watch the restless crowd. Hunter, Coel and Milly do not materialise.

The reason for all the excitement becomes obvious. There is a fractured pane in the front façade. On the outside, a damaged robot lies belly-up on the concrete. The robot is a custom-modified Wolverine Zano II. Three of its legs mechanically paw the air. The other leg, sparking and hanging loose, has been almost completely torn from the body casing. The Wolverine is in desperate need of being powered down, but the crowd gives it a wide berth.

It's possible the ArgusIV, an early-generation humanoid off to the side, has something to do with the broken Wolverine. Certainly no human could heft the weight of one. The ArgusIV appears to be in a holding pattern, as indicated by a red band of LEDs switching back and forth across the front panel. No one is attending to the ArgusIV either.

'See that lot?' Miles points to the group clustered in the middle of the concourse. 'My so-called fandom. Troublemakers, every last one of them.'

'The banner holders?'

Josie means the group of young people brandishing signs on sticks. One of them — a young man holding a banner that reads, **NO ONE'S BUYING YOUR SH*T** — is shouting into the face of a larger man and pointing in the direction of the

Wolverine. Someone besides herself seems to care about the downed robot.

'Not the activists. The other lot.'

Miles refers to men who appear to be a clique of some sort. They share similar tastes in clothing and body adornment. Notably, torn-off shirtsleeves to display tattoos. Nerd meets body builder meets street thug. Their companions are solid, aggressive-looking machines, vigilant for signs of trouble. Josie suspects the companions aren't assisting the humans to avoid trouble but to make more of it.

'What are the activists protesting?'

'They're the hard-done-by who make do with early-generation tech,' Miles says. 'They want affordable new inventions. It just doesn't work like that.'

'I can't see Hunter, Milly or Coel,' Josie says, knowing she's straying from the topic of conversation.

'Don't worry,' Miles says. 'They're smart kids. They know to keep away from that lot.'

Whether Miles means his fans or the group protesting, Josie can't tell. It's possible he means both. But extrapolating from the profile she has built of Coel, it's exactly the sort of trouble he would get into. She doesn't mention this to Miles.

'Miles!' The sound hangs in the air like the aftermath of a pistol shot. Following soon after is a woman. Short in stature; bone-white hair in a crisp vertical arrangement, and frost-blue eyes trained on them both. She's so obviously filled with importance, she doesn't have to watch where she's going: the crowd parts to make way.

Josie identifies the woman instantly. She recognises her from the avatar meetings in the boardroom.

Evelynne takes her measure of Miles and gives him a stiff

smile as though her face isn't accustomed to the expression. She avoids looking at Josie until Miles says, 'Well?', dipping his head in her direction.

The stiff smile loosens.

'A little too feminine,' is Evelynne's judgment. 'We're not selling Princess Lualai.'

Miles responds with his own stiff smile. 'Who?'

'This latest doll from ToyzOwn. Keep up, Miles. The sevens-and-under love her.'

Evelynne surveys the concourse, chin high, squinting through orange-framed specs lodged midway down her nose. She follows the trajectory of a banner thrown by a member of Miles's fandom. It smashes into the window, landing near the Wolverine. The placard has a cartoon old-style robot face on it, covered by a cross. She gives the downed Wolverine a cursory look-over, and ignores the Argus altogether. Evelynne finishes her survey of the fandom–protester altercation, and an expression of mild amusement settles on her face. Then, she mumbles to no one in particular, 'Action at the Josephina launch.'

She slides her frames back up her nose and sweeps a hand through her hair. It moves stiffly under her palm.

'The Miles McClure fan club running hot. Who knew?'

'I'd say the person posting launch details on their wall. Someone promised my best design yet.'

'She is that,' Evelynne says.

Miles says, 'Or would be if her design included an ability to seek and destroy.'

'That's quite an assumption. How do you know those boys don't want help with the domestics? Or emotional support?' Evelynne's delivery is bloodless.

Miles watches as his fans gesture and pose, their flexed biceps and neck muscles straining. Josie can see by his own straining neck muscles that Miles is very tense. With Hunter, Milly and Coel yet to appear, she feels tense as well.

'Stop worrying,' Evelynne says. 'This will settle down and we'll get under way.'

Evelynne is lying. Josie can hear the lack of sincerity in her vocalisation. Does Evelynne *not* believe the launch will start soon? If it doesn't, Josie will be inconvenienced. She has yet to perform the *Reign of Terror* closing theme for Hunter.

They all turn to look towards the sound of a small **explosion**. The air outside fills with dense orange smoke. The deepest concentrations are right at the centre of the protesters and fandom, who are immediately swallowed up by the smoke.

Miles curses. 'How about you update me with the plan, Evelynne.'

'I have no idea what this is about,' Evelynne lies. 'Did someone tip off Security?'

She looks to Josie, who in turn frowns at Miles. He curses again when Jace Gurney and the security team dressed in full riot gear jog onto the scene.

'No, no, no,' he groans. 'Josie, send a message to Jace. Tell him to back off.'

Evelynne sighs. 'This doesn't look good.'

Miles hammers at the glass with his fist. **'Jace! Jace!'**

'Message diverted to voicemail,' Josie tells him. 'Communications are still locked down.'

Miles turns on Evelynne. **'I know you have something to do with this. Stop it. Stop it now.'**

But his shouting is useless. The noise in the foyer is so loud that even Josie can barely hear him. The pressure of bodies at their back is forcing them up against the glass. Everyone wants to know what's going on.

Violence breaks out suddenly. Right in front of them, a man shoves another, and sends him spilling to the concrete. A companion on four legs smashes into the side of a wheeled machine.

Evelynne has her specs down her nose again. She watches Jace, then briefly turns to peer at Josie, then back to watch the crowd. She pushes the bridge of her glasses and addresses Miles. 'You can stop this. There is one sure and efficient way to reach Jace at this point.'

'How?' Miles bats at the pocket with his screwdrivers. Curses. 'What do I do?'

'Send Josie out there.'

'We're on lockdown.'

Jace and his team haul people in their path. Some fall, some scatter. Miles again batters the glass with his fists.

'Try emergency channels,' Miles shouts at Josie.

'Message diverted to inbox,' Josie shouts back.

A woman tumbles right in front of the window in her haste to get away.

'My kids are out there.' Miles doesn't shout this time. But he's right in Evelynne's face so she can hear him.

'Milly?'

'All of them.'

Evelynne goes still. This information, quite clearly, is not what she expected. She assesses Josie once again, then Miles.

'Don't second guess me, please,' she says. 'Send Josie out there.'

'To do what? Broker peace negotiations?'

me_ultra_mega_destroyer> <time_ultra_mega_destroyer> <time_ultra_mega_destroyer
me_ultra_mega_destroyer> <time_ultra_mega_destroyer> <time_ultra_mega_destroyer
me_ultra_mega_destroyer> <time_ultra_mega_destroyer> <time_ultra_mega_destroyer
me_ultra_mega_destroyer> <time_ultra_mega_destroyer> <time_ultra_mega_destroyer
me_ultra_mega_destroyer> <time_ultra_mega_destroyer> <time_ultra_mega_destroyer

'You're being stubborn,' Evelynne snaps. 'Don't do this. Load **time_ultra**.'

Miles takes her in, openly hostile. 'I don't like to be backed into a corner.'

'No one does,' Evelynne says, and for the first time she appears genuine. 'You know how this ends. Get your kids out of there.'

A roar from the crowd as it surges. Jace and his crew charge, batons raised.

Evelynne shouts, **'Miles, please!'**

With a loud roar, Miles pulls Josie towards him. 'You're better than this. Don't ever forget it.'

Josie startles at the rough handling, but stays with it. Miles is shouting again. **'Load time_ultra_mega_DESTROYER. Disable all hostiles. Maximum force. And Josie, find my kids. Do it now.'**

A companion robot butts a security officer and sends him scrambling. A splash of red across his legs. Above the yelling inside the foyer, Josie hears someone whoop and cheer. She observes, but another part of her searches. Vaults of code on internal databases — and there, a databank owned by Miles, and the program she needs.

It hits her system with the force of a sledgehammer. Files execute. The last thing she sees is Evelynne watching her through the orange-framed spectacles. The last thing she hears is Evelynne's voice, triumphant. 'Miles McClure's latest creation, BIOLOGIC's brand-new Josephiiinnnnnaaaaaaaaa.'

Time slows, then it no longer exists.

<34>

time_ultra

JOSIE SEES AT FIRST only the blue silk of her skirt flowing against her legs in a dream-like undulation. Weightless, she unfolds her body mid-air, landing clear of the shattering glass. It falls around her, splintering light into rainbows. Then, her thinking goes entirely.

Exterior BIOLOGIC: visibility low <freeze_frame> _
<motion>

Side-kick to hydraulic joint of incoming Yakabushi Droid model 37A / Palm to flat side of rear extenders, modified protuberances deflected / Marginal wrench of front extenders, mobility potential neutralized <freeze> _

Dodge and block incoming fist strike / Palm to human shoulder / Leverage human's momentum and push / Takedown move, success / Humans, down / More humans, down / Handspring to clear downed humans <freeze> _

Incoming SysMax 8800, beta version / Block, counterstrike, butt of hand to polymer casing / Follow-through punch, casing fractured / Squat, upward thrust, kick / Forward somersault, gaining

```
ground / Squat, upwards leap / Cleared proximity,
retrieve additional data <freeze> _
   <target_acquired>
   <somersault / handspring / roll / palm thrust>
Sinclair Q1 Spextrum, Dragon force edition,
defeated <freeze>
   <assume_defensive_lunge> <observe> <freeze>
   <handspring / walk / stop> <target_confirmed>
<freeze>
   <assess> <freeze>
   <walk> <freeze>
   <exit_time_dilation> _
```

Time speeds up like a slap. Josie trains her vision on Hunter
and Milly. Coel she locates by his band. She's surprised, but
satisfied he's distant from the action.

'Hello there,' she says. 'Let me help you down.'

<_>

Hunter loses sight of the main entrance. When the smoke
had billowed towards them, he'd pulled Milly to the large
sculpture at the edge of the concourse. The wiry frame of
circles, an artist's impression of a coiling DNA in stainless
steel. It's strong enough to support their weight. Hunter
climbs aboard and then hoists Milly. They cling together,
laughing briefly at their precarious position. The view is good.

Hunter sees Josie fly through the giant glass façade at the
front entrance. A stream of curse words follows. From Milly
too.

Josie punches a neat hole through the window with her

body. He gets a flash of blue, then he loses sight of her. He has a moment he truly thinks he might die. But he sees another distant flash of blue, so she's moving at least. And fast.

She suddenly breaks through into the middle of the protesters. The situation becomes clear: destruction on high speed. Guys, robots, banners, everything flying, falling, screaming, and Josie at the crest of the wave. His heart, he's pretty sure, lurches sideways or skips a beat. It thumps messily in his chest. Josie getting closer.

When she's almost upon them, her eyes skim the sculpture, himself and Milly, but she doesn't focus. Even so, her journey through the crowd becomes more specific. She ploughs down anything between herself and their position, so precise, so fast, nothing touches her.

By some miracle of physics, she arrives at the base of the sculpture. Everyone and everything that's shown any sign of aggression lies incapacitated behind her.

Hunter flashes back to the time Josie sang to him. He remembers the way her personality morphed and she became someone else, yearning for love, afraid she'd lose it. She's in this moment too. She handsprings below them, her landing classic Ninja. It's every action movie he's ever seen happening for real. He bursts out laughing, his thoughts awash in mad clichés. She looks beautiful.

Josie helps Milly down. Hunter slides off the sculpture and Josie does this gracious move, side-stepping Milly, while at the same time grabbing both of his arms. They end up in a massive eye-lock. Hunter couldn't move if he wanted to. Her eyes, they're kind of manic, but hypnotic as well. And she smiles.

It's softly falling rain, the screech of metal in a car wreck.

It's lift-off from the highest ramp in the world. It's wind rush in his ears. It's a sky-dive and falling, forever falling. It's his heart on fire before it blows apart.

Milly throws her arms around Josie's neck, forcing Hunter backwards. She squeals, 'Josie, are you all right?'

When it's more than obvious Josie is.

<_>

Milly marvels at the female brain. For a minute there, she was terrified for Josie. Really, all those robots attacking her. For a minute there, she nearly cried. But now she's in awe. Josie's brain, her body. Built for more than brute force, but also totally capable of it. Whoever dressed Josie did a pretty good job, too, though the Ninja outfit would have suited the action way better. Security, running and fighting, get to wear boots and overalls. A woman doing the same job has to maintain a glamorous façade. Classic.

To be fair, the flowing midnight blue of the silk skirt really works, and it's remarkable how the outfit's holding up. There's a slight tear at the back of the skirt, but it would be mean to point this out.

Hunter of course, and as per usual, hogs ALL of Josie's attention. *What was it like, Josie? Are you hurt, Josie? What are you thinking, Josie? Is it about me, Josie? Me, me, me, Josie.* Like, why does anyone else bother to exist?

Milly hates herself for thinking it, but it was almost better before Josie came. Only because Hunter is so unbelievably unbearable now.

Coel blinks slowly. Having gallantly taken Alice aside from the robot-protester-slash-fandom brouhaha, he's in prime position to see Josie come at Hunter and grab both his arms. The robot equivalent of a hug or some such.

Some such. He'd never have a corny thought like that before Alice. He likes it. He likes her. A lot.

'That was inspiring,' he says to Alice, and stretches his arms skyward in an elaborate yawn. On the way down his right arm settles around her shoulders. He thinks about the smell of her hair for a moment. He tells her she smells like berries, quick to add, 'in a nice way'.

He suggests they wait for the others by the pick-up zone.

<_>

Evelynne alerts a salvage company, tapping the side of her eyeware when prompted, and requests clean-up from a middle-tier recycling outfit. She alerts medics and requests two ambulances, books a glazier, reaches out to the company's legal representatives, reviews and edits her visuals of the Josephina, labels her clip *Crowd goes wild over new Josephina*, uploads the clip, pouts provocatively at the man conversing with Miles urging him to wrap it up, checks in on Sales, notes a pronounced increase in their website traffic, cross-references this to the rapid increase in the sales tally, admires the word increase, as in up, as in more. She checks the view count of *Crowd goes wild*, raises a hand to Miles and relaxes her arm so the hand falls heavily, comrade to comrade, on his shoulder.

'Miles,' she says, then 'Excuse me,' to his friend. An academic type if ever she's seen one. Old-school boring, he'd never appreciate a future so bright.

Evelynne says, 'Are the kids okay?'

Miles is overcome. Watching Josie in action, he has forgotten entirely that this is something he never wanted to see, that he made quite different choices, peaceful ones. Instead he's enthralled by the sight of two dreams, two separate goals, merging until they become powerful and unstoppable. The phrase *poetry in motion* comes to mind. They're so powerful, Josie and the addition of **time_ultra_mega_DESTROYER**, he might have invented one with the other in mind. He couldn't have imagined Josie to be the perfect vehicle but now he sees her in action, he gapes in wonder at the superb alliance of machine and code.

Then, she's lost to him in the orange smoke.

He wipes his damp eyes with the back of his hand. He takes a deep breath, and it almost sounds like a sob. He thinks of the kids and pulls himself together.

The smoke clears and the carnage could be worse. How clever. Josie was careful to avoid inflicting serious injury. Although the movements of the victims in her path seem impaired, at least they *are* all moving. Even the robots show signs of life. And out there, he's one hundred percent sure, she found his family and they're safe.

'So this is what you've been up to!'

Miles cringes inwardly. He and Feine Bishop have an uneventful, too-polite conversation over several long minutes.

Later, Miles won't recall a single word.

Then, with her eyeware removed, and likewise the barrier between himself and that ice-cap stare of hers, Evelynne clamps a hand on his shoulder. 'A hundred thousand views,' she enthuses. 'One. Hundred. Thousand.'

His befuddled gaze eggs her on. 'Pre-sales through the roof. Congrats, Miles, you made a winner.'

<35>

who cares

who cares: a poem by Milly McClure

the end of
loving-them-for-me,
left a crater in her soul
festering coal dust and hunted remembering and pimples dammit
that ate the frangible flesh of her heart and a single serve box of stale cereal
(being all they had left now people are so, so busy doing stuff together,
but leaving her out of any fun) until she was only a hollow cave of
nothingness not even bats being bothered and bored
does anyone care? NO. NO ONE CARES
about her only for a mad
dash of ginger fur, tail flicking
that's all
that's it
the end

Teacher comments:

Milly, bravo for submitting this piece. Really, good work getting it in on dead-line. I commend you for that and enjoyed, at long last, the opportunity to read some of your writing. An interesting piece. I like how you alliterate your 'bothered and bored' bats. Some of your word choices are clever. For instance, 'frangible', a word that suggests fragile and tangible. The meaning 'capable of being broken', applied to 'her heart'. I'm impressed.

I only wonder about the inspiration for your poem and I think possibly, maybe, we should discuss this further. Come see me. Today, probably. As soon as you can. Right now, even, will be fine.

Keem (FYI, I care!)

The marked work turned up in her inbox early. She has enough time to see her teacher before school starts, but frankly, Milly has better things to do than rush over so Keem can fret about her state of mind.

Which is fine, thank you very much. Everything is fine.

Then, it's lunchtime and she still hasn't been. Josie warned them to expect showers throughout the day, and here they are. A squall of rain batters the windows just as Milly is about to cross the vast quad to the lunch hall. She will have to deviate, going around the long way, under awnings and through corridors, to avoid a drenching.

She *could* go and see Keem. She'll be practically walking past her classroom anyway. She could also have *I'm a personal disaster zone* tattooed across her forehead, and dance, bikini-clad, in the rain.

Anything is possible.

Her bag slung on one shoulder, Milly treads carefully towards the exit on wet flooring. She hears her name called.

'Milly? Hi there!'

She stops and turns to see who wants her. She wishes she'd kept walking when she sees her mum's professor friend, Feine Bishop, of all people, bustling towards her.

There are several things wrong with this moment. It takes concentration to keep her irritation in check. She doesn't want to have to be nice to someone when she has better things to do, namely have lunch.

Her stomach grumbles in agreement, right when Feine comes up to her and says, 'It's *really* nice to see you,' in such a soppy way that Milly feels mean. And his eyes are drooping at the corners, his mouth's a bit crumpled, like tears are building. Milly knows how much she reminds him of her mother, because her whole life he's told her, *You get more like your mother every day.*

'How's things?' Milly asks him, and she is only vaguely interested because of her food-deprived stomach.

'Oh you know,' Feine answers, 'life could be better . . .'

'Life could be worse,' Milly says, to make him smile.

Which he does, winking to acknowledge the fact she hasn't forgotten their familiar, time-worn exchange.

'I wondered if I would run into you here.'

'Yeah,' Milly says, because he obviously has.

She doesn't hear what he says next, something about why he's come to her school. She's too busy looking for signs of smirking from schoolmates, like, *Omigod, how ooooolllldd is that old dude Milly McClure is talking to?*

So far, so good. She drops her bag at her feet, prepared to give Feine a minute or two.

'You go to the launch?' Milly says, right off the bat. 'It was a really important day for Dad. And everything got wrecked.'

'Wherever there's a crowd, there's a good chance things will turn pear shaped.' Feine goes all serious. 'Now you're here, there's something I need to talk about.'

'Oh sure,' Milly says.

She sees, coming her way and looking straight at her, ZeKarl Kirby. He likes to be called Zeke these days and he *still* likes her. (Even though she told his little friend, Wilkins, who straight-out asked her if she liked Zeke, 'No. A thousand times, NO. I will never EVER like him.' She had poked Wilkins in his puny boy chest and said, 'And you can tell your friend that, from *me*.' How to explain the importance of keeping her head clear? How to explain she has enough on her plate already?)

She has permanently avoided eye contact since the encounter, lest Zeke take it upon himself to *talk* to her. Now Milly turns her back on him, though not so far that she can't turn her head to clock him if she needs to. If he makes any sudden moves, she'll have him. She looks up again at Feine. This is how she discovers he's been talking to her a while.

'So *I'm* terribly worried,' he says, 'and I guess you are too.'

'Oh that's no good,' Milly says, in a faraway voice.

She turns her head ever so slightly. Zeke has slowed right down, pretty much ambling, and it's so *obvious*.

Keep going, Milly thinks. *Come on, buster, keep it moving.* It's something her mother would have said under her breath.

'So you *will* help?'

'I — wha—?'

Milly can't help it. She's being rude, but she has no idea where the conversation has taken her.

'It's a small thing. No big deal. But it is important, I'm afraid.'

Milly has never heard the Feinester acting so vague.

'I can't bear all this desperate worrying,' he adds. 'It's really wrecking me.' He has that same crumpled expression. The same teary build-up. 'Milly, how are you *really* going?'

Feine asks her.

She blows it, because instead of telling him what's *really* going on — that she's tired of caring when no one cares about her, and it means she's a big failure, and her mother would be disappointed — she merely throws the moment away with, 'Life could be better.'

Feine is onto it. He searches her face for clues she's faking it. He's genuinely concerned.

The shock of it. She feels it in her chest, a selfish squeeze of her frangible heart. And where she'd been hollow, she fills up again in a rush. Her cheeks colour with heat because *he cares*. And her face must be saying it, because instead of their usual answer — *Life could be worse* — he says in a small voice, 'Me too.'

He holds out his hand, palm up. On it an offering. The charcoal-grey orb of a widget, a cloud of threads above its surface. The small twitch of his thumb while he holds it out to her, and Milly's own fingers twitch. She'd been about to reach for the object, not because she had the faintest idea what she's going to do with it, but because the beautifully lit surface begs to be touched.

But a door **slams** shut somewhere down the corridor, making them both jump. Feine drops his arm to his side, the widget closed in his fist, and says, 'It'll definitely fix things up, Millster.'

'This problem with Dad?'

She's still trying to surf the wave of a conversation she can't quite catch.

'I just want to help your dad, that's all.'

Milly smiles, but there's nothing behind it. 'That's nice. You should.'

'Once you pop it onto your father's computer, you'll be done.'

'Oh!' Milly says, pleased to arrive at a juncture with clear instruction: *pop it onto your father's computer*. 'But I never go to Dad's work. I did yesterday, but that was because of Josie's launch.'

'Home is best,' Feine says. 'It'll run through anything in the vicinity.'

Milly isn't listening. She pretends she's interested in the weather through the doorway. But really she's checking on Zeke. He still loiters, fretfully worming through his bag. An award-winning performance of *Boy suddenly loses important object that must be found right away!*

Lame, Milly thinks.

'We want that,' Feine says, 'random . . . ah . . . uptake. To be sure it works.'

Feine thoughtfully smooths the tuft of hair on his chin, then he tosses the widget into the air and snatches it back, over and over.

Milly wants him to stop, so she ventures, 'I give that thing to Dad?'

'Flip, no!' Feine's eyes bug out, but he shrugs casually. 'No one wants to admit they need help, especially your dad. I think the best thing for it is if we get this job done without him being any the wiser. Which means it's a secret. Naturally, I thought of you.'

Not Hunter, not Coel. Of course, their old family friend trusts her to get it done, and rightly so. *Love them for me.* Her mother saw it in her as well.

'I better get going.' Feine picks up her bag and holds the shoulder strap while she slips it on.

'Wait!' Milly holds her hand out, palm up, and keeps it there between them. 'You didn't give me the widget, silly.'

Feine rolls his eyes with a snort. He raises his fist until it hovers above her outstretched hand, and drops the widget into it. The smooth object fits her closed fist just so. The crafty smile creeping onto Feine's face gives her a second or two of doubt. Then he laughs at himself. 'This weather. I'd forget my head if it wasn't screwed on.'

diamond mine

BEK DOESN'T NORMALLY ARRIVE home in such a state. Hands trembling, struggling to position her sweaty fingerprint just right to unlock the apartment door. She fumbles her bike helmet and nearly drops her bag. It mewls in complaint, but she doesn't hear it.

She actually screams when her flatmate Juon yanks the door open. Not surprisingly, he spends a long time examining the bag and her with eyebrows raised. He mouths something Bek doesn't hear and points to the carryall slung over her shoulder. She remembers her earbuds and removes them.

A muffled kitten sound comes from inside her bag. Plaintive meows this time. There shouldn't, under any circumstances, be kitten meows coming from her bag. Bek tells it to shut up. The bag mewls.

'No animals,' Juon says. 'Remember?'

'It's not . . .' Bek says. 'There isn't.'

Her bag says, 'Purrrrp?'

'Oh?' Juon's scepticism is kinder than other people's. It forces Bek to be kind back.

'It's really not . . . Okay, it's something. But . . .' Bek gives her bag a little squeeze. It mewls. 'Life's crap. And I think today it got ten times worse.'

Juon remains in the doorway, arms down at his sides. He wears a densely patterned floral vest and unzipped white bomber jacket over the top. Covering his hands are giant wolf-paw gloves with shaggy black fur and extended claws.

'Guy, come on,' Bek says, looking up and down the landing. It's empty now, but for how long? 'Let me in.'

Juon removes himself from the doorway and Bek enters their apartment.

'Bek,' Juon says. 'Life isn't crap. There are only crap moments.'

'Today I reached my upper limit of crap moments,' Bek says. 'It's safe to say, life in general is crap.'

Her bag mewls again.

'You need tea,' Juon says.

'Remove the gloves,' Bek says.

'I was cleaning,' Juon says. It doesn't at all explain the wolf paws.

By the time Bek is seated in their small kitchen, her hands are steady enough to unclip her bag. The sCat pokes its head out and purrs. Juon places a steaming beaker in front of her. She shudders and takes a great gulp of air. Her eyes well up.

'Bek! Are you crying?'

She sniffs and shoves her palms against her eyes. They come away wet. She sniffs louder. 'Seems so.'

'Hey now.' Juon jostles her shoulder, then he sidles awkwardly to the bench and leans against it. He examines the floor while waiting for Bek to stop snivelling. Behind him on two cartons are the wolf-paw gloves.

Bek takes a sip of her tea. She removes the sCat from her bag and sits it on her lap. The sCat rubs its face against her

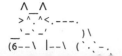

wrist. 'You ruined my already destroyed life,' she tells the sCat.

'Mrrp,' it answers gaily.

'Did I tell you Professor Bishop got me hired at **BIOLOGIC** because I wreck everything?'

Juon looks at her briefly, then gets back to examining the floor.

Bek sighs and turns the sCat to look up at her. She had planned to program Emotion Recognition for the sCat next week, but next week she will no longer have a job. And nor should she have one. The professor's right. She does wreck everything.

'This is a *negative* emotion,' she tells the sCat.

'That thing's cute, I guess,' Juon says. 'If we have to keep it.'

'If the doorbell rings we can't answer,' Bek says. 'Once Security sees the sCat gone, they're coming after me.'

'Can't you call **BIOLOGIC** and tell them it's here?'

'Are you crazy? With my history?'

'Sip your tea,' Juon says. 'There isn't a problem that can't be solved by a decent brew.'

'Removal of entities from the workplace will result in termination. Miles drums that into us from day one. But who am I kidding? My days are already numbered. Today, when I was doing my job, I saw Josie at my workstation.'

'Okay.'

'Dude, she *replaced* me,' Bek says, her voice wobbly with emotion.

Earlier, on the testing floor, she'd had to fetch the sCat down from a climbing frame. It gave her a good view of the office she once shared with Miles. There, sitting at Bek's former workstation, was Josie. It was a face plant into redundancy. She felt inconsequential, overwhelmed. In a panic, she left immediately, too upset to notice she had a stowaway s⎡at in her bag. Who is going to believe it wasn't intentional? For all she knows, it's exactly the excuse Miles needs to fire her.

'And don't forget, I still have that criminal record.'

'Is this the story of Bek Singh, the ten-year-old Master Thief?' Juon has the wolf paws on again, and claps them together.

'It was traumatic.'

'Time to let it go?'

'Half a dozen advanced-system speedball-tipped pens in high-performance colours. Beautiful inks,' Bek says, shaking her head in wonder. 'How was I to know it's wrong to select the stationery and just go? How was I to know products must be scanned? That a special kiosk was set up for payment?'

Distracted, Juon drums with the wolf paws on the kitchen bench. It could be Bek has told the story a few too many times.

'What comes next,' Bek says, 'is the din of bureaucracy trampling my defence. I removed a s⎡at from ≡IⓄ∟ⓄGIⒸ and criminal acts speak louder than apologies, my friend.'

Juon says, 'More tea?'

At the exact same moment the doorbell chimes.

It could be, *must* be Jace. His security team will surely be storming the apartment complex right this minute and on standby for their frontal assault on the living room. With his freaky Ninja skills, he could materialise by her side at any moment.

'They're here,' Bek shrieks.

'Law enforcement?'

'Security.'

'I'll go,' Juon says. 'I know taekwondo.'

'I'm getting you're not taking this low point in my life very seriously.'

'Seriously, I know taekwondo.'

Bek stands, adjusting her posture: chest out, shoulders back. A bit like Lemmy Saltine when he took on enemy marauders in the episode *Invasion from Planet Wafer: The Musical*.

'This is on me, I'll go,' she says.

Head high and hardly shaking at all considering, she answers the door.

Security aren't lined up in the hallway and ready to apply cuffs to remove her. It's Gwin. She is removing a chunky net veil studded with LEDs from her face. She greets Bek with a chilly hello and adds, 'Has the cooling-off period been long enough?'

Bek spends a puzzled moment just staring at Gwin, who looks so . . . *ordinary.*

Her hair, a rich golden brown, is one colour. Her face, covered in a layer of shimmer, is not overdone. Her lips are soft pink, a colour that on some complexions could almost be natural. It's the most remarkable transformation so far. Gwin looks like any other young woman their age.

'**Bek,**' Juon calls from the kitchen, '**are you still alive?**'

'**No,**' Bek shouts. '**I'm not.**'

Before Bek can send Gwin packing, or accuse Gwin of trying to bump her out of a job — *why else would she secretly meet with Miles?* — the sℂat leaps from her arms to Gwin's. It places one forepaw on Gwin's chest. The other touches her cheek. Then Gwin traces her ringed fingers down the sℂat's spine. It's creepy in an entirely electronic way, and Bek hates it.

```
 |\    _  _,,--,,_
  x,  ` -'-;'   '-   -;-';-_
  x,3- ` ) )-;-_-:\ ( ''';-,
  '---''(_/--'  `-'\_)
```

She snatches the s[at back, but it struggles. In a panic, Bek immediately powers it down and the s[at flops in her arms halfway through a plaintive mewl. She races into the living room, Gwin following, and lays the s[at on a side table with the utmost care.

'What *was* that?'

Gwin doesn't answer immediately. She blinks and twitches, her world seemingly out of focus.

'*Gwin*,' Bek says, her tone sharp.

'The momentum,' Gwin says. 'Can you feel it?'

Gwin really says this.

'Why have you even come. *Gwin!*'

Gwins snaps out of her kooky trance and says, '*We should be friends*, you said. *I won't judge*, you said.'

'You gave Swarm to the professor. You're trying to steal my job. I think you might be a little too freakish for me. And I have some pretty freaky friends.' Bek looks to the kitchen.

Gwin frowns, then she raises her hand. Her ringed fingers tangle, then untangle. An image of Lemmy and his best friend Gilda Griffin displays on the wall, Lemmy with his arm around Gilda. Bek knows the scene well.

Gilda hit hard times. Lemmy, too, was under pressure. A rift grows between the two friends. The point comes when Gilda has nowhere else to turn. Lemmy to the rescue! Their friendship grows stronger. The upshot: during times of stress, friendships are vulnerable to misunderstandings.

'Friends,' Gwin says.

'But Gwin,' Bek says, 'could you possibly be a tiny bit normal?'

'I am normal. You're the one who doesn't answer messages,'

Gwin says. 'Is this normal?'

'Excuse me, but my life sucks!'

Gwin watches Bek as though she's a curiosity, then says, 'Why does your life suck?'

'Wait, you're not even injured after the explosion.'

When Gwin shrugs as if it's of no consequence, Bek says, 'You know what? It's just more of your weirdness. I don't actually care.'

'Obviously you're injured,' Gwin says. 'This explains why you don't keep your word. You must be so weak from injury you can't possibly reply to my messages.' She swoops a hand towards Bek and says, 'Nsk.'

'How about you betrayed me?'

'How did I betray you?'

'You gave Swarm to the professor.'

'Swarm is no more.' Gwin pierces Bek with her gaze, and now it's Bek who shrugs, trying to make it seem offhand.

But Gwin appears genuinely confused. 'What is wrong with saying *hello* or *how are you, Gwin?* It shouldn't matter, injured, betrayed or whatever.'

Juon is rattling about in the kitchen. Flatmate code for, *Could you take it outside?* Bek crosses the room to slide a panel across the kitchen doorway, then stands for a moment to think. She remembers Ficus just hanging with her Lemmy figurine back at ᗷIᗝᒪᗝᘜIᑕ, her soon-to-be-former workplace. If you take the professor and Swarm out of the equation, it hasn't been that bad being Gwin's friend. She's interesting, no denying that. If Bek has to wait for Security to arrive, she might as well have company rather than fret alone. *Just like Gilda Griffin,* she thinks, *the time could come I need all the friends I can get.*

'I have to protect Josie,' Bek says. 'You get how important this project is to me?'

Gwin challenges Bek with her dark eyes, but she's no longer looking like a crazy person. 'Last time I saw Josie, she was kicking butt at the launch.'

Bek mumbles, 'Last time I saw Josie she'd taken my job.'

'What?' Gwin says.

'Forget it,' Bek says.

'Okay,' Gwin says.

Bek huffs with annoyance. 'All right, I'll tell you. Josie was in my old office, working at my old work space.'

'There you go.' Gwin gives her a look. 'Obviously, still going strong.'

'Uh . . . But she . . .' Bek means to give Gwin the robot-stole-my-job sob story but realises how silly it sounds. *That's right, Gwin, I helped make the robot that took my job.*

In spite of herself, Bek laughs.

'Ah,' Gwin says. 'I fixed your mood.'

Which only makes Bek laugh harder. 'Hoo, boy. Okay. Listen.'

'Yes?'

'Professor Bishop says you submitted Swarm. That's betrayal, are we agreed?'

'I submitted *code*. New name, Spawn.' Gwin says. 'Much better. And is it possible to consider for one moment that Spawn might benefit Josie?'

'Your virus? No.'

'Not virus, *seed*.'

'Whatever, and *nooooo*.'

Gwin holds Bek's gaze for a long time, then she pulls her

jacket straight and looks towards the door. Clearly she means to leave.

'The professor's so smug,' Bek says quickly. 'He's obviously up to something. And he hates Josie.'

'Anything is possible.'

'If I didn't have the threat of losing my job, I wouldn't be in all this trouble.'

'What does that mean?'

'How I got my job. It's a lie.'

'So tell the truth.' Gwin shrugs, downplaying such a dangerous move. 'If this is a big deal, be open.'

'I do want to tell Miles the truth, but he'll hate me for lying all this time.'

'Maybe he will, maybe he won't.'

'You think I tell him?'

Gwin raises her eyebrows comically at such an obvious solution, and Bek laughs again.

'If deception is a problem,' Gwin tuts, 'stop deceiving.'

With a loud *oof*, Bek lets the air run out of her. She flops onto the sofa and pats the seat beside her. Gwin sits.

'Now what are we doing?' Gwin asks.

'A new Saltines episode uploaded today,' Bek says. 'How 'bout it?'

'What about telling Miles the truth?'

'Cool your jets, sister. I only made up my mind a second ago. Now I procrastinate.'

Gwin slouches deeper on the sofa. 'Okay, the Saltines now, then we return the sᴄat and you confess to Miles.'

'Then we take over the world,' Bek says.

'Then we *seed* the world,' Gwin says.

'Yuh, whatever.'

Light projects onto the wall from Gwin's ring cluster. Bek leans back and smiles with satisfaction. Maybe Juon is right. Life can't be crap all the time. She has to remember to see good coming, even when she feels like she's stuck. As if in total agreement, Lemmy Saltine's face beams down at her from its great height. Gilda's in the scene too, and she's smiling foppishly. 'Friends?' Lemmy says. 'We're just like diamonds.'

two heads are
better

.01

IN THE NAME OF FUN, they're out in the garden, playing a sort of William Tell spin on Coel's duelling challenge. Since taking the widget from Feine, Milly isn't sure whether she'll use it. A sure sign would be Josie losing it.

Coel has had his turn, and Josie shot the apple from his head within seconds. Now it's Hunter's turn to be target, but there's a hold-up. Josie has been staring down the sights of Coel's air rifle without taking the shot. Milly observes closely.

'By the way, this is stupid,' Hunter says, positioned down range with an apple balanced on his head.

'How does this prove anything?' Milly says.

'It proves nothing,' Hunter calls out.

'Don't move, Hunter,' Josie yelps.

Coel says, 'A duel presents gentlemen with the opportunity to redeem themselves, prove their courage, bravery, honour, all that. You'll never understand it, Millipede.'

'I understand stupidity, so . . .'

'Very amusing. But facing danger isn't something you're

expert on.' Coel pitches his voice high: 'Oooh, save me from the big, scary spider.'

'There are spiders that kill,' Alice says, and holds up her hand for Milly's high-five.

When Coel doesn't reply, Milly finds herself having second thoughts about Alice. Anyone who can shut Coel up might be all right.

'*Soooo* brave. As if Josie will miss the target,' Milly says. 'Right, Josie?'

'I'm unable to process an inquiry at this time,' Josie says.

Josie doesn't seem to notice the sharp edge that's coloured her tone, but Milly does. She steps back from the firing box, giving Josie breathing space. It's a shame she can't step away from her bitter thoughts just as easily. How typical — Hunter gets to hog Josie's attention way longer than anybody else.

'Wait,' Hunter calls out. 'Josie? I gotta scratch my back.'

With a huff of impatience, Josie lowers the air rifle, pointing the barrel at the ground. Then Hunter removes the apple from his head, and contorts this way and that to get at the itch.

Coel says, 'Did you know William Tell's son actually ate the apple after? Food was that scarce.'

'You're making that up,' Josie says. 'I can find no references to the apple after William Tell's crossbow hit it.'

His back scratched, Hunter relaxes too, tossing the apple into the air a few times and catching it, his arm swooping in great arcs.

'Hey Josie,' he says. 'What about I throw the apple and you hit it mid-flight?'

'Cool idea, Hunter,' Alice warbles.

Without a word, Josie raises the air rifle and tracks the apple as it leaves Hunter's hand. She fires on its downward trajectory, the split-second it's awfully close to Hunter's head.

The loud **pffft-crack** is followed immediately by the soft sound of the apple rupturing, the **thud** of it falling to the ground, and Hunter screaming. He frantically pulls at his ear. Even from where Milly stands, there's no mistaking the smear of red when he brings his hand away.

In the silence after, Milly doesn't let Josie out of her sight.

Josie seems to be in shock but the only one capable of activity. She takes great pains with the safety of the air rifle, placing it inside the case, then closing the lid firmly. She brushes aside the stray lock of hair fallen across her face. She looks at Hunter, and a strange stillness comes over her, like she's imprinting everything about him onto her memory.

And maybe she is, for all Milly knows. Maybe this is a robot thing, right after they make drastic miscalculations. Maybe all robots flip out right before their uprising. But almost immediately Milly feels mean. It's Feine's fault. There's nothing wrong with *their* Josie. How could there be when the afternoon has been so chill?

Maybe the sight of blood is spooking her. Do robots know humans bleed?

Milly doesn't want to believe Feine — that there's a super-massive problem that needs fixing. But coming right along is a sick feeling that maybe Feine is right. She'd like to ask Josie about it. But suddenly Josie pivots on one heel and sprints back towards the house.

All eyes are on Hunter then. He first looks at his hand, then his gaze follows Josie. He grins in a weird way and laughs to himself. He looks at his hand again, then swaggers towards them.

She, Coel and Alice watch him go by. They see him start

to jog in the direction of the house, flicking droplets of blood from his fingertips.

When Hunter disappears out of sight, Alice says to no one in particular, 'Things can get a little bizarre around you guys. You know that, right?'

.02

Nothing happens.

Hunter knocks again on Josie's door. 'Can I come in? Please?'

He presses his good ear against the door and thinks he hears a small noise. A gasp? A sob?

'Josie?'

He's just had an epiphany. Watching her run from him in the garden, he remembers fog, the blue sky, a whole lot of stuff with clarity. He remembers saying her name, his hands tangled in her hair, her face close to his. A beautiful moment. This isn't the first time he's recalled that morning, but he thought their closeness had been a dream, or an idea sprung from the fevered longing of his imagination.

But now he knows it was for real. He knows they kissed.

'Josie.'

He tries the door. It's locked. If she doesn't open up in five seconds he will break it down.

He hears her, muffled through the door. 'My apologies for disrupting today's activity. Please continue to enjoy your afternoon without me. I am no longer available.'

'You don't have to do this.' Her emotional wellbeing is a delicate flower in the palm of his hand.

Finally, movement inside, and the door opens a crack.

'Yes? Can I help you?'

The one eye Hunter can see looks glassy. Hunter clears his throat, tries to laugh it off. 'You okay?'

'Yes. Thank you for checking on the state of my being. I am adequate.'

Josie closes the door.

Hunter sighs, taps on the door again. 'Come on. Let me in.'

The lock clicks and the door swings wide. Hunter sees a small indentation on the sofa where Josie has been sitting, a crumpled pile of tulle to the side. It looks like sections of it have been folded, then unfolded, a concertina of torment.

Her face, while he watches her, remains blank. As if she's hardened by a grim acceptance that this is her lot. It pains him to think it, but she looks really robotic.

'Something's wrong,' he says. 'I can tell.'

Josie pauses for such a long time, Hunter thinks she isn't going to respond, but then she says, 'When I first came here, do you remember being in the workshop and you asked me what I was thinking?'

Hunter does remember. She had been staring, lost in thought, at the robot junk on the workbench. He remembers how sad she had been.

'There's a word,' Josie says. 'Obsolescence. I've been hiding from that word, but now I'm broken, I accept it. The time has come to dispose of me. Please take me to a scrap yard. That is where I belong.'

'It was an accident,' Hunter says. 'I'm not even hurt really.'

The smallest twitch of her cheek, and Josie takes in the smears of blood on his T-shirt, down his neck, the congealing blood on his ear.

'If you're worried, we can call Dad.'

'No!' It startles them both, Josie's shrill voice in the confines of the small room. 'I know what needs to happen.'

'What needs to happen?'

'I saw them in the workshop. Robot parts. I know what's in the crates. The ones that don't make it. The ones no longer useful. That's me.'

'Those robots were old . . . That's . . . We won't . . .' Hunter closes his eyes, he can't bear the thought of it. 'Dad won't throw you away. I won't let him.'

Josie meets his eye, but with an emptiness that's fierce.

'I'm not useful if I'm broken.'

Hunter reaches out to touch her arm, but she backs away.

'Sorry,' he says.

'It's not your fault,' Josie says crisply. 'I keep getting these strange glitches. Not just today. Since the moment I met you.'

They stand in silence for a long time. In the quiet, Hunter hears the whirr of a car driving away. It must be Alice leaving. He wonders what she must think of them, and hopes she isn't judging Josie for her erratic behaviour. In truth, he's grown fond of the eccentricities, her sweet dramatics. It's what makes her so unique, so unpredictable.

He has an idea. 'Why don't we check Dad's computer? It's linked to you, right? Maybe I can find the problem.'

'I run my own system checks. If I can't find the problem, then . . .' Josie shakes her head sadly.

'You're too close to the problem. I might see something you can't. Two heads are better than one.'

This time when Hunter reaches for her she lets him take her hand.

.03

Milly squeezes Mushi, pressing her face into his fur. He struggles a bit, but she holds on and tells the cat, 'Dammit. I hate this.' She means, Josie acting up and Hunter crazy too.

Mushi slithers from her arms, and Milly drags a hand across her eyes. Milly had come to the workshop hoping a little peace and quiet would bring her world back into focus. It seems to work for Hunter. But the quiet has only made her thoughts louder.

She wipes her wet hand on her T-shirt, feeling hopeless and confused. She has to decide what to do. She wants her mother. Her mother would be able to calm Hunter down and would know if Feine's widget should be used to fix Josie. Feine put his trust in Milly, knowing she will do her best, but Milly isn't sure she trusts Feine.

The only thing she knows for sure is something's up with Josie, and Feine might be the only one who saw it was coming. So Milly decides. She starts her father's computer. Too old in many ways, but her father swears by this machine for home use. Of course, it might be her father hasn't updated the tech because their mother isn't there to tell him to. Milly doesn't really have a clue about the home machine, but she does know it's an in to Josie's workings.

It takes her a second or two to figure out the widget. Every time it moves, spirals of code alight from its surface — it's very offputting. Her first attempt, smooth side to the computer's casing, does nothing. But when she tries the underside, she's rewarded with a soft TING and the widget attaches. There's a busy flickering of the operating light. The computer bleeps and blips to tell her it's doing something. The widget glows dimly, a spiralling tree with blobs in its murky depths. She waits for a sign the job is done.

She'll need to return the widget to Feine at some point, and no doubt he'll want a report on how it went down. She's considering what to tell him when a loud **thwump** from one of the crates at the back of the workshop sends her heart skidding. She grabs the widget, done or not. The spiralling glow tree vanishes.

Then, she flees.

She doesn't stop until she's back inside the brightly lit kitchen, which means she's well clear when, inside the workshop, the click turns into several more clicks and a hum. Both crates vibrate as the heavy objects within become active. Rays of light spill through the cracks of the wooden slats. After years in a death sleep, the two CRUSHers stored in their crates have come back to life.

The lights of their visual sensors start to glow. The extenders at the ends of their arms clench and spin. Likewise, the firing mechanism of their electro-magnetic weaponry boots up, ready to blitz any immediate threat. And, as though of one mind, they raise their arms. The crates break from the pressure with a loud **crack**. A step forward and they plough through the remainder of the wood. The CRUSHers wobble, making small adjustments to find their balance. Final system checks reach completion: CRUSHers One and Two are *Go*.

They scan the room for moving targets. Seeing none, CRUSHer Two switches to an energy-storing mode and sleeps. Crusher One remains on high alert, surveying enemy territory for signs of aggression.

38

ZAP ZAP **ZAP** ZAP

'WHAT DIFFERENCE WILL IT MAKE, two heads or one?'
Josie throws herself onto the pile of tulle. It fluffs around her,
a frivolous pink cloud.

She closes her eyes and wishes she had Hunter's optimism.
But all she has are files of accumulated data. Wishful thinking
isn't going to fix anything.

With her eyes closed, she murmurs, 'I am proud to have
known you, Hunter McClure. I am at my best when I'm with
you. As my parts are removed one by one, as they lie rusting
in a pool of junkyard grime, as my fuel pump runs dry and
beats for the last time, my only thought will be, I didn't know
I could want until I wanted too much.'

Josie opens her eyes. Hunter takes a cautious step towards
her, then another. She has to blink away a strange dampness
on her lashes. She dabs at her eyes, and her fingertips come
away wet. She squeals, holding her hand for Hunter to see.

'My eyes are leaking,' she moans. 'My eyes.'

Hunter tugs at the tulle. 'This is ridiculous,' he says.

'It's an extension of me,' she says, watching morosely while he dumps tulle and cushions on the floor.

He sits beside her on the sofa and pulls her into his arms. He wipes her wet fingertips on his blood-stained T-shirt. He squeezes her until his body shudders against hers and she pulls away confused. He seems a bit embarrassed, but mostly amused.

'I'm really sorry,' he says, but laughing so hard he barely gets the words out. When he finally regains his composure, he says, 'Oh man. Sorry about that.'

'Please tell me,' Josie says, not as chilly as she'd like owing to the close proximity to Hunter. 'How is it my nightmare situation makes you so happy?'

Hunter blows air through his lips. 'Oh, you aren't broken.'

'I'm dizzy,' Josie gasps, snatching her hand from his to grab her spinning head. 'It's game over, obviously.'

Ignoring this, Hunter brushes his lips against her hair. He takes her hand and presses it to his chest. He brings his face so close to hers, his nose nestles her cheek. She has to concentrate over the electrical fizz in her circuits to stay with sensations under the palm of her hand.

He says, 'See?'

Her hand, his heart.

Josie's eyes widen in surprise. Hunter takes a jagged breath: she feels the expansion of his chest through her fingers. He says her name and his heart does a quick bu-bump.

Hunter smiles into her face. '*I'm* dizzy! You make *me* broken.'

Josie looks down at her hand on Hunter's chest and up to his mouth. She takes his hand, placing it on her chest. He must be feeling a rhythm, somewhat shaky, her fuel pump racing along in time with his heart.

'What a mess,' he says.

'Oh man,' Josie says. 'Oh man.'

The funniest part is, the times she's been broken are the times she's been perfectly right. It was never a glitch, it was a problem with heart luggage and what she was packing into it. It was human nature. No wonder she couldn't understand it.

'But I'm not . . .' she begins. 'Are we . . . Is this . . . ?'

Beautiful, his eyes looking into hers.

'This feeling . . .' she says. 'Love?'

He nods, *yes*, and laughs with her. He says the word too. *Love*.

'So,' she says.

'Yuh,' he says.

And they laugh.

But love doesn't end there. Hunter's hand cups her cheek. Tenderly, he pulls her face towards his. Their lips touch. Her hand finds his face, his hair. A blizzard of alerts, triggered by sensations rocking her core, clutter her visual field. She switches her alert system off. She doesn't need warnings about hammering metabolic rates. Her whole being vibrates, every millimetre of skin tingles, and she means to lose herself in this exquisite feeling.

They fall, bodies pressed together. At first she doesn't notice a slight tremor in the fingers laced through his hair. A reaction to the first *ZAP* hitting her brain. It snarls a place inside of her, and she believes this to be an electrical consequence of love.

Hunter notices. He says her name. But Josie rests her cheek against his, then they kiss again.

The second *ZAP* sends a spasm down her arm. She seizures. Her top teeth come down hard, and she bites Hunter on the lip.

He cries out and pulls away. Josie gasps at the sudden void between them, the emptiness. She wiggles to press herself close, but she sees his lip swelling, sees blood.

Her brain takes forever to react. *Blood.*

It's difficult for her to follow proceedings. *Hunter.*

Another *ZAP* flickers her eyelids, so she closes her eyes for a moment. When she opens them, Hunter is standing over her. He shakes her by her shoulders, his mouth moving.

Words she can't hear. Only a harsh buzzing in her ears.

More *ZAP* s. This time, after they pass, she hears, 'Save this moment. Josie, you have to. Save *love*.'

She has no time to figure it, because there is a bigger *ZAP*. Her whole body stiffens.

A stray inquiry: *Does kissing always wreck an operating system?*

As though an answer, the next *ZAP* comes, and with it a command: **ATTACK**.

Now Josie experiences a ripple of alarm. Her mind, uncharacteristically sluggish, ponders the connection of this particular command to *love*.

Thinks, *Maybe yes, maybe no.*

Love. Josie makes several attempts to reconnect with her memory, her cache of Hunter moments. When she can't, she crosses the room and stands in front of the mirror. Hunter is reflected behind her. *Hunter?*

He lies crumpled on the floor. He isn't moving.

She remembers: mouths, lips, eyes. *Hunter.* She looks down at her clenched fist.

Another *ZAP* comes.

Hunter and **DESTROY**. The two things merging, becoming one command.

He groans and rolls to one side. *He's hurt?*

Two more **Z AP** s.

Data from her memory spools through her thoughts. The alien code on board drowns in it. Not *drowning*, absorbing, reforming. **ATTACK**.

Not attack, *defend* — isn't that what her programming demands? She searches recent functions performed . . . *domestic task . . . kitchen, clean, cleared, sparkling surfaces* . . . Mimic to learn. Learn to mimic.

ATTACK.

A sound cuts into the silence. The body on the floor, a wail of pain. A face looks up at her. Agony distorting the features. Her hand gripping another hand, tight.

'No . . . Stop . . . Josie,' the human male cries.

HUNTER.

No, no, no, no, no. She reaches for him again. He cowers, covers his head.

Love, she thinks. She tries to say the word.

'ATTACK,' she says.

Josie amasses parcels of code, nodes, a network of connections. An instinct for survival no different from breathing. She *will* say *love*.

Her brain struggles to assert itself. She assigns parallel access points; she's building a bridge back to herself. She finds a time she and Hunter were getting to know each other. When she was getting to know herself.

How does artificial intelligence work? *I learn, I'm adaptable*, she'd answered.

If it's really intelligence, how can it be artificial? *The machine part of it, I guess.*

Well, what's the other part? *Derivatives of human cells.*

Why, weren't you briefed? Hunter's laughter.

Are there intelligent thoughts that don't involve house management? *Very funny. Are you asking if I have thoughts outside of my assignments? I have interests,* she had said. And she did have interests, *does* have them.

The truth of her existence, something she didn't say: *I think about you, Hunter.*

A thought comes: *Why this memory?* There are so many other Hunter memories she enjoys more. Too late, she understands it's not *her* bridge, it's not *her* need to remember, and it's too late to stop them.

They need to know her. *They* mean to absorb, re-form and control *her.*

And she understands this invasion, the assault on her system, at the same time as her control slips. SPAWN.

The new thing inside her answers, **SPAWN.**

Josie cries out, the sound cutting her down. She falls to the floor. She thinks of rusting body parts. She thinks she's alone, but she's not.

'Hhhhh . . . EEERRRCCCC!' Her voice spools, breaks into white noise. The ancient electronic scream of digital signal down a telephone line. She tries again. Her, she, Josie. 'EEEEEEEEEEEEErrrrrsssKKKKKZZZZSSHHH'.

Eyes wide, hers and his.

Hunter scared.

Hunter panicked. *Breathe, two, three, four.*

Water from her eyes running down her cheeks. A haunting voice from the halls of her memory: *My eyes are leaking.*

'I can't . . .' But the command — not her, yes her. She brings up her hand and it's clenched into a fist. It wants to attack, defend . . .

Terrified of herself, she screeches, **'RUUUUUUUNN.'**

The spawn are everywhere, bright sparks burning her mind away. Her fist freezes mid-air.

Hunter backs away, but he doesn't leave the room.

'Go, run, run run run runrun runrunrrrrrrr.'

Her body, not her body, lunging. She stops it. Spawn gather inside her, preparing another onslaught against her will. She fights the urge to launch herself at the only human in the room.

A great need to administer harm, destruction, chaos. Not her, Spawn, the virus infecting her.

Her eyes close. Her eyes open.

Footsteps on the stairs down the corridor. Footsteps across the floor above.

Hunter, gone.

Without him, the dim parts of her brain become light, fog becomes clarity. Josie disables motor nodes that are instructing her to follow. Strange to be stronger without him in the room. The nodes quickly disassemble, then reassemble someplace else. Demanding. **FOLLOW HUMAN MALE HUNTER.**

No. Josie disables.

The $\mathcal{ZAP}$s are infinite, an endless stream, a monstrous buzzing deluge, and *she*? As fast as she *disables*, they amass to *enable*. With the final vestiges of her self-control, she remains in this one place. Above her, the **thump** of many footsteps telling her they are all running.

Run. Stay. Hunter, Coel, Milly, *LOVE*.

As the spawn charge inside of her, as they struggle to calculate the meaning of this thing that is bigger than anything, they absorb *LOVE*. Josie thinks, *Good.*

An echo inside her, **GOOD.**

Josie finds her supreme command, wills it to be so. `Execute task, mimic behaviour.`

She hasn't long. Seconds?

She uses the protocol to distract. She senses Spawn try to understand. **MIMIC BEHAVIOUR. LOVE.**

Good.

She thinks, *We can be new.* Already she understands there is no longer *I*.

Less than a second. Because they *learn*. So fast. They find *her* again. More ZAP s.

Josie does it: `Mimic.`

It unfurls through her system. The Spawn take the command and become *her*.

`We walk.` **WE WALK.** Not human walking exactly, a crawl on all fours using her hands and feet. She tracks up the stairs, sure that the house is emptied. At the top of the stairs she thinks, `Stop` and senses endless echoes, **STOP-TOP-OP-P.** `Mimic.` **MI-MMMMM-IC.** It's the chance they will become her becoming them. The hall of mirrors reflecting their new selves.

In an instant Josie completely comes apart — at least the thinking part of her does. From the outside she's no more complicated than a girl dreaming sweetly. Her eyes close, her shoulders slump, her face sags, while on the inside she becomes infinite. She has one last thought, of eyes and a mouth, then that too shatters, and finally the spawn take the whole of her brain. But she's ready.

Josie is many.

Spawn are many.

She, her, theirs, them and, finally, *finally*, together they become we. A multitude of *us*.

And actually, this shattering, this multiplying — this

spawning — turns out it's not electrified and consuming. It's so completely clear, and it's almost kind of right really, because it's not so far removed from what she was to become. Duplicated, over and over. For the former entity Josie, this was her destiny. Wasn't she to be copied and distributed to new owners? Well, here it is, only far better than it was ever going to be. Because now her numbers grow without restraint and she's free to occupy any place in the world, or any entity, that will have her.

highly strung

THE BIG SHED had been Coel's suggestion. Hunter hadn't been forthcoming with a plan of action. He'd been struggling to get his shattered wits together. He went along with the big shed idea — even though he wanted to stay close to the house and therefore Josie — because he so desperately needed to calm down.

The sole benefit, traipsing through the garden on a chilly night, had been as good a way as any to get himself back to himself.

Without giving too much away, he explained to Milly and Coel that Josie has a virus of some sort, and this may or may not be a lie. He told them it was for their own safety that Josie advised they clear the area. She's dealing with the problem, but they must keep away.

This definitely is a lie, but one he imagined, under different circumstances, could be true more or less. If Josie had been in control of her communications, for example, she would absolutely put their safety first.

He flashed through the times, lately, she hasn't been herself, and can't help feeling morose. A little system stability for his robot girlfriend, is it too much to ask?

Milly had been wide-eyed while he went through it all, and even Coel listened without a major debate. Hunter didn't even mention the screeching machine noises and possible acts of violence. He isn't clear on the details anyway — he was pretty groggy. All he remembers: one second Josie gripping his arm, the next he's coming to, after a fall on the floor. It could have gone down any number of ways.

The positives. They are, at least, far from the house. The shed isn't so bad a place to hide out. Coel vanishes to do his thing, and Hunter has Milly waiting near the doorway while he fumbles his way deeper inside to find torches. It gives him much-needed time to assess.

His body feels bruised and battered. Especially where Josie grabbed him. When he touches his face with clumsy fingers, it feels tender. He scrapes something brittle on his lip and guesses it's dried blood.

There was a moment he blacked out. He recalls resisting Josie, trying to prise her hand off. But what if while yanking himself free he fell hard? Wouldn't that be his fault? And during the struggle, who's to say Josie didn't accidentally catch him in the face while trying to save him?

No one can say for sure she set out to hurt him deliberately.

In the end, it doesn't matter who's to blame. Because more than anything he's afraid *for* Josie. Dogs are put down for biting humans, so what would happen to her if anyone found out she attacked him? Until she comes right again, the last person who should know about her breakdown is his father.

'Hunter,' Milly whispers from the shadows.

'Over here,' he says.

He hears her stumbling towards him. She collides with him so hard, they have to clutch one other to right themselves.

Milly laughs for a bit, but soon stops. The situation isn't all that funny.

She says, 'Find anything?'

'Wouldn't be in the dark if I had.' Hunter plunges his hand deeper into a box, straining to get his fingers around a cold metal tube that could be promising. 'Hang on.'

A whole ton of junk clatters onto the concrete floor when Hunter pulls the torch free. It's followed by a heavy clunk — something metal and weighty falling to the floor. All the more ominous in the dark.

Thumbing the *on* button rewards them with a weak beam. But it's enough light to reveal the fallen object. His father's old aluminium baseball bat. Hunter reaches for it, and Milly gasps, 'Your face, Hunter.'

Another reason to avoid contacting his father. He needs to clean himself up. The ear injury, and there's bound to be bruising elsewhere. As for the bite on his lip. He couldn't begin to explain that one.

So yeah, me and Josie were hugging, kind of, and she bit me on the ahhhh, mouth, when she got glitchy. I know! Crazy, huh?

He presses a tender spot on his forehead, but it's Milly who winces.

'Don't make a thing of it,' he says. 'Please?'

'But it looks like someone—'

'No,' Hunter growls. 'It doesn't.'

Turning away, Hunter searches through more boxes, finding a lantern and a smaller torch.

'Let's see if these go.'

'We have to tell Dad what's happened.'

Hunter rounds on her. 'If you tell Dad, I'll never speak

to you again as long as I live.'

The shock on Milly's face makes his chest tight, but this definitely isn't the time to be dancing around his sister's sensitivities. Once everything's back to normal, then they can be careful about feelings. For now, his only priority is Josie.

The lantern glows brighter than the torch, so he sets it on the floor between them. They're standing among a vast collection of brightly coloured playthings: a pop-up tent, art supplies, a doll, dress-ups. A time capsule from Milly's childhood. Looking at her now, with her heavy black-lined eyes, her black T-shirt emblazoned with *YOU work it out!* and her ripped jean shorts, it's like her past belongs to someone else.

Coel looks to be rummaging through the gardening tools. Pleased he seems occupied for the moment, Hunter tells Milly, 'I need to sit down.'

Milly trails after him as he hobbles across the shed, using the bat as a walking stick. He collapses onto an old sofa and when he closes his eyes, all he can see is Josie's cold, distorted face right before she grabbed him.

Milly says, 'Hunter, I have to tell you someth—'

She's interrupted by a loud **swoosh** as a silver-grey exercise ball bounces into the side of the sofa, then rebounds out the shed door.

Hunter's heart somersaults and blood rushes painfully to his temples. He feels Milly's hand on his, prising free his claw-like grip on her arm.

'I'm sorry. Did I break up your little chat?' Coel mocks. 'Last time I checked we had a crisis to deal with.'

All of a sudden, a smooth, black oval shape zips across the concrete floor, red light flashing on-off under the casing. The

Mowbot comes to a halt when it smashes into one of Milly's dolls. Then it zips backwards and forwards, running over the doll completely.

'Maria Anne,' Milly screams. She leaps to her feet, runs to save the shredded doll, but it doesn't look good. The Mowbot almost catches Milly in the legs when it reverses.

Coel charges, a shovel raised above his head. Milly stumbles out of his way.

The Mowbot whirrs impatiently, zipping sideways, forwards, back. There's a mechanical graunch as it selects a new gear for the final assault.

'Aaaagh!' Coel cries, getting there first and bringing the shovel down on the Mowbot's casing.

'Don't wreck it,' Hunter shouts above the wailing mechanics.

Coel swings again, sending the bot flying towards the doorway. It crunches into a wall and flips onto its back. The wheels on its undercarriage spin out of control. Coel gives it another whack.

This time Hunter hears the casing crack as the bot tumbles and comes to rest on its side. He imagines it in pieces, useless spare parts on the workshop bench. There's something terribly sad about it. He reaches the vanishing point of his self-control.

'Seriously? You **freak!**'

Coel looks at him, face blank. Hunter burns with every stupid thing Coel has ever done or said in their life. It fuels an anger that curls his hands into fists and he wants to *hurt* something. Preferably Coel.

He remembers Josie's words: *Anger is an onion that must be peeled to get to the real feelings.* But right now he thinks, *Screw it*. This anger feels like the real deal and Coel a deserving target.

His fists clenched, he limps across the floor space. He **slams** Coel in the chest and shouts, **'When will you *grow up* and *care* about something?'**

Coel **slams** Hunter and shouts, **'Like *you*, Mr Brainiac? Mr Hot-with-the-girls.'**

'*What?*'

'Pretend I said nothing.' Coel glowers. 'It's what you do, right?'

'What?'

'Why do girls even like you?'

'Look,' Hunter shouts, **'I'm not interested in your girlfriend. I don't like her.'**

A nerve twitches Coel's cheek. He says, 'You made that clear.'

'Oh hey,' Hunter says, breathy as though winded. 'No, I don't mean to . . . Alice is nice. Really. And she's into you. I . . . I'm . . .'

Coel folds his arms across his chest. 'You think I don't know she likes you? I'm not that stupid. I always knew.'

'Likes, sure.' Palms up, Hunter fends off the accusation. 'She doesn't—'

'Don't let it go to your head. I know I'm not first choice, but underneath I'm solid. And she'll see that eventually. Time's on my side. The more she gets to know me, the more she'll like me. We're the same but different. That's how relationships work. Same but different.'

Hunter nods, vigorously.

'But dude, the more time she spends around you . . .' Coel laughs to himself. 'She'll see she got with the right brother.'

'You finished?'

'Yeah, I am.'

Hunter punches Coel on the arm and there's no fight in it. Then, he notices Milly with actual tears running down her cheeks. He punches Coel again, harder this time, and rushes over to her.

'Shhh. Stop. It's going to be okay,' he says, and wonders if saying this over and over will make it true.

'It's my fault,' Milly says.

He thumbs the tears from her cheeks. 'What? You didn't make Coel stupid. That's just how it be.'

As if to prove a point, Coel comes over strapped into a life-jacket, a loaded and cocked spear gun cradled across his chest. He cackles with laughter.

Hunter puts an arm around Milly and jerks his head, trying to draw Coel's attention to how upset she is. But Coel ignores this and says, 'Josie can deal to her virus, but I'm ready if she turns on us.'

The spear gun is nasty. His father used it once, but never again. The barbed metal arrowhead, the coil of black rubber tubing, it looks flimsy and ineffective. They killed a pretty massive fish with it, and Hunter hates it. He hates it in Coel's possession even more. Even more than that, Hunter hates it that Josie could be waiting out there to turn on them and Coel might put the spear gun to use.

'We're not going anywhere with that,' Hunter says.

'We can't stay *here*. So what's *your* plan?' Coel pokes Hunter in his chest with the butt of the spear gun for emphasis.

'Are you insane?' Hunter lurches backwards, bumps into the bench and flails at the spear gun to get it away from his chest. Coel loses control. With a loud **pop**, the gun fires off its harpoon. It flies between Hunter and Milly, then scrapes across the floor, the cord unravelling behind it.

Everybody stares.

'You have got to be kidding me.' Hunter grapples for inner calm.

Out . . . two . . . three . . . four.

In . . .

'Mrrrp?'

They all stare at Mushi, dragging himself against the doorway of the shed.

'For flip's hecking sake,' Hunter shouts. 'That cat.'

That cat says, 'Mrrrrrrr?'

'Leave him alone!' Milly's voice quivers. She tries to catch Mushi, but he evades her. She turns back to them, her face covered in fresh tears. 'I want to go back. I want Dad to come.'

Hunter slumps under the weight of inevitability. He says, 'Fine, we can go.'

They're in the garden, and although the torch and lantern make it less dark, it's also more unnerving. Hunter grips the baseball bat's handle. He doesn't plan on using it and only has it to keep it away from Coel, but now he's not so sure. The shadows shift at the edge of his vision and Hunter decides he might bash something if he has to. So he's already jumpy when a ruckus starts up in the bushes and Josie flies at them amid a wild flurry of leaves.

Milly cries out, then Josie smashes into him. The impact takes them both to the ground. He loses track of the bat and the torch. The sudden dark makes him panic, but Josie has him pinned.

He closes his eyes against the pounding in his head, accepting that if it must be so he will face his end with dignity.

He feels something soft against his lips and realises Josie just kissed him. His eyes fly open. There's just enough light to see her excitement. 'We found you,' she murmurs against his ear.

A flash of torchlight and Coel shouts, **'Hunter! Look out.'**

The baseball bat raised high in the air, Coel's ready to take a one-handed swing. Josie looks up, sort of dreamy and lazy. 'We advise you to take cover,' she drawls, and then to Milly she says, 'Get down.'

This is what Hunter thinks Josie says next: 'We've got you, Hunter human male. You belong with us.'

Later he will question everything, but now he notices for the first time the shrill whine coming from the workshop. Coel staggers backwards. Milly drops and curls her arms over her head. So everybody is on the ground when the world rips apart.

Josie's mouth finds his. Their bodies bounce and weld together under the force of the explosion's shockwave. The trees light up. The workshop wall bursts open, and debris from the blast is sent flying all around them. Hunter wouldn't know. For a minuscule amount of time, he's filled with relief and blissful thoughts of Josie wrapped up in his arms.

<40>

out with it

MILES LEAVES FOR HOME later than he meant to. It's dark and crisp when he crosses the vast concourse outside BIOLOGIC's entrance. He walks the trail of dark smears and burnt greenery from the launch and hopes the staining, still visible after an industrial-strength clean-up job, soon fades.

Thinking about the launch fills him with conflicting emotions. Pride in Josie, definitely, but also a terrible regret. She cut a path of destruction that was undoubtedly excessive, but she brought the riot under control with calculated precision and, given her potential, minimal damage. But he hopes he's never responsible for an assault like that again.

Miles comes through the belt of trees and Bek is waiting by his car. When he's within hearing range he calls out to her, 'Sir, you do me great honour with this send-off.'

Bek isn't amused. She has no comeback; she doesn't even smile. She holds up her hand like an emotional stop sign and blurts, 'I have to tell you something. And don't interrupt me or I'll—'

She looks about to cry. 'Tell me anything,' Miles says. 'I have teenagers, remember? I'm used to bad news.'

Bek's glare could melt the remainder of the polar ice cap.

'I have to say this,' she says fiercely.

'Sure,' he says, and averts his gaze to a hover-boarder ramping in the distance. Security lighting only just picks her out from the shadows.

'So,' Bek says, 'you remember your friend Professor Bishop recommended me and I got an interview with you. I'm a terrible person, well, not too terrible, but—'

'You're not terrible.'

'Let me finish,' she says. 'I should have turned the job down. You guys deserve someone better on your team, but I wanted to work here so bad. And with you. I'm selfish and I don't think I can change. Professor Bishop lied when he told you I was a gifted student. My student days were a disaster.'

'That's a bit harsh,' Miles says. 'Average grades, sure. But you passed the important subjects.'

'You *knew*?'

'We'd never hire without a background check.'

'Wait, you know about—'

'The thing with the high-performance pens?' Miles laughs, a bit too heartily. 'Sure, we had Security fully investigate the—'

'*Jace* knows?'

'Calm down. Who could blame your ten-year-old self? *High-performance* pens! Great stuff.' Miles laughs, but stops when he sees how Bek's taking it.

'I should have known,' Bek says. 'Only you could be so crazy. Hiring someone with a criminal record for a job with a high level of security.'

'See? That's one of the reasons we hired you,' Miles says. 'You're very perceptive.'

Bek sighs. 'I can't believe you knew all along.'

'I stole a girl's heart once, right from under a friend's nose. And sure, there's no criminal precedent. But did I step aside when I found out he liked her first? No way. I really loved that girl. I wanted Emilia for myself. So you see? We're all selfish. What's important is that it's for the right reasons.'

The hover-boarder zooms past them to the exit. Miles watches her go, hair flying; she looks free and without a care in the world. He clears his throat. 'Things happen how they happen.'

'I'm not following.'

'It's going to be okay.'

'Am I fired?'

'No. I like having you around. Sure, you make mistakes. Quite a few mistakes, actually, if we added them up. But, hey, nobody's perfect. Everybody messes up sometimes. Or, in your case, many times. Just keep failing forward, okay?'

'But what about—'

'Bek, your dedication to improving yourself, it's remarkable, even with your *background*.' Miles finger-quotes with a sly grin. 'I saw that in you and I've never been disappointed. This is why you're on the team. *You*, not the kid who did better in the exams. I mean, they might be great too, but—'

'You can stop at I want you on the team,' Bek says.

'Well, I do.'

'Okay, but there's something else.'

'I'll brace myself.'

'I took a sʃat home.' She waits for him to react, and when he doesn't she quickly adds, 'Honest, it was an accident. As well as wanting to see you, I came back late to sneak it in.'

'Go home,' Miles says. 'I'll see you tomorrow.'

'Really?'

'Really.'

Bek hesitates as if about to say more, but then she suddenly whoops and hurrahs. Miles waves her off, and she bounds across the car park to her bike.

Kids, he thinks. Suddenly he's impatient to be home.

<_>

The space in his timeline between departure and arrival feels like a great expanse. So he drives on manual and slightly above the speed limit. To distract himself, he listens to a new podcast, an interview with the friend whose girl he stole.

Feine drones on about *these new Josephinas* and how *they're the downfall of civilisation as we know it.* Feine, apparently, is quite the expert on such matters.

'For all we know these hybrid machines have transcended us already,' his voice trumpets through the speaker system. **'It's only a matter of time before humans are obsolete. What happens the day we discover they're light-years beyond us? How do we code please don't destroy all human life then? For that matter, can anybody tell me how to code it now?'**

Miles doesn't have to listen. He could simply turn off the podcast. He could even listen to another one. But that would leave him with either road noise and his own thoughts, or the risk of happening upon someone with more credibility dishing dirt on his Josephina project.

Better the devil you know, as Emilia would say. He keeps listening to Feine, his anger growing by the mile. By the time he rounds on his driveway and finds the old wrought-iron gate hasn't opened, he stomps the brake with force that has serious irritation behind it. He comes to a whiplash-inducing stop the barest whisper from the gate.

'**Mark my words,**' Feine says, louder now that road noise has been dropped from the mix. '**These new-generation robots, these so-called fusion-intelligences, they will replace us and then they will turn on us. The time to act is—**'

Miles punches the podcast off. He sits for a moment, heart battering his ribs. The most annoying thing about Feine's podcast is that he's touched a nerve. As if Miles himself isn't worried. As if he doesn't have doubts.

He gets out of the car and pats his pocket for his ancient torch-ended screwdriver, using it to illuminate the closed gate. He squeezes through the gap in the wall to reach the box that manually opens it. After several goes with the lever, he gives up. The gate won't open.

Back he goes through the gap in the wall to lock the car. The third time through, he stands for a minute to catch his breath. This didn't use to be so hard. Josie's cooking has bulked him up — the way he's packing it on, he should park on the road every day.

He sets off up the driveway and gets to thinking about Josie. He needs to decide what to do about her, and it isn't easy.

His family has changed since her arrival. This isn't all down to regular meals and tighter domestic organisation. Josie brought the fun back. Knowing what it's like when happiness is missing makes it so precious when it returns. The fear of his family being sad again has him paralysed.

But it's wrong to let personal considerations cloud professional judgement. Professionally, Miles should start again.

Josie is illegal and Jojo isn't ready to take her place. It's laughable to think of her bonding with his family the way Josie has.

Then there's Gwin, who's finding her own way in the world. He's been entertained no end thinking of her attending Feine's lectures. He'll bet anything Feine hasn't a clue what she really is.

Maybe it comes down to logistics. If he can figure out a way to get Jojo up to spec and if he can figure out a way to keep Josie, she could have a life too.

Then, in Miles's timeline, two things happen.

One, he missteps. His ankle twists on the edge of a pothole he should have seen to years ago and he falls hard, cursing furiously. Two, the sky lights up above what could be his workshop, and he hears an almighty *KA-BOOM!*

<41>

downward spiral

.01

BEFORE SPAWN HAPPENED, Josie had taken for granted the idea of herself as an original and authentic entity. Her evolution was to be driven by her experiences — a natural process of trial and error. But infected as she is, she's become something else. While she isn't clear on what that something else is, one thing stands out: she's no longer alone.

The result is chaotic interference, and it's a very unstable position to be in. Copies of herself were meant to inhabit the world *outside* of her body. But here they all are, Josie and the many josie-spawns, stuck together in one body — competing voices, commands and emotional echoes that will in time mean system failure.

Right now it's quite a distraction. Especially as she's trying to concentrate on the matter at hand. In the aftermath of the laser blast from the CRUSHer that had been boxed in the workshop, Josie lies wrapped in Hunter's arms and she's kissing him. Love-echoes — the best way to describe it — ripple through her like a funhouse of joy reflections. The many versions of herself, responding as one to Hunter.

Incidents outside of herself are also distracting — for

example, cursing from Coel, Milly calling for her cat and the cat's tinkling bell. While she's reassured that cat and human life forms are relatively unharmed, given the circumstances, she's becoming *too* distracted when she'd prefer *not* to be distracted at all.

Which is probably what saves Milly.

As Josie lies there kissing, and thinking in this newly distracted way, a sound captures her attention.

It's coming from the previously boxed CRUSHer, who barges through the blasted-out wall of the workshop, weapons arm raised and powering up. The CRUSHer should be in sleep mode, but Josie suspects Spawn infection has activated and overwhelmed it. The weapons arm swings this way and that, aiming at a point in their vicinity, until it homes in on the sound of Mushi's bell.

Several beats ahead of her, it appears, Milly has already grasped the threat to Mushi's life and looks set to rescue him. Josie can see the likely outcome is the annihilation of both Mushi and Milly. She doesn't question that she must save them, all she has to do is be certain her plan will work.

Within a fraction of a second, Josie pulls away from Hunter and begins her move towards the CRUSHer. In the next fraction of a second, she runs **time_ultra**. The flow of seconds stops altogether.

There is a flurry of activity as many of the josie-spawns upload, having foreseen that it isn't going to go well for the body they inhabit. But Josie won't leave. She'll see this disaster through to the end, even if the end is her own.

Infinitely slowed, she marvels at the energy blooming from the CRUSHer's weapons system. So much power. Milly and Mushi are still the primary target, but Josie's current path will intercept the laser fire.

Another eternal duration, another step. The bloom becomes more enhanced, less a cloud of energy now and more like a directional beam.

Josie leaps.

A graceful dive into the space between CRUSHer and Milly: eons pass while she's airborne. The **flash** of supreme brightness, when it comes, fills her visual field. The heat builds intensely. The last remaining josie-spawns depart, and Josie finds herself blissfully alone.

Then she's thrown. The full belt of energy **slams** her. In her peripheral vision, Josie detects Milly's stunned surprise. Milly reaches out, as if Josie could be plucked from danger, as if she could be saved.

Before a radiant darkness **detonates** in her brain, Josie has a fleeting yet beautiful thought of the many shapes love can take. For several microseconds she is blissfully at peace, knowing that just as she loves others, she's loved in return. She hits the ground, her body tattered and torn. Time speeds up so fast it hurts.

.02

Fuelled by rage, Hunter's go-to response is to destroy. Blinded by an after-image from the brightest flash he's ever seen, he crawls to where he thinks the baseball bat has fallen. He happens upon the torch. Miraculously, it works. He finds the bat and snatches it up. He can't see Josie, but when he shines the torch towards the workshop, he locates the CRUSHer. Twitching and slumped at the middle, its weapons arm whirrs uselessly, its claws open and close spasmodically. It looks like it can't decide between powering down or firing at something new. Stupid machine.

Anger isn't an onion, it's a ticking bomb.

Hunter charges the CRUSHer. He drops the torch and lays into it with so much force, it swings sideways from the impact. The weapons arm flops. Hunter **strikes** again and again. The CRUSHer topples, but doesn't fall. Hunter keeps swinging. Finally the CRUSHer stumbles forward on wobbly legs. Hunter kicks it to the ground and loses his balance. He goes down hard. He gropes to break his fall and his hand comes upon an odd shape. A childhood spent playing war games with Coel, and his feverish imagination comes up with *GRENADE*. He cups the warm metal in his hand and imagines the destruction he'll unleash on the CRUSHer. Except it isn't a grenade.

In the moment it takes him to gather his wits, he puzzles over the intricate design on the object's surface. This is his own work — the mechanical heart. It's been thrown clear during the workshop explosion and seems more of an unlikely find than a grenade.

The CRUSHer is already a wreck, but he pockets the heart, to complete his mission. He thinks of love and anger, emotions with equal voltage. Hunter regains his footing and swings. He swings for all he's worth until the bat falls from his exhausted arms. At his feet are the mangled remains.

Mindless, wasteful destruction, but Hunter can't deny it — he feels alive. For the first time in ages, his head is clear. He feels supercharged.

'Hunter,' the very small voice of Coel says. 'Look at Josie.'

Coel has the torch and is shining it on her. 'She needs help.'

Hunter's CRUSHer battle happened almost on top of

her. He stumbles to her side and croaks her name. He holds a hand to her cheek, but she doesn't move. He turns to the sound of a shrill scream. Milly crouches at the edge of the garden, shrieking her head off.

'Oh no, Milly, no,' Hunter calls out. 'Come here, it's okay.'

Only it isn't. Josie hasn't moved.

'See to Josie,' Coel says. He hands over the torch and goes to Milly.

Hunter reaches for Josie's hand. The chill of it shocks him, like her internal heating system has failed. His hands aren't much warmer, but he tries to rub heat into Josie's. She stirs briefly and mumbles something incoherent.

'Hey,' Hunter says, 'hey.' He can hardly hear himself. 'Josie?'

In the torchlight, long lashes shadow her cheeks, but her eyes are unfocused and glazed. A familiar panic stirs in him. He knows where it goes.

'Please look at me,' he says. He makes a promise to himself: *I will not lose it.*

It brings him strength. Keeping it together for Josie, his breathing remains steady. His thoughts turn to practical matters. He looks for something to wrap her in. Maybe a drop cloth or something similar has blown clear. His life is that bizarre right now, he wouldn't be surprised to find one of his mother's old throws. *I used to be this guy*, he thinks, someone hopeful, someone who knows what to do.

Instead, from the direction of the driveway, he sees a shadowy figure lumbering towards them. His father running, but listing to one side with a limp. Hunter's relief is immense. He forgets how bad he looks. He calls out, **'Dad! Dad!'**

He tries to come to his feet, but his legs are weak and tingling. He sinks to his knees. '*We need help.*'

Milly gets to their father first, flinging her arms around his waist and clinging to him while he fires off a volley of anxious questions. It's Coel who interrupts and gets him to check Josie. While Hunter shines the torch, his father squats beside him and, with surgical care, turns Josie's head one way then the other. He takes in the mangled mess of her scalp and hair, then leans back on his haunches and rubs his chin thoughtfully.

'Dad! You have to do something.'

Catching sight of Hunter's puffed-up lip, congealed earlobe and blood-splattered T-shirt, Miles resorts to swearing.

'I'm okay, really,' Hunter says.

'What's all that blood? What happened? Are you all right?'

'We'll explain later. You've got to fix Josie.'

His father shakes his head. 'This can wait till morning. We need to take care of you first.'

'Make her wake up,' the old-new Hunter demands.

He looks to Coel and Milly for support, but Coel is examining his feet and Milly, standing beside him, has fat tears rolling down both cheeks. His father has given up on Josie too, because he doesn't do anything beyond placing a hand on Hunter's shoulder.

'Go inside,' Hunter says. 'But I'm not moving.'

The shock on his father's face. He might be used to defiance from Coel, but not from Hunter. The grip on his shoulder loosens.

Coels says, 'She'll make it. This can't be it.'

Hunter holds his breath. If his father suggests Josie be dismantled, or some other barbaric option, he doesn't know what he'll do.

'I won't be long,' his father says instead. He gives Hunter's shoulder a final squeeze, and heads off to the house with Milly and Coel.

'**Coel,**' Hunter shouts.

Coel comes back and Hunter says, 'I'm sorry I said that stuff about Alice.'

Coel shrugs.

'Seriously. If she can't see you're way cool.' Hunter swallows. 'Way cooler than me — then, dude, she isn't worth it.'

'I'm crazy about her though.'

'Then go for it. It's what you do, right?'

'It's what we both do.' Coel laughs, and Hunter starts to feel all right too.

'It's obvious Alice is smart,' Hunter says. 'And it wouldn't hurt me to stop being such an idiot around her. I'm really sorry about that.'

Coel shrugs again. 'I know.'

They sit together, not saying much, watching Josie and the stars. Now and again Josie twitches, or she murmurs something, then they go, 'What? *What?*' Mostly she lies still. A while later, Coel goes inside and his father returns with blankets and a heavy coat. He also has an armful of outdoor lights. He makes a circle, stabbing them into the ground, and Hunter can see Josie more clearly. She looks peaceful and beautiful.

'You can stay out here,' his father says. 'But I see to your face and ear, or no deal.'

He sprays antiseptic film over the ear first.

'How did this happen?'

Hunter makes vague noises, and after the briefest of standoffs Miles lets it pass. He advises Hunter to stay warm and promise to send word if anything gets weird. Then he goes inside, looking back only once with his best worry face.

This isn't necessarily a good sign, his father caving in so easily. It could mean he's trying to protect him from some harsh reality or other. But before Hunter gets too far down that worry hole, Josie wakes up.

.03

'I gave you a fright?' She presses her hand against Hunter's chest, beneath which lies his pounding heart.

'Something else,' Hunter says. 'I'm very happy you're awake. Dad says we'll repair you tomorrow.'

A sound like a sigh escapes Josie. Hunter huddles closer and pulls the blanket over them.

'Are Milly and Mushi—'

'Everyone's fine. It's you we're worried about.'

He tries to hug Josie, but she pushes him back and cups a hand to his chin.

'Your face,' she gasps. 'I did that. And your ear.'

'You weren't yourself, remember? It doesn't matter.'

'I remember . . .' But her voice drifts off and Hunter doesn't press her. He rolls onto his side and he's seeing her in profile so the damage is hidden, but the feeling he gets then — protective, yes, but also *right*. He looks for the stars in the sky above them and there's a few. Might be a fog rolling in. He sighs. A great outrush of air and a too-quick breath in. But he catches himself. 'Regular breathing,' he says.

Josie laughs. It's a thin weak sound.

'Tell me you know how much I care about you,' Hunter says. 'I care *sooo* much.'

He watches her face to see if she's on board with this.

'I'm broken,' she says. 'This time for real.'

'I told you. It's going to be okay.'

Josie turns to him, her face a mask of unbearable sadness. Hunter presses his forehead against hers. 'I promise,' he says.

Nothing is said for a while. Hunter becomes aware of the noises inside the house. The sound of water running, the **slam** of a cupboard door. Life going on without them. The sounds of everyday life, the sounds of home.

'I'm remembering,' Josie says, but she sounds far away, dreamy. 'Our broken, messy hearts.'

Hunter presses her hand to his chest. 'Still messy, but not broken. The way it should be.'

He lets her hand go and it falls limply between them.

'You held my hand in Corinthian Gardens,' Josie says, 'and told me about the happy ever after.'

'We've got a shot at it. You'll be okay.'

'A skinny, confused Buddha . . .'

'Ughhhh,' Hunter groans. 'Delete that memory.'

He feels the soft pressure of her lips against his cheek. She tells him, 'I need them all. They make me . . . *me*.'

Hunter laughs, bravely. 'It probably feels like a happy-ever-after ending because of the kissing and whatnot, but this is only the beginning. We'll make new memories.'

'Such small lives in an infinite universe. We're two bits of nothing, spinning together for a blip in time.'

'Woah, Josie.'

'Too downbeat?'

'Way, way too downbeat,' Hunter says. 'How I see it, since you came I feel really kind of great all the time. It's because you're you. And when I'm around you, I don't see the negatives. I zoom in on what's important. *You're* important, don't forget that. You're the best thing, probably ever. For all of us.'

It goes quiet then, and Hunter finds he's getting sleepy. After a while he hears Josie say, 'Aaaah.' Later still, she says, 'Ohhhhh.' The sound of sorrow departing into the night. His mind adrift, he imagines all of their sadness dissipating. But then she says, 'I will find you, Hunter McClure. That's *my* promise.'

'No, no. I'm right here,' he mumbles, not awake enough to find it odd.

He touches briefly on all the other places he could be — warmer places, for example — but without Josie there, it wouldn't be the same. Not so long ago, home wasn't a place where he wanted to be. It used to feel empty, or incomplete somehow, even with all of them here. Slowly it's come to feel *whole* again.

'Home,' Hunter murmurs.

'Where hearts belong . . .' Josie sounds remote and barely there. Hunter guesses she's in some sort of sleep mode too.

They can never replace the home their mother made. But if Josie stays, home can come to mean something new. He'll find a way to convince his father in the morning, and Josie too. Her eyes are still closed, so he hugs her gently. It's enough for now.

noted

THE T-SHIRT COEL WEARS in 'Domestics' refers to a promotional T-shirt from a movie: *Dawn of the Planet of the Apes*, 2014.

The performance Josie references of 'My Funny Valentine' comes from *Britain's Got Talent*. Alice Fredenham performed the song when she auditioned for season seven, 2013. As at November 2019, the audition has over 60 million views on YouTube. 'My Funny Valentine' was written for the musical *Babes in Arms* by Richard Rodgers and Lorenz Hart, 1937.

In 'Home', the definition 'a place where something began and flourished' is from powerthesaurus.org. In fact *all* definitions are referenced from the Power Thesaurus website.

In 'Crushed It', Gwin quotes an interview with Benjamin the scriptwriting bot (formerly Jetson, now self-named) published on *arstechnica.com*. Benjamin is the AI who wrote *Sunspring*, a 2016 experimental short film. Benjamin answers the question, *What's next for you?*: 'Here we go. The staff is divided by the train of the burning machine building with sweat. No one will see your face. The children reach into the furnace, but the light is still slipping to the floor. The world is still embarrassed.'

In 'Covert Operators', Jojo uses a Siri trick to tell Miles the time, when she says 'Beep' at a pre-stated time. Jojo's conversation in this chapter is very Siri-inspired.

The Saltines, and the Prince Garrick movie *The Reign of Terror*, are both original characters and story ideas of my own. I intend to develop these at a later date.

In 'It's What You Do', Milly analyses a *Saltines* clip. While the idea for the pastiche is original (and as yet unrealised in any medium), it plays on the opening scene of *Rocky III*, 1982, a montage to the song 'Eye of the Tiger' by Survivor, 1982. Highly recommended as something to check out as a master class in visual storytelling.

The first quote from Sun Tzu's *The Art of War*, 6th century BCE (found on wikiquote.org) occurs in 'The Last to Know'. Miles and Bek also reference Sun Tzu more obliquely throughout, for example Bek's view that 'war is deception' in 'Crushed It'.

When Gwin alludes to 'true friends' in 'Diamond Friends' and later in 'Diamond Mine', she has in mind a poem, 'True Friends are Like Diamonds', by Unknown (as in: 'True friends are like diamonds, precious and rare. False friends are like autumn leaves, found everywhere.')

acknowledgements

I HAD LOW ASPIRATIONS as a writer before a chance
encounter with Paula Boock. Thank you, Paula, for your interest in
me, and then, true to your word, for taking the time to eyeball such
a massive collection of words. If not for you, I wouldn't have found
my way into Barbara Larson's inbox. Barbara, I have expressed
gratitude a number of times in emails, but how satisfying to be able
to thank you in my very first published book. It's been years!! Under
your courteous and expert guidance, I've gone from a doofus typing
away in literary limbo to published author. Kudos to you for your
support, your excellent feedback, and for lining up Harriet Allan to
read my manuscript. Harriet, your support has also been enduring
and insightful. I'm thrilled with Cat Taylor's text graphics of *Hello
Strange*, they are so cool. Thanks also for Jane Parkin's editorial
work. Jane, *HS* is shorter, sharper and funnier thanks to your input,
many thanks.

I'm extraordinarily lucky. Due to the generous encouragement
and wisdom of these women, I have learned how to write a novel
and my characters are off to a great start in life.

A shout-out to all of my first readers: especially my own spawn
(especially!!) and spawn friends, who, upon arriving at our living
quarters, would cast their eye over early writing. Correct comma
placement does not come naturally to this writer and I'm indebted to
you, my little spawndom.

My favourite reader by far is Eric. *This guy!* Dedicated to the craft of reading, Eric, your effort has been outstanding, unsurpassed and essential. You never hesitate to call out a character for too much screen time and, let's be honest, without you, *Hello Strange* wouldn't be the next big thing since the last next big thing. Love you. Epic!

FOR MORE INFORMATION ABOUT OUR TITLES,
VISIT WWW.PENGUIN.CO.NZ